# MAIGRET AND THE LONER

## AND

# MAIGRET AND THE MAN ON THE BOULEVARD

The body of a vagrant—a man with beautifully manicured nails—is found in a derelict house near Les Halles, and Maigret discovers that the victim was a cabinet-maker called Marcel Vivien, whose past seems increasingly mysterious. What happened to him after he deserted his wife and daughter twenty years ago? What became of his pretty young mistress, Nina Lassave, and why was he leading the miserable and lonely existence of a tramp? An anonymous telephone call provides Maigret with a clue and causes him to make a journey to the holiday resort of La Baule, where he begins to solve the riddle of Vivien's strange past.

\*     \*     \*

Louis Thouret is found, stabbed in the back, in a cul-de-sac off the Boulevard Saint-Martin, wearing brown shoes and a garish tie which his wife has never seen before. Each day he used to leave his home in Juvisy and travel up to Paris. His family understood that he worked as a storekeeper for the firm of Kaplan and Zanin, but Maigret discovers that the firm closed down three years ago. So why had Louis concealed the truth from his wife and what did he do in Paris during the day? His daughter Monique and her lover, Albert Jorisse, play a strange part in the story, but the unexpected appearance of a former circus performer, Fred the Clown, provides Maigret with the vital link he needs.

*Also by*
# GEORGES SIMENON

★

# MAIGRET AND THE LONER

*and*

# MAIGRET AND THE MAN ON THE BOULEVARD

★

## GEORGES SIMENON

THE
COMPANION BOOK CLUB
LONDON AND SYDNEY

This edition, published in 1976 by
The Hamlyn Publishing Group Ltd,
is issued by arrangement with
Hamish Hamilton Ltd

## THE COMPANION BOOK CLUB

The Club is not a library; all books are the property of members. There is no entrance fee or any payment beyond the low Club price of each book. Details of membership will gladly be sent on request.

Write to:
The Companion Book Club,
Odhams Books, Rushden, Northants.

Or, in Australia, write to
The Companion Book Club,
C/- Hamlyn House Books, P.O. Box 252,
Dee Why, N.S.W. 2099

*Made and printed in Great Britain
for the Companion Book Club
by Odhams (Watford) Ltd*
600872068
9.76/306

# CONTENTS

\*

# MAIGRET
# AND THE LONER

*

*Translated from
the French by*
EILEEN ELLENBOGEN

# Chapter One

IT WAS ONLY nine o'clock in the morning, but it was already very warm. Maigret, who had taken off his jacket, was indolently opening his mail, pausing from time to time to glance out of the window at the motionless leaves on the trees in the Quai des Orfèvres, and at the Seine, which was flat and smooth as silk.

It was August. Lucas and Lapointe, along with over half the other inspectors, were on holiday. Janvier and Torrence had taken their holidays in July, and Maigret himself was planning to spend most of September at his house, which looked like an old rectory, in Meung-sur-Loire.

Every day towards early evening, for almost a week now, a brief but violent storm, accompanied by lashing rain, had sent the people in the streets scurrying for shelter under the buildings. These storms dissipated the intense heat of the day, and the cooler evenings which followed were a welcome relief.

Paris was empty. Even the street noises were different, with intervals almost of silence.

Everywhere there were brightly coloured coaches from many different countries, all invariably converging on the familiar tourist attractions, Notre-Dame, the Louvre, the Place de la Concorde, the Etoile, the Sacré-Coeur and, inevitably, the Eiffel Tower.

Walking about the streets at this time of year, it was almost a shock to hear anyone speaking French.

The Chief Commissioner was also on holiday, so Maigret was spared the drudgery of the daily briefing. There was very little correspondence and not much crime, other than the occasional robbery with violence.

The ringing of the telephone roused the Chief Superintendent from his torpor. He lifted the receiver.

'It's the Superintendent of the First *Arrondissement*. He's asking to speak to you personally. Shall I put him through?'

'Yes, I'll speak to him.'

9

Maigret knew him well. He was somewhat affected in manner and always exquisitely turned out, but he was a genuinely cultivated man, who had been at the Bar for some years before joining the police force.

'Hello! Ascan?'

'I hope I'm not disturbing you?'

'Not in the least. I've got all the time in the world.'

'I'm ringing because I've had a case dumped in my lap this morning that I thought would be just up your street.'

'What's it all about?'

'A murder. . . . But it's no ordinary murder. It would take too long to explain over the telephone. When will you be free?'

'I'm free now.'

'Would it be asking too much to suggest you came over to my office? The thing is, it happened in an obscure little cul-de-sac near Les Halles.'

This was 1965, and the fruit and vegetable market of Les Halles had not yet been transferred from Paris to Rungis.

'I'll be with you in a few minutes.'

He grumbled to himself, indulging in the pretence of being inconvenienced, whereas, in reality, he welcomed any excuse to get away from the boring routine of the past few days. He went into the Inspectors' Duty Room. Ordinarily he would have taken Janvier with him, but it was essential, in his absence, to leave someone in charge at the Quai des Orfèvres who could be thoroughly relied upon, and who was capable of acting on his own initiative.

'Come with me, will you, Torrence? We'll take a car from the forecourt.'

It was not far to the police station of the First *Arrondissement* in the Rue des Prouvaires. Maigret was shown straight into Superintendent Ascan's office.

'You'll be flabbergasted when you see what I have to show you. I've never seen anything like it in all my life. I'd rather say no more for the present. Ah! Torrence. . . . You'd better leave the car here. It's no distance.'

They skirted Les Halles, where it was business as usual, even in August. The smell, in the intense heat, was overpowering. They threaded their way through narrow little streets, hemmed in by small shops and somewhat dubious-looking rooming houses. There were vagrants loafing around here and there, one of them, a woman, so drunk that she was able to stand upright only by leaning against a wall.

Having arrived at the Rue de la Grande-Truanderie, Ascan turned into a little passage so narrow that it would not have admitted a lorry.

'Here we are,' he announced. 'Vieux-Four Passage.'

There were not more than ten old houses on either side, with a gap in the middle where a building had already been pulled down. The whole street was scheduled for demolition, and the houses had been evacuated.

Some were shored up with planks to prevent the walls from collapsing.

The Police Superintendent stopped at a house which had no glass in any of its windows. Indeed, some of the window frames had been ripped out bodily. The front door had gone, and the entrance was boarded up. Ascan removed two of the boards, which were loose, to reveal a long passageway beyond.

'Watch out for the stairs! They're very rickety, and some of the treads are missing.'

There was a strong smell of dust and mildew mingled with the stench of Les Halles.

With all this in their nostrils, they went up two flights of stairs, and came upon a boy of about twelve squatting with his back against the flaking wall. As the men came up to him, he sprang to his feet, his eyes shining.

'You're Chief Superintendent Maigret, aren't you?'

'Yes.'

'If anyone had told me I should actually be seeing you in the flesh . . . ! I keep a scrapbook of newspaper cuttings about you. . . . All your photographs and everything. . . .'

Ascan intervened to explain:

'This is young Nicolier. . . . Your Christian name is Jean, isn't it?'

'Yes, sir.'

His father keeps a butcher's shop in the Rue Saint-Denis. It's the only one hereabouts that stays open all through the month of August. . . . Go on, Jean, let's have your story.'

'It's like I told you. Most of my mates are away at the seaside. . . . Well, as there's no one to play with, I spend my time poking about the neighbourhood. Even though I was born here, there are lots of odd corners I don't know. This morning, I spotted this house. I tugged at the boards nailed across the doorway, and found they were loose. . . . I went in and called out:

' "Anybody at home?"

'There was no answer but the echo of my own voice. I didn't really expect there would be. I went on in, just to have a look round. You see that rickety old door over there, to the right . . . ? Well, I pushed it open, and that's where I found the man. . . . I couldn't run away fast enough. I was all out of breath when I got to the Police Station.

'Do I have to go back into that room?'

'I don't think that will be necessary.'

'Shall I wait here?'

'Yes.'

The door was so rotten that it would no longer serve even as firewood. It was Maigret who pushed it open. Standing on the threshold, he could see what the Police Superintendent had meant when he had promised him a surprise.

It was a fair-sized room, and the panes of both windows had been replaced with cardboard or stout paper. The uneven floor, with gaps of more than an inch between the boards, was covered with an incredible litter of bric-à-brac, most of it broken, all of it useless.

Dominating the room was an iron bedstead where lay, fully dressed on an old straw mattress, a man who was unmistakably dead. His chest was covered with clotted blood, but his face was serene.

His clothes were those of a tramp, but his face and hands suggested something very different. He was elderly, with long silvery hair shot through with bluish highlights. His eyes, too, were blue. Maigret was beginning to feel uneasy under their fixed gaze, when the Superintendent closed them.

He had a white moustache, slightly turned up at the ends, and a little Van Dyck beard, also white.

Apart from this he was closely shaven, and Maigret saw,

12

with renewed surprise, that his hands were carefully manicured.

'He looks like an elderly actor got up as a tramp,' he murmured. 'Had he any papers on him?'

'None. No identity card, no old letters, nothing. Several of my inspectors, all assigned to this district at one time or another, came and had a look at him, but none of them recognized him, though one thought he might have seen him once or twice rummaging in the dustbins.'

The man was very tall and exceptionally broad-shouldered. His trousers, which had a tear over the left knee, were too short for him. His tattered jacket, fit only for the dustbin, was lying crumpled on the filthy floor.

'Has the police surgeon been?'

'Not yet. I'm expecting him any minute. I was hoping you'd get here before anything had been touched.'

'Torrence, find the nearest bistro, and ring Headquarters and ask them to tell the Forensic Laboratory to send someone along as soon as possible. They'd better let the D.P.P. know as well.'

He was still much intrigued by the face of the man on the battered iron bed. His moustache and beard were so neatly trimmed that it seemed certain that he had been to a barber as recently as the previous day. As for the carefully manicured hands, with their varnished fingernails, it was difficult to imagine them scrabbling in dustbins.

And yet the man must have been doing just that for a very long time. The whole room was crammed with the most unlikely assortment of objects. Nearly all broken. An old coffee grinder. A number of badly chipped enamel jugs, several battered buckets with holes in them, a paraffin lamp with no wick or paraffin, a pile of odd shoes.

'I'll have to make an inventory of all this stuff.'

There was a wash-basin fixed to the wall, and Maigret went across and turned on the tap, with no result. As he had expected, the water had been cut off. The same went for the electricity and gas. It was standard procedure with houses scheduled for demolition.

How long had the man been living here? Long enough to have collected a formidable pile of junk. There was no possibility of questioning a concierge or neighbours, since there were none. The local superintendent went out on to the landing and spoke to the Nicolier boy.

'How about making yourself useful? Go downstairs and wait outside. Some men should be arriving in a few minutes. When they get here, show them up.'

'Yes, sir.'

'Don't forget to warn them about the missing treads on the stairs.'

Maigret was wandering about the room, picking things up and putting them down. In the process, he came across a bit of used candle and a box of matches. The candle was stuck to the bottom of a chipped cup.

In all his professional career, he had never seen anything like this room. The more he looked, the more puzzled he became. 'How was he killed?'

'He was shot several times in the chest and stomach.'

'With a large calibre gun?'

'Medium. . . . A .32 most probably.'

'Wasn't there anything in the pockets of his jacket?'

He could just imagine the revulsion with which the elegant and fastidious police superintendent had forced himself to handle those filthy rags.

'A button, some bits of string, a hunk of stale bread. . . .'

'No money?'

'Just two 25-centime pieces.'

'And what about his trouser pockets?'

'A filthy rag, that he must have used as a handkerchief, and some cigarette ends in a cough-lozenge tin.'

'No wallet?'

'No.'

Even the vagrants from the Quais, those who slept under the bridges, usually had papers in their pockets or, at the very least, an identity card.

Torrence, who by now had returned, was no less dumbfounded than Maigret.

'They're coming right away.'

Moers and his men from the Forensic Laboratory were, in fact, already being led up the stairs by the Nicolier boy. They looked about them in amazement.

14

'Is it murder?'

'Yes. There's no gun in here, so there's no question of suicide.'

'Where should we start?'

'With finger-prints, because we can't go very much further until he's been identified.'

'He certainly looked after his hands. It seems a shame to have to mess them up.'

Nevertheless, they took his finger-prints.

'Photographs?'

'Of course.'

'He's a fine figure of a man, isn't he? He must have been as strong as a horse.'

At this point, cautious footsteps were heard mounting the stairs, followed by the appearance of the D.P.P.'s representative, the Examining Magistrate, Cassure, and his clerk. All three gaped in amazement when they saw the room and its extraordinary contents.

'When was he killed?' asked the D.P.P.'s representative.

'We shall soon have the answer to that. Ah! here is Doctor Lagodinec, who should be able to tell us.'

The police surgeon was young, brisk and cheerful. He shook hands with Maigret, nodded to the others, and went straight up to the bed, which stood unevenly on crooked legs, another piece of wreckage picked up in the street, no doubt, or on some patch of waste ground.

They all looked anxiously at the floor. With so many people in the room, it was sagging dangerously and seemed on the point of collapse.

'It wouldn't surprise me if we all fell through to the floor below,' remarked the young doctor.

He waited by the bed until the photographers had completed their work, and then proceeded to examine the body. He bared the chest to reveal three black holes where the bullets had penetrated.

'Three shots were fired from a distance of three feet or less. The assailant took careful aim. The spacing is very neat, as you can see, which suggests to me that the victim was asleep at the time.'

'Instantaneous death, would you say?'

'Yes. One of the shots went clean through the left ventricle.'

'Do you think the bullets will have gone right through?'

'I'll tell you that when I've turned him over.'

One of the two photographers helped him. There was only one exit wound in the mysterious vagrant's back. No doubt the bullet would be found lodged in the mattress.

'Is there any water in the room?'

'No. It's been cut off.'

'I wonder how he managed to wash himself so thoroughly. As you can see, he kept himself very clean.'

'Can you give us a rough idea of the time of death?'

'Between two and five this morning. I daresay I'll be able to narrow it down a bit after I've done the autopsy. Has he been identified?'

'Not yet. We'll have to get a picture into the papers. By the way, how soon can you let us have the first prints?'

'In about an hour. Will that do?'

The photographers departed, leaving the other technicians to get on with the job of finger-printing everything in the room.

'I don't suppose we can be of any further use?' murmured the D.P.P.'s representative.

'Do you want me to stay?' put in Judge Cassure.

Maigret, with an abstracted air, was slowly puffing at his pipe. It took him a second or two to realize that he was being spoken to.

'No. I'll keep you informed.'

And to the police surgeon:

'Was he drunk, would you say?'

'I very much doubt it, but we'll know for sure when we've examined the contents of the stomach. At first sight, at any rate, he doesn't strike me as a man who was given to drinking.'

'A non-drinking vagrant?' murmured the local superintendent. 'You don't often come across one of them.'

'Maybe he wasn't a vagrant?' suggested Torrence.

As for Maigret, he spoke not a word. His glance travelled about the room, resting here and there, as though he were making a kind of private photographic record of everything he saw, down to the smallest detail. In less than a quarter of an hour, while the technicians were still at their work, the mortuary van from the Forensic Laboratory drove into the little passage, and the Nicolier boy went downstairs to show the two stretcher-bearers the way up.

'Yes, you can take him away.'

One last look at the noble patriarchal head, with its elegantly trimmed beard.

'The old fellow weighs a ton!' remarked one of the stretcher-bearers.

They had considerable difficulty in manœuvring their burden down the rickety stairs, with so many of the treads missing.

Maigret called out to the boy:

'Come here, laddie. Do you happen to know if there is a School of Hairdressing anywhere in the neighbourhood?'

'Yes, Monsieur Maigret. In the Rue Saint-Denis. Just three doors down from our butcher's shop.'

Maigret had had occasion, ten years ago or more, to visit one such school in pursuit of a criminal. No doubt in some districts of Paris such places were quite luxuriously appointed, but one would hardly expect to find anything on a very grand scale in the neighbourhood of Les Halles.

Presumably, the one in the Rue Saint-Denis, like many others, relied mainly on vagrants and beggars for the inexperienced and clumsy apprentices to practise on. The apprentices would be of both sexes, some of them training as manicurists.

But there was no point in going there until he had photographs of the dead man to show. For the time being, all Maigret could do was to hang fire, hoping that something useful might be gleaned from the finger-prints.

He left Moers and two of his men to carry on with their work in the room, and went downstairs, accompanied by Torrence and the local superintendent. It was a relief to breathe the relatively clean air of the cul-de-sac.

'Why was he killed, do you think?'

'I haven't the remotest idea.'

Beyond the archway, there was a courtyard. It was littered with old packing cases and other debris. Still, it did provide

Maigret with the answer to one of the doctor's questions. Set into one of the walls was a pump with a bucket in fairly sound condition underneath. He tried the pump. At first, nothing happened, but, with a little persistence, he soon got the water flowing.

Here, surely, was the explanation of the unknown man's personal cleanliness. The Chief Superintendent could picture him, naked to the waist, sluicing himself down with buckets of water.

Parting company with Superintendent Ascan, he turned into the Rue de la Grande-Truanderie and made towards Les Halles. It was growing hotter and hotter and, on the pretext of having to make a telephone call, he went into the nearest fairly decent-looking bistro and ordered a half of beer for himself and Torrence.

'Put me through to Records, will you?'

He asked to speak to Inspector Lebel, the officer who had taken the dead man's finger-prints.

'Hello . . . Lebel? Have you had time to go through the records yet?'

'I've just come from there. There are no prints corresponding to those of the dead man.'

Here was another anomaly. There were few vagrants who had not, at some time or other, come into conflict with the law.

'Thanks, anyway. Do you happen to know if the photographs are ready?'

'They should be in about ten minutes. . . . Ten minutes, Mestral, is that right?'

'Let's say a quarter of an hour.'

It was not far from Police Headquarters, and it took the two men no more than a few minutes to get back to the Quai des Orfèvres. Maigret went straight up to the Photographic Section. He had to wait a little while for the prints to dry. He had left Torrence in the Inspectors' Duty Room.

A number of photographs had been taken and, armed with three copies of each, he returned to his office, and instructed Inspector Lourtie to give them to the newspapers, especially those which printed afternoon editions.

'Come with me, Torrence. We've got an hour before

lunch. We'll use the time to make a few house-to-house calls.'

Maigret handed Torrence a sheaf of photographs.

'Show these around in all the little shops and bars near Les Halles. I'll meet you at the car.'

He himself made for the Rue Saint-Denis. It was a narrow street, crowded and noisy even at holiday time. For this little local community, seaside holidays were a rarity.

The Chief Superintendent peered at the numbers on the houses. The one he was looking for was a seedsman's shop. To the left of the shop window was a little passage leading into a courtyard. A flight of steps jutted out into it, beside which, fixed to the wall, were two enamel plaques which had once been green, but which by now had faded to an indeterminate grey.

JOSEPH
SCHOOL OF HAIRDRESSING and MANICURE.

Beneath this was an arrow pointing to the steps, and the word: MEZZANINE.

Flush underneath this plaque was another, which read:
MADAME VEUVE CORDIER
ARTIFICIAL FLOWERS

Here, too, there was an arrow pointing to the steps, but this time accompanied by the words: SECOND FLOOR.

Maigret mopped his brow, climbed to the mezzanine, opened a door, and found himself in a fairly large room inadequately lit by two narrow windows. A few naked light bulbs hanging from the ceiling did little to relieve the gloom.

There were two rows of armchairs, apparently one for men and the other for women. Several boys and girls were working under the direction of older men. Keeping a general eye on things was a skinny little man, almost bald, with a moustache dyed coal-black.

'You are the proprietor, I take it?'

'I am Monsieur Joseph, yes.'

He could have been any age between sixty and seventy-five. Mechanically, Maigret scrutinized the men and women in the armchairs, which had undoubtedly been bought as a job lot. He might have been in a Salvation Army shelter or under the bridges, since all the men and women being combed and clipped and shaved by the boys and girls were vagrants. It was really rather a gruesome spectacle, the more so in that dim light. On account of the heat, the two little windows were open, and the street noises were clearly to be heard, which made the school-room atmosphere of the place seem even more incongruous.

Not wishing to try Monsieur Joseph's patience any further, Maigret got the photographs out of his pocket and handed them to the little man.

'What am I to do with these?'

'Just look at them. Then tell me if you recognize . . .'

'What's he done? You're from the police, aren't you?'

He was visibly on the defensive.

'I'm Chief Superintendent Maigret of the *Police Judiciaire*.'

Monsieur Joseph was not impressed.

'Are you looking for him?'

'No. I'm sorry to say we have already found him. He was shot three times, full in the chest.'

'Where did it happen?'

'At his home . . . if you can call it that. . . . Do you know where he lived?'

'No.'

'He had moved into a house scheduled for demolition. . . . A small boy poking about in the building found the body, and reported it to the police. . . . Do you recognize him?'

'Yes. . . . He was known to us as the Toff.'

'Did he come often?'

'It varied. Sometimes we wouldn't see him for a whole month, and then for a few weeks after that he'd be in as often as two or three times a week.'

'Do you know his name?'

'No.'

'Not even his Christian name?'

'No.'

'Did he talk much?'

'He didn't talk at all. He'd sit down in the first vacant chair with his eyes half-closed, and let us do whatever we

20

liked with him. It was at my suggestion that he grew a moustache and a beard. . . . They're coming back into fashion again, and our apprentices need practice in trimming them—a trickier job than you might suppose. . . .'

'How long ago was this?'

'Three or four months.'

'Before that, was he clean-shaven?'

'Yes. He had a magnificent head of hair, there was nothing you couldn't do with it.'

'Had he been coming to you for long?'

'Three or four years.'

'You seem to work mostly with vagrants.'

'Almost entirely. . . . You see, they can always be sure I'll give them a five-franc piece at the end of the morning or afternoon session.'

'Did that apply to him, too?'

'Of course.'

'Was he friendly with any of your regulars?'

'I never saw him speak to anyone, and if anyone spoke to him, he pretended not to hear.'

It was close on midday. The scissors snipped more rapidly. In a few minutes there would be a stampede for the door, as in an ordinary school.

'Do you live in this district?'

'My wife and I live in this building, on the first floor, right overhead. . . .'

'Did you ever run into him in the street?'

'I don't think so. Or at any rate, if I did, I don't remember. . . . You must excuse me now, it's time. . . .'

He went behind a counter of sorts, in front of which a queue had formed, and pressed an electric buzzer.

Maigret went slowly down the steps. After so many years in the *Police Judiciaire*, not to mention those earlier years of pounding the beat and policing the railway stations, he surely knew all there was to know about the human flotsam of Paris. And yet he could not remember ever having met anyone remotely resembling the man they called the Toff.

Slowly he walked to the corner of the Rue Rambuteau, where the car was parked. Torrence arrived almost at the same moment, and he, like Maigret, was mopping his face.

'Did you have any luck?'

'Well, first of all, I found the bakery in the Rue du Cygne where he bought his bread.'

'Did he go in every day?'

'Pretty well. Usually in the morning, late.'

'Were they able to tell you anything about him?'

'Nothing. Apart from asking for his bread, he never spoke.'

'Did he never buy anything else?'

'Not there. There's a place in the Rue Coquillière, though, where he used to buy slices of sausage or a hot saveloy. There's an open air stall as well, on the corner, which also sells hot sausages, especially at night. He'd go there occasionally round about three in the morning for a bag of chips and a sausage.

'I went into two or three bistros with the photographs. He'd been seen in all of them from time to time, but he never had anything but a cup of coffee. He didn't drink wine or spirits. . . .'

The picture that was emerging was more and more odd. The Toff, to use Monsieur Joseph's nickname, seemed to have had no contact whatsoever with any other human being. It looked as if he had worked through the night in Les Halles, whenever there was work going, unloading fruit and vegetables from a lorry.

The Chief Superintendent suddenly remembered that he had to telephone the Forensic Laboratory, which gave him an excellent excuse for ordering his second glass of beer that morning.

'Would you be so good as to put me on to Doctor Lagodinec.'

'One moment, please. He's just on his way out. I'll call him back.'

'Hello! Lagodinec? Maigret here. . . . I suppose you haven't begun the autopsy yet?'

'I'll be doing it straight after lunch.'

'Could you leave his face alone, do you think? I shall need some more photographs.'

'No problem. When will you be sending the photographer?'

'Tomorrow morning, in company with a barber.'

'Whatever for?'

'To shave off his moustache and beard.'

Torrence drove him home to the Boulevard Richard-Lenoir. 'Will you be wanting me to carry on this afternoon?'

'Yes.'

'The Les Halles district again?'

'Yes, and possibly the Quais as well. I fancy he may have been in the habit of sleeping under the bridges at one time or another.'

Madame Maigret could see at once that he was preoccupied, and pretended not to notice.

'Are you hungry?'

'Not really.'

It was he rather than she who wanted to talk about the events of the morning.

'I've just come across the most extraordinary character you could possibly imagine.'

'A criminal?'

'No. A victim. The man is dead. . . . He had dug himself in in an empty house long scheduled for demolition. He lived in one more or less habitable room, and crammed it full of the oddest assortment of junk, fished out of dustbins and rubbish dumps. . . .'

'In other words, a tramp.'

'Except that he has the looks of an Old Testament patriarch.'

He told his wife about the School of Hairdressing, and showed her the photographs.

'Of course it's hard to tell much from a dead man's photograph.'

'But surely he must have been known in the district?'

'No one knows his name, not even his Christian name. At the School of Hairdressing, they called him the Toff. . . . The afternoon editions of the newspapers will carry his photograph . . . I wonder if any of their readers will recognize him.'

As he had said, he was not hungry, and he picked at his food. He hated to be mystified, and everything he had discovered that morning had only deepened the mystery.

By two o'clock he was back in his office and, after filling his pipe, he went through the rest of his mail. Soon afterwards, the newspapers were brought in to him. Two of them, he noted, had printed the photograph on the front page. In one, the caption read: *Do you know this man?* and in the other: *A corpse without a name.*

There were a number of journalists outside in the corridor. Maigret agreed to see them. He had practically nothing to tell them, apart from assuring them that every effort was being made to identify the man found dead in Vieux-Four Passage.

'He didn't commit suicide?'

'There was no weapon in the room or anywhere in the building.'

'Can we take photographs?'

'Well, the body has been moved, of course.'

'It's background material we want.'

'Very well. There's a man posted at the door. You can tell him you have my permission.'

'You seem worried.'

'I'm trying to puzzle it out, that's all. Sooner or later, no doubt, I shall succeed. This time, I can assure you, I've got nothing up my sleeve. I've told you all I know. The more publicity the better, as far as I'm concerned.'

At about four, the phone calls started coming in. Among the callers were the usual hoaxers and nut-cases. This was unavoidable.

One caller, a young girl, asked:

'Has he a wart on his cheek?'

'No.'

'Then he's not the man I thought he was.'

Four or five people actually turned up in person. Patiently, Maigret interviewed them all. He showed them the photographs, taken from various angles.

'Do you recognize him?'

'He reminds me a bit of an uncle of mine who has disappeared a couple of times before. But . . . no . . . it isn't him. . . . This man was tall, wasn't he?'

'About six foot.'

'My uncle was short, very small and very thin. . . .'

For the first time that week, there was no cloudburst, and the air was stifling.

It was nearly five when Torrence got back.

'Any luck?'

'Nothing to speak of. There was an old tramp under the Pont-Marie who thought he vaguely remembered our man, but I'm not sure how far he is to be believed. It seems that, some years back, our friend was in the habit of sleeping under the bridges. . . . He was never very forthcoming. It was generally believed that he spent part of the night working in Les Halles, but that was all that anybody knew.'

'Christian name? Surname? Nickname?'

'He was known by a nickname, yes: the Mute.'

'Anything else?'

'Every now and then he would buy a candle.'

It was six o'clock before he had anything more definite to go on. He had a call from Doctor Lagodinec, to let him know the result of the autopsy.

'My written report will be ready in the morning, but meanwhile I thought you'd like a rough idea of my findings. It's my belief that the man is a good deal younger than he looks. How old would you say he was, Maigret?'

'Sixty-five? Seventy?'

'Judging from the state of his internal organs and his arteries, I'd say he wasn't a day over fifty-five, if that.'

'He'd had a hard life, that's for sure. What about the contents of his stomach?'

'First of all, I can now say for certain that he was killed between two and five in the morning, most likely about three. His last meal, which was only partly digested, consisted of sausages and chips. He must have eaten at about two, and gone straight home to bed.'

'And, finding him asleep, someone took the opportunity to . . .'

'To do what?' objected the doctor. 'Couldn't his visitor have been someone he trusted?'

'I can't see him trusting anyone. What was his state of health?'

'Perfect. . . . No congenital disabilities either. . . . He was an extremely robust man, and unusually resistant to . . .'

'Thank you, Doctor, I shall look forward to reading your report. If you like, I'll send over for it in the morning. . . .'

'Not before nine, please.'

'Very well, I'll make it nine o'clock.'

The thing that surprised Maigret most was the Toff's real age. To all appearances, he had been a vagrant for some years, probably for many years, and, as a general rule, vagrants were on the elderly side. What was more, they were a gregarious lot. From one end of the Quais of Paris to the other, up stream and down stream, there was scarcely a single vagrant not known to all the others, and all took an immediate and lively interest in any newcomer.

'What have you found out, Torrence?'

'Practically nothing. Except for the old boy at Pont-Marie, no one remembers him. And yet some of them have been living rough for ten years or more. I went into the tobacconist's nearest to where he lived. He used to go in occasionally for a box of matches.'

'What about cigarettes?'

'No. It seems he only smoked fag-ends that he picked up in the streets.'

The telephone rang. 'Hello! Monsieur Maigret?'

It was a woman's voice, a young voice.

'Yes, speaking. . . . Who is that, please?'

'My name wouldn't mean anything to you. Did the man who was found dead this morning have a scar on his scalp?'

'I must confess I don't know. No doubt, if he had, it will appear on the police surgeon's report, which I shall be receiving in the morning.'

'Have you any idea who the man is?'

'I don't know yet.'

'I'll ring you again sometime tomorrow.'

She hung up without another word. Whereupon it occurred to Maigret that he had no need to wait until next day to get the answer to the young woman's question. He rang the School of Hairdressing, and was put on to Monsieur Joseph.

'This is Chief Superintendent Maigret. There's one thing I forgot to ask you this morning. Did you ever do the Toff's hair yourself?'

'Yes. . . . Occasionally, when I was doing a demonstration for the apprentices.'

'Did you notice a scar on his scalp?'

'Yes. . . . But I could never pluck up the courage to ask him how he got it.'

'Was it big?'

'About three inches long. And it hadn't been stitched up, so it was fairly wide.'

'Was it visible through his hair?'

'Not when it was properly brushed. As I think I told you, he had a magnificent head of hair.'

'Thanks.'

So he was on the scent at last, even though he had lost it again after only a few seconds. Somewhere in Paris there was a girl or young woman who must have known the Toff, since she was aware that he had a scar on his head. She had taken good care to hang up before Maigret could ask any questions. Would she ring again next day, as she had said she would?

Maigret was running out of patience. He couldn't wait to put a name to the unknown man and discover why he had chosen to live as he had.

The extraordinary collection of junk assembled in the room in Vieux-Four Passage suggested a madman, or at least an obsessional. Why else should anyone hoard a quantity of objects which were not merely unsaleable but useless?

But Maigret could not bring himself to believe that the man had been mad.

Once again the telephone rang. This was what Maigret had been expecting and hoping for ever since the photographs appeared in the papers.

'Hello! Is that Chief Superintendent Maigret?'

'Yes. Who is that, please?'

Like the earlier caller, this woman, who, however, sounded a lot older, did not give her name, but making it sound as casual as possible, she asked the same question.

'Has he a scar on the crown of his head?'

'Do you know someone who has, and who looks like him?'

Silence at the other end of the line.

'Why don't you answer me?'

'You haven't answered my question.'

'There is, in fact, a scar about three inches long across the top of his head.'

'Thank you.'

Like the previous caller, she hung up at once. So there were two women who had known the Toff, though, on the face of it, they were not in communication, otherwise there would have been no need to make two separate telephone calls.

How was he going to find them among five million people? And why were they both so anxious to remain anonymous?

Maigret was very much put out, and he left Police Headquarters fuming. Still, he had learned one thing, which was that his mysterious recluse had not always been that much of a recluse.

Two women had known him. Two women remembered him, but did not want to answer questions.

Why not?

Although there had been no storm, it was a little cooler. A light breeze had sprung up, and it was puffing a few little pink clouds across the sky, as on a stage set.

He decided to treat himself to a glass of beer. He had promised Doctor Pardon to moderate his drinking. But, surely, three glasses of draught beer in a day could not be called immoderate?

He resolved to banish the Toff from his thoughts. All the same, he would very much like to know who had tracked him down to his extraordinary lair, and why whoever it was had killed him.

He shrugged his shoulders irritably. He knew well enough that he had no right to expect, as he invariably did, to find out everything all at once at the very beginning of a case. Every time, he behaved as if fate had dealt him an unkind blow.

Then, in the days that followed, the truth would gradually come to light. Was that how it would be this time, too?

Defiantly, he whistled as he went up the stairs to his flat.

# Chapter Two

BY THE NEXT MORNING, Maigret had shed his ill-humour and, once again, he decided to walk from his home to the Quai des Orfèvres. The municipal road sweepers were moving slowly through the empty streets, leaving broad, wet tracks behind them, and a misty heat-haze shimmered over the Seine.

On his way up the stairs of Police Headquarters, he overtook a photographer, loaded with photographic equipment, who was on his way to see him. He knew him well. He was always hovering about when a case was in progress. He worked for an agency, and was prepared to wait hours in the hope of getting a break. He was redheaded, with the eagerness of an overgrown schoolboy, and if he was turned away at one door, he would come in by another, or climb through a window.

He was known to his colleagues as Coco. His real name was Marcel Caune.

He took a quick shot of Maigret on the stairs. It must have been at least his two-hundredth picture of the Chief Superintendent.

'Have you interrogated any witnesses yet?'

'No.'

'There's one waiting for you in the corridor.'

'It's the first I've heard of it.'

And, indeed, there was a man sitting on a bench. He was very old, but spry, and he sprang eagerly to his feet.

'Could I have a word with you, Chief Superintendent?'

'Is it about that business in Les Halles?'

'Yes. The murder in Vieux-Four Passage.'

'I'll see you in a moment.'

First, as was his invariable habit, he looked in on the inspectors.

They were all in shirt sleeves, and the solitary window of their room was wide open. Torrence was there, reading a newspaper article under the headline: *Chief Superintendent Maigret on the scent.*

Which was pure fabrication, of course.

'Any news, lads?'

'The usual anonymous letters. And letters from a couple of our regular correspondents, lunatics, of course.'

From his office, Maigret telephoned the School of Hairdressing.

'Monsieur Joseph? I wonder if I could ask you a favour? Could you spare one of your young men to go to the mortuary and shave off the Toff's beard and moustache . . . ? Needless to say, he'll be paid for his trouble.'

'I'd rather go myself. It's a job that requires skill.'

Next, he rang Criminal Records and spoke to Moers.

'Is Mestral in?'

'He's just arrived.'

'Would you mind sending him over to the mortuary? He'll find a barber there shaving off our man's moustache and beard. As soon as it's done, I want some good, clear photographs taken from all possible angles. It's urgent.'

No sooner had he hung up than the telephone rang.

'Hello! Chief Superintendent Maigret?'

He thought he recognized the voice.

'I'm the person who rang you yesterday about the murder in Les Halles.' The young voice. Not the other one.

'You want the answer to your question, I presume?'

'Yes.'

'You're not the only one.'

'Oh?'

'Another woman rang, after you did, and asked me the very same thing. . . .'

'What did you say to her?'

'Come and see me here, and I will tell you. Alternatively, you could give me your name and address.'

'I'd rather not.'

'As you wish.'

And this time it was Maigret who rang off, grumbling: 'Little madam!'

The long and the short of it was that there were at least three people who knew the Toff's identity: the two women who had telephoned about the scar and, needless to say, the murderer.

Maigret went across and opened the door. His visitor, who was small and thin, sprang to his feet and came towards him.

'I was afraid you might not be willing to see me.'

There was something about his walk, his bearing and his speech which struck a chord in the Chief Superintendent, though he could not have said why.

'My name is Emile Hugon and I live in the Rue Lepic in the flat where I was born. . . . It belonged to my parents then. . . .'

'Take a seat.'

'Though I may not look it, I am eighty-five years old.'

He was obviously very proud of having reached his present age in such good condition.

'I walked here from Montmartre; I make a point of walking for at least two hours every day.'

There was no point, Maigret realized, in bombarding him with questions.

'I am known in the district as the Colonel. Mind you, I never was a colonel, only a captain. When the 1914 war broke out, I was a cadet at the Military Academy. I was at Verdun and the Chemin des Dames. I came through Verdun unscathed. . . . It was at the Chemin des Dames that I got a shrapnel wound in the leg, which has left me, even now, with a limp. By the time the second war broke out I was over age, and they had no further use for me.'

He radiated self-satisfaction. The Chief Superintendent could only exercise patience, and hope that the Colonel was not going to tell him his entire life story in detail.

Instead of doing so, however, the old man broke off abruptly to ask, 'Have you identified him?'

'Not yet.'

'Unless I'm very much mistaken, which I am pretty sure is not the case, his name is Marcel Vivien.'

'Did you know him personally?'

'He rented the workshop overlooking the courtyard, just underneath my flat. Whenever I went out, I always made a point of passing the time of day with him.'

'When was this?'

'Soon after the end of the Second World War, in 1945. . . .'

'How old was he then?'

'About thirty-five. He was a tall, well-built young man, with an intelligent open face.'

'What did he do for a living?'

'He was a cabinet maker. What's more, he had done a course at a School of Arts and Crafts. . . . His speciality was the restoration of antique furniture . . . I saw some marvellous stuff there, the very finest marquetry.'

'Did he live in the same building?'

'No, he just rented the studio-workshop. He came in in the morning and left at night.'

'Is there really a very close resemblance between him and the man in the photograph?'

'I could swear it was the same man, except that he was clean-shaven. . . .'

'Do you know if he was married?'

'Certainly. . . . A woman of about his own age used sometimes to come and fetch him at the end of his working day. And there was a little girl of about seven or eight who often looked in on him on her way home from school.'

'When did you lose sight of him?'

'Somewhere about the end of 1945 or the beginning of 1946. He just failed to turn up one morning at his workshop, and he wasn't there the next day or the next. . . . At first I thought he must be ill. Then, a few days later, his wife came. . . . She had the key. . . . She went into the workshop and stayed there a long time. . . . I thought she must be making an inventory. . . .'

'Have you seen her since?'

'She still lives in the neighbourhood, and she often comes to the Rue Lepic to buy vegetables and such off the little barrows. . . . For years I used to see her daughter around too. . . . She was growing up. . . . I daresay she's married by now.'

'What happened to the furniture that was left in the workshop?'

'It was taken away by a firm of upholsterers. There's a locksmith there now.'

Maigret showed him all the photographs he had of the man from Vieux-Four Passage. The Colonel studied them attentively.

'I'm still of the same opinion. I'm almost sure it's him. I've been retired for many years. In the summer I spend hours every day sitting on a park bench or a café terrace watching the people go by. I try to guess at their occupation, their life-style. In other words, I've trained myself to be observant.'

'Do you happen to know if this man ever had an accident?'

'He didn't own a car. . . .'

'There are other sorts of accidents. Do you happen to know if he ever had a scalp wound?'

Suddenly the Colonel slapped himself on the forehead.

'But of course! It was in the middle of the summer. . . . It was very hot, as hot as it is now. . . . He was working out in the courtyard, fitting a new leg to a chair. . . . I was watching him out of the window, and I saw a pot of geraniums fall on his head. . . . It was Mademoiselle Blanche on the third floor. . . . She was watering her plants, when she accidentally knocked it over. . . .

'He wouldn't see a doctor or go to the hospital. He just dabbed some disinfectant on the wound, and the chemist opposite bandaged it up for him.'

'Was there a visible scar?'

'He had a lot of hair, very thick, and he wore it quite long, so that the scar was hidden.'

'Is there anything else you can tell me about him? Have you ever seen him since about the neighbourhood?'

'Never.'

'And yet his wife and daughter went on living there? So he obviously didn't take them with him. . . .'

'That is so.'

'Did he drink, do you know?'

'Far from it. Every morning at about ten, he would shut up shop for a few minutes, and go and have a cup of coffee in the little bistro nearby.'

'Is there anyone living in your block, apart from yourself, who was there in 1945?'

'Let me think. . . . The concierge. . . . Yes, it's still the same one. . . . Her husband is dead . . he was a policeman. . . . She's aged a lot. . . . Mademoiselle Blanche—I mentioned her just now—she's still alive but chairbound and, so it's said, not quite in her right mind. . . . The other floors . . . ? There are the Trabuchets, on the third. . . . He used to be a tallyman. . . . He's retired, too. . . . Needless to say, we're none of us getting any younger.'

'Do you think any of them would remember Marcel Vivien?'

'It's possible, but the Trabuchets' windows overlook the street. They hadn't the same opportunities as I had to see what went on in the courtyard. . . .'

'I'm much obliged to you for having come, Monsieur Hugon. All that you have told me will be most helpful, I'm sure. Would you be so good as to go into one of the little rooms at the end of the passage with one of my inspectors, and repeat your story to him?'

'Will I be called as a witness at the trial?'

He was highly delighted at the prospect.

'Not so fast! We must first apprehend the murderer, and have the victim formally identified.'

Maigret opened the communicating door to the Inspectors' Duty Room. Lourtie had the fastest typing speed in the Department. He called him over, told him what was required, and gave the Colonel into his charge.

It really did begin to look as if he had a lead at last. Maigret was anxious to be on his way to the Rue Lepic, but he had to wait for the photographs. Mestral was a fast worker, he knew, so he stifled his impatience and filled in the time by opening his mail.

At half past ten, the photographer arrived with a whole sheaf of pictures in his hand.

'It makes him look younger, don't you think?'

'Yes. . . . And, in fact, it seems he isn't all that old. Fifty-five at the most, the police surgeon says. How many copies have you made?'

'I've brought you five of each pose, if one can call it that in the case of a dead man. Incidentally, that barber of yours was so overcome that I thought he was going to pass out.'

'Thanks. I shall need some more copies. I'll have to send them out to all the newspapers.'

Maigret stuffed two sets of photographs into his pocket, and handed another to Coco, the most persistent newshound in Paris.

'Here. . . . We've done half your work for you. . . . Pictures

34

of the dead man with his moustache and beard shaved off. Your agency can make copies and send them to as many newspapers as they like.'

Maigret also gave two sets to Leduc, one of the youngest inspectors in the Department.

'Deliver these to the two main evening papers. Come to think of it, you'd better get a move on. The first editions go to press in the early afternoon. See to it that they get to the editor himself, or at least to the chief sub-editor.'

Finally, he went to the end of the corridor, where Lourtie was typing the Colonel's statement. The old man sprang to his feet, as he had done before.

'Don't get up. I just wanted to show you these. . . .'

And he held out the new photographs. The retired military man glanced at them and looked up, his face wreathed in smiles.

'That's him. Now I'm quite sure there's no mistake. He's aged, of course, but it's Vivien all right.'

Maigret nodded to Lourtie to carry on, and returned to the Inspectors' Duty Room.

'Get your hat, Torrence.'

'Are we going far?'

'To Montmartre. The Rue Lepic, to be precise.'

He showed the photographs to the inspector.

'You've had him shaved, I see.'

'This morning. . . . I've just had a visit from an old retired army captain of eighty-five who says he recognizes him, although he hasn't seen him for the best part of twenty years.'

'Who is he?'

'A cabinet maker, so it would seem. He had a workshop in the Rue Lepic, until, from one day to the next, he suddenly vanished. . . .'

'Twenty years ago?'

'Yes.'

'Had he any family?'

'A wife and daughter, apparently.'

'Have they vanished as well?'

'No. They lived on in the district for some years.'

They took one of the little black *Police Judiciaire* cars,

and drove to the Rue Lepic, which was jammed with barrows selling fruit and vegetables. Number 65B was at the bottom of the road, on the left.

'Try and find somewhere to park, and then come and join me. I'll probably be with the concierge.'

The concierge was still quite young and attractive. She watched the Chief Superintendent through the glass panels of the lodge door. Maigret knocked. She opened the door.

'What can I do for you?'

'I'm Chief Superintendent Maigret of the *Police Judiciaire*.'

'Is it about one of my tenants?' she exclaimed, in amazement.

'It's about one of your former tenants. . . .'

'Ah! So I wasn't mistaken. . . .'

'What do you mean?'

'Yesterday, as soon as I saw the picture in the paper, I was reminded of Monsieur Vivien. In fact I said as much to someone in the dairy, but in fairness I had to add: "It can't possibly be him. . . . Such a respectable, hardworking young man. . . . I can't believe he'd ever have sunk to being a down-and-out." '

As Maigret held out the new photographs, Torrence came into the lodge.

'This is one of my inspectors. . . . Have a good look at these pictures.'

'Oh! There's no need . . . I can see at a glance that it's him. . . . What put me off a bit yesterday was the moustache and the beard. . . . You've had him shaved. . . .'

Still staring at the photographs, she added: 'It's knocked me all of a heap.'

'Do you remember the circumstances in which he left? Did he give notice? Did he return the furniture he was working on to its owners?'

'Nothing of that sort at all. He just simply stopped coming, and no one hereabouts ever saw him again.'

'Didn't anyone report his disappearance to the police?'

'I don't know. . . . His wife may have done. She seldom came to see him at work. . . . His daughter, now, that was different. She used to pass here on her way to and from school, and she'd look in almost every day, to give him a hug. He lived not far from here, in the Rue Caulaincourt. I don't know the number, but it's next door to a dry cleaner's.'

'Have you ever seen his wife since?'

'Quite often. She still buys her fruit and vegetables off the little barrows in the Rue Lepic. . . . Her hair has gone grey, and she's grown very thin. . . . She used to be quite plump in the old days. . . .'

'Have you ever spoken to her?'

'I caught her eye two or three times, but she didn't seem to recognize me.'

'How long is it since you last saw her?'

'Some months. . . . A year, perhaps.'

'And the daughter? She must be twenty-eight now.'

'Someone, I can't remember who, told me that she was married, with children of her own.'

'Does she live in Montmartre?'

'Apparently, but I don't know exactly where.'

'Would it be possible for me to have a look at the work-shop?'

'The door leading to the courtyard is at the end of the passage. You'll find Monsieur Benoît, the locksmith, at his work there.'

The locksmith was a very pleasant-looking man of about thirty.

'What can I do for you?'

Maigret introduced himself.

'I presume you've come about the man who was shot three times in the chest? Everyone was talking about him this morning in the bistro where I regularly go for a drink.'

'Did you know him?'

'How could I? I was only ten years old when he left here. The tenant after him was an upholsterer. He stayed for about fifteen years. But he was getting on in years and, in the end, he decided to retire to the country. It was then that I took over the lease.'

'Has anyone ever come in here making inquiries about Marcel Vivien?'

'Never. But now everyone is talking about him. . . . This

morning, while I was having my coffee and croissants, I heard some of the older residents discussing him. Most of them remember him, and they can't understand how he can have been driven to vagrancy. . . . He was a fine-looking man, it seems, very big and strong, skilled at his trade and making a very good living. . . . And yet, from one day to the next, he disappeared without a word to anyone. . . .'

'Not even his wife?'

'Apparently not. . . . Whether that's true or not, I can't say. I'm only repeating what I've heard. . . . Several days went by after he disappeared, it seems, possibly as much as a week, before she came here making inquiries. . . . That's all I know, but if you want to hear more you have only to go to the bistro nearby. . . .'

'I'm much obliged to you.'

He returned to the Rue Lepic, accompanied by Torrence. He was beginning to get a clearer picture of the dead man from Les Halles. They both went into the little local bar. It was immediately obvious that all the people standing at the old-fashioned bar counter were regulars.

'What will you have?'

'A beer.'

'And the same for me,' said Torrence.

There was a pleasant smell of fruit and vegetables, wafted in from the little barrows that lined both sides of the street outside.

The proprietor brought them their drinks.

'Aren't you Chief Superintendent Maigret?'

'Yes.'

'I presume you've come about the man whose picture was in the afternoon editions of yesterday's papers?'

Everyone was staring at him now. It was only a question of who would speak first.

The first to speak was a powerfully built man, with huge arms, wearing a blood-stained white apron. He was a butcher.

'Who's to say that he didn't slink off with some little piece or other, much younger than himself? And no doubt, when she ditched him, he hadn't the face to go back to his old woman. I had an assistant like that once. He worked for me for almost ten years. A quieter, more reliable fellow you would never meet. But that didn't stop him from disappearing one day without a word to anyone. He had run off with an eighteen-year-old girl. As for him, he was all of forty-five. Two years later, he was seen queueing up for the dole in the employment exchange in Strasbourg.'

The others nodded sagely. It was a typical local in a working class district. Most of those present were manual workers, small traders or old age pensioners, who came in regularly for a mid-morning drink.

'Did anyone here ever see him again after his disappearance?'

They exchanged glances. A spindly man in a leather apron expressed the general view.

'He wouldn't have been such a fool as to show his face here.'

'Do you know his wife?'

'No. I don't even know where he lived. I only ever saw him when he came in here for his morning coffee. He wasn't very sociable. . . .'

'A bit toffee-nosed, was he?'

'No, not toffee-nosed. He just liked to keep himself to himself.'

Maigret drank his beer. His first that day. He was keeping count. Next time he saw Pardon, he would be able to report, not without pride, that he had cut down considerably. Admittedly, the same could not be said of his smoking. He was as dependent on his pipe as ever. But surely a man wasn't to be deprived of all his pleasures, just because he was coming up to fifty-five?

'I believe I saw him once in the Rue de la Cossonnerie, but his hair was quite white, and he was dressed like a beggar. I decided it couldn't be him, and went on my way. . . .'

The speaker was a little old man who was drinking a brand of aperitif that was very popular forty years earlier, but for which there was now very little demand.

'How long ago was this?'

'About three months ago. . . . No, longer than that. . . . Admittedly, spring was late this year, but it was still winter.'

'I'm very much obliged to you, gentlemen.'

'Think nothing of it. Anything I can do . . . I sincerely hope you get the scoundrel who shot him in the chest. . . .'

They set out on foot for the Rue Caulaincourt. Was it really going to be necessary to ring at every door and question every concierge in order to find Vivien's wife, always assuming that she was still living in the district?

Owing to the heat, Maigret could not face the prospect. Instead, he made his way to the police station in the Rue Lambert.

Years ago he had known a man who had disappeared in the same manner as the cabinet maker, though whether for similar reasons it was hard to tell.

The man had been a prosperous industrialist living in Paris, seemingly without a care in the world. Aged a little over fifty, he had had a wife and two children. The elder, a boy of twenty-one, had been at university. As to the daughter, three years younger, there was no reason to suppose that she had ever given her parents a moment's anxiety.

One morning, he had set out at the usual time for his factory in Le Vallois. He was driving himself. It was to be several years before anything more was heard of him.

His car had been found not far from the Rue du Temple. As far as anyone knew, he had never had a mistress. According to his doctor, he had never been seriously ill, and had many years of life still to look forward to.

The police had searched for him everywhere, except where he was actually to be found.

He had, in fact, decided overnight, as it were, to become a tramp. He had been to a pawnbroker in the Rue des Blancs-Manteaux, and there exchanged his clothes for a set of filthy rags. From that moment onwards, he had stopped shaving.

Three years later, in spite of the disguise of a heavy beard, he had been recognized in Nice by one of his former suppliers. He was selling newspapers on the café terraces. The supplier, with the best of intentions, had informed the police, and telephoned the man's wife, but although a thorough search was made for him, he was never found. Maigret thought of him often.

'My advice is to give up the search, Madame. You know

now that he is alive and in good health. . . . He has chosen to lead his own life in his own way. . . .'

'You're not suggesting, surely, that he has become a down-and-out from choice?'

She had failed to understand. This man, however, had kept his identity card, so that it had been possible to inform his family when he died, fifteen years later, in the old quarter of Marseilles, which, at that time, had not yet been pulled down.

'Good morning, Dubois,' said Maigret to the constable on duty at the desk. By some miracle, or perhaps because so many people were away, the entrance hall of the police station was empty.

'The Chief has gone out, but he should be back soon.'

'It's not him I want to see. I just wanted to ask you if you'd be so good as to look up your records, and tell me whether a Madame Vivien, Madame Marcel Vivien, is still living in this district.'

'Do you happen to know her last address?'

'Rue Caulaincourt. I'm afraid I don't know the number.'

'Is that a recent address?'

'No. It goes back twenty years.'

The constable leafed through several big black ledgers, pausing here and there to run his forefinger down the page.

It took him a quarter of an hour to find what he was looking for.

'Christian name of Gabrielle?'

'That's right.'

'Her address is still registered as 67 Rue Caulaincourt.'

'I'm most grateful to you, Dubois. Considering the length of the Rue Caulaincourt, you've saved me at least an hour. . . . I'd have had to plod from door to door. . . .'

Although it was a journey of only a few hundred yards, the two men got into the car. Number 67 was near the corner of the Place Constantin-Pecqueur.

'Do you want me with you?'

'I'd better go alone, I think. It might put her off if there were two of us.'

'I'll wait for you at *Chez Manière*.'

There are few Frenchmen who have not heard of *Chez*

*Manière*, which was only a few doors away. Maigret knocked at the door of the lodge, where he could see a young woman arranging fruit on a dish.

'Come in.'

He pushed open the door.

'What can I do for you?'

'I'd be grateful if you could tell me if Madame Vivien still lives here.'

'On the fourth floor.'

'Is it the same flat she lived in with her husband?'

'I was too young to be a concierge in those days. But I think she moved from a larger flat on another floor. Her present flat has just two rooms and a kitchen, overlooking the courtyard.'

'You don't happen to know if she's at home?'

'It's more than likely, I should think. She goes out very early in the morning to do her shopping. And not every morning, at that.'

There was a small lift. The Chief Superintendent was about to get into it when the concierge caught him up and said, 'It's the door on the left.'

'Thanks.'

Maigret could hardly wait. He had the feeling that he was within touching distance of his goal, and that in a few minutes he would know everything there was to know about the man from Vieux-Four Passage.

He pressed the bell and heard it ring inside the flat. Then the door opened to reveal an elderly hard-featured woman. Frowning, she stared at him.

'Madame Vivien?'

'What do you want? Are you a reporter?'

'No. I am Chief Superintendent Maigret of the *Police Judiciaire*. I believe you telephoned me yesterday.'

She neither confirmed nor denied this, nor did she invite him in. They looked at one another uncertainly for a moment, then the Chief Superintendent took the bull by the horns, pushed the door wider, and went inside.

'I have nothing to say to you,' she declared emphatically, intending him to understand that this was her last word on the subject.

'I only want to ask you a few questions.'

An open door led from the entrance lobby into a sort of sitting room, most of which, however, was taken up with the paraphernalia of dressmaking. There was a sewing machine on a small table, and a larger table covered with dresses in various stages of completion.

'You've taken up dressmaking, I see.'

'One has to earn a living as best one can.'

As with the table, dresses were hung over all the chairs. Maigret remained standing, and so did the woman.

The most striking thing about her was the hardness of her expression, reinforced by the rigidity of her body. It was evident that she had suffered a good deal and, in consequence, had turned in upon herself and had become, as it were, atrophied.

Colourfully dressed she could have been quite attractive, but she had ceased to care about her appearance.

'Two people, both women, telephoned me yesterday, and both asked me the same question. And then they both hung up on me, presumably because they wanted to remain anonymous. I take it that the second caller was your daughter . . . ?'

She didn't answer.

'Is she married? Has she any children?'

'What has that got to do with you? Why can't we be left in peace? At this rate, it won't be long before we are besieged by reporters and press photographers. . . .'

'They won't get your address from me, I promise you.'

She shrugged, apparently accepting the inevitable.

'Your husband has been identified by several independent witnesses, so there is no longer any doubt as to who he is. Did you know what had become of him?'

'No.'

'What did he say to you, twenty years ago, when he left you?'

'Nothing.'

'Did you notice any change in his attitude towards the end?'

She seemed to give a little start, but her self-control was such that it was difficult to be sure.

43

'He was just the same as usual.'

'Were you and he on good terms?'

'I was his wife.'

'Some husbands and wives quarrel from morning to night, and make life hell for one another.'

'It wasn't so in our case.'

'Did he ever go out alone at night?'

'No. We always went out together.'

'Where did you go mostly?'

'To the pictures. Or sometimes just for a walk in the neighbourhood.'

'Did he seem preoccupied in the last few days before he disappeared?'

'No.'

Maigret had the feeling that she was resorting to monosyllables to conceal the fact that she was not telling the truth.

'Did you ever entertain friends?'

'No.'

'What about relations?'

'Neither of us had any relations living in Paris.'

'Where did you meet him?'

'In the shop where I used to work.'

She had the pale, dull complexion of someone who never went out, and all her movements were stiff and awkward.

'Have you done?'

'Have you a photograph of him?'

'No.'

'That's him, isn't it, on the mantelpiece?'

This was a young Marcel Vivien, good-humoured, almost jocular.

'That stays where it is, in its frame.'

'You shall have it back as soon as I've had copies made.'

'I said no. . . . You surely don't want to deprive me even of the little I have left. . . .'

She took a step towards the door.

'May I have your daughter's address, please?'

'Where did you get mine from?'

'The police station.'

She seemed on the point of telling him that he could get her daughter's address from the same source, but then, apparently changing her mind, she said, with another little shrug of her shoulders:

'She was barely eight years old when he left.'

'She's married, isn't she?'

Also on the mantelpiece there was a photograph of two children, aged about six and four.

'Yes, she is married. Her married name is Odette Delaveau, and she lives at 12 Rue Marcadet. Now, I'd be obliged if you would leave. I have someone coming for a fitting this afternoon, and I still have some work to do on the dress.'

'I'm much obliged to you,' said Maigret, not without a touch of sarcasm.

'Don't mention it.'

He would have liked to ask her a good many more questions, but he could see that they would get him nowhere. It would take time to win her confidence, if it could be done at all.

Torrence was waiting for him on the terrace of *Chez Manière*.

'Will you have a half?' suggested the inspector.

Maigret succumbed to the temptation. It was his second that day.

'What's she like?'

'Hard as nails.'

Although he was a bit fed up with her for complicating the issue by her stubborn reserve, nevertheless he could see her point of view.

Would she want her husband's body returned to her, so that he could have a conventional burial? Had she even considered the question before Maigret ran her to earth in the Rue Caulaincourt?

Torrence, as if reading his thoughts, murmured:

'Someone will have to bury him, anyway.'

'Yes.'

'And the reporters and photographers will turn up in force. . . .'

'Drive me to the Rue Marcadet, number 12.'

'It's no distance.'

'I know. It's no distance to anywhere in Montmartre.'

It was also one of those districts of Paris whose inhabitants very rarely moved house. Some of the people there scarcely ever left it, not even to go to the city centre.

'Are we going to see the daughter?'

'Yes.'

The building was similar to that in the Rue Caulaincourt, except that it was slightly newer, and the lift was more spacious.

'Will you see her alone?'

'Yes. . . . If her mother is anything to go by, I don't suppose she'll keep me long.'

He inquired at the lodge. The concierge, in this case, was an elderly woman.

'Second floor. . . . The door on the right. She and the children only came in about a quarter of an hour ago.'

'Does her husband come home to lunch?'

'No. He can't spare the time. He has an important job. He is head of one of the departments at the *Bon Marché*.'

Maigret went up to the second floor, and rang the bell beside the door on the right. From inside, he could hear children's voices. The flat was well-lit and, at this time of day, bathed in sunshine.

The young woman who opened the door looked at him mistrustfully.

'Aren't you Chief Superintendent Maigret?'

'Yes.'

'Who gave you my address?'

'Your mother. I've just come from seeing her.'

'Was she willing to see you?'

'Yes. Why shouldn't she be? She's done nothing to be ashamed of, has she?'

'She has certainly done nothing to be ashamed of, but she hates being reminded of the past.'

'And yet she keeps a photograph of your father on her mantelpiece.'

The two children were kneeling on the floor, playing with a small electric train.

'What puzzles me is why you should have hung up on me before I had time to ask you any questions.'

'I didn't want the neighbours gossiping about me.'

'Why should they?'

'They believe my father died twenty years ago, and that my mother is a widow.'

'I presume, nonetheless, that she will wish formally to identify the body, and to exercise her right to give him a respectable funeral.'

'I hadn't thought of that.'

'Do you mean to say that you and your mother would have left him to be buried in a pauper's grave?'

'I repeat, I hadn't given any thought to the matter.'

'How well do you remember your father?'

'Very well. I was eight years old, don't forget, when he went away.'

'What was he like?'

'Handsome, very strong, and nearly always full of fun. Sometimes he used to take me out, just the two of us together. He'd buy me ices and let me do anything I liked.'

'What about your mother?'

'She was much stricter. She didn't like me to get myself dirty. . . .'

'How did you hear that your father wasn't coming back? Did he write?'

'If he did, Mother never told me. . . . I don't think he ever did write. . . . We were completely in the dark. . . . My mother spent all her time looking out for him, and she used to go to the workshop in the Rue Lepic every day, to see if he was there.'

'Did you notice anything out of the way towards the end?'

'No. What did my mother tell you?'

'I could hardly get a word out of her. Was there anything for her to tell?'

'I don't know. I've never asked her, but I've always had the feeling that she was hiding something from me.'

'Forgive me, but you are no longer a child: was there ever any talk of your father having a mistress?'

She flushed.

'It's odd that you should ask that. The thought had crossed my mind. . . . But, really, having regard to the life he led, it doesn't seem possible. He wouldn't have left us for another woman, or if he had done he would have made no secret of it.'

'Had he many friends?'

47

'I didn't know of any. No one ever came to the house. He wasn't the sort of man who spends his evenings playing cards in a café.'

'Did he and your mother ever quarrel?'

'Not in my presence.'

'Have you any idea why he should have become a vagrant?'

'None. Indeed, until yesterday, I wouldn't have thought it possible.'

'Was he a Catholic?'

'No. He had no religion, and he brought me up to have none. It wasn't that he had anything against religion, it just didn't mean anything to him, that's all.'

'Is that how you feel, too?'

'Yes.'

'And your mother?'

'As a girl she was quite keen on religion, but she'd grown out of it by the time she was married. All the same, they were married in church, purely as a matter of form, I should imagine.'

'Do you often go and see your mother?'

'No. She comes to us almost every Sunday, to see the children.'

'Does she bring them sweets?'

'That's not her way.'

'Does she play with them?'

'No. She just sits very upright on a hard chair—she wouldn't dream of lounging in an easy chair—and watches them play. Sometimes, my husband and I take advantage of her being here to go to the cinema.'

'I'm much obliged to you. Is there anything else you can tell me?'

'No. I do hope I won't be badgered by a lot of reporters and photographers.'

'I'll do what I can, but once your mother has been to identify the body, it will be difficult to keep the newsmen out of it.'

'Please do the best you can, anyway.'

Just as he was about to open the front door, she added:

'Would I be allowed to see him?'

'Yes.'

48

'I'd like to, very much.'

Unlike her mother, the daughter had unbent considerably. No doubt she had been one of those little girls who worship their fathers.

## Chapter Three

AT HALF-PAST TWO, Maigret knocked at the door of the Examining Magistrate's chambers. All the benches in the long corridor were crowded, mostly with prisoners, some handcuffed, with a guard on either side. It was as silent as a cloister.

'Come in.'

Judge Cassure's chambers were in a part of the *Palais de Justice* which had not yet been modernized. It was like stepping into a scene from a Balzac novel. As in an old-fashioned school, the desk, painted black, was scarred and scratched, and, in one corner of the room, there were stacks of files on the floor. The clerk, though not actually wearing protective cuffs over his sleeves, still looked like something left over from the nineteenth century.

'Take a seat, Maigret.'

Cassure was barely thirty. In the old days it would have been inconceivable for a man of his age to have attained the eminence of a magistracy in the capital.

Maigret, as a rule, mistrusted the younger magistrates, who were usually full of theories, gleaned from recently published books, which they could not wait to put into practice. In appearance, Cassure was typical of the breed. He was a tall, lithe young man, exquisitely dressed, with a whiff of the lecture-room about him.

'I take it, since you asked to see me, that you have fresh news.'

'I did want to put you in the picture as to how things were going, yes.'

'As a rule, that's the very last thing the police want to do, unless they are ready to make an arrest and need me to sign the warrant.'

49

He smiled a little wryly.

'You have a reputation, Maigret, for getting out and about, talking to concierges in their lodges, calling on craftsmen in their workshops, and housewives in their kitchens and dining-rooms. . . .'

'That's right, I do.'

'That's something we are not permitted to do. The etiquette of our profession demands that we should confine ourselves to our chambers, except on those occasions when we have to appear publicly as experts among experts, hemmed in by formalities.

'I gather from the newspaper reports that the name of our vagrant was Vivien, and that he had been, at one time, a cabinet maker.'

'That is so.'

'Have you any idea what made him desert his work and his family to become a tramp?'

'I've spoken to his wife and daughter. Neither was able to answer that question. I came across a similar case years ago in London, a well-known English banker who did precisely the same thing.'

'When exactly did Vivien disappear?'

'In 1945.'

'Do you think he was keeping a mistress, running a second home?'

'So far, it's impossible to tell. My men are going through the neighbourhood with a fine-tooth comb. What makes things more difficult is that the only people who can help us are the elderly. This morning I spoke to a number of shop-keepers, workmen and residents, to no avail. This was in the bistro where Vivien went every day for his mid-morning coffee. They remembered him well, but knew almost nothing about him. He kept himself very much to himself. . . .'

'It does seem odd that, after twenty years, someone should suddenly decide to kill him.'

'That's why I'm digging as hard as I can into his past life. The only alternative is to believe that some crank or lunatic just happened to stumble on him, and shot him on the spur of the moment, which doesn't seem very likely. . . .'

'What sort of a woman is his wife?'

'Disagreeable. Admittedly, it can't have been easy for her to wake up one morning and find herself destitute, with a little girl of eight to bring up. Fortunately for her, she was handy with her needle. She began by making dresses for the neighbours, and then gradually built it up into a modest little business.'

'Did she leave the district?'

'No. She still lives in the Rue Caulaincourt, in the same building as when her husband was with her. Only she's moved into a smaller and less expensive flat on another floor. Like other women who no longer have any reason for living, she seems ageless. Her eyes have that slightly glazed, lustreless look that is so often a mark of great unhappiness. . . .'

'Has she no idea why her husband left her?'

'I could hardly get a word out of her. If she knows anything, she isn't telling, and I doubt if she will ever be persuaded to change her mind.'

'What about the daughter?'

'She is now twenty-eight. She's married to the head of one of the departments in the *Bon Marché*. I haven't met him yet. She was a little more communicative than her mother, but she, too, was on the defensive. She has two children, a girl and a boy, aged six and four.'

'Is she on good terms with her mother?'

'More or less. They see each other almost every Sunday, mostly on account of the children. I fancy there isn't much love lost between them. Odette, that's the daughter, hero-worshipped her father, and she still reveres his memory. They'll probably be visiting the mortuary this afternoon or tomorrow, to identify the body.'

'Together?'

'I very much doubt it. If I know anything, they will go separately. I gave them both the go-ahead to make arrangements for the funeral. They are terrified of reporters and photographers. . . . If you agree, I'll arrange to keep that side of things private. . . .'

'Of course. I can understand how those two women feel. Have you still no idea who committed the murder?'

'So far, there's nothing to go on. I don't think, in the whole of my career, I've ever come across a man so completely cut off from the rest of the world. It's not just that he lived alone in a condemned house without even the amenities of light and water, it's virtually impossible to imagine how he can have filled his days.'

'What does the police surgeon say? Was Vivien in good health?'

'His physical condition was excellent. In appearance, he could have been sixty-five, but it seems that he was, in fact, only fifty-five, and all his internal organs were perfectly sound.'

'Thank you for putting me in the picture. Am I right in thinking that your inquiries are likely to take some considerable time?'

'Unless something wholly unexpected turns up. . . . If, for instance, Madame Vivien should suddenly take it into her head to talk, I fancy she could tell us a good deal.'

Maigret returned to his office, and telephoned the Forensic Laboratory.

'Hello! Could you tell me whether a Madame Vivien has called in to identify her husband's body?'

'She left half an hour ago.'

'Is there any doubt that it is her husband?'

'No. She recognized him at once.'

'Did she cry?'

'No. She stood there quite still for a while, holding herself very stiffly, just looking at him. She asked me when she could start making arrangements for the funeral, and I referred her to you. Doctor Lagodinec has finished with the body. There's nothing more he can learn from it.'

'Thanks. I expect you'll be visited by a young woman in the course of the day. She's his daughter.'

'I'll attend to her.'

Maigret went over to the door leading to the Inspectors' Duty Room, and summoned Torrence. 'Any news?'

'I have arranged, as you suggested, for six men to cover the area around the Rue Lepic and the Rue Caulaincourt, and I have instructed them to question everyone—the shopkeepers, the customers in the bars and cafés, even the passersby in the streets—in fact anyone who looks old enough to have known Vivien before his disappearance.'

There was no evidence that, having abandoned his business and his family and vanished without trace, Vivien had turned vagrant overnight. He might simply have moved to another district, or he could have gone to live in the provinces for a time.

It was impossible to search the whole of France. Maigret was pinning his hopes on Montmartre, though he would have found it hard to explain why.

A little later, he telephoned Madame Vivien, having looked up her number in the phone book. She had returned home from the mortuary. Answering the telephone, she sounded resentful, as though she had given up all hope of ever hearing anything but bad news.

'Hello! Who is that speaking?'

'Maigret. I understand that you have been to identify the body. Is it, in fact, your husband?'

'Yes,' she said dryly.

'Did you find him much changed after twenty years?'

'No more than anyone else.'

'I've just come from seeing the Examining Magistrate. I spoke to him about the funeral arrangements. He says you may remove the body and arrange for burial whenever it suits you. Furthermore, he shares my view that the press should be kept in the dark, as far as possible.'

'Thank you.'

'I take it you won't be wanting the body laid out in your flat in the Rue Caulaincourt.'

'Of course not!'

'When will the funeral be, do you think?'

'The day after tomorrow. I was only waiting to hear from you before getting in touch with the undertakers.'

'Do you own a plot in one of the Paris cemeteries?'

'No. My parents hadn't that kind of money.'

'In that case, I fancy it will have to be the cemetery at Ivry.'

'That's where my mother is buried.'

'Have you spoken to your daughter?'

'Not yet.'

'I'd be obliged if you'd let me know the time of the funeral.'

53

'Do you intend to be there?' She sounded far from friendly.

'Don't worry. You won't even see me.'

'What if the newsmen latch on to it, and follow you?'

'I'll make it my business to see that they don't.'

'Well, I can't stop you from coming, can I?'

She was bitter. She had nursed her bitterness for twenty years. Was it perhaps congenital? Had she always been of a sour disposition, even before her husband left her?

Maigret felt it his duty to consider every possibility, however remote or even absurd. He was striving, vainly so far, to form a picture in his mind of the character of Marcel Vivien, that loneliest of lonely men.

Most people, however self-reliant, needed some contact with others. But he had not. He had installed himself in a big empty house which was due to be pulled down at any moment, and he had filled his room with an incredible jumble of utterly useless junk.

He was known only by sight to his fellow vagrants. Some of them had attempted to get into conversation with him, but he had gone on his way without so much as a word. Two or three times a week he had visited Monsieur Joseph's establishment to earn a five-franc piece, but here too he had kept silent, gazing fixedly at his reflection in the glass opposite.

'The funeral is to be the day after tomorrow,' Maigret told Torrence. 'I promised we'd do all in our power to keep it from the press.'

'Some of those reporter fellows ring up two or three times a day.'

'You'll just have to tell them that there have been no developments.'

'That's what I have been telling them, and that's what the other inspectors tell them when I'm not there. But they're getting restive, they're convinced we're keeping something from them. . . .'

And so, needless to say, they were. What was there to prevent any reporter from finding out all that Maigret had discovered?

The following day, the six detectives continued with their work of showing the photographs of Marcel Vivien to all and sundry, and asking questions, with precious little result.

Maigret had telephoned Odette Delaveau. She too had recognized her father.

'Do you know when the funeral is to be?'

'Hasn't my mother told you?'

'Last time I spoke to her, on the telephone, she hadn't yet got in touch with the undertakers.'

'The funeral is to be at nine o'clock tomorrow morning.'

'Will there be a religious service?'

'No. We'll be going straight to the graveside. There will be no one there except my mother, my husband and myself. We'll be following the hearse by car to the cemetery.'

Maigret regretted having been made to promise to keep the newspapers in the dark. Had it been otherwise, the murderer, as had so often happened in the past, might have been seen lurking near the Forensic Laboratory, or even at the cemetery itself.

Had he or had he not known Vivien twenty years ago? There was no evidence one way or the other. The dead man might well have made an enemy of someone later on, after he had become a vagrant.

Alternatively, some other vagrant might have got it into his head that Vivien had saved money and kept it hidden away in his room.

This, however, was unlikely. Vagrants seldom, if ever, owned firearms, still less a ·32 pistol.

In the course of twenty years, any number of things might have happened. And yet Maigret kept returning to that day twenty years ago, when Vivien had left home as usual in the morning, but never got as far as his workshop in the Rue Lepic.

Had there been a woman in the case? But if so, why had he left her later to become a vagrant? Among the letters received at Police Headquarters after the publication of the photographs and the reports in the press, not one had even hinted that there had been an unknown woman in Vivien's life.

That evening, to stop himself from endlessly chewing over the problem which, by now, was beginning to sicken him, Maigret watched a Western on television. When she had finished the washing up, Madame Maigret came and sat beside him, being careful to avoid disturbing him with questions.

'Will you please wake me half an hour earlier than usual tomorrow morning?'

Although she had not asked him why, he volunteered: 'I'm going to a funeral.'

She did not need to be told whose funeral, and she brought him his first cup of coffee at seven.

He had instructed Torrence to pick him up at half-past eight in one of the little *Police Judiciaire* cars. Torrence arrived punctually.

'I take it we'll be going first to the mortuary?'

'Yes.'

The motor hearse was already waiting in the road outside, along with a car provided by the undertakers. The two women and Odette's husband were in the car, and Torrence stopped some way off to avoid notice. There were no reporters or photographers in sight. The coffin, which seemed unusually heavy, was carried out by four men, and a few minutes later the little procession set off for Ivry.

Since yesterday, the sky had clouded over, and the heat was less intense. The weather forecast was of rain in the west, reaching Paris by the evening.

Torrence kept a long way behind the car occupied by the dead man's family. Maigret smoked his pipe, not saying a word, staring straight ahead of him. It was impossible to guess what he was thinking.

Torrence did not attempt to break the silence, though it was a struggle, for he was well known to be the most garrulous inspector in the Department.

The hearse travelled almost half the length of the cemetery before it stopped beside an open grave in the new section, where there were a number of vacant plots. Maigret and his colleague stationed themselves more than a hundred yards away. Madame Vivien and her daughter and son-in-law stood motionless at the edge of the grave, while the coffin was lowered into it. Both women were carrying bunches of flowers.

One of the undertaker's men held out a spade to the dress-maker for her to throw the first spadeful of earth into the grave, but, to Maigret's surprise, she shook her head, and contented herself with dropping her flowers on to the coffin. Odette did the same and, in the end, it was Delaveau who took the spade in hand.

He had never known Marcel Vivien. He was not old enough. Maigret put his age at about thirty. He was dressed in black, in what was no doubt the working suit he wore at the *Bon Marché*. He was a good-looking man on the whole, with a moustache which, like his hair, was very dark brown, almost black.

It was all over. The ceremony, if one could call it that, had lasted only a few minutes. The hired car reserved for the family drove off. Maigret throughout had kept his eyes skinned, but had seen no suspicious characters lurking in the vicinity. It seemed to him, now that the vagrant was buried, that he was farther from the truth than ever.

He was in a pretty foul mood. He continued to preserve a gloomy silence, endlessly mulling over the unresolved problem.

Why had the killer of Marcel Vivien not even bothered to slit open the mattress? After all, that was where people of small means usually hid their money.

In spite of himself, Maigret could not get away from the time of the man's disappearance, twenty years back, and that was why he had detailed six inspectors to comb Montmartre.

A pleasant surprise awaited him on his return to Police Headquarters. He found one of the six inspectors in his office, in a state of great excitement.

'What have you got to tell me?'

'What was the exact date on which Vivien disappeared?'

'December the twenty-third.'

'And he was never seen again?'

'That is so.'

'Had he already bought his daughter's Christmas present?'

'I should have asked his wife, but it never occurred to me.'

'Do you know the *Brasserie Cyrano* in the Place Blanche?'

'Yes.'

'One of the waiters there, a man of about sixty, recognized Vivien from the photographs I showed him.'

'When did he first get to know him?'

'Later than December the twenty-third, at any rate. It was at the end of January of the following year.'

'How can he be sure, after all this time?'

'Because he didn't start work at the *Cyrano* until the January.'

'Did he see Vivien more than once?'

'At least ten times, during the January and February of 1946. He was never alone. There was always a very young woman with him, a little dark girl, and they were forever holding hands.'

'Did they always turn up at the *Cyrano* at the same time of day?'

'Usually between eleven and half-past at night, after the cinemas had closed.'

'Was this waiter fellow sure he recognized Vivien?'

'He claims he remembers him specially because he never drank anything but mineral water, whereas his companion always ordered a Cointreau. . . .

'It was his first job as a café waiter. Before that, he had been employed as a floor waiter in one of the smart hotels on the Boulevards.'

'Did he ever see him anywhere other than in the brasserie?'

'No. Julien—that's the waiter's name—lived some distance away, in the Boulevard de la Chapelle.'

'When did the pair of them stop coming in?'

'About two months later.'

'And he's never seen Vivien since?'

'No.'

'Nor the young woman, either?'

'No.'

'Did he ever hear the man call her by her surname?'

'No. It seems he knows nothing more than I've already told you.'

Assuming that Julien had got his dates right, the one fact to emerge from all this was that, whatever Vivien's reason for deserting his family and his workshop, it was not in order to become a vagrant.

He had left on account of a woman. No doubt, he had intended to begin a new life.

One would have expected him to have kept well away

from his old haunts, and yet the *Cyrano* was barely two hundred yards from his workshop, and less than a mile from the flat where his wife and daughter were still living.

Had he had no fear of being recognized? Or was it simply that he didn't care? Had he told his wife that he was leaving her for another woman? Was that the explanation of Madame Vivien's grim manner?

'I want you to go back there after lunch. And keep at it. There may be more than one elderly waiter working at the *Cyrano*. The proprietor himself. . . .'

'The proprietor is under thirty. He has recently taken over from his father, who has retired to the country.'

'Find out where he's gone to.'

'O.K., Chief.'

'There are innumerable small hotels round about. I want you to inquire at all of them. In those days, almost more than at any other time, it was practically impossible to get a flat. . . .'

Maigret knew perfectly well that, in the end, he would not be able to resist going to the *Cyrano* himself, and roaming around the Rochechouart district.

He went home for lunch in a taxi, but not before he had treated himself to an aperitif in the *Brasserie Dauphine*.

At about half-past two, Maigret stood facing the terrace of the *Cyrano*, as he had known he would. There was considerable activity in the Place Blanche, owing to the coach-loads of tourists, bunched in clusters like grapes, with cameras slung round their necks. All or nearly all of them were taking photographs of the *Moulin Rouge*, next door to the brasserie.

The terrace was crowded, and there was not a seat to be had. The waiters—there were three of them—weaving in and out among the tables were all youngish, but in the dim interior Maigret could see one who could not have been much under sixty.

He went inside and sat down.

'A half. . . .'

He had not brought Torrence with him, because he felt a little shamefaced over his increasing preoccupation with

59

the mystery of Marcel Vivien. When the waiter brought him his drink, he asked: 'Is your name Julien? Was it you one of my men was talking to this morning?'

'Are you Chief Superintendent Maigret?'

'Yes.'

'It's an honour to meet you. I believe I told the inspector everything I know.'

'You are sure that it all took place in 1945?'

'Yes. The reason being, as I explained this morning, that it was my first experience of the fizzy drinks trade.'

'Was it the end of December or the beginning of January?'

'I can't be absolutely positive about exact dates. Christmas week is such a mad rush, one scarcely has time to notice the customers. . . .'

He was summoned away to another table, but soon returned to Maigret.

'I'm terribly sorry, but I'm on my own in here. The other waiters are all out on the terrace. What was I saying? January? Yes, I saw them then, and in February too, I believe. I'd come to think of them as regulars, and that takes a bit of time. . . .'

'Do you positively identify this man as Vivien?'

'I never knew his name, but there's no doubt that he was the man who used to come in almost every night in company with a very pretty girl.'

'And this would nearly always be just after the cinemas had closed?'

'Yes. I remember I was struck by it at the time, though I can't think way.'

'Would you recognize the young woman again?'

'Well, you know how it is with women. They're not so easy to recognize after twenty years.'

Then a thought struck him.

'But that girl. . . . Yes, I would recognize her.'

'How is that?'

'She had a small strawberry mark on her cheek.'

'Which one, right or left?'

'Let me think. . . . They nearly always sat at this table, so, if I saw the mark when I was serving them, it must have been on her left cheek.'

'Did the young woman ever come in with anybody else?'

'No. At least not as far as I can remember. I think I should have noticed, because I had grown accustomed to her face and style of dress.'

'How was she dressed?'

'She always wore black. A plain black silk dress, and a black coat with a fur collar.'

'Did they have a car?'

'No, they always came on foot. I imagine they lived nearby.'

'Did they ever take a taxi?'

There was a taxi rank opposite the brasserie.

'Not to my knowledge.'

'When they left here, did you notice if they went towards the metro?'

'No. I had the impression that they were locals. It's a different thing after midnight, when you get people of all nationalities crowding into the cabarets. But here, it's like being in another world. There's a great difference between this side of the boulevard and the other.'

Suddenly, he struck himself on the forehead.

'What was it I was saying just now? Didn't I say it was in 1945? I'm getting thoroughly muddled by all these questions. . . . What I meant to say, of course, was 1946. In 1945, I was still employed as a floor waiter at the Grand Hotel. . . .'

Once again he was summoned away, by someone calling for his bill. When he came back, he went on:

'I'm fond of this district. It's different from the rest of Paris. There are still a lot of craftsmen, with their work-shops in the various courtyards. There are lots of service workers, too, shop assistants and the like. And then there are the retired people of modest means, who are so attached to Montmartre that they are determined to end their days here, rather than retire to the country as others do. . . .

'Is there anything else I can do for you?'

'I don't think so. . . . If you should happen to remember anything else that might be of interest, be so good as to ring me at the Quai des Orfèvres.'

'I'm coming! I'm coming!' he called out to four newly arrived customers, who were showing signs of impatience.

Clouds were starting to gather in the west. From time to time, there was a little gust of cool air.

Slowly Maigret sipped his beer, telling himself that it would be his last that day. He was just about to pay for it, when the man at the next table leaned across to him.

'Did I hear you say that you were Chief Superintendent Maigret? Please don't think I'm taking a liberty . . .'

He was very fat, very red in the face, with three chins and an enormous stomach.

'I was born in Montmartre, and I've lived here all my life. I'm a picture framer, and I used to have a little shop in the Boulevard Rochechouart. I retired three years ago, but old habits die hard. . . .'

Maigret looked at him inquiringly, wondering what exactly he was getting at.

'The fact is, I couldn't help overhearing part of your conversation with the waiter. It was about that tramp who was murdered in a tumbledown house in Les Halles, wasn't it? I've had a good long look at the photographs in the papers, and I'm sure I'm not mistaken.'

'Did you know him?'

'Yes.'

'Have you seen him recently?'

'No. Not for almost twenty years. It was when I saw the pictures without the beard and moustache that I was sure.'

'Used you to go to his workshop in the Rue Lepic?'

'No. If what the papers say is right, he had already left there. Like Julien, I first got to know him in 1946.'

'What time of year was this?'

'February, I think. And for about six months after that, I used to see him regularly.'

'Was he a neighbour of yours?'

'No. I don't know where he and the girl lived, but they always had lunch in the same restaurant as I did, the *Bonne Fourchette* in the Rue Dancourt. It's a small place, frequented only by regulars. There aren't more than half a dozen tables. Naturally, everyone knows everyone else.'

'You're sure this went on for as long as six months?'

'I know they were still going there in August, before I went off to the Riviera for three weeks' holiday.'

62

'And when you got back?'

'Naturally, I looked out for them, but they were no longer there. I asked Boutant—he's the proprietor—what had become of them, but all he knew was that, from one day to the next, they had stopped coming.'

'Mightn't they, too, have gone away on holiday?'

'No. In that event, they would have come back in the autumn. I never once ran into them on the Boulevard or in the back streets.'

Maigret was somewhat disturbed by what he had just heard. The man was undoubtedly genuine, and seemed to have an excellent memory. His story, added to that of the café waiter, pointed plainly to the conclusion that, having abandoned his wife and daughter in the Rue Caulaincourt and his workshop in the Rue Lepic, Marcel Vivien had, to all intents and purposes, set up house with a very young woman, probably no more than a teenager, without even bothering to move to another district.

For two months, they had patronized the *Cyrano* fairly regularly after having been to a cinema. Right up to the middle of August, they had been in the habit of lunching at a restaurant in the Rue Dancourt, a few blocks away.

What had they lived on? Vivien's savings? Was it conceivable that he should have taken all his money with him, leaving nothing for his wife and daughter?

This was something else he would have to ask Madame Vivien herself, as her daughter might well have been kept in the dark about it. Would she be willing to give him a straight answer?

He sighed, paid for his beer, and thanked Julien. Then he turned to his neighbour, the retired picture framer, and thanked him also.

'I hope that what I've told you will prove to be of use.'

'I'm sure it will.'

He filled his pipe and smoked it, walking the whole length of the boulevard. He had no difficulty in finding the *Bonne Fourchette* restaurant in the Rue Dancourt. The dining room was small, and the door had been left open to let in a little air. Seated at the cash desk, reading a newspaper, was an elderly man wearing a chef's overall and hat.

It was an old-fashioned restaurant. It even had a wall-unit with pigeon holes in which the regular customers' table napkins were kept. The dining room and kitchen were separated only by a glass door.

Needless to say, at this hour there were no customers.

'Would you care for a drink?'

Maigret went across to the zinc bar counter.

'I'm not thirsty, thanks, but there are one or two questions I should like to ask you.'

'Who are you?'

'Chief Superintendent, *Police Judiciaire.*'

'I was sure the police would be on to me sooner or later.'

'Why?'

'Because that tramp fellow, Vivien, was by way of being a regular customer of mine for some months.'

'When was this?'

'In 1946.'

'Used he to come in alone?'

'No. He was always with a very attractive girl and, I can tell you, she never missed an opportunity of snuggling up to him.'

'How come you remember them so clearly?'

'Because one just couldn't help smiling when they came in. Everyone did, the waiters, the customers. . . . They were obviously so very much in love. Even while they were actually eating, they would stop to kiss one another full on the mouth, right there in front of everyone.'

'Didn't that strike you as odd?'

'Well, you know, in this business one sees all sorts. Nothing surprises me. He looked about fifteen years older than she was, but there are lots of couples like that.'

'Do you happen to know where they lived?'

'No. Locally, I should imagine, because they always walked, arm in arm, as if they had all the time in the world.'

'Did they never take a taxi from here?'

'Not as far as I know.'

'Did they ever dine here?'

'No. Not that there was anything unusual in that. Most of our lunch-time customers work in the neighbourhood,

64

and go home for dinner. In the evening, we get a different lot altogether.'

'When did they stop coming?'

'Round about the fifteenth of August. . . . We closed for a fortnight, so that my wife and I could get a breath of country air, and I could do some fishing. . . . I never saw them again after I got back . . . I daresay they decided to go somewhere else. . . .'

Maigret thanked him and went out. Back in the Boulevard Rochechouart, he strolled along at a leisurely pace, as if he were on home ground. He was puzzled. There was something wrong somewhere.

Marcel Vivien had left home two days before Christmas. To all appearances, he had been devoted to his little eight-year-old girl, and yet he had been unwilling to postpone his departure even for three days.

Had he only just met the young woman or teenage girl with whom he was about to join forces?

There was a telephone-box nearby. Maigret went in, looked up Madame Vivien's number and dialled it. He recognized her harsh voice as she asked:

'Who is that speaking?'

'It's me again. Chief Superintendent Maigret. This time, I have just one question to ask you, but a great deal may turn on your answer. When your husband disappeared, did he leave any money with you?'

'No!'

'Had he no bank account, no National Savings?'

'He did have a bank account, because some of his customers paid by cheque.'

'Did he withdraw the whole of his credit balance?'

'Yes.'

'Was it a surprise to you when he left?'

'Do you imagine that I was expecting it?'

'Did you know he was having an affair with another woman?'

'No. And I don't want to hear any more about it.'

Whereupon she rang off.

In August 1946, Marcel Vivien was still living in Montmartre with his mistress. From then on, all trace of him was lost. Had he moved to the provinces or gone abroad? Or was it at this point that he had decided to become a vagrant?

And what had become of his companion, who had seemed so much in love as to evoke indulgent smiles from the patrons of the *Bonne Fourchette*?

Maigret was lucky enough to get on to a bus with an open platform. It was one of the last in service. Soon there would be none left.

Contentedly, he smoked his pipe while gazing down on the ever-changing panorama of Paris.

What conclusions should he draw from the new facts available? The opening chapter of the story was clear enough: Marcel Vivien, owner of a prosperous little business, with a wife and child, had mysteriously vanished, having made up his mind overnight to abandon everything and throw in his lot with a very young woman.

How long would his savings last? And what would he do when they were exhausted?

His life had undergone a violent upheaval.

When last seen, in August 1946 in Montmartre, he had been a regular patron of the *Cyrano* and the *Bonne Fourchette*.

Thereafter, he had vanished again, leaving a great void. Had he grown tired of his mistress, or had she, rather, grown tired of him?

He had left no trace behind, but, nineteen years later, he had been found dead in one of the rooms of a derelict house. He had lived there all alone. He had had no friends. Two or three times a week, he had gone to the School of Hairdressing, to be practised on by an apprentice.

His murder must have been premeditated, since people do not, as a rule, go around with ·32 firearms in their pockets.

Where was the motive for the murder likely to be found? In those last few months in Montmartre, or in Vivien's subsequent life?

There was no way even of knowing how many years ago Vivien had decided to take up residence round and about Les Halles.

What had happened to his companion? What was her name? Before he was aware of it, Maigret was back at Vieux-Four Passage. There was a constable on guard at the door of the house where Vivien had lived.

He must have lived there for some considerable time to have amassed the enormous quantity of junk which filled the room. Had he been completely sane or had he, towards the end, gone out of his mind? Monsieur Joseph, the proprietor of the School of Hairdressing, had not noticed anything amiss, but he, admittedly, was more used to seeing alcoholics and cranks than normal people.

Maigret went upstairs. This was the first time he had been alone in this dark, dank house, full of unexpected creaking sounds. He was not searching for anything in particular. He just wanted to take another look at the surroundings in which Vivien had lived.

No finger-prints other than those of the dead man had been found in his room, which suggested that the murderer had worn gloves.

Among the junk on the floor was a battered hanging paraffin lamp. What could he possibly have hoped to do with it? And there was a pile of odd shoes, all of different sizes, and a gutted suitcase which had once been handsome and expensive.

Had he perhaps formerly occupied other rooms in the house, abandoning them only when they became intolerably overcrowded? Maigret went farther up the stairs, which were now very rickety, with many of the treads missing. On the fourth floor, there were no longer any windows or doors, and the floors were bare, except for a few old packing cases and cardboard boxes.

He went down again, still ferreting about, and trying to avoid getting covered in dust. He could picture the old man coming home at night, striking a match to light himself up the stairs. The question now was not who he was or what his life had been in the distant past, but how long he had lived here in this way.

He spoke a word in parting to the policeman on guard, and then made his way to the police station in the Rue des Prouvaires. Ascan did not keep him waiting.

Maigret went into his office and sat down.

'I think I'm going to need your help.'

'Have you any news, apart from what's in the papers?'

'Yes. But for the time being I don't want it to leak out. When he vanished from his home on the 23rd of December, Vivien didn't leave the district. I don't know where he went, but he turned up in January in company with a pretty girl in a brasserie in the Place Blanche, the *Cyrano*.'

'That's no distance from his workshop.'

'That's right. He doesn't seem to have made any attempt at concealment. Maybe, he was just insensitive. . . . A month later, still in company with the same girl, he began lunching in a restaurant, almost entirely patronized by regulars, in the Rue Dancourt. He didn't leave the district. He withdrew all the money he had in the bank. I may be able to find out how much that was. He left his wife and daughter penniless. He kept on going to the same restaurant until the middle of August.

'From then on, all trace of him is lost until he turns up again, alone and a vagrant in Les Halles. This is where I need your help. Les Halles is in your jurisdiction. It's teeming with vagrants, not to mention old lags and elderly prostitutes. . . . Among your men, there must be some who have specialist knowledge of that class of person. . . .'

'There are four, no more.'

'Could you possibly get them to ask some questions for me? My men wouldn't know whom to approach or where to start.'

'That's easy. Can you let us have some photographs, especially those taken before you had him shaved?'

'I have a set with me, but I'll ring my office and arrange for several more to be sent over to you.'

'I can't be sure my men will have any success, but I can promise you they'll do their best. What really do you want to know?'

'How long Vivien had been living as a vagrant, which may well turn out to be the best part of twenty years. All these vagrants know one another by sight, at least, and they take an interest in any newcomer, even if they don't go as far as asking personal questions.'

'Yes. It may be necessary to go farther afield than Les Halles, and question that lot on the Quais.'

'I have that in mind. May I use your telephone?'

When he got through to Police Headquarters, he asked to speak to Moers.

'Maigret here. . . . Is Mestral in? . . . He is? . . . I'd like him to do an urgent job for me. I want five or six more sets of those photographs, especially the ones taken before our man was shaved. They must be delivered today without fail to Superintendent Ascan personally, at the police station in the Rue des Prouvaires. Thanks, Moers. Goodbye for now.'

And to Ascan: 'They'll be with you in an hour's time.'

'I'll put my men on to it this very night.'

It was pouring when Maigret got outside, and, here and there, hailstones bounced on the pavement. The sky was heavily overcast, and the Chief Superintendent was thankful to find a free taxi cruising by.

'Police Headquarters!' he barked.

He was sick and tired of repeating the same questions to himself over and over again, and getting no satisfactory answers.

He went into the Inspectors' Duty Room and asked, 'Which of you are free tomorrow morning?'

They looked at one another, and three of them put up their hands.

'You'll have to get some sets of photographs from Criminal Records, and then I want you to go to Montmartre. Concentrate on the Boulevard Rochechouart and the surrounding streets, and inquire at all the litle hotels with furnished rooms to let. The chances are that Marcel Vivien and his girl friend lived in one of them for about six months. I'm especially interested in the girl. You might do well also to make inquiries in the local shops, the food shops in particular. And the best of luck to you.'

He went back into his office, followed by Torrence.

'Any fresh news, Chief?'

Feeling too weary to go over the whole story again, he murmured, 'I'll tell you tomorrow. Tell Janvier he can call off his six men.'

He dozed in his armchair for a full half-hour, during which time the rain splashed in through the open window and made a puddle on the floor.

## Chapter Four

HE WAS IN HIS OFFICE very early next morning, and by the time the inspectors arrived, he had already been through his mail. In his opinion, the greater the speed of the inquiry, the better the chance of success.

No doubt the men of the First *Arrondissement* had been at work on his behalf all through the night, but he was reluctant to telephone Superintendent Ascan, as he did not wish to appear to be putting pressure on him. Janvier was dealing with the various matters in hand, assisted by such other inspectors as were available. Most of the offices in the Department were empty.

It had stopped raining. The sky was blue, except for one or two little white clouds edged with pink in the strong sunlight.

'Come along, Torrence, we're going out.'

He had no definite plan in mind, preferring rather to follow his instinct. Besides, how could one plan in a case like this, with no solid basis to build on and no real clues to follow up?

'The Rue Lepic. . . . I seem to remember noticing a branch of the Crédit Lyonnais almost opposite Vivien's workshop.'

It did not take them long to get there. There was very little traffic, especially at this time of the morning.

'Try and find somewhere to park, and wait for me.'

He went up to the counter.

'I would like a word with the manager.'

'What is your name, please?'

'Chief Superintendent Maigret.'

'You're in luck. He was away on holiday until yesterday.'

He was not kept waiting. He was received in the manager's office by a man of about forty, with a pleasant, suntanned face, and invited to take a seat.

'What can I do for you, Chief Superintendent?'

'If you happen to have seen the papers during the last few days, you will have read of the Vivien case. Marcel Vivien was a cabinet maker with a workshop just across the street from here. This was twenty years ago. I was wondering if you still had copies of his bank statements?'

'Not after twenty years. When an account is closed, that is to say, when a customer withdraws the whole of his credit balance, we keep his file for a few months, and then send it on to the Department of Social Security in the Boulevard des Italiens.'

'And how long do they retain such files?'

'I'm not absolutely sure, but certainly not more than ten years. Otherwise, the work of classifying them, and the space required to house them, would be enormous.'

'One of your clerks, I noticed, is an elderly man.'

'Old Frochot. . . . He's the oldest member of our staff. He's been with us for forty years, and is due to retire at the end of this month. . . .'

'Could I have a word with him?'

The manager pressed an electric buzzer. A young man put his head round the door.

'I want a word with Monsieur Frochot.'

Frochot had a humorous face, and his eyes twinkled behind the thick glass of his spectacles.

'Take a seat, Monsieur Frochot. Allow me to introduce you to Chief Superintendent Maigret, who has some questions to ask you.'

'I'm honoured.'

'Have you a good memory, Monsieur Frochot?'

'I believe I have that reputation.'

'The customer I want to ask you about left this district twenty years ago, and I have every reason to believe that, before doing so, he closed his account. . . .'

'Do you mean Marcel Vivien?'

'How do you know that?'

'I read the papers, and seeing that you have taken the trouble to come yourself. . . .'

71

'You're quite right. Can you tell me approximately how much money Vivien had in his account?'

'Never any great sum, though, of course, it fluctuated according to the receipts from his business. On average, I'd say his credit balance was in the region of ten to fifteen thousand francs. . . . At the end of each month he would withdraw sufficient funds to meet his current expenses, which usually amounted to about two thousand francs. . . .'

'When did you see him last?'

'It was early one morning, just after we had opened. He told me that he was moving house, and that he wished to withdraw the whole of his credit balance. I asked him where he was moving to, and he said to Montparnasse.'

'What was the sum involved?'

'Round about twelve thousand five hundred francs.'

'Did he seem at all on edge?'

'No. He was a man of cheerful disposition, and his business was thriving. Even the very top antique dealers used to send him their furniture for restoration.'

'How long had he had the workshop in the Rue Lepic?'

'Not quite ten years. Eight or nine years, I'd say. He was a steady sort of chap. His home address was in the Rue Caulaincourt. . . .'

'I'm much obliged to you, Monsieur Frochot. . . . Oh! yes, there's just one other thing. . . . Did you ever, by any chance, subsequently run into him in the street?'

'Once he'd gone out through the door, I never set eyes on him again. I find it hard to understand how he can have ended up as a tramp. He always seemed so well-balanced.'

Maigret returned to the *Police Judiciaire* car, in which Torrence was waiting.

'Did you find what you were looking for, Chief?'

'Yes and no. What I did find out doesn't seem to have got me very much farther, at any rate.'

'Where to, now?'

The little barrows, piled high with fruit and vegetables, were surrounded by a throng of housewives, their voices filling the air with a continuous hubbub.

'Back to the Quai.'

At this very moment, three inspectors were combing the

district, going from one hotel to another, in the hope of finding some trace of Vivien. And, since this was an area swarming with small hotels and lodging houses, the search might take days and days, unless one of the men were to strike lucky by accident.

And this, more or less, was how it turned out. Maigret had hardly had time to sit down at his desk, when he received a phone call from Inspector Dupeu, one of the three men on the job.

'Where are you speaking from, Dupeu?'

'From the *Hôtel du Morvan* in the Rue de Clignancourt. Vivien lived here for a time, and the proprietor remembers him very well. I think it would be as well for you to speak to him yourself.'

'Come on, Torrence. We're going out again.'

There was nothing Torrence liked better than to be out and about, playing chauffeur to the boss. He was delighted.

'The *Hôtel du Morvan* in the Rue de Clignancourt.'

They found Dupeu outside on the pavement, smoking a cigarette. Beside the entrance to the hotel was a fake marble plaque, inscribed: *Rooms to let by the day, week, or month.*

They all went inside. The proprietor had a bulging stomach, and shuffled about on flat feet encased in carpet slippers. He was unshaven. He looked as if he had not even washed, and his shirt was unbuttoned, revealing a hairy chest. He seemed to be suffering from chronic weariness.

'So you are Maigret,' he said, holding out a grubby hand.

'I understand that you were here as far back as 1946. . . .'

'I've been here a lot longer than that.'

'Have you found the name of Marcel Vivien in one of your old registers?'

'I don't keep my registers for twenty years.'

'But you do remember him?'

'I remember him very well. He was a fine-looking man, and pleasant with it.'

'How long did he stay?'

'From January to June.'

'Are you sure he didn't stay until August?'

'Quite sure, because as soon as he left, I let his room to a woman who was such a pest that I had to throw her out.'

73

'Vivien was not alone. Can you tell me the name of his companion? No doubt you also filled in a form for her. . . .'

'There was no need for that, as she didn't sleep here.'

'Do you mean to say they weren't living together?'

'Yes.'

Maigret was staggered. This was the last thing he had expected.

'Did she ever come to the hotel?'

'Occasionally she'd come and fetch him some time about noon. He always got up late, because he seldom got back here before two or three in the morning. . . .'

'Are you quite sure he lived alone?'

'If he hadn't, I would have had to fill in a form for his girl friend. The lodging-house inspectors are very hot on things of that sort.'

'Did she ever go up to his room?'

'Quite often, but only in the daytime, and I have no way of preventing that.'

'Do you happen to know her name?'

'I only know that Vivien called her Nina.'

'Had she any distinguishing marks?'

'A strawberry mark on her cheek.'

'What sort of clothes did she wear?'

'She was always dressed in black. At least, whenever I saw her she was.'

'Did Vivien have much luggage with him?'

'Only one suitcase, a cheap one. It was brand new. I fancy he'd bought it just before he booked in here.'

The three men stood looking at one another. One thing only was certain: Vivien had left the *Hôtel du Morvan* in June. It therefore followed that he must have spent July and part of August elsewhere.

As to the young woman, nothing was known about her, not even her surname. Had she lived in another hotel, or with relations, or had she perhaps had a little flat of her own?

It was a morning of comings and goings. The previous night's rain had not been succeeded by a cooler day. On the contrary, it was, if anything, hotter than it had been, and a lot of men in the streets were carrying their jackets.

Maigret had not been back in his office a quarter of an hour when the telephone rang. This time it was Lourtie. He, too, was speaking from Montmartre. Both of them had struck lucky.

'I'm in the Place des Abbesses, Chief. I'm speaking from a bistro opposite the *Hôtel Jonard*. The proprietor hasn't much to say for himself, but I thought you might like a word with him yourself.'

'Here we go again, Torrence.'

'Where to, this time?'

'The *Hôtel Jonard*, in the Place des Abbesses.'

The front of the hotel was faced with white tiles, and there was a strong smell of garlic-flavoured cooking in the vestibule. The proprietor was uncommunicative and somewhat surly.

'Do you remember him well?'

'I wouldn't go as far as that. But I do remember he had a pretty little girl friend.'

'Was she registered with you?'

'No. She never spent the night in the hotel, though she sometimes called in during the day. . . .'

'When did he book in here?'

'In June, if my memory serves me right.'

'And when did he leave?'

'Some time in August. Towards the end of the month. He was always very correct, very polite, which is more than you could say of some of the people we get here.'

Apart from the fact that she had a strawberry mark on her left cheek, they still knew nothing about the young woman. It was very discouraging.

'You may as well go back to the Quai,' Maigret said to Lourtie.

As for himself, he told Torrence to drive him to the police station in the First *Arrondissement*. Superintendent Ascan, whose door was open, sprang up to greet him.

'Did you get my telephone message?'

'No. I came straight here from Montmartre.'

'I rang to let you know that we're beginning to get results. Nothing spectacular as yet, but I thought it might be of use to you. Do sit down, won't you?'

Slowly, Maigret filled his pipe and, before lighting it, mopped his forehead.

'My men have tracked down the oldest vagrant in Les Halles. He's known to everyone as Toto. Mind you, he's only been around these parts for the last fifteen years. I gave orders that he was to be kept under close guard until you got here. You know what these people are like, once you lose sight of them, it's no easy job to find them again.'

Ascan sent for a constable and instructed him to produce the aforementioned Toto, who turned out to be an elderly man. Though not actually drunk, he smelt strongly of wine.

'How much longer do you intend to keep me locked up here? I'm a free man, aren't I? I've got a clean record. . . .'

'Chief Superintendent Maigret has a few questions to ask you.'

'Where did you live, before you came to Les Halles?'

'In Toulouse.'

'What did you do for a living?'

'Much the same as I do here. Except that you get badgered a lot more in the provinces.'

'Have you never had a regular job?'

He was silent for a moment, apparently deep in thought.

'I've humped crates and baskets all my life.'

'Even as a young man?'

'I ran away from home when I was fourteen. I was caught and brought back three times, and each time I got away again. They'd have to tie me up. . . .'

'How long have you been in Paris?'

'Fifteen years. . . . I've known every tramp there is in my time . . . I've seen the older ones die, and others come to take their place. . . .'

'Did you know Marcel Vivien?'

'I didn't know his name until this gentleman told it me. . . . He came here before I did. . . . He didn't give much away. He was always on his own, and when spoken to, would reply in words of one syllable or not at all.'

'Where did he sleep?'

'At that time? I don't know. I saw him occasionally at the Salvation Army shelter. . . . Then I heard that he was living in an old pile that was due to be pulled down. . . .'

76

'Did you ever see him in company with a woman?'

At this, he burst out laughing. Apparently, the question struck him as highly comical.

'No, Chief Superintendent. There's not much of that sort of thing here. . . . Especially with a man like him, who—I'd take my oath on it—was a gentleman. Mind you, we get all sorts . . . I remember one who had actually been a doctor, but he was a tippler, and he didn't last long.'

'Did you ever see Vivien talking to a stranger?'

'No. . . . But then I didn't take any particular interest in him. There was no reason why I should.'

'I'm much obliged to you.'

Toto turned to the local superintendent.

'Can I go?'

'Yes.'

Then, addressing the constable, Ascan added: 'Send in the next one!'

'A woman?'

'Yes.'

She was a monstrous-looking creature, so bloated that she was scarcely able to sit down. Her legs and wrists were grossly swollen. She was more than half drunk, and she looked about her with an air of defiance.

'What have you got against poor old Nana this time?'

'Nothing,' replied the superintendent. 'We just have a few questions to ask you.'

'What about letting me have the price of a litre?'

'Very well.'

She stood up and held out her hand, preferring to be paid in advance. The superintendent slipped five francs into the grubby outstretched hand.

'Be quick about it, then. I'm thirsty.'

'You told the inspector who questioned you last night that you had seen someone go into the house in Vieux-Four Passage. . . .'

'God's truth, I did.'

'When was this?'

'Three or four nights ago. . . . I never know what day it is. Every day is the same to me. . . . What I do know is that it was the night they found the body of that tramp. . . .'

77

'What time was it?'

'Round about three in the morning.'

'Can you describe the man you saw?'

'He was getting on in years, but he wasn't an old man. He had a very straight back. You could see that he wasn't a Les Halles man.'

'How could you tell?'

'I don't know. It's just something one senses at once.'

'Had you ever seen him before?'

'Yes.'

'When?'

'That same night, round about ten o'clock. He came out of the restaurant, *Chez Pharamond*, and stood on the pavement watching the unloading of the vegetables, fruit and fish. You could tell he was a newcomer. He seemed fascinated by it all.'

'Was Marcel Vivien there?'

'The one whose picture was in the papers? I believe he was helping with the unloading, yes.'

'Did this man, whom you saw again later at three in the morning, speak to Vivien?'

'No. . . . I don't know. . . . You're confusing me with all these questions. . . . And, besides, I've got a raging thirst . . .'

Maigret, with a nod, indicated that he had done with her, and they let her go. She would lose no time in buying a litre of cheap red wine and, in an hour's time, would be found lying paralytic on the pavement.

Ascan was saying:

'My men will carry on with their inquiries tonight, but I fancy those two are the only ones with anything interesting to tell.'

'Yes,' replied Maigret, as he relit his pipe, which had gone out.

'First, we now know that Vivien had been living here for fifteen years, and second, that a man who did not normally visit Les Halles was in the vicinity on the night he was killed. . . . He must have seen him unloading vegetables. . . . Was he there looking for him? . . . Impossible to say. . . . But, be that as it may, he was seen again in Vieux-Four Passage round about three in the morning. . . .

78

'If he was the one who shot him, then presumably, in the interval, he went home to get his gun. He'd hardly be likely to go out to dinner at a place like *Chez Pharamond* carrying such an unwieldy weapon. . . .

'But unfortunately we have no idea who this man is or where he lives. . . . He could just as easily have come into town from the provinces. . . . You don't suppose the fat woman could have been making the whole thing up?'

'I doubt it very much. . . . These vagrants are wary of getting mixed up with the police. . . . They only make a lot of trouble for themselves. . . .'

'There are five years unaccounted for between the time when Vivien was living in small hotels in Montmartre and when he was first sighted in Les Halles. I suppose he could have been here all that time?'

'Toto is the oldest of the fraternity. . . . People of his sort don't live to a great age. . . . The School of Hairdressing didn't yet exist. . . . As to the shopkeepers, their one ambition is to make their little pile as quickly as possible, and return home to their villages. I doubt if you'd find a single one who had been here since 1946. . . .'

'Thanks,' said Maigret, standing up with a sigh. 'Your help has been most valuable, which is more than I can say of my investigations in Montmartre.'

'Haven't you found any trace of him?'

'Yes. Not only in one hotel but in two. The trouble is that his girl friend wasn't living with him. She never spent a night in either hotel. So either she was living in yet another hotel, or she had a place of her own. If she had been living with her parents, she would hardly have been able to go home every night in the small hours. No name. No address. Nothing to go on but a strawberry mark on the left cheek. . . .'

'You'll find her in the end.'

'That'll be the day! As for the man who dined at *Chez Pharamond*, he's hardly likely to turn up again in Les Halles. If he's the murderer, he wouldn't want to run the risk of being recognized.'

'All the same, we'll go on looking.'

'Thanks again, Ascan.'

Maigret went out to the car, and was driven back to the Quai des Orfèvres. After all too brief an interval, the stifling heat had returned. Maigret, too, would have liked to carry his jacket over his arm. As soon as he was back in his office, he took it off.

'Any news?'

'A woman telephoned. . . . A Madame Delaveau.'

Vivien's daughter.

'Did she say what it was about?'

'No. But you can ring her back. She said she'd be in for the rest of the morning.'

Maigret asked for her number, and, when she answered, he could hear a hubbub of children's voices in the background. 'Hello! Chief Superintendent Maigret?'

'Yes, Madame.'

The young woman no longer sounded aggressive, as she had at their first meeting.

'I don't know whether the little I can tell you is worth bothering you with, but if you would care to come and see me soon after lunch, I'll tell you all I know. Don't make it too late, because I have to take the children out for their walk. Somehow, I believe that, when I've spoken to you, I shall feel more at peace with myself.'

He went home to lunch. His wife had made him a *coq au vin,* which was one of his favourite dishes, but he ate without seeming to notice what was on his plate, nor did he remark upon it in any way.

'You're a bit on edge, aren't you?' she ventured. 'Ever since the start of this case, you haven't been quite yourself. I get the feeling that you've got something nagging away at the back of your mind.'

'You know how it is. There comes a stage in every inquiry when one seems to lose confidence in oneself. In this particular case, I feel I'm going round in circles. Every time I think I've taken a step forward, I find all I'm really doing is marking time. And then, don't forget, most of what I want to know about happened twenty years ago. . . . And what's more, there's Marcel Vivien himself, the man who was killed in Les Halles. . . . I just can't make up my mind whether to like him or loathe him. . . .'

'It will all work out, you'll see.'

'I shall certainly have to bring it to a conclusion, one way or another. Which reminds me that I really ought to look in on the Examining Magistrate.'

He returned to the Quai des Orfèvres to enlist Torrence's further services as a chauffeur.

'Where to? Les Halles? Montmartre?'

'Montmartre. Odette Delaveau's flat in the Rue Marcadet.'

She was looking remarkably cool in a brightly coloured flowered dress.

'Do please sit down.'

The children must have been resting, because they were not making a sound, and there was no sign of them in the living room. Besides, when Odette Delaveau spoke, she was careful to keep her voice down.

'Have you managed to track down the young woman?' she asked.

Now there had so far been no mention in the newspapers of any young woman. He had considered it advisable to keep that aspect of the inquiry to himself for the time.

All innocence, he asked: 'What young woman?'

She gave him a shrewd look, and smiled.

'I see you don't want to commit yourself. I daresay you don't altogether trust me.'

'You haven't answered my question.'

'The young woman for whom my father left us. I didn't know at the time. My mother never said a word about it. Whatever she may say to the contrary, my mother was very jealous, and, several times, she followed my father when he left the workshop.

'What I'm saying, in fact, is that she knew about my father's connection with the girl before he left us. She never spoke of it to him, but she withdrew into herself more and more. Even much later, when I was old enough to understand, I was not the one she chose to confide in.

'I'm talking now of several years ago, when I was still living with her. I have an uncle, Uncle Charles, who lives in Meaux. He was in a big way of business, in fertilizers, and he used to come and see my mother every time he came to Paris. When we were left penniless, with nowhere to turn for support, it was he, I'm certain, who tided my mother over until she could find some means of earning a living.'

Mechanically, Maigret filled his pipe, but he did not light it.

'Do smoke if you feel like it. My husband smokes like a chimney in the evenings, when he's watching television.

'One day I was in my bedroom, and the sitting-room door had been left ajar. Uncle Charles was there, and I could hear him and my mother talking. I can still hear my mother's voice:

' "All in all, I'd say it was a good riddance. I couldn't have stood it much longer, living with a man who came back straight from the arms of another woman."

' "Are you sure you're not imagining it?"

' "I followed them on several occasions. By now, I could tell you every detail of their daily routine, and I know where she lives. . . . They haven't even bothered to leave the district. Marcel is crazy about her. I've never seen a man in such a state. He'd do anything so as not to lose her. . . ."

'Take note of that, my mother told Uncle Charles:

' "I know where she lives. . . ."

'It came back to me quite suddenly, and that's why I telephoned you.'

'Did she mention the address to your uncle?'

'No. They went on to discuss money matters. My uncle asked if she had any outstanding bills, and wanted to know whether there was anything owing from my father's customers. . . . I presume you'd be interested to have the young woman's address?'

'Very much so. Several of my men have been searching for her, without results. We don't even know her name.'

'I'm sure my mother does. Only don't tell her that it was I who sent you.'

'Have no fear on that score. . . . And I really am most grateful to you. . . . I don't suppose you have any recollection of a very tall, extremely thin man, with a long, narrow face and blue eyes?'

82

'When might I have seen him?'

'I don't know. Twenty years ago, possibly, or perhaps much more recently.'

'I can't think of anyone who answers that description. Is it important that he should be found?'

'According to one witness, he's the man who murdered your father.'

For an instant her eyes clouded over.

'No. I don't know him.'

In parting, she shook hands with him.

'I wish you luck with Mother.'

He had himself driven to the Rue Caulaincourt, where he was kept waiting for some little time on the doorstep.

'Oh, it's you again!' sighed Madame Vivien, evidently somewhat vexed. 'You'll have to wait in the lobby, I'm in the middle of a fitting.'

She pointed to a chair that looked far from comfortable. Obediently, he sat down, with his hat on his knees, and his pipe, still unlit, in his right hand. He could hear women's voices in the room beyond, but only as a murmur in which, here and there, a word could be distinguished.

She kept him waiting about half an hour. The customer was a blonde with an ample bosom and a flashing smile. She looked at him searchingly as she made for the door. Having shut it behind her, Madame Vivien turned on him.

'How long do you intend to go on harassing me?'

'You may rest assured that I try to avoid bothering you more than I have to.'

'Very considerate of you, I'm sure. I shudder to think what my life would be like if you didn't.'

'I do feel for you in your bereavement.'

In a hard voice, she replied:

'There's no question of bereavement. I attended the funeral only because you made such an issue of it. . . . Well, anyway, I did attend the funeral, and now he's well and truly buried. Isn't that enough for you?'

'You sound as if you hated him.'

'I did.'

They had gone into the room beyond, where a dress, bristling with pins, was spread out on the table.

'Because he had a mistress?'

She shrugged, as though she considered the question beneath her notice.

'Listen to me, Chief Superintendent. Maybe I'd have done better to speak my mind from the first. . . . For years, Marcel was a man of the highest character, a dedicated craftsman and an excellent husband. He virtually never went out without my daughter or me. . . . Then one day, quite suddenly, everything changed. . . . He was out almost every night, and he didn't even put himself to the trouble of inventing excuses. He went out, and that was that. . . . It was always well after midnight when he got home. . . .'

'So you decided to follow him?'

'It's only what any normal woman would have done, surely?'

Had she ever loved him? Maigret was by no means sure that she had. Certainly, he had been her life's companion, and the family breadwinner. But had she ever had any real affection for him?

'Yes. I did follow them. I say "them" because, of course, he wasn't alone. They were like a couple of kids in love for the first time. They were dazed and dazzled by one another. The girl was barely twenty, and he was thirty-five.

'I daresay he didn't realize what a fool he was making of himself. He always had his arm round her waist. Sometimes they would break into a waltz right there on the pavement, and then they would kiss and burst out laughing. And do you know why? Because they'd done it again, without realizing it they had once more kissed right under a gas lamp.

'I followed them into a cinema, and their conduct couldn't have been worse. Then they went into a nearby brasserie for a drink.'

'The *Cyrano*.'

'So you knew?'

'This must have been in January or February of 1946.'

'Yes, January. . . . He had only just left me. But I had followed him before, when he was still living here. . . .'

'Did you ever speak to him?'

'No. . . . What was there to say? I couldn't force him to

come back, could I? Besides, he had become a different man altogether, one I never knew existed. . . .'

'Was he living in the *Hôtel du Morvan*?'

'You seem to know a great deal. How did you find out?'

'In June, he took up residence at the *Hôtel Jonard*, in the Place des Abbesses.'

'It was after that I lost sight of him.'

'The girl didn't live with him.'

'She had her own flat in the Boulevard Rochechouart. She inherited it from her mother, who had died the year before.'

'Do you know the name of the girl?'

'Yes. I found out from the concierge. Her name is Nina Lassave. . . .'

'All this was twenty years ago. Have you ever seen her since?'

'No.'

'Did you never think of going to the Boulevard Rochechouart to find out what had become of her?'

'It never entered my head. . . . I had my work to do. . . .'

Her tone was cold and hard, without the smallest hint of emotion.

'Do you know the number of the house in the Boulevard Rochechouart?'

'No. . . . But it's not very far from the Place Pigalle. There's a chemist's shop on one side and a bakery on the other.'

'Did it surprise you to learn that your husband had become a vagrant?'

'It proved, at any rate, that they were no longer together. How long had he lived in Les Halles?'

'At least fifteen years. Probably longer.'

'It serves him right!'

He had to repress a smile. She was positively brimming over with hatred.

'It was very good of you to see me.'

'Now that you know how I feel, I trust you will leave me alone.'

'I'll do my best to bother you as little as possible. You did say Nina Lassave, didn't you? You don't happen to know whether she had a job, do you?'

'When they first got together, she was still working in a lingerie shop in the Rue Lepic. But she soon gave that up. She didn't have to go on being a shop-girl. She had an easier way of earning a living. . . .'

'I'm obliged to you, Madame.'

He parted from her with an almost absurdly formal bow, and left her to the regurgitation of her bitterness and spite.

Torrence was sitting in the car, reading the early edition of an evening paper.

'Take me to the Rue Lepic.'

'To his workshop?'

'No. There's a lingerie shop, I think I've seen it, it's quite a long way down.'

It was a poky little place with a narrow window. Inside, behind the counter, a stringy old maid was folding a pile of slips. She was obviously not used to seeing an unaccompanied man come into the shop.

'Can I help you?'

'I am a chief superintendent from the *Police Judiciaire* . . . I'm making inquiries about a woman who used to work here. How long have you had this shop?'

'Forty years, Monsieur.'

'So you were here in 1945 and 1946?'

'In the whole of my life, I haven't had what would add up to three months' holiday. Until recently, my sister was with me, but she died last year.'

'Do you remember a girl called Nina Lassave?'

'She worked here for two years. She was not quite eighteen when she applied for the job. She was a pretty girl, very fresh and unspoilt.'

'Did she ever give you cause for complaint?'

'I was a bit worried about her towards the end. I noticed that there was a man always waiting for her across the street when we closed the shop. He was much older than she was. This went on for about two months, and at the end of that time she gave in her notice.'

'I asked her if she was going to be married, and she burst out laughing, as if I'd said something very funny.'

'Did you ever see her again?'

'No. I have no idea what became of her. I'm very much

86

afraid that she must have gone to the bad. And yet, as I said before, when she first came here, she was so very fresh. . . . A sweet child. . . .'

Maigret thanked her, and returned to the black *Police Judiciaire* car.

'Since when have you been interested in ladies' under-wear?'

'I have at last found out the name of Vivien's mistress. . . . Twenty years ago, she worked in that little shop, there. . . . And now we're going to take a look at the house where she used to live. She may still be there, because it was her own flat, which she inherited from her mother.'

'Where is it?'

'In the Boulevard Rochechouart. Not far from Pigalle. There's a chemist's shop on one side and a bakery on the other. . . .'

'I see! You got her address from the woman in the shop?'

'No. . . . I got it from Madame Vivien. She quite literally spat it out. I've never seen such a look of hatred in anyone's eyes as in that woman's, when she spoke of her husband and his mistress. . . .'

The streets and the boulevards were very quiet. They came first to the chemist's shop, and then saw the bakery. Between the two was a gateway painted brown, with a smaller open door let into it.

At the far end of the entrance lobby could be seen a paved courtyard with a magnificent lime tree.

Maigret knocked at the door of the lodge. A trim young woman in a white apron came to open it.

'Who are you looking for?'

'I presume, in view of your age, that you haven't been here very long?'

'All of five years.'

'I wonder if, by any chance, a tenant by the name of Nina Lassave still lives here?'

'I've never heard that name.'

'Does the name Vivien ring a bell?'

'Isn't he the man that was killed somewhere near Les Halles? I've read about him in the papers in the last few days.'

'You don't happen to know where your predecessor is now?'

'She retired and went back to her home village, where one of her sons has a vineyard. It's somewhere near Sancerre. . . .'

'Do you know her name?'

'Let me think. . . . I only knew her very slightly. . . . Michou, that's it. It's a name one wouldn't easily forget . . . Clémentine Michou.'

'I'm much obliged to you.'

And to Torrence:

'We're going back to the Quai.'

'What about stopping for a half first?'

They each had a half of beer in a bar in the Rue Notre-Dame-de-Lorette. Maigret was beginning to see a glimmer of light. Now that he had the name of the young woman, it ought not to take too long to find her.

'As soon as we get back to the office, I want you to go up to Records and see if they have anything on Nina Lassave. . . . If you find nothing there, see if the Vice Squad has anything. It's a long shot, but you never know. . . .'

'Right you are.'

As for Maigret, as soon as he was back in his office, he took off his jacket and, standing by the window, filled his pipe. In spite of everything, he was not wholly satisfied, and Madame Maigret would have said he was on edge.

And so he was. He had conducted his inquiries to the best of his ability, concentrating as much on the past as on the present. And with substantial results. And yet, he had a nagging feeling that he had missed something. But what? He could not put his finger on it, and it worried him.

'Would you get me the police station at Sancerre, please, miss . . . I'd like to speak to the man in charge, of course, if he's there. If not, put me on to one of his assistants.'

He began restlessly pacing the room. Within the next two weeks, he told himself reassuringly, the case would be solved, and he and his wife would be able to go and relax in their house at Meung-sur-Loire, which incidentally was not so very far from Sancerre.

'Hello! Yes. . . . Is that the Chief of Police in Sancerre? Chief Superintendent Maigret of the *Police Judiciaire* speaking . . . I'm sorry to trouble you personally over what may seem a small matter, but it could turn out to be of great importance. . . . I believe you have a vinegrower of the name of Michou living in your district . . . ?'

'There are two Michous, as it happens, and the odd thing is that they're not related.'

'One of them probably has his mother living with him. She's been there for about the last five years, and before that, for many years, she worked as a concierge in Paris.'

'That would be Clémentine Michou.'

'Does she still live with her son?'

'She died last year.'

It was the same old story, one step forward and another step back.

'Would you like to speak to the son?'

'No. She was the only one who could have told me what I want to know. It's about something that happened all of twenty years ago.'

'In that case, I can guess. . . . It's to do with the Vivien business, isn't it? How is it going?'

'Badly. . . . Especially after what you've told me. . . . I was relying on old Madame Michou, and she had to go and die a year too soon. Thanks all the same, Chief. What sort of a vintage are you expecting this year?'

'If the weather holds, it should be an exceptional year.'

'I hope you're right. Thanks.'

He had been standing by the window during this conversation, watching fascinated as a string of four black and red barges went by in tow. He now went across to his desk and sat down.

'I've just come from upstairs, Chief.'

'Did you find anything?'

'Nothing in Records, and the Vice Squad have never heard of her either.'

The telephone rang. 'There's someone on the line who won't give his name, Chief Superintendent.'

'Never mind, put him on.'

The voice at the other end of the line was muffled. The caller was probably speaking through a handkerchief to disguise his voice.

'What would you say to a really good tip, Monsieur Maigret?'

'What about?'

'About the case you're on at the moment. Take careful note of this: The name is Mahossier. . . . That's all. The rest is up to you. . . .'

And the line went dead.

## Chapter Five

'TORRENCE! Bring me the phone book from next door.'

Maigret turned to the name Mahossier, little dreaming that he would find eleven subscribers of that name listed in the Paris directory. Which of them was the one referred to by the anonymous caller?

Maigret, having warned the switchboard operator that he would be making a number of calls, began working down the list.

No occupation was given for the first subscriber. He tried the number and got no reply. There was no reply from the second, either. The third name was that of a florist in Passy.

'May I speak to your husband, please?'

'I have no husband. I divorced him five years ago.'

No reply from the next number. Most of the people living in Paris were away on holiday, of course.

His next call was to a Secretarial College in the Boulevard Voltaire.

No reply. That made four. He got seven no replies in all, and Torrence, who was standing by the window, marvelled at his patience.

He missed out the next number, as the subscriber was a doctor, with a surgery in the Place des Vosges. But he got through to the one after that, a firm of decorators in the Avenue Trudaine.

'Hello! Who are you calling?'

'May I speak to Monsieur Mahossier, please.'

'Monsieur Mahossier left for La Baule yesterday.'

'Will he be away long?'

'At least three weeks. Possibly four. Who is that speaking?'

'Is that his home number?'

'No. These are his business premises. Monsieur and Madame Mahossier have a flat in the Rue de Turbigo.'

'Have they a house in La Baule?'

'Yes. It's called the *Umbrella Pines*. They've had it for about ten years.'

The Avenue Trudaine was in Montmartre, and the Rue de Turbigo just a stone's throw from Les Halles.

He began pacing up and down the room. He didn't want to look a fool, even in front of Torrence, and he certainly would, if the anonymous caller were leading him up the garden path.

'Put a call through to *Air Inter,* will you. Find out if there's a flight to La Baule tomorrow morning, and whether it's possible to get back the same day.'

Torrence went into the inspectors' room to make the call. Within a very few minutes he was back.

'There's a flight to La Baule at ten past ten, returning at half-past six. Shall I make a booking for you?'

'Yes, please.'

'Mahossier . . . Mahossier . . .' Maigret murmured the name to himself, with an almost painful effort at recollection. He knew the name. He must have heard it somewhere, or possibly seen it on the front of a building.

He went upstairs to see the Examining Magistrate.

'Any new developments, Monsieur Maigret?' asked young Judge Cassure, in his friendly way.

'Nothing much, except that I now know the name and former address of the young woman on whose account Vivien walked out on his wife and daughter.'

'What's become of her?'

'Unfortunately, the concierge of the flats is fairly new to the place. The old concierge retired to Sancerre, where she died last year. All the present tenants are under forty.'

For an instant he hesitated, then, taking his courage in both hands, said:

'I've just had an anonymous phone call.'

'A crank?'

"I don't know. It's a risk I'll have to take. The name Mahossier was mentioned. There are eleven subscribers of that name in the phone book. Seven are away on holiday. Of the other four, only one is a possible suspect. He owns a firm of decorators.'

'Are you going to see him?'

'With your permission. The fact is, he and his wife left for La Baule yesterday. They have a house there. They won't be back for at least three weeks. I have no proof whatever that he is in any way mixed up in this case. But for some reason, I can't think why, I won't be easy in my mind until I've seen and spoken to him.'

'You want to go to La Baule?'

'I've booked on a domestic flight leaving Paris in the morning and returning in the late afternoon.'

'It's your case, and it's up to you to do what you think best.'

'Thank you. I think, maybe, I ought to have a warrant, in case he turns out to be the sort who stands on his rights.'

Judge Cassure signed the warrant there and then.

'The best of luck to you, Maigret.'

He went home early, had cold meat, salad and cheese for dinner, and spent the rest of the evening looking at television.

Every now and then he would murmur, like an incantation: 'Mahossier ... Mahossier. ...'

But whatever it was he was trying to remember, it still eluded him.

'By the way,' he said to his wife, 'I won't be in to lunch tomorrow.'

'Pressure of work?'

'No, not specially, but I have to go to La Baule.'

'La Baule?'

'Yes, there's someone I have to see there. I'll be flying there and back the same day. I should be home by about half-past eight.'

He knew by experience that many a criminal would escape scot-free but for a tip-off from an informer or an anonymous caller. When he got up next morning, the sun was already high in the sky, brilliant as ever, and there was not a breath of air. This was satisfactory, as he did not much care for flying, and indeed always suffered a mild sense of claustrophobia in an aircraft.

'See you this evening.'

'You might even manage to find time for a dip in the sea,' she said, teasingly.

The point was that Maigret could not swim, which was one of the reasons why they always went to the country rather than the seaside for their holidays.

The aircraft was a small two-engined machine, which looked like a toy beside the giant transatlantic planes. There was room only for eight passengers. Maigret gazed at them absently. Among them were two children who refused to sit still, and talked incessantly.

He shut his eyes, hoping to doze off, but failed to do so. At last, after two hours' flying, they touched down at the airport of La Baule. For some time before they came in to land, they had had a view of the glittering sea and, in the distance, a single ship apparently sailing on a course parallel with the horizon.

He hailed a taxi.

'Do you know a villa called the *Umbrella Pines*?'

'Don't you know the address?'

'No.'

'Do you know who owns it?'

'Yes. The name is Mahossier . . . Louis Mahossier. . . .'

'Hang on a minute.'

The driver went into a little bar, to consult the local telephone directory.

'Got it!' he said, when he came back.

'Is it far from here?'

'It's behind the *Hôtel Hermitage*.'

He was in a completely different world. Here, all the men wore shorts, with their shirts unbuttoned to the waist. All along the several miles of beach rows of umbrellas were set up, and thousands of holiday-makers could be seen sunbathing, while as many more splashed about in the sea.

The villa, set well back from the road, a shady avenue, was impressive.

Maigret looked for a bell to ring, but could not see one. The door, which was painted white, was ajar. He could see a terrace furnished with a table and garden chairs. He pushed the door a little wider, and called out:

'Anyone at home?'

At first, there was no reply. It was only after he had called out for the third time that a very young servant-girl in a white apron emerged from the shadows of the entrance hall.

'Who are you?'

'Can I have a word with Monsieur Mahossier?'

'Monsieur and Madame are always down on the beach at this time of day. If you'd like to come back this afternoon. . . .'

'I'd rather go down to the beach now and find them.'

'Do you know them by sight?'

'No.'

'Take the first turning on the left, go to the end of the street, and there you will see some stone steps leading down to the beach. Their tent is the fourth you will come to. You'll see the number 24 painted on the canvas. . . .'

'You wouldn't like to come with me, and point them out to me?'

'I can't leave the house unattended.'

'How old is Monsieur Mahossier?'

'I don't know exactly. I only work for them in the holidays. About fifty, I should think.'

'What does he look like?'

'He's still a good-looking man, very tall and slim, with hair greying at the temples.'

'And Madame Mahossier?'

'She's much younger. I shouldn't think she's more than forty.'

'What number was the tent, did you say?'

'Twenty-four.'

There were whole families going down to the beach, already in bathing suits. In some cases, their skins glowed with health, from exposure to the sun.

He found the way down to the beach, and threaded his way through the bodies stretched out on the sand. He had no difficulty in finding the orange tent with the number 24 stencilled on it.

In front of the tent was a woman. She was stretched out prone on the sand, so that he could not see her face. Her back, covered with suntan oil, glistened in the sun.

He looked around for a man answering the description of Louis Mahossier. Not far from the edge of the sea, where the waves lapped lazily, was a row of some twenty men doing physical exercises under the guidance of an instructor. One of them stood out as being taller and slimmer than the rest. Mahossier?

Maigret did not feel he could interrupt the class, so he stood waiting, not a yard away from the woman outside tent number 24. Was she never going to notice him? She pulled up the top half of her bathing suit, which was not much less scanty than a bikini, and turned over on her side.

The sight of a man standing there in a city suit gave her a start. Sure enough, Maigret was the only man fully clothed on the whole of the beach.

'Are you looking for something?' she said at last.

Her face was smothered in some sort of cream or oil. She was plump, and she appeared to be of a pleasant disposition.

'Madame Mahossier?'

'Yes. How did you know?'

'Your little maid gave me the number of your tent. I should very much like to have a word with your husband.'

'I'm afraid you'll have to wait. What time is it?'

'Nearly half-past twelve.'

'He's in the middle of a P.T. class. They should finish in just a few minutes.'

'He's the tall one, isn't he?'

'Yes. The third on the right . . . In spite of being so thin—he hasn't an ounce of fat on him—he never misses a day's physical training when we're here in La Baule.'

She looked at him inquiringly, but had not the courage to ask him outright what his business was.

'Have you just got here?'

'Yes, this morning.'

'By road?'

'By plane.'

'We always fly ourselves, unless we need the car. Are you staying at the *Hermitage*?'

'I'm not staying anywhere. I'm going back this afternoon.'

The physical training class had ended, and the tall thin man was coming towards the tent. When he saw Maigret in conversation with his wife, he frowned.

'This gentleman has come all the way from Paris to see you. He came by air this morning, and is going back this afternoon.'

Mahossier was visibly uneasy. 'Monsieur . . . ?'

'Maigret of the *Police Judiciaire*.'

'And you've come to see me?'

'Yes. I have one or two questions to ask you.'

He fitted the description given to Maigret of the man who had been seen coming out of *Chez Pharamond*, and who had stood watching Vivien unloading crates of vegetables. He had been seen again in Vieux-Four Passage, going into the crumbling ruins of the house in which the vagrant had taken refuge.

'You're in the decorating business, are you not?'

'That's right.'

There was something bizarre about this conversation, having regard to the setting in which it was taking place, the hurly-burly of the beach, the shouts of children and, not least, the fact that one of the participants was wearing nothing but bathing trunks.

'Is it an old-established business?'

'I've built it up over the past fifteen years or so.'

'And before that?'

'I was an employee in another firm.'

'Also in Montmartre?'

'Where is all this leading, Chief Superintendent? I'm here on holiday. I don't see what right you have to intrude on my privacy in this way.'

Maigret showed him the warrant, which he studied with close attention.

'What does it all mean?'

'Some days ago, you had dinner in Les Halles, at *Chez Pharamond.* . . .'

He looked at his wife, as if hoping that she would be able to refresh his memory.

'That was the night my mother came to dinner. As you can't stand the sight of her, you decided to eat out. . . .'

'What did you do next?'

'I walked about a bit, then I went home.'

Maigret noticed that the woman suddenly seemed a little flushed. She opened her mouth, as if to intervene, but she did not speak.

'Yes, you did return home briefly. . . .'

And then, looking his suspect in the eye, Maigret let him have it straight.

'What calibre is your pistol?'

'I haven't got a pistol.'

'Take care, Monsieur Mahossier. I warn you your statement can easily be checked. You had better be frank with me, otherwise I shall ask the Examining Magistrate to issue a warrant empowering me to search your business premises and your flat in the Rue de Turbigo.'

The woman stared at her husband in amazement. As for Mahossier, his expression was stony, almost threatening.

'I do have an old automatic, but it must be covered in rust by now. I don't even know where I've put it.'

'Is it a .32?'

'Very likely. I don't know anything about firearms.'

'It's a pity you don't know where you've put it. I was hoping you'd authorize one of your staff to hand it over to me.'

'What is this all about? Are you going to tell me, or aren't you?'

'It's a very serious matter, Monsieur Mahossier. It concerns a murder. When I have found your gun, I shall be able to say within a matter of hours, after the ballistics experts have examined it, whether or not you are involved.'

'Do what you like. I refuse to answer any more of these idiotic questions.'

He turned away to shake hands with a **fat man** in a

bathing suit, who went on to stretch himself out in front of the tent next but two to his own.

'Twenty years ago, you made the acquaintance of a young woman named Nina Lassave, did you not? And then, through her, you got to know Marcel Vivien. . . .'

'Wasn't that the vagrant killed in Les Halles?'

'He wasn't a vagrant then. He was a cabinet maker with a workshop in the Rue Lepic.'

'And I'm supposed to have known him?'

'Yes.'

'I'm sorry to disappoint you, but I know nothing about these people.'

'Does the Boulevard Rochechouart mean anything to you?' Maigret had never before conducted an interrogation on a beach. Mahossier's wife had raised herself up on one elbow, and was listening intently.

'Naturally, like any other Parisian, I know the Boulevard Rochechouart.'

'Where were you living in 1946?'

'It's a long time ago, and in those days I moved around a good deal, living in various small hotels.'

'In Montmartre?'

'As a matter of fact, yes. My place of work was in that neighbourhood.'

'Did you ever stay in the *Hôtel Morvan*?'

'I can't remember.'

'Or the *Hôtel Jonard*, in the Place des Abbesses?'

'I may have done.'

'Were you in the habit, in the course of that summer, of taking your meals in the *Bonne Fourchette* restaurant in the Rue Dancourt? Old Boutant, the proprietor, is still alive, and, as he has an excellent memory, he may still be able to identify you.'

'I know nothing about all this.'

'You don't know the restaurant?'

'I may have had lunch or dinner there once or twice. How many more questions?'

'Not many. Especially as I'm getting nothing but evasive answers. I suppose you can at least tell me in what year you were married?'

98

'In 1955.'

'Did you break it off with Nina?'

'You must be out of your mind, Chief Superintendent!'

'Do you still not remember where the pistol is? Can you really not recall where you put it?'

'I'm not even sure I still have it.'

'When did you buy it?'

'I didn't buy it. It was given to me by one of my workmen. He had two small children, and he thought it safer not to keep firearms in the house.'

'Does this man still work for you?'

'Yes.'

'What is his name?'

'Oscar Raison. You'll find him at the Avenue Trudaine. He's one of my oldest employees. Now I hope you really have finished.'

'I have nothing more to ask you. Thank you for your help. I do apologize, Madame, for having intruded upon you while you were sunbathing.'

She did not reply, but looked up inquiringly at her husband.

In a side street, Maigret chanced upon a little Italian restaurant. At the sight of the oven, he was seized with a sudden fancy for a pizza. While he was waiting for it, he ordered a plate of seafood and a bottle of Muscadet. They had no half-bottles.

He looked grave but calm. He had a feeling that he had not had a wasted journey. After he had had his coffee, he took a taxi to Saint-Nazaire, where he felt certain of finding a police station. He made inquiries at the Town Hall, and was sent on to Nantes. The police station was rather poky, and staffed only by three men.

All three recognized him, and seemed surprised to see him there.

'Is La Baule in your territory?'

'Yes, but we seldom have occasion to go there. It's just a seaside resort for family holidays. Nothing ever happens there. . . .'

'I want a round-the-clock watch kept on a man who is at present on holiday there. Is that possible?'

'Of course, nothing is impossible. But there are only the three of us.'

Maigret showed them the warrant.

'We'll do our best to oblige, Chief.'

He described Louis Mahossier and his wife, and gave their address.

'If either of them should suddenly leave La Baule, I want you to telephone me immediately, at home if need be.'

He gave them his private telephone number.

'I shall want to know, naturally, where they are heading for.'

'Of course, Chief Superintendent. And now will you join us in a glass of Muscadet?'

'I've just had one. My doctor has prescribed moderation.'

He left them, and returned by taxi to La Baule. One or two men walking along the front were dressed, like himself, in city clothes. They were carrying their jackets folded over their arms. He decided to do likewise.

He drove straight home in a taxi from Orly. Madame Maigret was waiting for him out on the landing. When she saw him, she couldn't help laughing.

'What would you look like, I wonder, after a month at the seaside?'

'What do you mean?'

'You've been away less than a full day, and you've caught the sun good and proper. Take a look at yourself in the glass. . . .'

She was right. Maigret's face was flaming red. And he couldn't wait to take off his sand-filled shoes. He had been unable to resist the childish urge to walk the whole length of the beach, within three feet of the water, with its narrow white border of tiny waves. He had walked thus for nearly two hours, amid a riot of noise and colour, with children's balls coming at him from all directions.

'Have you had dinner?'

'I had a snack on the plane. I must ring the Quai right away.'

He was put through to the Inspectors' Duty Room and, to his amazement, recognized the voice of Janvier.

'What are you doing in the office at this hour?'

'There's been an armed robbery in a post office. It's kept us very much on the run. We've arrested the two villains, and recovered the money. All we need now is to get the third man, the look-out, who managed to escape in the confusion. And what about you, Chief?'

'It will be a couple of days before I can be sure that my journey was really worthwhile. Meanwhile, can you let me have two inspectors tonight? I want a couple of addresses kept under surveillance.'

'We're terribly short-handed, but we'll manage somehow.'

'Write this down: The Avenue Trudaine, near the Lycée Rollin. I want the warehouses and workshops of the firm of Louis Mahossier, decorators, watched. I haven't the least idea what, if anything, is likely to happen there, but I'd be easier in my mind if I knew that the premises were under surveillance. Next, I want someone posted in the Rue de Turbigo to watch the residence of this same man, Mahossier . . . the flat isn't empty. Their old cook is living there alone for the moment. . . .'

'I've got it. . . . What if Mahossier should show up at either place?'

'He's to be followed, and note taken of where he goes and what he does.'

Maigret slept badly, because as soon as he began to perspire in bed, his face started smarting. He could still hear the murmur of the waves, and the brilliant colours of the beach seemed imprinted on his retina.

Next morning, he was once again up very early, and hailed a taxi to take him to the Rue de Turbigo. The building was typical of the architecture of the Old Quarter. The façade had recently been restored, and had regained the appearance of a luxurious private mansion.

'Excuse me, Madame. Can you please direct me to Monsieur Mahossier's flat?'

'He's not here. He and his wife are on holiday at their villa in La Baule.'

'I know. But I understand that their cook, Mademoiselle Berthe, is in residence.'

'Oh! very well. It's on the first floor, the door on the right, though in fact either door would do, as their flat occupies the whole floor.'

There was no lift, but the staircase was wide, with shallow treads. The door was of old wood, gleaming with wax polish. He rang, and was kept waiting for some time before anything happened. Eventually, he heard light footsteps approaching, and the door was opened.

'Monsieur and Madame Mahossier are . . .'

'They're in La Baule, I know. It's you I've come to see.'

'Me?'

'Yes. You are Mademoiselle Berthe, the cook, are you not?'

'Come in. There's no point in hovering out there on the landing.'

She led him into the vast drawing room, which was lit by three tall windows. Most of the furniture was contemporary with the house.

'Please sit down. Are you a vacuum cleaner salesman?'

'No. I'm from the *Police Judiciaire.*'

She subjected him to a bold stare. She was obviously not without courage, and doubtless would not hesitate to speak her mind.

'You're Chief Superintendent Maigret, aren't you?'

'Yes.'

'You're in charge of that murder case. . . . The tramp . . . what was his name? I can't remember names as I used to.'

'Vivien.'

'Yes. What an extraordinary thing to do, to kill a tramp, don't you think? Unless he was one of those who kept a fortune sewn up in his mattress.'

'He wasn't. I saw your employer yesterday in La Baule.'

'Oh?'

'Did you know him before he was married?'

'Well, I first met him when he became engaged to Mademoiselle Cassegrain. At that time, I was in service with her parents. Monsieur Cassegrain is a notary. He lives in the Avenue de Villiers. His wife is in very poor health. She had a personal maid, who looked after her and did the cooking. It was Monsieur Cassegrain who persuaded me to go with his daughter when she got married.'

'How long ago was that?'

'About fifteen years. The only difference here is that Madame has no personal maid, and I have to do everything myself. . . . Well, perhaps that's not quite fair. Madame helps me a lot, and she's as good a cook as I am myself. . . .'

'Do they go out a lot?'

'Very seldom. . . . Just occasionally to the theatre or the cinema. They entertain very little, just one or two close friends.'

'Do they get on well together?'

'They don't fall out over every little thing, if that's what you mean.'

'Do you think they are still fond of one another?'

Her reply to this was an eloquent silence.

'Has Monsieur Mahossier a mistress?'

'I've no idea. He'd hardly be likely to tell me if he had.'

'Does he ever go out alone at night, and come back home very late?'

'Never. . . . At least not until one night last week. . . . It was about eleven o'clock. Madame had had her mother to dinner here, and was driving her home. He rushed in like a whirlwind, and made straight for his bedroom. And then he went out again, as suddenly as he had come. When Madame returned, she decided not to wait up for him, and went straight to bed. I don't know whether she heard him come in, he crept in so quietly, but I did. . . . And I can tell you that it was past three o'clock in the morning. . . .'

'How long have they had separate bedrooms?'

'Almost since they were first married. Monsieur has to be up very early in the morning, to supervise his workmen. Madame, who likes to sleep late, found that it disturbed her. . . .'

One only had to hear her allude to Mahossier to realize that she disliked him, whereas she spoke of her mistress with positive adoration.

'How old was she when she married?'

'It was just a month after her twentieth birthday.'

'Do you happen to know where they met?'

'No. She was out and about all the time, when she was a girl. And, as you know, girls nowadays go everywhere unchaperoned.'

'Is she happy?'

Another eloquent silence.

'Has her marriage been a disappointment to her?'

'She's not the sort of woman to complain or go into a decline. She takes things as they come.'

Maigret noticed that there was a photograph of the Mahossiers on the piano. Louis Mahossier was wearing a moustache, which he had since shaved off, and the young woman had blonde curls all over her head.

The cook, following Maigret's glance, abruptly asked:

'What's he done?'

'Why do you ask? He hasn't necessarily done anything.'

'If that was so, you wouldn't be here. When a man like you takes the trouble. . . .'

'Would you show me his bedroom?'

'He'd be furious if he knew, but I don't care. I'm not afraid of him.'

They went through the dining room and out into a passage.

'Here,' she said, flinging open a door, 'this is Madame's bedroom.'

It was a cheerful room. The colour-scheme was pale grey, with touches of blue. The floor was covered with a white carpet. Maigret felt his feet sinking into it.

Mahossier's room, adjoining, was naturally more subdued, but everything was in the best of taste.

'Who chose the colour schemes and the furniture?'

'Madame. She attended classes on the history of art at the Louvre, and she also did a course at the School of Interior Design.'

'Is she the one who plays the piano?'

'Yes, but only when she's on her own.'

This room was done up in soft shades of beige and brown.

'Tell me, does Mahossier own a pistol?'

'Yes. I saw it quite recently, about a fortnight ago.'

'Is it a revolver?'

'Do you mean has it a kind of cylinder to hold the bullets?'

'Yes.'

'No. It's quite flat.'

'An automatic.'

'You can see for yourself.'

She went to the bedside table, and opened the top drawer.
. . . A look of shocked bewilderment came into her face.

'It's not here.'

'Perhaps he took it with him to La Baule?'

'That he did not. I packed the cases myself.'

'Could he have put it somewhere else?'

She opened the two other drawers, which contained keys,
a penknife and a quantity of club membership cards.

'It's been in this drawer here ever since I came to this
house.'

'And you say you saw it as recently as a fortnight ago?
Were there any cartridges with it?'

'A whole boxful. They've gone too.'

She looked in all the cupboards and drawers, and even
searched in the bathroom.

When she came face to face with Maigret again, she looked
grave and a little pale.

'I think I'm beginning to see why you're here.'

'Does it surprise you?'

'A little. Not all that much. If I tell you why, I daresay
you'll laugh at me. He doesn't like animals. He won't have
a dog or a cat in the place. Madame used to have a cocker
spaniel—it was company for her—but he made her get rid
of it.'

'I'd be obliged if you would remain in Paris for the next
few days. I may have need of you very soon now.'

'I'll be here.'

And, after a slight pause, when they were on their way
back to the drawing room:

'Did you see Madame in La Baule?'

'Yes.'

'I bet you she was sunbathing.'

'She was.'

'When she's at the seaside, she spends every minute she
can soaking up the sun. She used to go to La Baule with
her parents, as a child.'

'Don't they want any children?'

'They've never discussed it with me, but I don't think
they're all that keen.'

105

'Many thanks, Mademoiselle Berthe. You have been most helpful.'

'I did my best, I'm sure. . . .'

But she did not add:

'And I also did my best to land my employer in the soup.'

He returned by taxi to the Quai des Orfèvres. Torrence announced that there had been a phone call from Nantes, to say that there was nothing to report from the villa so picturesquely named the *Umbrella Pines*. They wanted to know if they were to keep up the watch.

'Ring them back and say yes.'

He found Janvier in the Inspectors' Duty Room.

'Have you posted two men, as I asked?'

Janvier was the only one whom he regularly addressed by the familiar *tu*, though occasionally he also addressed young Lapointe, the most junior of the inspectors, in the same fashion. As for the others, he normally stuck to the more formal *vous*, except in moments of absent-mindedness or stress.

'Who have you sent to the Rue de Turbigo? Whoever it is is keeping himself well hidden. I've just come from there, and I didn't see anyone. Admittedly, there is a bistro just opposite the house. . . .'

'Baron is there, and Neveu is in Montmartre.'

Maigret went across to the wing which housed the examining magistrates, and knocked at Judge Cassure's door.

'Come in,' called out the judge.

'Are you making any progress?'

'In a way, yes. As a matter of fact, I would be obliged if you would sign a warrant empowering me to keep my man under surveillance.'

'Tell me about it.'

Maigret subsided into an uncomfortable chair, and began giving the details of his peregrinations in the course of the past two days.

'I have no guarantee that Mahossier is the murderer of Vivien, but I have found enough evidence to justify a more searching interrogation than I was able to carry out on the beach. . . .'

'I agree with you. How are you going to set about it?

Are you going to send two men to arrest him, or will you leave it to the local police?'

'I'll send two of my men if they can possibly be spared. We're so short-staffed at the moment that if the criminal fraternity got to hear of it, they would have a field day.'

'I'll sign the surveillance warrant right away.'

He began filling in one of the forms so familiar to Maigret.

'Christian name?'

'Louis.'

'Is there an "h" in Mahossier? I don't know why, but I seem to have an urge to spell it Marossier.'

'Thanks, Judge.'

'Have you been to the Avenue Trudaine?'

'I intend to go there this morning.'

Returning to his own floor, he sought out Janvier.

'Look, I absolutely must have two more men. . . .'

Poor Janvier did not know which way to turn.

'Will you need them for long?'

'Just long enough to bring someone back from La Baule.'

He looked searchingly at Maigret, and understanding began to dawn.

'I get it! You can have Véran and Loubet.'

Maigret took them both into his office, gave them his instructions, and then handed them the surveillance warrant.

'There's a plane leaving in an hour. You should be able to catch it. But I would prefer you to return by train.'

'Is he to be handcuffed?'

'Only if he tries to give you the slip. Otherwise, I don't think it will be necessary.'

He called out to Torrence:

'Come on. I shall be needing my chauffeur again.'

In point of fact, Torrence had been pretty well his full-time chauffeur for the past few days.

'The Avenue Trudaine. . . . Just opposite the Lycée Rollin.'

'Are you having him arrested?'

'I'm bringing him in for questioning. We'll see how things go after I've put him through it a bit more thoroughly than I was able to do on the beach. . . .'

He found himself in a large courtyard, with ladders lying about all over the place and, at the end, a kind of garage full of huge drums of paint. An enamel plaque inscribed OFFICE with an arrow directed Maigret to the place he was seeking.

The office turned out to be a single, fairly large room, whose sole occupant was a grumpy-looking little man, bent over a pile of invoices.

'I am Chief Superintendent Maigret.'

'Are you sure it's me you're looking for?'

'What is your name?'

'Vannier . . . Gérard Vannier, and I can't think what the police can . . .'

'It doesn't concern you personally.'

'Is it one of our workmen? They'll all out on the various sites. . . . And besides, they're all reliable men, who have been with us for years. . . .'

'Does that door there on the left lead to the boss's office?'

'Yes, but he's hardly ever in it. He's always at one or other of the sites.'

'Is it a profitable business?'

'We have no cause for complaint.'

'Are you a partner?'

'Alas, no. I'm just the book-keeper.'

'How long has the business been going?'

'That I can't tell you. All I know is that the former owner went bust in 1947. Admittedly, he spent most of his time in one bistro or another, and there was a good deal of waste. . . . Anyway, Monsieur Mahossier took over the business, and sacked all the old staff.'

'What about you?'

'At first a book-keeper was only needed two days a week. Then, as business started to pick up, he took me on full time. This was towards the end of 1948.'

'Is he a hard worker?'

'He keeps a personal eye on every detail of the business. Some days he barely has time to slip out for a quick lunch.'

'How does he get on with his workmen?'

'He's very friendly with all of them, but he won't allow them to overstep the mark, and they know it.'

'How many workmen does he employ?'

'For the moment, eight, including one apprentice.'

'Do you know if he keeps a pistol in his office?'

'A pistol? No. Why ever should he? Most of his customers pay by cheque, and these are taken straight to the bank at the corner of the Avenue.'

'Do you mind?'

To the intense indignation of the little man, he went into Mahossier's office and opened all the drawers, one after the other. There was no gun in any of them.

'What, precisely, are you here for?'

'I'm conducting an inquiry.'

'When Monsieur Mahossier hears about this . . .'

'I saw him yesterday.'

'You mean you went all the way to La Baule?'

'Yes, and by tomorrow morning at the latest, he will be back in Paris.'

'He was intending to be away for three weeks or a month. . . ?'

'I persuaded him to change his mind.'

'Didn't he object?'

The little fellow's hackles were up, and no mistake. He looked like a fighting cock about to strike.

'I'd very much like to know what all this is about.'

'You'll find out soon enough.'

'Making yourself at home in the boss's office. . . . Opening drawers. . . . Asking preposterous questions. . . . And now telling me that you have persuaded the boss to return from La Baule. . . .'

Maigret, without saying another word, left the little fellow to fulminate in solitude.

## Chapter Six

NO SOONER was Maigret back at the Quai des Orfèvres than he received a telephone call from La Baule. It was from Véran, one of the two inspectors sent to bring Mahossier back to Paris.

'How did it go?'

'Not too good to begin with. At first, he got on his high horse, and refused to come with us to Paris. He spoke of friends in high places, and threatened big trouble for the Department.'

'How did his wife take it?'

'She just listened. She was obviously surprised. I gave them a few minutes to talk it over, then I took the handcuffs out of my pocket, and told him that if he didn't come quietly, he'd find himself wearing them all the way to Paris. He was furious.'

'Would you have actually had the nerve to do that?'

'Yes.'

'But what on earth for, in God's name?'

'I realized that what he dreaded more than anything else was public humiliation. At any rate, he eventually agreed to come with us to the station, to catch the night train. His wife wanted to come too, but he wouldn't have it. He told her he'd be back within forty-eight hours.

'"I tell you, they've got nothing on me. They're only storing up trouble for themselves."'

Next morning, Maigret went straight into the office. He sat down at his desk, chose a pipe, and filled it with great deliberation. Then he summoned Torrence, and told him to sit at one end of the desk, ready to take shorthand. It was usually Lapointe who took down statements in shorthand, as the most highly skilled stenographer in the Department, but Torrence was competent enough.

Maigret pressed a buzzer, and Véran appeared with Mahossier, who subjected him to a hard, unwavering stare.

'Take a seat.'

'I protest. I have been wrongfully arrested, and I reserve the right to bring an action against you, even though you are the great Maigret himself.'

Maigret was impassive.

'Would you be so good as to tell me, Monsieur Mahossier, where your pistol is to be found?'

'What pistol?'

'The one that, until only a few days ago, was kept in the top drawer of your bedside table. A ·32, if I'm not mistaken.'

'I know nothing about firearms, and I couldn't tell you what calibre this one was. As I said before, it was given to me a long time ago.'

'Where is it now?'

'Where it always has been, I shouldn't wonder.'

He spoke snappishly, and when his glance rested on the Chief Superintendent, his eyes were full of hatred. But was there not also a hint of fear in those eyes?

'The pistol is no longer in the drawer. What have you done with it?'

'I'm not the only person with access to the flat.'

'Are you suggesting that Mademoiselle Berthe might have taken it? All I can say to that is that flippancy will get you nowhere.'

'I wasn't suggesting that the cook had taken it.'

'Who then? Your mother-in-law, perhaps? She was, after all, in your flat on the night when you dined alone at *Chez Pharamond*, and returned home at three in the morning.'

'I have never returned home as late as three in the morning.'

'Do you wish me to confront you with the witness who saw you clearly, and who will not hesitate to identify you?'

Torrence, his forehead bathed in perspiration, was scribbling away as fast as he was able.

'Not only is there a witness here at hand, who saw you go down Vieux-Four Passage shortly before three, but there is another witness who heard you coming into your flat a few minutes after three.'

Sardonically, he said:

'Are you, by any chance, referring to my wife?'

'If it were your wife, she could not testify against you.'

Maigret, in contrast to his suspect, was very composed.

'Then it must have been that old bitch, Berthe. Just because she brought up my wife more or less single-handed, she's so jealous of anyone else at all close to her that she can't stand the sight of me.'

'Where did you first meet Marcel Vivien?'

'I don't know anyone of that name.'

'Don't you read the papers?'

'I don't pay much attention to the news items.'

'All the same, you do know that he was murdered? He was asleep in his bed, when he was shot three times in the chest.'

'What's that got to do with me?'

'It may have a great deal to do with you. It would be a great help, if you could produce your pistol.'

'First, I'd need to know who had moved it, or stolen it.'

He was the sort of man who would go on professing his innocence in the teeth of the strongest evidence. He lit a cigarette with trembling fingers. He might have been trembling with rage.

'Are you saying that you've never been in Vieux-Four Passage?'

'I don't even know where it is.'

Abruptly, Maigret changed the subject to the discomfiture of his suspect.

'What happened to Nina Lassave?'

'Am I supposed to know her? The name means absolutely nothing to me.'

'In 1945 and '46, you lived in Montmartre, in a private hotel, a mere stone's throw from the Boulevard Rochchouart.'

'I did live round about there at one time, but I can't remember what year it was.'

'The girl in question had a flat in the Boulevard Rochechouart.'

'Maybe she did. But then so do thousands of others. Am I supposed to know every one of them?'

'The probability is that you did make her acquaintance, as well as that of Marcel Vivien, who was her lover at that time. Please take time for reflection before you answer my next question. Were you, also, Nina Lassave's lover?'

'I don't need time for reflection. The answer is no. At that period, which was before my marriage, I did have a succession of mistresses, but no one of that name, and I never knew anyone called Marcel Vivien.'

'In other words, you have no connection with anyone concerned in this case?'

'None whatsoever.'

He was growing bolder, yet, at the same time, he was

noticeably more tense, and he could not prevent his hands from trembling.

'I am sending you back to your cell, to give you time to think things over.'

'By what right . . . ?'

'Aren't you forgetting the warrant for your arrest, duly signed by the Examining Magistrate?'

'If you insist on putting me through another interrogation, I demand that my lawyer should be present.'

'I should be within my rights to refuse at this stage. It is not until the Examining Magistrate takes over that you become entitled to legal representation. But I don't wish to be obstructive. What is the name of your lawyer?'

'Maître Loiseau. His address is 38 Boulevard Beaumarchais.'

'I'll let him know in good time.'

Maigret got up, lumbered to the open window, and gazed out at the glaringly blue sky. Everyone, except for those who were at the seaside, was longing for the rain, which persisted in holding off. The temperature was still rising.

Inspector Véran took Mahossier back to his cell.

'He won't be seeing this one off to a better world,' muttered Véran under his breath, referring no doubt to Chief Superintendent Maigret.

Maigret, for his part, was remarking to Torrence:

'He's very stubborn. Get those notes of yours typed out, will you? I'll get him to sign his statement next time.'

'Do you really believe he knew Nina Lassave?'

'It's a possibility. I was only flying a kite. I thought I detected some reaction. He certainly wasn't expecting me to mention her name. . . .'

He chose a fresh pipe from the rack, and put on his hat. 'If I'm wanted for anything urgent, I'll be at the office of the *Parisien Libéré.* . . .'

Torrence looked surprised, but said nothing. First, Maigret stopped off for a half of beer in the *Brasserie Dauphine*, then he got into a taxi.

'The office of the *Parisien Libéré.* . . .'

He recalled that this was one of the first newspapers to

appear after the Liberation. He himself had been out of Paris in 1946. Shortly before, he had fallen out with the then Chief Commissioner of Police, who had retired a few months later. He had been posted to Luçon, where there had been practically nothing to do, and to pass the time, he had spent most of the day playing billiards. He had had to stay there, eating his heart out, for the best part of a year. Madame Maigret, too, had not taken to life in the Vendée.

Fortunately, the new Commissioner had summoned him back to Paris. At that time Maigret was only a Superintendent. He had not yet been promoted to Chief Superintendent and Head of the Crime Squad. Maigret now looked back on his time in Luçon as not merely a gap in his career but a blank in his memory.

'I would like to see the editor.'

'Your name, please.'

'Chief Superintendent Maigret.'

The editor, whom he had never met before, and who turned out to be a very young man, came out of his office to greet him.

'To what do I owe this honour?'

'It's about a case I'm working on,' Maigret explained.

'What can we do to help you?'

'I presume you file all the back numbers of your paper?'

'Of course. They are bound, and arranged in chronological order.'

'I'd like to look up the years 1945 and '46. . . .'

'Come with me.'

He followed the editor through a bewildering maze of corridors, and came at last to a dark room fitted with bookshelves, which were filled with rows of huge books bound in black cloth.

'Do you need any help? I could let you have someone to lend a hand.'

'I don't think that will be necessary. The fact is that it may take hours.'

This, Maigret felt, was what he ought to have thought of doing at the outset. It had occurred to him, fleetingly, but then it had gone right out of his mind.

'Would you like me to send out for some beer? There's a bistro just over the way. We often . . .'

'Thanks, but I've only just had a glass.'

As soon as he was alone, he took off his jacket, rolled up his shirt sleeves, and went to the shelves to find the bound volume for the year 1945.

It took him an hour to work through it. Needless to say, he read only the headlines. None of them seemed to have any bearing on the lives of Marcel Vivien, Nina Lassave or Louis Mahossier.

He returned the volume to its place on the shelves and, oppressed by a slight headache, started on the year 1946. Twice, the editor looked in to ask if there was anything he could do to help.

'Still not feeling thirsty?'

'I could do with a half now, I must admit.'

The air was blue with smoke from his pipe. The room smelt of old paper and printer's ink.

Some of the headlines took him by surprise, recalling old scandals and sensations which were now completely forgotten.

January . . . February . . . March . . . April. . . .

He plodded his way through to August and there, in the issue for the 17th, he was confronted with the following headline:

*Young woman found strangled in the Boulevard Rochechouart*

The headline was not particularly prominent, nor was it on the front page. At the time, presumably, it had not attracted much attention.

*A young woman, Nina Lassave, aged twenty-two, was found strangled in the bedroom of her flat in the Boulevard Rochechouart. She was lying naked on the bed. Nothing seems to have been disturbed either in the bedroom or elsewhere in the flat. In reply to questioning, the concierge was unable to supply any significant information.*

*For several years, Nina Lassave was employed as a sales girl in a lingerie shop in the Rue Lepic. The proprietress expressed herself as being well-pleased with her work.*

*At the end of 1945, she suddenly gave in her notice. It was* known that there was a man in her life, but he seldom visited her flat. What precisely was it that occurred on the night of her death? The facts will be hard to establish. The concierge, as it happens, is an elderly woman, not much interested in the comings and goings of her tenants and their visitors.

*The inquiry is being conducted by Chief Superintendent Piedboeuf.*

The following day, under the headline:

*No new developments in the Boulevard Rochechouart case,* it was stated in a brief paragraph that nothing fresh had come to light regarding the young woman's private life. According to the police surgeon's report, couched in technical language, the cause of death was strangulation. There were no signs of any other injuries on the body.

In response to further questioning, the concierge had confirmed that the girl had occasionally returned home in company with a youngish man, who usually went up with her to her flat, though he had never once spent the night there.

She had caught a glimpse of him once or twice. Nevertheless, she had thought it unlikely that she would recognize him again. During the last two months of her life or thereabouts, the young woman had had another regular visitor, who had been in the habit of calling in the afternoon. The light being better at that time of day, the concierge had had a good look at him, and was able to give a fuller description.

He was exceptionally tall and thin, with dark eyes. He always bounded up the stairs, two at a time, and left, unaccompanied, about an hour later.

There followed three blank days before it was announced in the *Parisien Libéré* that:

*A man has been at Police Headquarters helping Chief Superintendent Piedboeuf with his inquiries.*

*An atmosphere of great secrecy surrounds the interrogation of a suspect at present being held at Police Headquarters. The fact of the matter is that the tall, thin man known to have visited Nina Lassave on several occasions in her flat in the Boulevard Rochechouart has been identified as one Louis M, a housepainter, who lives in lodgings in the vicinity.*

*He does not deny having been the lover of the young woman, but maintains that he did not see her on the day she died. The concierge, however, claims to have seen him on the stairs, on his way up to her, on that very day, at approximately four o'clock in the afternoon.*

*In the absence of any concrete evidence, the police have released M, but their inquiries continue.*

*As to Marcel V, cabinet maker, who was Nina Lassave's lover for at least six months before her death, there are witnesses to prove that he was in a café in the Boulevard de la Chapelle at the time when the murder was committed.*

Maigret made notes in his old black notebook. The waiter from the local brasserie had brought him a half of beer with a good head on it, and this, combined with the interest aroused by the newspaper revelations, had dispelled his headache.

He tried to find his way back to the editor's office, but got hopelessly lost in the maze of corridors, and had to ask for directions.

Would you mind if I had photostat copies made of one or two items from your archives?'

'Not in the least.'

'May I use your phone?'

He asked to be put through to Moers.

'Is Mestral there . . . ? Send him along to the office of the *Parisien Libéré*, will you? Tell him to ask at the desk for the Archives Room. I'll be there, waiting for him.'

Maigret returned to his researches among the old newspapers. As time went on, less and less space was devoted to Nina Lassave, as a sensational political trial got under way and riveted the attention of readers all over France.

*It now appears that Louis M, allegedly seen by the concierge going upstairs to Nina Lassave's flat at about four o'clock on the afternoon of her death, also has an alibi. Chief Superintendent Piedboeuf and his team of inspectors are continuing their inquiries, but apparently have been unable to discover any fresh evidence.*

This more or less sounded the death knell in the Boulevard Rochechouart affair. There was no photograph of Mahossier or Marcel Vivien in any issue of the paper.

Mahossier had been summoned to the Quai des Orfèvres for questioning on two or three further occasions. The interrogations had taken place under the auspices of Judge Coméliau, who was still alive at the time, but there had been no follow-up.

Half an hour later Mestral arrived, with a regular arsenal of cameras and flash-light equipment.

'How much is there to photograph?'

'Only about half a dozen shortish paragraphs.'

Maigret watched him at work, indicating the relevant material as required.

'Could you manage to let me have some roughs by this afternoon?'

'They should be ready by four o'clock, unless it's so urgent that you'd rather I skipped lunch.'

Maigret went in to thank the editor.

'Did you find what you wanted?'

'Yes.'

'Presumably you want it kept under wraps for the time being?'

'When the time comes to release the story, I promise you'll be the first to know.'

'Thanks. See you again very soon, I hope.'

It was a few minutes past twelve. It was not much more than half an hour's walk from the Rue d'Enghien to the Boulevard Richard-Lenoir. Maigret, in good spirits, enjoyed looking at the people, the coaches and the goods displayed in the shop windows. Two or three coaches were parked near the Bastille, and cameras clicked as the tourists snapped it, to take its place alongside the Arc de Triomphe, the Sacré-Coeur and the Eiffel Tower. Most of them looked a little weary, but all were determined to miss none of the sights they had been promised.

He was humming as he let himself into his flat.

'Things are looking up, it seems,' remarked Madame Maigret, as she helped him to hors-d'œuvre.

'I fancy I've done a good morning's work. I can't say yet what it may lead to, but it will lead to something, that's for sure. There's one man, unfortunately, who will never come forward as a witness.'

'Who is that?'

'Marcel Vivien. I've learnt one thing, at any rate, and there's no reason why I should make a secret of it. Nina Lassave was murdered in her flat in August 1946.'

'Was she shot?'

'No, strangled.'

'No wonder you couldn't trace her!'

'Quite. And the more I question Mahossier, the more stubborn he gets.'

He tucked into his food with a will. They had a leg of lamb which was pink and succulent, with the merest bead of blood forming on the bone.

'Delicious,' he said with a sigh, and had another slice.

'Would you say the end was in sight?'

'I can't say anything definite at this stage, but I fancy we still have some way to go. The joke is that everything I found this morning in the back numbers of the *Parisien Libéré* must have been available from the first, only in greater detail, on the files of Criminal Records. The reason it slipped my mind was that it all happened during the time we were in Luçon.'

'I was never so bored in my life!'

'You can say that again!'

'Would you like a peach? They're beautifully ripe and juicy.'

'I wouldn't say no.'

He was at peace with himself and the world.

This time, returning to the Quai, he treated himself to a taxi. As on the previous day, the windows in his office were wide open, and little eddies of cooler air frolicked about the room.

'Torrence!'

'Yes, Chief?'

'Have you finished typing that statement?'

'It's been ready since well before lunch.'

'Let me have a copy, will you?'

When Torrence had brought it to him, he went on:

'I want you to go up to Records. Somewhere in the files for 1946, you're bound to find some material on the murder of Nina Lassave in the Boulevard Rochechouart.'

'That seems to ring a bell. . . . Ah! I remember now. It was one of Chief Superintendent Piedboeuf's cases.'

'Quite. I want to see the file as soon as you can lay your hands on it.'

Pausing occasionally for thought, or to relight his pipe, he read carefully through the transcripts of the questions and answers which he and Mahossier had exchanged that morning.

Every word was significant.

On paper, Mahossier's statement looked a lot more incoherent than it had sounded at the time.

When he had finished, Maigret sat very still, with his eyes half closed. Anyone watching might have supposed him asleep, but his mind was more active than ever. He was endeavouring to recall every aspect of the inquiry, down to the smallest detail, to build up a coherent picture in his mind.

He was in no hurry to reach a conclusion. On a sudden impulse, he decided to telephone Ascan, the Superintendent of Police in the First *Arrondissement*.

'I'm terribly sorry, Chief Superintendent, I have no further progress to report.'

'That's not why I rang you. I'd be most grateful if you could possibly get hold of those two vagrants, the man and the woman, whom I spoke to in your office. If you do manage to lay your hands on them, I'd be obliged if you could send them both to see me here. . . .'

'I hope you don't catch their fleas!'

'It wouldn't be the first time. It's an occupational risk.'

'We get more than our share of them in this district. What time do you want them to be there?'

'About four, if possible.'

'We'll do our best. Some of my men here specialize in that sort of work. . . .'

Maigret asked the switchboard operator to put him through to Maître Loiseau in the Boulevard Beaumarchais. She rang him back almost at once, to say that he was not in his office, and it was thought that he was in the *Palais de Justice*.

'Try and get hold of him there.'

This time Maigret was kept waiting for a quarter of an hour, while minions scurried to and fro looking for the lawyer.

'Maître Loiseau speaking. . . .'

'Chief Superintendent Maigret here. . . . The point is this, Maître. In connection with a recent case of murder, I brought a man in for questioning. His name is Louis Mahossier, and I understand that he's a client of yours. . . . This morning, I endeavoured to question him, but virtually to no avail. He refuses to talk except in your presence. Well, I have no objection to that. . . . I wonder if you could possibly manage to be here, in my office, at about four?'

'I'm afraid I couldn't make it four. My case doesn't come on till three. . . . Would five o'clock suit you?'

'Fine. I look forward to seeing you then.'

Scarcely had Maigret replaced the receiver, when Torrence came in with a slim file containing the documents relating to the murder of Nina Lassave in 1946. Having taken off his jacket and relit his pipe, he sat down at his desk to study it.

The first document was a signed statement made at the local police station by the concierge. Although the girl had come in early the previous night, she had still not appeared downstairs by two o'clock the following afternoon, so the concierge had gone up to her room and knocked.

Finding the door on the latch, she had gone into the flat. Everything seemed in order. The contents of the drawers had not been disturbed. The same was true of the bedroom, where she discovered the poor young woman lying, stark naked, on the bed, with her tongue hanging out, and her lifeless eyes turned up towards the ceiling.

Next followed a statement from the local Superintendent of Police, whose name was Maillefer. He had visited the scene of the crime accompanied by a Constable Patou. They had found the victim in the condition described by the concierge. Her clothes, among which was a print dress, were neatly folded on a chair not far from the bed.

'Robbery was plainly not the motive for the murder. Furthermore, having regard to the victim's state of undress, and the fact that she made no attempt to cover herself up or fend him off, she must have been on terms of intimacy with the murderer. . . .'

Using the telephone in the girl's bedroom, the local Superintendent had rung the Chief Superintendent of the *Police Judiciaire*. Piedboeuf had said he would be coming at once, reminding him that everything should be left exactly as it was and nothing touched, and had asked him to inform the D.P.P.

If Maigret's memory served him right, Piedboeuf, at that time, must have been a little under fifty-five. He knew his job inside out, and was not a man to be trifled with. If anything, he was rather too brusque and impatient.

He had been accompanied by two inspectors, one of whom still worked in the General Information Section.

Piedboeuf's report was fairly long, and attached to it was a plan of the flat.

'None of the furniture seems to have been disturbed in any of the rooms, and I found three hundred francs in the victim's handbag, which was lying on the bedside table for all to see.'

He referred to the arrival of the people from the D.P.P.'s office, which, as usual, had been no more than a formality.

Attached to the Chief Superintendent's report were two more, in addition to several photographs of Nina as she had been found. The first of these two reports was Moer's. He stated that his men had searched in vain for finger-prints. Apart from those of the victim, there were none, except for those of the concierge on the doorknobs.

Maigret was making notes.

The other report bore the signature of Doctor Paul, with whom Maigret had worked for many years, but who was regrettably now dead. He had been Chief Medical Officer of Police, and a great expert on good food.

Expressing himself in more technical language, he concluded that the victim had suffered death by strangulation. The marks of the murderer's fingers were clearly distinguishable on the girl's neck, and these indicated that the killer had unusually powerful hands.

The other tenants in the building had been questioned.

There were not many of them. No one had heard anything. No one had seen any suspicious comings or goings on the stairs.

'Did Nina Lassave have many visitors?'

'No.'

'But surely she had at least one fairly regular visitor?'

'There were two men who used to visit her.'

'Together?'

'No. Separately. The taller one usually came round about mid-afternoon. . . . The other one would call to fetch her in the evening. They used to go out together. I don't know where they usually went, but I did catch sight of them one day, or rather I should say one night, on the terrace of the *Cyrano.* . . .'

'Which of the two had she known longer?'

'The one who came in the evening. . . . The other one had only been coming for a couple of months or so.'

'Did you see either of them on the stairs on the day of the murder?'

'To tell you the truth, I didn't set foot outside my flat until after six.'

The other tenants had even less to tell. One of them, an elderly bachelor who worked in a bank on one of the Grands Boulevards, was in the habit of leaving the house at eight in the morning, and not returning until nine at night.

'I didn't even know of the woman's existence, let alone anything about the comings and goings of her men-friends.'

It was through the concierge that they had got on to Mahossier's track. He had turned up one day in a mini-van inscribed in gold letters: *Lesage et Gélot, decorators, Boulevard des Batignolles.*

More reports and statements. Even the most trivial questions put to a witness were faithfully recorded in the usual stilted language. If he were to come across one of his own reports written at that period, Maigret wondered, would he have found it equally quaint?

'As instructed by Chief Superintendent Piedboeuf, I visited the premises of Messrs Lesage et Gélot, decorators, at 25 Boulevard des Batignolles. Monsieur Lesage was absent, but I obtained an interview with Monsieur Gélot. I inquired of him how many workmen he employed, to which he replied that, this being the slack season, he had, at present, only four men on his books.

'He supplied me with their names. I asked him their ages. Three of them were over forty, one, in fact, being a man of sixty.

'Only one, a man of the name of Louis Mahossier, was young, aged twenty-six. I had to wait for nearly half an hour, as Mahossier was out delivering materials to a site. He was driving the van described by the concierge at the Boulevard Rochechouart.

'Mahossier took it very much amiss. He demanded to know by what right I was subjecting him to such questioning, and at first denied ever having met Nina Lassave. I asked him to accompany me to the Boulevard Rochechouart. The concierge remembered him very well. He was undoubtedly the man she had met on the stairs, two nights previously, at about the time at which the young woman was killed.

'In view of this, I asked him to accompany me to the Quai des Orfèvres, where I handed him over to my superior officer, Chief Superintendent Piedboeuf.'

Maigret mopped his face.

Mahossier had been questioned on four separate occasions, and he had stuck to his original story throughout. On the day in question, he claimed, at about the time when the murder was taking place, he had been in one of the firm's vans, delivering drums of paint to an address in the Rue de Courcelles.

His fellow-workmates, who had taken delivery of the paint, had confirmed his story, but had been much more vague about the time of delivery.

Coméliau, the Examining Magistrate on the case, had sent for him and questioned him on his own.

Other witnesses questioned had been Marcel Vivien, and the proprietor and waiter from the café in the Boulevard de la Chapelle.

Vivien appeared stunned. The death of his mistress, it seemed, had left him drained of all energy. For want of any evidence against him, he had been allowed to return to his lodging house in the Place des Abbesses.

They had persisted longer with Mahossier, but in the end, having so little to go on, they had decided to leave him in peace.

The file was not actually marked *Case Closed*, because the police never formally close an unsolved murder case, but in practice it came to the same thing.

'Torrence! Be a good fellow and bring Mahossier here to me from the cells in about a quarter of an hour.'

As for himself, he intended to nip out to the *Brasserie Dauphine* for a quick half. If Maître Loiseau were to prove as stubborn as his client, the forthcoming session was going to be no picnic.

When he got back, Mahossier was already installed in a chair in his office, and Inspector Torrence had his short-hand notebook open on the desk.

'We can't start without Maître Loiseau.'

Mahossier pretended not to have heard. Maigret idly turned over the pages of the file, committing to memory one or two final details.

Maître Loiseau arrived, still in his robes, having come straight from the *Palais de Justice*, by way of the communicating door, to Police Headquarters.

'I'm terribly sorry, but my case started a quarter of an hour late. . . .'

'Do please sit down. I have a number of questions to put to your client. Up to now, he has persisted in denying everything. I take it you know what the charge is?'

'The charge! Aren't you getting a bit ahead of yourself? As I understand it, the interrogation hasn't even started.'

'Very well, let's put it another way. Your client is suspected of the murder of a vagrant, Marcel Vivien, in a condemned building in Vieux-Four Passage.'

Maigret turned to Mahossier.

'To begin with, I can prove that you were in Les Halles on the night in question.'

'Are your witnesses reliable?'

'You may judge for yourself.'

He sent Torrence out to fetch the man known as Toto,

who had been brought to the Quai des Orfèvres along with
the gross Nana by an inspector from the First *Arrondissement*. Toto, who was quite at home with the police, was
not in the least overawed. He looked boldly from one to
another of those present. When his glance fell on Mahossier,
his face lit up.

'Well! Fancy seeing you, mate! How are you, old fellow?
I hope you're not in any trouble.'

'So you know this man?' asked Maigret. 'Can you tell me
exactly where and when you met him?'

'In Les Halles, of course. Where else? I spend every night
of my life there. . . .'

'Can you tell us exactly where you were at the time . . .?'

'Not ten yards away from *Chez Pharamond* . . . I was
watching a lorry being unloaded. . . . One of my buddies
was working on it . . . if you could call him a buddy, because,
to tell the truth, he wasn't really buddies with anyone. . . .
His name was Vivien. . . . He was unloading vegetables, and
I was waiting for another lorry to turn up, so that I could get
myself taken on. . . .'

'What happened next?'

'The door of *Chez Pharamond* opened, and this gentleman came out of the restaurant. He stood there for quite a
time, watching the fellows unloading. I made the most of it
by going up to him and asking him to let me have the price
of a glass of red wine. . . . Instead of giving me a franc as I
expected, he gave me a five-franc piece, enough to buy myself
a whole bottle. . . .'

'Had you ever seen him in Les Halles before?'

'Never.'

'Do you go there often?'

'I've been going every night for the past fifteen years.'

'You are at liberty to question this witness if you wish,
Maître.'

'The night you were telling us about, what date was that?'

'As if I keep account of dates! I can tell you one thing, at
any rate, it was the night Vivien was done in. . . .'

'Are you sure?'

'Yes.'

'Were you drunk, by any chance?'

'Sure I was, by three o'clock in the morning, but not at ten o'clock at night.'

'Are you quite certain you recognize him?'

'As sure as I am that he recognizes me. Just take a look at his face. . . .'

Maigret turned to Mahossier.

'Is that true?'

'I've never set eyes on the old rag-bag before.'

'Rag-bag! Rag-bag, did you say?'

Torrence propelled him, protesting, from the room, and ushered in the fat woman with the swollen legs and fingers like sausages. She was not yet completely drunk, though somewhat unsteady on her feet.

Having sat down, she looked about her, and then raised her right hand and pointed to Mahossier.

'That's him,' she said, sounding very hoarse, as no doubt she always did.

'What are you talking about?'

'I mean he's the man I saw coming out of that place where the toffs go for their grub—about ten o'clock at night, it was.'

'Do you know the name of the restaurant?'

'*Chez Pharamond.*'

'Are you sure this is the same man?'

'Certain sure. And I'm just as sure I saw Toto talking to him. He told me afterwards that this same fellow had given him a five-franc piece, and he even went so far as to buy me a drink on the strength of it.'

'Do you recognize her, Mahossier?'

'Certainly not. I've never seen the woman in my life, and she certainly never saw me in Les Halles.'

Maigret turned to the fat woman known as Nana.

'Did you see him again?'

'That same night, at about three in the morning. I was sitting sheltering in a doorway on the corner of the Rue de la Grande-Truanderie and Vieux-Four Passage. I heard footsteps, and then someone brushed past me. A very tall, thin man he was. I knew him at once. You couldn't mistake him, especially as there is a gas lamp just at the entrance to the passage.'

'Did you see where he went?'

'Into one of those tumble-down houses that have been under a demolition order for the last ten years. I'm surprised they haven't collapsed already. . . .'

'Mahossier, do you or do you not recognize this woman?'

'I've never seen her. . . .'

Maître Loiseau remarked with a sigh:

'Is this the best you can produce by way of witnesses . . .?'

'Take her outside, Torrence, if you please.'

'Shall I bring in the next witness?'

'In a minute. . . . The first time I put the question to you, you denied having dined at *Chez Pharamond* on the night in question. Do you still deny it?'

'Certainly, I do.'

'In that case, where did you dine? Not at home, according to your own admission, as your mother-in-law was expected to dinner, and you and she are not on the best of terms.'

'I went to a snack bar on one of the Grands Boulevards.'

'Could you find it again?'

'I imagine so.'

'Did you have anything to drink?'

'I don't drink, except for a glass of wine with my meals.'

'In other words, you're saying you never set foot in *Chez Pharamond*?'

At a sign from Maigret, Torrence went out and returned with a man in his early fifties, who was dressed from head to foot in black.

'Please be seated, Monsieur Genlis.'

'In my professional capacity, I am generally known as Robert.'

'Tell us about that. What is your profession, and where do you work?'

'I am assistant head-waiter at *Chez Pharamond*.'

'And in that capacity, I presume you pay particular attention to the arrival and departure of your patrons?'

'It's mostly my job to show them to their tables.'

'Is there anyone in this room whose face is familiar to you?'

'Yes.' And he pointed to Mahossier, who this time turned a little pale.

'When did you last see him?'

'I only saw him once. That was on Monday evening. He was on his own, which is fairly unusual for our patrons. He ate his meal rather fast, and then I showed him to the door and let him out.'

'What do you say to that, Monsieur Mahossier?'

'It's ten years or more since I last set foot in *Chez Pharamond*. According to this man's own statement, he only saw me once in a room crowded with people.'

'How do you know if it was crowded?'

'I presume it was, considering what a well-known place it is. . . .'

'I should point out,' remarked the assistant head-waiter, 'that one seldom sees a man so tall and thin. . . .'

'Any questions, Maître Loiseau?'

'None. My client reserves his defence for his official interrogation before an examining magistrate.'

'Thank you, Monsieur Genlis. I needn't trouble you any further.'

'Have you any other witnesses, Chief Superintendent?'

'As far as this particular matter is concerned, that's as far as we need go for today.'

The lawyer, looking somewhat relieved, stood up.

'But there is still another matter to be considered.'

'Another matter? Isn't it enough that you have accused my client of murdering a tramp whom he has never set eyes on?'

As for Mahossier himself, he now turned very pale indeed, and this accentuated the dark circles under his eyes and the harsh lines at the corners of his tight-lipped mouth.

'Please go on.'

'Do you, by any chance, recall the 6th of August, 1946, Mahossier?'

'Certainly not. What reason could I possibly have for doing so? It must have been a working day like any other, because in those days I was saving every penny I could earn, and I couldn't afford holidays?'

'You were an employee with the firm of Lesage et Gélot. . . ?'

'That is so.'

He seemed taken aback and a little uneasy.

'You frequently drove a mini-van bearing the name of the firm on the side?'

'Quite often, yes.'

'On that day you delivered a number of drums of paint to your workmates on a site in the Rue de Courcelles.'

'I can't remember.'

'I have here a statement that you made to Chief Superintendent Piedboeuf. You won't attempt to deny, I presume, that you answered questions put to you by the Chief Superintendent on a number of occasions?'

So saying, Maigret passed the open file to him across the desk.

'What are you getting at?'

'Where were you living at the time?'

'I can't remember. I lived in hotels, and I never stayed anywhere for very long.'

'Allow me to refresh your memory. You lived in the *Hôtel Jonard*, in the Place des Abbesses. Do you know who else lived in that hotel?'

'I didn't know any of the other occupants.'

'You saw him again very recently, in Les Halles, for the first time in twenty years. I am referring to Marcel Vivien, who was, at that time, Nina Lassave's lover.'

'That's no concern of mine.'

'Oh! yes, it is, indeed. She visited Vivien frequently. I don't know whether you followed her home, or what, but the fact remains that the concierge of the flats where she lived recognized you as a man who came to see her regularly during the last two months of her life.'

Maître Loiseau asked:

'Is the concierge here?'

'She died some time ago, having returned, on her retirement, to the village where she was born. . . .'

'In other words, you can't call her as a witness, which, I dare say, suits your book very well. So far, all you have been able to produce is a couple of squalid, sottish drunks and a man who makes a living out of tips, and now we are asked to take the word of a dead woman. What next, I wonder?'

'All in good time,' murmured Maigret, refilling his pipe.

# Chapter Seven

THE LAWYER consulted his watch, which no doubt showed that it was ten past six, as did Maigret's. He was still young, and given to affecting an air of importance. Brusquely, he stood up.

'Have you done with my client, Chief Superintendent?'

'I'm not sure.'

'I'm afraid I shall have to go. I have an appointment in my office in twenty minutes, and I must on no account be late for it.'

The Chief Superintendent shrugged, as if to say: 'That's no concern of mine.'

Loiseau turned to Mahossier.

'Let me give you a word of advice. If you are asked any more questions, don't answer. That is your right under the law. No one can compel you to say anything.'

Mahossier did not respond. His manner was more sober, less aggressive. He was beginning to appreciate the gravity of the situation, it seemed, and also to realize that the lawyer's chief concern was his own self-importance.

Maître Loiseau bustled out, looking as pompous as when he had come in.

Maigret murmured, as if in passing:

'Let me give you a word of advice. If you are committed for trial at the Assizes, change your lawyer. That fellow will only antagonize the Court.'

He went on:

'He's quite right in saying that you cannot be compelled to answer questions, but in the eyes of many silence is taken to indicate, if not to prove, guilt. I'm not going to ask you any more questions, but I should be obliged if you would listen to what I have to say, and please feel free to interrupt, if there is any comment you wish to make.'

He was watching Mahossier very closely. It seemed to him that his manner was less aggressive than it had been in La Baule or when he had first been brought in for questioning. Now, his expression was more that of an overgrown schoolboy, keeping up a pretence of sulking even when he no longer feels like it.

'Chief Superintendent Piedboeuf was an excellent police officer, and by no means the sort to resent being proved wrong. Is it not a fact that Nina Lassave had a strawberry birth mark on her left cheek?'

'Is this a trap?'

'Nothing so subtle. There is evidence enough here on this file to prove that you were indeed this woman's lover.'

'The concierge is dead.'

'That doesn't invalidate her testimony. Here, for instance, is the transcript of an exchange between the two of you when you were brought face to face:

'You asked her, somewhat defiantly:

' "How did you know my name?"

'Apparently, you thought she would be hard put to it to find an answer to that. This, however, is her reply:

' "I was in my lodge one afternoon, having tea with a friend who calls in to see me from time to time. I can give you her name and address if you wish. As we were sitting there, this man" (pointing to you) "came in under the arch-way, and we got a clear view of him through the glass door. My friend started in surprise.

' "Well! Well!" she said, "If it isn't my decorator! He's the one who painted my kitchen and laid the carpet in the dining room. His name is Louis Mahossier, and he works for a firm in the Boulevard des Batignolles."

'This friend of the concierge, whose name was Lucile Gosset, was interviewed, and she confirmed what she had previously said. It was as a direct result of this that you were traced so soon.

'On the day Nina was killed, at about four o'clock in the afternoon, you were working in the widow Gosset's flat in the Rue Ballu. At about that time, she went out to do her shopping, and you at once seized the opportunity of driving straight to the Rue Caulaincourt. . . .'

Mahossier was watching him, frowning. He seemed puzzled, as though searching for some explanation which continued to elude him.

'I can, if you wish, read you the concierge's statement. The postman called with an express letter for one of the tenants on the third floor, and she took it up to her. As she was coming downstairs after delivering the letter, she passed you on the way up to Nina's flat. Do you still persist in denying all this?'

There was no answer. As he listened to Maigret, Louis Mahossier seemed to grow calmer, though it was clear that he was still under considerable strain.

'You were both crazy about her. I don't know what it was about her that aroused such intense feelings. For her, Marcel Vivien abandoned his wife and child. And yet she wasn't prepared even to go and live with him. She never spent the whole of a single night in his company. Nor in yours, for that matter. I don't know whether it was just some lingering inhibition due to her up-bringing. . . .'

Maigret's voice was muted. From time to time, mechanic-ally, he riffled through the pages of the file in front of him.

'To get back to the afternoon of Nina's murder, undeni-ably Marcel Vivien had an alibi, but it was by no means watertight.'

Mahossier was now watching the Chief Superintendent more intently.

'This morning I came across a note written in the margin of the file by my predecessor, Piedboeuf. It reads as follows:

' "Received an unsolicited visit from an old man, a regular of the bistro in the Boulevard de la Chapelle, name of Arthur Gilson, nicknamed Peg-Leg because he has a stiff knee joint and walks as if he had a wooden leg. He was obviously tiddly.

' "He claims that on the afternoon in question Marcel Vivien came into the bistro at about half-past three, and tossed off two brandies, one after the other. He was very much struck by this as, normally, the cabinet maker drank nothing but coffee. According to him, Vivien then made off in the direction of the Boulevard Rochechouart." '

Maigret looked up, and there was a moment's silence as he gazed searchingly at Mahossier.

'It is only fair to tell you that of all the other people who were in the bistro at the time, not one was able to confirm his story. Or rather, the proprietor did confirm that the events as described did take place, but on the day after Nina's death.

'One of the two witnesses must have been right, and the other wrong. My predecessor seems to have favoured the proprietor's version.'

Mahossier could not resist asking:

'And you?'

'I'm inclined to believe Peg-Leg. He was old, but perfectly coherent. He is now dead. All we have to go on is this marginal note by Chief Superintendent Piedboeuf. . . . Nina had been Vivien's mistress for more than six months. Having severed all ties with his family, he looked upon her as his own exclusive property. . . . Then she met you, and having given herself to you, she still maintained her intimacy with Vivien.

'Vivien seldom visited her in the afternoon. They had formed the habit of lunching together in a restaurant, and meeting again in the evening.'

Once more Mahossier's expression hardened.

'At the time of the inquiry, the concierge could not recall having seen him arrive or leave. Asked what she had been doing at the time, she replied that she had been sitting by the window, knitting and listening to the wireless. Now from that part of the room, she would not necessarily have seen everyone coming in and going out through the arch-way. . . .'

'What are you getting at?'

'I am suggesting that it was Vivien who killed his mistress, who was also your mistress. It's possible that he actually saw you leave the building. We shall never know. One thing we can be sure of is that he was beside himself, literally torn apart by grief.

'It's unlikely that he went to the Boulevard Rochechouart with the intention of killing her, and he was certainly un-armed. It may be that all he had in mind was to surprise you together.

'He found her lying naked on the bed. Why should she have taken off her clothes unless she was expecting a lover?

'He felt that he had done everything for her sake. Had he not shamefully abandoned his wife and daughter, leaving them without a penny? And now here she was, deceiving him with the first man who came along.

'I don't know what they said to one another. But one thing is clear, Nina Lassave was unable to quieten him down. She was not frightened, witness the way she was lying when they found her. . . . But he was working himself up into a state of frenzy, driving himself, screwing himself up to such a pitch that he could find it in his heart to strangle her. It was his whole life that he could see crumbling in ruins. . . . He could never again return to the Rue Caulaincourt, still less to his workshop in the Rue Lepic. . . . Nothing mattered to him any more. . . . Though it might have given him some satisfaction if they had succeeded in pinning the murder on you. . . .'

'It's what they tried to do, more or less, and you, too, at the beginning. I always said I hadn't killed her.'

'When did you find out that she was dead?'

'A quarter of an hour later. I saw Vivien hurry out of the building. He almost ran as far as the Place Blanche. I suddenly felt I had to go in and ask Nina what he had come for.

'I went inside, and that was when I bumped into the concierge on the stairs. When I got to the flat, the door was on the latch. . . . That struck me as odd. . . . A couple of minutes later, I found the body. . . . That was when I removed all the finger-prints. . . . I wiped everything I had touched, not only then but on former occasions. That meant I also had to get rid of Vivien's finger-prints. . . .'

'Why didn't you report him to the police?'

'Because I'd made up my mind to deal with him myself. . . .'

Poor Torrence was having difficulty in keeping up with the rapid tempo of his speech. There was no more question of a monologue delivered by Maigret. A genuine dialogue was developing.

Maigret had penetrated Mahossier's defences, and he was cracking up.

'You really loved her to that extent?'

'She's the only woman I have ever truly loved.'

'What about the woman you married?'

'I'm very fond of her, and so she is of me, I believe. But it was never an overwhelming passion for either of us.'

'Twenty years have gone by, Mahossier.'

135

'I know. All the same, never a day passes when she is not in my thoughts.'

'Don't you realize that the same was true of Vivien? He loved her every bit as passionately as you did, passionately enough to kill her. He never tried to make a new life for himself, but rather chose to spend the rest of his days in misery. . . . He became a derelict, and so remained until you saw him again quite by chance after twenty years.'

## Chapter Eight

MAHOSSIER, in silence, gazed fixedly down at his shoes. His face had undergone a change. He looked much less arrogant and, in consequence, much more human.

'You have had twenty good years . . .'

He looked up at Maigret, his thin lips twisted in a half-smile, expressing his awareness of the irony of the situation.

'I didn't kill her, it's true. And yet it is no less true that, indirectly, I was the cause of her death. . . .'

'You worked hard, and you saved. You managed to set up in business on your own, and things went well for you. . . . You have a charming and attractive wife, a magnificent flat, and a villa in La Baule. . . . And yet you were prepared to risk losing all that you had built up, to kill a man whom you hadn't met for twenty years, and who, in the meantime, had degenerated into a wreck. . . .'

'I had sworn an oath that I would punish him.'

'Could you not have left that to the Law?'

'He would have claimed that it was a *crime passionnel* and got off with a light sentence. By this time, he would have been a free man for many years. . . .'

'Your lawyer will also claim on your behalf that the killing of Vivien was a *crime passionnel*. . . .'

'It's a matter of indifference to me now. . . . As short a time ago as yesterday, I was determined to deny everything . . . to defend myself. . . .

'The fact is, that whatever you may think, the burden is too heavy for me to bear. . . .'

The telephone rang.

'Ascan speaking, First *Arrondissement*. All going well?'

'Fine. I've had Mahossier here with me in my office for the last two hours.'

'Has he confessed?'

'Yes.'

'He would have had to anyway, however reluctantly. Some kids who were playing on a patch of waste ground near the derelict house where Vivien shacked up have just handed me a ·32 pistol. Three bullets are missing from the magazine. One of my men is on the way to the Quai now, to hand it over to you personally.'

'It will be very useful as corroborative evidence.'

'Did he kill Nina Lassave too?'

'No.'

'Who did it then? Vivien?'

'Yes.'

'Do you mean to say that Mahossier was still so much in love with Nina Lassave after twenty years that he was prepared to kill, to avenge her murder?'

'Yes. . . . I'm much obliged to you, Ascan. You've been a tremendous help to me. . . . In fact, you and your men have done most of the work in this case.'

'Oh! I wouldn't go as far as that! . . . Anyway, I mustn't keep you from your work any longer.'

Mahossier had been doing his best to follow this conversation, but he could only hear Maigret's side of it, which gave away very little.

'So you spent the last twenty years searching Paris for him?'

'Not in any systematic way. . . . I looked at the faces of the people in the streets. . . . I was convinced, I don't know why, that one day I should see him again. . . . You were right in saying that I dined at *Chez Pharamond* that night. I walked from my flat to Les Halles. It brought back old memories. In the old days, I looked upon *Chez Pharamond* as the height of luxury, a mecca of self-indulgence far beyond my means. I went in, was shown to a table, and dined alone. . . . My mother-in-law can't stand me, and she's forever making little digs at me. She can't forgive me for having started life as a house-painter. . . . Besides, she somehow found out that I was born in Belleville, and that I was illegitimate.'

A few minutes later, old Joseph, the messenger, knocked at the door.

'There's an inspector here from the First *Arrondissement*. He has a parcel which he says he has instructions to hand over to you personally.'

'Send him in.'

The inspector turned out to be young and very keen.

'I came as soon as I could, Chief Superintendent. I have instructions to give you this. . . .'

He held out a parcel wrapped in grubby, wrinkled brown paper. He looked at Mahossier with frank curiosity.

'Do you wish me to stay?'

'That won't be necessary. Thank you.'

As soon as the inspector had gone, Maigret opened the parcel. 'This is your gun, isn't it?'

'It looks like it, at any rate.'

'So you see, even without your confession, we should have arrived at the truth. Of course, we shall have to check that the bullets in the gun match those removed from Vivien's chest. . . . You were so scared of being caught with this gun in your pocket that you got rid of it by dropping it on the first patch of waste ground you came to. . . .'

Mahossier shrugged.

'It's quite true that I gave a five-franc piece to a tramp. I also saw the fat woman, who seemed to be dead drunk. When I recognized Vivien, unloading crates of vegetables, all the old rage boiled up in me again, and I rushed home to get my pistol. . . .

'I waited there in the dark street. . . . I had to wait a long time, because another lorry had arrived, and he was taken on, among others, to unload it.'

'And all this time your hatred remained at white heat?'

'No. I just felt I had a duty to accomplish.'

'A duty to Nina?'

'Yes. But there was something else as well. This man, this fellow Vivien, seemed at peace with himself. After all, he had chosen his way of life for himself, hadn't he? And through it, he seemed somehow to have found peace. I was infuriated. . . .'

'And, in this frame of mind, you hung about until three in the morning?'

'Not quite that long. . . . Till about half-past two. . . . Then I followed him as far as Vieux-Four Passage. . . . The fat woman I had seen in Les Halles was crouching in a doorway. I thought she was asleep or in a drunken stupor. I never dreamed that she could be dangerous. Maître Loiseau will be furious with me for telling you all this, but it's all one to me. . . .

'I watched Vivien go into the house. . . . Shortly after, I followed him in, and began creeping upstairs. I heard him shut his door. . . . I waited on the stairs for nearly half an hour. . . .'

'Were you waiting for him to fall asleep?'

'No. It was just that I couldn't make up my mind.'

'What decided you in the end?'

'It was the thought of Nina, or, more precisely, the little strawberry mark on her cheek. It gave her such a fragile look, somehow. . . .'

'Did you find him awake?'

'After the first shot, he opened his eyes. He looked surprised. I can't say whether he recognized me. . . .'

'Didn't you speak to him?'

'No. Maybe I was sorry I'd come, but it was too late by then. The only reason I fired the other two shots was to spare him pain. Believe it or not, as you please.'

'You tried to get away with it.'

'That's true. I fancy it was more instinctive than anything else. Vivien also failed to give himself up after he had killed the woman he loved. . . .'

A spasm of anguish passed over his face as he spoke these last words. Then, once more, he shrugged.

'By the way, what became of Madame Vivien?'

'She's still alive, living in a smaller flat in the same block in the Rue Caulaincourt. She's become a dressmaker. She seems to have built up quite a nice little business.'

'There was a daughter as well, wasn't there?'

'She's married and has two children.'

'I hope all this hasn't been too painful for them.'

On this point, Maigret preferred to say nothing.

'What are you going to do with me?'

'For the present, you will return to your cell. Tomorrow, you will be formally interrogated by the Examining Magistrate, who will probably sign a warrant for your arrest. Until this stage of the proceedings is completed, you will probably be detained in the Santé. Later, I fancy, you will be moved to Fresnes Prison, where you will remain until your trial.'

'Won't I be allowed to see my wife?'

'Not for the first few days, I'm afraid.'

'When will the news of my arrest be in the papers?'

'Tomorrow. I believe a reporter is already waiting outside with a photographer.'

Maigret felt a little weary. He, too, had been suddenly relieved of a heavy burden, and it had left him feeling hollow inside. His voice sounded strained. Certainly he felt easier in his mind, but he did not appear triumphant.

Searching for one murderer, he had found two. Was that the solution he had been groping towards all along?

'I am going to ask you a favour, which I daresay you won't be able to grant me. I would like to spare my wife the distress of learning of my arrest from the newspapers or, worse, through a phone call from her mother or a friend. She should be in the middle of dinner by now. At any rate, I'm sure she's back at the villa. . . .'

'What is her telephone number?'

'La Baule 124.'

'Hello! Mademoiselle, would you please get me La Baule 124. Yes, it is urgent. . . .'

It was he rather than the accused man who was longing to be free. Within three minutes, he was through.

'Is that the *Umbrella Pines*?'

'Yes.'

'Madame Mahossier? This is Maigret speaking. Your husband is here with me in my office. He would like a word with you.'

Maigret stumped over to the window and stood there, puffing furiously at his pipe.

'Yes. I'm at Police Headquarters. Are you alone?'

'Except for the maid.'

'Listen carefully. . . . You're in for a grave shock. . . .'

'Do you think so?'

'Yes. . . . I have just confessed. I had no other choice.'

Contrary to his expectation, she took it very calmly.

'To both of them?'

'What do you mean?'

'I mean both murders.'

'I wasn't responsible for the murder in the Boulevard Rochechouart. That was Vivien. . . .'

'I had a feeling. . . . And when you saw him again after twenty years, all the old jealousy built up again. . . .'

'You knew?'

'I was sure of it, from the first.'

'How could you be?'

'Because I know you. . . .'

'What's to become of you?'

'To begin with, I'll stay on here, unless the Examining Magistrate wants me in Paris. After that, I'm not sure yet. There's never been any great love between us, after all. . . . The fact is, I was never anything more than a substitute. . . . I daresay my mother will nag me into divorcing you. . . .'

'Oh!'

'Does that surprise you?'

'No. . . . I suppose not. . . . Good-bye, Odette. . . .'

'Good-bye, Louis.'

As he put back the receiver, he swayed and almost fell. He had not expected things to turn out quite like this. It was not so much what had been said as all that it implied. Fifteen years of his life had been wiped out by a conversation lasting a few minutes.

Maigret went to his cupboard, and poured a little brandy into a glass. 'Here, drink this.'

Mahossier, hesitating, looked at Maigret in amazement.

'I had no idea. . . .' he stammered.

'No idea that your wife had guessed the truth?'

'She's going to divorce me.'

'What else could you expect? That she should wait for you?'

'I don't understand anything any more.'

He gulped down his brandy and coughed. Then, making no attempt to sit down again, he murmured:

'It was good of you not to harass me. . . .'

'Take him back to the cells, Torrence.'

Fat Torrence looked upset, Mahossier stood waiting for him in the middle of the room. In a curious way, he appeared to have shrunk, and in his bewilderment he seemed all at once insignificant.

He made as if to hold out his hand, but then changed his mind.

'Good-bye, Chief Superintendent.'

'Good-bye.'

Maigret felt drowsy. Heavily, he paced the room while awaiting Torrence's return.

'Do you know?' Torrence remarked when he got back. 'At one point, I really felt quite moved.'

'What about coming with me to the Place Dauphine for a glass of something?'

'I'll be glad to.'

They walked side by side from the Quai des Orfèvres to the bar they knew so well. There were several inspectors already in the bar, but only one from the Crime Squad.

'What's it to be, Chief Superintendent?' asked the proprietor.

'A long beer. In the tallest glass you've got.'

Torrence ordered the same. Maigret drank the whole lot down almost in one gulp, and held out his glass for a refill.

'It's thirsty weather today,' remarked the proprietor.

Maigret repeated the words mechanically, as though they had no meaning for him:

'Thirsty weather, yes.'

He went home in a taxi.

'I was wondering whether you'd be home in time for dinner.'

He flopped into his armchair, and mopped his face.

'As far as my part in the business is concerned, the case is over.'

'Has the killer been arrested?'

'Yes.'

'The man you went to see in La Baule?'

'Yes.'

'How about going out to a restaurant? All I've got for you is some cold meat and Russian salad.'

'I'm not hungry.'

'It's all on the table. You might as well eat it.'

That evening he felt no inclination to look at television, and by ten o'clock he was in bed.

*Epalinges, 7th February 1971*

# MAIGRET AND THE MAN ON THE BOULEVARD

★

*Translated from*
*the French by*
EILEEN ELLENBOGEN

# 1. The Brown Shoes

AFTERWARDS, Maigret had no difficulty in recalling the date, October 19, because it also happened to be his sister-in-law's birthday. He even remembered the day, a Monday, since as everyone at the Quai des Orfèvres knows, murder is rarely committed on a Monday. And furthermore, as it happened, this case, unlike any other that year, had a flavour of winter about it.

A thin, cold drizzle had been falling all that Sunday, and the roofs and pavements were black and glistening. A kind of yellowish fog seeped in through the chinks in the windows, so much so that Madame Maigret had said:

'Maybe I ought to get them fitted with draught excluders.'

For the past five years at least, as autumn approached, Maigret had been promising to fit them himself the following Sunday.

'You'd better wear your winter coat.'

'Where is it?'

'I'll get it.'

It was half-past eight, and still so dark that lights were on in all the houses. Maigret's coat smelt of moth balls.

It did not rain that day, at least not noticeably, although the pavements were still wet, and as the day wore on, and more and more people trampled them, they grew very slippery. Then, round about four in the afternoon, the yellowish fog, which had cleared since the morning, returned, blurring the light from the street lamps and windows.

When the telephone rang, neither Lucas nor Janvier nor even young Lapointe was in the Inspectors' Duty Room. It was answered by Santoni, a Corsican, who was new to the Crime Squad, having spent ten years first in the Gaming Squad and then in the Vice Squad.

'It's Inspector Neveu of the Third *Arrondissement*, Chief. He's asking to speak to you personally. He says it's urgent.'

Maigret lifted the receiver: 'What is it, laddie?'

'I'm speaking from a bistro in the Boulevard Saint-

Martin. A man has just been found. He's been stabbed with a knife.'

'Right there on the boulevard?'

'No, not quite. In a sort of cul-de-sac.'

Neveu, who was an old hand at this game, knew very well what Maigret must be thinking. There is seldom much of interest to the investigator in a stabbing. Usually, especially in over-crowded areas, it is the result of some drunken brawl or a quarrel between rival gangs of Spaniards or North Africans.

Neveu hastened to add:

'There are one or two odd features about this case. I think you ought to come and see for yourself. The cul-de-sac runs between the big jeweller's and the artificial-flower shop.'

'I'll come right away.'

Maigret had never before worked on a case with Santoni. In the confined space of the little black *Police Judiciaire* car, he was uncomfortably conscious of the powerful smell emanating from the Inspector, a little man who wore high-heeled shoes. He used hair-oil, and, on his fourth finger, wore a big yellow diamond, probably paste.

People flitted by like black shadows in the dark streets, and their shoes went flip-flop on the greasy pavements. In the Boulevard Saint-Martin, two policemen wearing capes were holding back a crowd of some thirty people. Neveu, who was watching out for Maigret, opened the door of the car.

'I persuaded the doctor to stay until you got here.'

The Grands Boulevards are always jammed with people, but at this time of day the crowds were at their thickest. Above the jeweller's shop was a big clock. The hands on the illuminated dial stood at half-past five. As for the artificial-flower shop, which had only one window, grimy and thick with dust, it was so dimly lit and looked so neglected that one wondered if anyone ever went into it.

Between the two shops ran a little cul-de-sac, so narrow as to be easily missed. It was no more than a gap between two walls, unlit, and apparently leading to the sort of paved courtyard to be found all over this district.

Neveu, followed by Maigret, elbowed his way through the

crowd. A few yards inside the dark cul-de-sac, several men were standing about. Two of them had electric torches. Their faces were a blur.

It was colder and damper here than on the boulevard. There was an unremitting draught. A dog, though roughly shoved aside by all and sundry, kept slinking back and getting under everyone's feet.

On the ground, against the dripping wall, lay a man, one arm bent under him, the other stretched out, so that the ghostly hand almost touched the opposite wall, barring the way.

'Is he dead?'

The doctor, a local man, nodded:

'Death must have been instantaneous.'

As if to underline these words, one of the torches played its circular beam back and forth over the corpse, throwing the projecting handle of the knife into eerie relief. The other torch illuminated the man's profile, a staring eye, and a grazed cheek where he had scraped it against the wall as he fell.

'Who found the body?'

One of the uniformed men, who had been waiting for this opportunity, came forward. His features were barely visible. All one could tell was that he was young and distressed.

'I was on my rounds. I always take a quick look into all the little passages, because people get up to all sorts of beastliness in the dark in this sort of place. I saw someone lying on the ground. At first I thought it was a drunk.'

'Already dead, was he?'

'Yes, I think so. But the body was still warm.'

'What time was this?'

'A quarter to five. I blew my whistle, and as soon as rein-forcements arrived, I went off to telephone the station.'

Neveu interposed: 'I took the call myself, and came straight over.'

The local police station was only a few yards away, in the Rue Notre-Dame-de-Nazareth.

Neveu went on: 'I left it to a colleague to call the doctor.'

'Did no one hear anything?'

'Not as far as I know.'

149

Maigret noticed a door a little farther on, with a dimly lit fanlight above.

'Where does that lead?'

'Into the offices at the back of the jeweller's shop. It's hardly ever used.'

Before leaving the Quai des Orfèvres, Maigret had been in touch with the Forensic Laboratory. The technicians had just arrived with their cameras and other equipment. Like all specialists, they concentrated solely on their job, asking no questions, worrying about nothing except how they were going to be able to manage in such a restricted space.

'Where does the courtyard lead to?' Maigret asked.

'Nowhere, just blank walls. There's only one door, which was condemned years ago, leading to a building in the Rue Meslay.'

The man, it was plain to see, had been stabbed in the back when he was ten paces or so inside the cul-de-sac. Someone had silently crept in after him, and the crowds on the boulevard had streamed past unawares.

'I slipped my hand into his pocket and found this.'

Neveu held out a wallet to Maigret. Without having to be asked, one of the men from Criminal Records shone a torch on it, much more powerful than the Inspector's.

It was just an ordinary wallet, not new, but not particularly worn either. The best one could say of it was that it was of quite good quality. It contained three thousand-franc notes, a few of a hundred francs, and an identity card in the name of Louis Thouret, storekeeper, of 37 Rue des Peupliers, Juvisy. There was also an Electoral Roll card in the same name, a sheet of paper on which there were five or six words scribbled in pencil, and a very old photograph of a little girl.

'Can we make a start?'

Maigret nodded. Cameras clicked and bulbs flashed. The crowd at the entrance to the little passage was growing, and the police were having difficulty in holding them back.

Next, the technicians carefully withdrew the knife and put it in a special box. Only then did they turn the body over, to reveal the face of a man between forty and fifty, with a fixed expression of utter bewilderment.

He had been unable to understand what was happening to him. He had died without understanding. There was something so childlike about his bewilderment, so incongruous in the tragic circumstances, that someone tittered nervously in the darkness.

His clothes were respectable and clean. He was wearing a dark three-piece suit and a beige spring coat, and his feet, oddly twisted, were encased in light-brown shoes, which seemed out of place on a day as sombre as this.

Apart from his shoes, he was so ordinary-looking that no one would have given him a second glance in the street or on one of the many café terraces on the boulevard.

All the same, the policeman who had discovered the body remarked, 'I have a feeling I've seen him before.'

'Where?'

'I can't remember, but the face seems familiar. I fancy he's one of those people one sees about every day without really noticing them.'

Neveu confirmed this. 'He looks vaguely familiar to me too. Very likely he worked somewhere around here.'

Which did not go anywhere towards explaining what Louis Thouret was doing in a cul-de-sac leading nowhere. Maigret turned to Santoni, who had served for years in the Vice Squad. For there are always a certain number of eccentrics with the best of reasons for lurking in lonely places, especially in this district. Nearly all are known to the police. Occasionally one of them proves to be a person of some prominence. From time to time they are arrested. As soon as they are released, they return to their old habits.

But Santoni shook his head. 'I've never seen him before.'

Maigret's mind was made up.

'Carry on, gentlemen. When you've finished with him, have him sent to the Forensic Laboratory.' And to Santoni he said. 'We're going to see his family, if he has one.'

If it had been an hour later, he would probably not have gone to Juvisy himself. But he had the car, and he was more than a little intrigued. The man was so utterly commonplace, a very ordinary man doing a very ordinary job.

'Let's be going then, to Juvisy.'

They stopped for a minute or two at the Porte d'Italie,

to have a half of beer standing at the bar. Then they sped along the motorway, dazzled by headlights, overtaking one heavy lorry after another. When they reached the railway station at Juvisy, they had to ask five people before they found one able to direct them to the Rue des Peupliers.

'It's part of the new estate, right at the far end of the town. When you get there, you'll just have to look at the street names. They're all called after trees, and they all look exactly alike.'

They drove alongside the vast marshalling yard, where an endless stream of goods wagons was being shunted into one siding or another. There were twenty engines, belching smoke, whistling and panting. Wagons clashed together, shuddering on impact. On their right lay the new estate, where building was still going on. The network of narrow streets was picked out in electric lights. There were hundreds, maybe thousands, of detached houses all exactly alike in size and shape. The noble trees, after which the streets were named, had not yet had time to grow. In some places the pavements had still not been surfaced, and consisted of rough verges interspersed with black holes. Elsewhere, on the other hand, there were neat little gardens, in which the flowers of late autumn were beginning to fade. Rue des Chênes . . . Rue des Lilas . . . Rue des Hêtres. . . . One day, maybe, it would look like one great park, always provided the jerry-built houses, which were like units in a toy construction kit, didn't disintegrate before the trees attained their full height.

Behind the kitchen windows, women were preparing dinner. The streets were deserted, their uniformity broken here and there by a little shop, brand-new like everything else here, and seemingly run by amateurs.

'Try the next turning on the left.'

They went round in circles for ten minutes before finding the street-name they were looking for inscribed on a blue plaque. They overshot the house, because number 37 came immediately after number 21. There was only one light showing, on the ground floor, in the kitchen. Through the net curtains they could see the somewhat bulky figure of a woman moving about.

'Let's go in,' sighed Maigret, extricating himself with some difficulty from the little car.

He emptied his pipe by tapping it on the heel of his shoe. As they went towards the house, the curtain twitched, and they caught a glimpse of a woman's face pressed against the window. Presumably a car parked at her door was an unusual sight for her. He went up the three front steps. The door was of varnished deal, with wrought-iron trimmings and two small, dark blue glass panes. He looked about for a bell, but before he could find it, a voice called out from inside: 'What do you want?'

'Madame Thouret?'

'Yes?'

'I'd be glad of a word with you.'

She was still none too eager to open the door.

'It's police business,' added Maigret, keeping his voice down.

At this, she slid back the chain and unbolted the door. Then, opening it a crack through which only a narrow segment of her face could be seen, she looked searchingly at the two men waiting on the threshold.

'What is it you want?'

'I have something to tell you.'

'How do I know you're really from the police?'

By the merest chance, Maigret happened to have his badge in his pocket. As a rule, he left it at home. He held it out to her so that it was illuminated by the beam of light from inside the house.

'Very well! It *is* genuine, I suppose?'

She let them in. The entrance lobby was poky, the walls were white, and the doors and door frames were of varnished wood. The kitchen door had been left open, but she led them past it into the adjoining room. Having switched on the light, she ushered them in.

She was about the same age as her husband, but a good deal more heavily built, although she couldn't be called fat. It was her frame that was large, and covered in firm flesh. The grey dress she was wearing, covered with an apron which she now mechanically took off, did nothing to soften her appearance.

The room to which she had taken them was a dining-room furnished in rustic style. Presumably, it was also used as a sitting-room. There was an impersonal tidiness about everything which was reminiscent of a window display, or the interior of a furniture shop. Nothing had been left lying about, not even a pipe or a packet of cigarettes. There was not even a newspaper or a piece of needlework to be seen, nothing to suggest that people actually lived here. She did not ask them to sit down, but kept a wary eye on their feet, fearful lest they might dirty the linoleum.

'I'm listening.'

'Your husband's name is Louis Thouret, is it not?'

She nodded, frowning as she tried to guess the purpose of their visit.

'Is his place of work in Paris?'

'He's assistant manager with the firm of Kaplan et Zanin, in the Rue de Bondy.'

'Has he ever worked as a storekeeper?'

'That used to be his job.'

'How long ago?'

'Some years. Even then, he was the one who really kept the business going.'

'Have you by any chance, a photograph of him?'

'What do you want it for?'

'I want to be sure . . .'

'Sure of what?' She was becoming even more suspicious.

'Has Louis met with an accident?'

Mechanically, she glanced at the kitchen clock, then frowned, as if trying to recall where her husband should be at this time of the day.

'I'd like to satisfy myself that he is the man in question.'

'On the sideboard,' she said.

There were five or six photographs in metal frames on the sideboard, one of a young girl standing beside the man who had been found stabbed in the cul-de-sac. He looked a good deal younger, and was dressed in black.

'Do you know if your husband had any enemies?'

'Why on earth should he have enemies?'

She went out for a moment, to turn down the gas under a saucepan that was bubbling on the stove.

'What time does he usually get back from work?'

'He always catches the same train, the 6.22 from the Gare de Lyon. Our daughter comes on the train after that, as she finishes work a little later than he does. She has a very responsible job. . . .'

'I'm afraid I'll have to ask you to return with me to Paris.'

'Is Louis dead?'

She looked him up and down, defying him to lie to her.

'I want the truth.'

'He was murdered this afternoon.'

'Where did it happen?'

'In a little passage off the Boulevard Saint-Martin.'

'What was he doing there?'

'I've no idea.'

'What time was it?'

'As far as one can tell, round about half-past four.'

'At half-past four, he's still at work. Have you made inquiries at Kaplan's?'

'There hasn't been time. And, besides, we didn't know where he worked.'

'Who killed him?'

'That's what we are trying to find out.'

'Was he alone?'

Maigret was beginning to lose patience.

'Don't you think you'd better get ready? The sooner we leave, the better.'

'What have you done with him?'

'By this time, he will have been taken to the Forensic Laboratory.'

'The morgue, you mean?'

What could he say to that?

'My daughter will have to be told.'

'You could leave her a note.'

She considered this.

'No. We'd better call in at my sister's. I'll leave the key with her. She can come over and wait for Monique here. Will you be wanting to talk to her as well?'

'I would like to, yes.'

'Where should she meet us?'

'In my office in the Quai des Orfèvres. It would save a lot of time. How old is she?'

'Twenty-two.'

'Couldn't you give her a ring, and break the news to her yourself?'

'Well, for one thing, we're not on the phone, and for another, she'll have left her office and will be on her way to the station by now. I won't keep you long.'

She went up the stairs, which creaked at every step, not because they were old but because they had been constructed of flimsy planks of wood. It was obvious that the house and everything in it was built on the cheap. Doubtless, it would not survive to be old.

The two men exchanged glances as they listened to the comings and goings overhead. She was changing into a black dress, they were sure, and probably brushing her hair. When she came downstairs, they once more exchanged glances. They had been right. She was already wearing mourning, and smelt of eau de cologne.

'Would you wait for me outside while I switch off the lights and the gas?'

She looked doubtfully at the little car, as if afraid that there wouldn't be room for her. Someone was watching them from the house next door.

'My sister lives just two streets away. Go right at the next turning, driver, and then it's the second on the left.'

The two little houses were identical, except that the panels of glass in the door were a different colour here, apricot instead of blue.

'I won't keep you a moment.'

But she was gone about a quarter of an hour. When she returned to the car, she had another woman with her, who was also dressed in black, and was so like her in every way that they might have been twins.

'My sister is coming with us. I daresay we'll manage to squeeze in somehow. My brother-in-law will go to my house and wait for my daughter. It's his day off. He's an inspector on the railways.'

Maigret sat next to the driver, Santoni and the two women squeezed uncomfortably into the back. The sisters could be heard whispering to one another from time to time, as if in the confessional.

When they got to the Forensic Laboratory, near the Pont d'Austerlitz, they found the body of Louis Thouret still fully clothed, in accordance with Maigret's instructions. He was laid out temporarily on a marble slab. It was Maigret, his eyes on the two women, who uncovered the face. It was the first time he had seen them together in a good light. Just now, in the darkened street, he had mistaken them for twins. Now he could see that the sister was three or four years younger, her figure having retained a measure of suppleness, though probably not for much longer.

'Do you recognize him?'

Madame Thoret, with a handkerchief crumpled in her hand, did not weep. Her sister took her by the arm, desirous of offering comfort and support.

'Yes, that's Louis. That's my poor Louis. I'm sure he never dreamed, when he left the house this morning. . . .'

She broke off abruptly to say:

'Why are his eyes still open?'

'You may close them now, if you wish.'

She and her sister exchanged glances, as though uncertain which of them should undertake the task. In the end, it was the widow who did it, with ritual solemnity, murmuring: 'Poor Louis.'

Then, all of a sudden, she caught sight of the shoes projecting beyond the sheet covering the body. She frowned.

'What's this?'

Maigret couldn't imagine what she was talking about.

'Who put those shoes on him?'

'He was wearing them when we found him.'

'It's not possible. Louis never wore brown shoes. At any rate, never during the twenty-six years that we were married. As he very well knew, I wouldn't have permitted it. Do you see, Jeanne?'

Jeanne nodded.

'I think, perhaps, you'd better make sure the clothes he is wearing are his own. I take it you are in no doubt as to his identity?'

'None whatever. But those are not his shoes. I should know, I polish them every day. When he left this morning, he was wearing black shoes, the pair with the reinforced soles that he always wore to work.'

Maigret removed the sheet.

'Is this his overcoat?'

'Yes.'

'And his suit?'

'Yes, that's his. But that isn't his tie. He would never have worn anything so garish. Why, you could almost call it red!'

'Was your husband a man of regular habits?'

'He certainly was. Ask my sister. Every morning he caught the bus at the corner, which got him to Juvisy station in time to catch the 8.17 train. He always travelled with our neighbour Monsieur Beaudoin, who works in the Inland Revenue. From the Gare de Lyon, they went on to Saint-Martin by metro.'

The employee of the Forensic Laboratory made a sign to Maigret. Realizing what was required of him, he led the two women towards a table on which the contents of the dead man's pockets had been laid out.

'I take it you recognize these things?'

There was a silver watch and chain, a plain handkerchief without initials, an open packet of Gauloise cigarettes, a lighter, a key, and, lying beside the man's wallet, a couple of bluish ticket stubs.

The first things that caught her eye were the ticket stubs.

'Those are cinema tickets,' she said.

Maigret examined them, and said:

'A newsreel cinema in the Boulevard Bonne-Nouvelle. The figures are a bit rubbed out but, as far as I can see, they were issued today.'

'That's not possible. Did you hear that, Jeanne?'

'It does seem odd,' said her sister, without emotion.

'Would you please take a look at the contents of the wallet?'

She did so, and frowned. 'Louis didn't have as much money as this on him when he left this morning.'

'Are you sure?'

'I always see to it myself that he has money in his wallet. At most he had a thousand-franc note, and two or three hundred-franc notes.'

'Could he, perhaps, have collected his pay?'

'He didn't get paid till the end of the month.'

'How much did he usually have left at the end of the day?'

'All of it, less the price of his metro ticket and his cigarettes. He had a season ticket for the train.'

She seemed about to put the wallet in her bag, but thought better of it.

'I daresay you'll want to keep this for a while?'

'For the time being, yes.'

'What puzzles me is why they should have changed his shoes and tie. And what he was doing away from the shop at the time when it happened.'

Maigret, not wishing to harass her, asked no further questions, but merely handed her the necessary forms to sign.

'Are you going straight home?'

'When can we have the body?'

'In a day or two, I should think.'

'Will there have to be a post mortem?'

'That's up to the magistrate. He may not think it necessary.'

She glanced at her watch.

'There's a train in twenty minutes,' she said to her sister. And to Maigret: 'Would you mind taking us to the station?'

'Don't you want to wait for Monique?'

'She can make her own way.'

The Gare de Lyon was a good deal out of their way. They watched the two almost identical figures going up the stone steps.

Gruffly, Santoni said: 'She's as hard as nails! The poor fellow can't have had much of a life.'

'Not with her, at any rate.'

'What do you make of that business of the shoes? The obvious answer would be that he bought them today, except that they aren't new.'

'He wouldn't have dared. You heard what she said.'

'He wouldn't have dared to buy a loud tie, either.'

'It will be interesting to see whether the daughter is like her mother.'

Before returning to the Quai des Orfèvres, they stopped for a meal at a *brasserie*. Maigret telephoned his wife, to tell her to expect him when she saw him.

The *brasserie* too smelt of winter, with damp coats and hats hanging from all the hooks, and dense clouds of steam rising from the dark windows.

At the gatehouse of Police Headquarters, Maigret was met by the man on duty, who announced:

'There's a young woman waiting to see you. She says she has an appointment. I sent her straight up.'

'Has she been here long?'

'Twenty minutes or so.'

The fog had turned to a thin drizzle, and the dusty treads of the main staircase were intricately patterned with damp footprints. Although most of the offices were empty, here and there a crack of light showed under a door.

'Do you want me to stay?'

Maigret nodded. Santoni had been with him on the case from the start. He might as well see it through to the end.

There was a young woman sitting in an armchair in the waiting-room, though all that could be seen of her was a pale blue hat. There was only one dim light on in the room. The desk clerk was reading an evening newspaper.

'She's waiting to see you, Chief.'

'I know.' And to the young woman: 'Mademoiselle Thouret? Will you come with me, please.'

He switched on the green-shaded light that hung above the chair across the desk from his own, and invited her to take a seat. She did so, and he could see that she had been crying.

'My uncle has told me of my father's death.'

He did not say anything at first. Like her mother, she had a handkerchief in her hand, but hers was rolled into a ball, and she was kneading it, as Maigret used to knead plasticine when he was a child.

'I thought my mother would be with you.'

'She's gone back to Juvisy.'

'How is she?'

What could he say?

'Your mother was very brave.'

Monique was not unattractive. She did not look much like her mother, though she was of the same heavy build. This was less marked in her case, because her young skin was softer and her body more supple. She was wearing a well-cut suit. The Chief Superintendent found this a little surprising. She had certainly not made it herself, nor had it been bought in a cheap shop.

A few drops of moisture gathered on her eyelashes as she asked, 'What happened exactly?'

'Your father was stabbed with a knife.'

'When?'

'This afternoon, between half-past four and a quarter to five.'

'I simply can't understand it.'

Why was it that he had a feeling she was not being altogether sincere? Her mother too had expressed incredulity, but being the sort of woman she was, that was only to be expected. Basically, as far as Madame Thouret was concerned, it was a disgraceful thing to get oneself murdered in an alleyway off the Boulevard Saint-Martin. She had planned her life in every detail, and not only her own life but also that of her family, and murder had no place in her scheme of things, especially this murder, with the corpse wearing brown shoes, and a tie that might almost be described as red!

As for Monique, though she seemed on the whole a sensible girl, she was obviously apprehensive. There would be questions that she would prefer not to answer, and revelations that she would prefer not to hear.

'Did you know your father well?'

'But . . . of course.'

'Of course you knew him in the way that most children know their parents. What I mean is, were you and he in one another's confidence? Did he ever talk to you about his private life and private thoughts?'

'He was a good father.'

'Was he a happy man?'

'I suppose so.'

'Did you and he ever meet in town?'

'I don't understand. Do you mean did we ever run into one another in the street?'

'You both worked in Paris. I know you didn't go to work or return home on the same train.'

'We kept different office hours.'

'You might have met for lunch, occasionally.'

'We did sometimes.'

'Often?'

'No, not very often.'

'Used you to go and fetch him from the shop?'

She hesitated.

'No. We would meet in some restaurant or other.'

'Did you ever telephone him at work?'

'Not as far as I can remember.'

'When did you last meet for lunch?'

'Several months ago. Before the summer holidays.'

'Whereabouts?'

'At *La Chope Alsacienne* in the Boulevard Sébastopol.'

'Did your mother know?'

'I daresay I mentioned it to her. I don't remember.'

'Was your father of a cheerful disposition?'

'Fairly cheerful, I think.'

'How was his health?'

'I've never known him to be ill.'

'Had he many friends?'

'We saw hardly anyone, apart from my aunts and uncles.'

'Have you many?'

'Two aunts and two uncles.'

'Do they all live in Juvisy?'

'Yes. Not very far from us. It was my Uncle Albert, my Aunt Jeanne's husband, who told me of my father's death. My Aunt Céline's house is a little farther away.'

'Are they both sisters of your mother?'

'Yes. And Aunt Céline's husband, my Uncle Julien, also works on the railways.'

'Is there a man in your life, Mademoiselle Monique?'

She looked a little flustered.

'Surely this is no time to go into that. Don't you want me to see my father?'

'What do you mean?'

'I understood from my uncle that I would be required to identify his body.'

'Your mother and your aunt have already done that. However, if you wish to . . .'

'No. I presume I shall see him when he's brought home.'

'Just one more thing, Mademoiselle Monique. When you met your father in town for lunch, can you remember if you ever saw him wearing brown shoes?'

She didn't answer at once. To gain time, she repeated: 'Brown shoes?'

'Well, very light brown would perhaps be a better description, what, in my day, if you'll pardon the expression, used to be called goose-dung shoes.'

'I can't remember.'

'Did you ever see him wearing a red tie?'

'No.'

'When did you last go to the cinema?'

'Yesterday afternoon.'

'Here in town?'

'In Juvisy.'

'I won't keep you any longer. I hope you haven't missed the last train.'

'It leaves in thirty-five minutes.'

She glanced at her wrist watch, and stood up. There was a pause. 'Goodnight,' she said, at last.

'Goodnight, mademoiselle, and thank you.'


## 2. The Pug-Nosed Virgin

MAIGRET, though he could not say why, had always had a special affection for the section of the Grands Boulevards that stretches from the Place de la République to the Rue Montmartre. To put it another way, he felt that he was on his home ground. It was here, in the Boulevard Bonne-Nouvelle, just a few hundred yards from the passageway in which Louis Thouret was killed, that Maigret and his wife went to the pictures almost every week. Arm in arm, they walked the short distance from their flat to what they regarded as their local cinema. And opposite was the *brasserie* where he enjoyed going for a plate of *choucroute*.

Farther on, approaching the Opéra and the Madeleine, the boulevards were more spacious and elegant. In the area between the Porte Saint-Martin and the Place de la République the streets were narrower and darker, and so densely packed with people on the move as to make one feel dizzy.

He had left home at about half-past eight, and, walking at a leisurely pace in the grey morning light, had taken barely a quarter of an hour to reach the intersection of the Rue de Bondy and the Boulevard, which formed a little square dominated by the Théâtre de la Renaissance. The weather was less damp than on the previous day, but colder. Maigret was looking for the premises of the firm of Kaplan et Zanin where, according to his wife, Louis Thouret had spent the whole of his working life, including his last day on earth.

The number he had been given was that of a very old building, visibly subsiding. On either side of the gateway, which was wide open, were a number of white enamel plaques, with black lettering, indicating that among the lessees were a mattress-maker, a secretarial college, a wholesaler in feathers (third floor, on the left, Staircase A), an upholsterer and a qualified masseuse. The concierge in the lodge, which faced the archway, was engaged in sorting the mail.

'Could you please direct me to Kaplan et Zanin?' he asked her.

'My dear sir, they closed down three years ago, three years next month.'

'Were you here then?'

'I shall have been here twenty-six years in December.'

'Did you know Louis Thouret?'

'Know him? Why of course I knew Monsieur Louis. By the way, what has become of him? It must be all of four or five months since he last called in to say hello to me.'

'He's dead.'

Abruptly, she pushed the letters aside.

'But he was such a healthy man! What did he die of? A heart attack, I'll be bound, the same as my husband.'

'He was stabbed with a knife, not far from here, yesterday afternoon.'

'I haven't seen a paper today.'

Anyway, there was nothing much in the papers, just a few terse lines reporting the murder, as if it were an everyday occurrence.

'Whoever could have wanted to kill a fine man like him?'

She was a worthy soul herself, a little creature, but full of life.

'For more than twenty years he went past this lodge four times a day, and never once did he fail to stop and say a pleasant word or two. When Monsieur Kaplan gave up the business, he was so shattered that . . .'

She had to stop, to wipe her eyes and blow her nose.

'Is Monsieur Kaplan still alive?'

'I can give you his address if you like. He lives in the Rue des Acacias, near the Porte Maillot. He's a fine man, too, in his own way. I believe old Monsieur Kaplan is still alive.'

'What did the firm deal in?'

'You mean you don't know?'

She seemed to think that the whole world ought to have heard of the firm of Kaplan et Zanin.

Maigret explained: 'I'm from the police. I have to find out all I can about Monsieur Thouret and everything to do with him.'

'We always called him Monsieur Louis. Everybody did. Most people didn't even know his surname. If you wouldn't mind waiting a moment. . . .'

She returned to the mail, murmuring to herself as she sorted the last few letters: 'Monsieur Louis murdered! I wouldn't have believed it possible! A man of such . . .'

Having slotted the letters into the various pigeon-holes, she wrapped a woollen shawl about her shoulders, and turned down the anthracite stove.

'Come and I'll show you.'

When they were under the archway, she explained:

'This building was due to be pulled down three years ago, to make way for a cinema. At that time, the tenants were

165

given notice, and I myself made arrangements to go and live with my daughter in the Nièvre region. That was the reason why Monsieur Kaplan gave up the business. Though the fact that business was none too brisk may also have had something to do with it. Young Monsieur Kaplan, Monsieur Max as we called him, didn't see eye to eye with his father. This way. . . .'

Beyond the archway was a courtyard, at the end of which could be seen a large building with a glass roof which looked like the entrance hall of a railway station. On the rough-cast wall only a few letters of the name *Kaplan et Zanin* were still legible.

'There were no longer any Zanins in the firm, when I came to this place twenty-six years ago. At that time old Monsieur Kaplan was running the business single-handed. Children would stop in the street and stare at him, because he had the look of an Old Testament patriarch.'

The door was not shut. The lock had been wrenched out. Everything around him was now in decay, though a few years earlier it had been part of a living world, the world of Louis Thouret. What precisely the place had been used for, it was hard to tell. It was a huge room, rising to a very high glass roof, the panes of which were now either missing or opaque with grime. Two galleries, one above the other, such as are often to be seen in big stores, ran right round the room, and there were marks on the wall where there had once been rows of shelves.

'Whenever he came to see me. . . .'

'Did he come often?'

'Every two or three months, I'd say, and he never came empty-handed. And each time, I may tell you, Monsieur Louis insisted on coming in here to take a look round, and you could tell that his heart was heavy. I've known there to be as many as twenty girl packers in here, even more towards the end, and especially round about Christmas time, and, quite often, they worked late into the night. This wasn't a retail business. Monsieur Kaplan sold direct to the cheap multiple stores up and down the country, and to market traders of all sorts. There was so much stuff in here that one could scarcely move. Monsieur Louis was the only one who knew where everything was. Heaven knows, there was variety enough, false beards, cardboard trumpets, Christmas tree decorations of every sort, paper streamers, carnival masks and seaside holiday souvenirs.'

'Was Monsieur Louis in charge of the stock?'

'Yes. He always wore a grey overall. Over there in the right-hand corner, see, Monsieur Kaplan sat in his glass-walled office. The young Monsieur Kaplan, I mean, after his father had his first heart attack, and stopped coming in. He had a secretary, Mademoiselle Léone, and an elderly book-keeper, who worked in a little cubby hole upstairs. No one had the least inkling of what was in store for them. One day, without warning—I'm not sure exactly when, but it must have been in October or November, because there was a nip in the air already—Monsieur Max Kaplan called his staff together, and told them that the firm was to be closed down, and that he had found a buyer for the stock.

'Everyone believed at the time that the building was to come down the following year, to make way for a cinema, as I told you.'

Maigret listened patiently, looking about him, and trying to picture the scene in all its former glory.

'The front of the building is due for demolition as well. All the tenants have been given notice. Some have already left. The others have hung on, and, as things have turned out, they made the right decision, seeing that they're still here. The only trouble is that, since the building was sold, the new owners have refused to maintain it. There are goodness knows how many lawsuits pending. The bailiff turns up once a month or so. I've packed up all my things twice already.'

'Do you know Madame Thouret?'

'I've never set eyes on her. They lived in the suburbs, in Juvisy.'

'She's still there.'

'Have you met her? What's she like?'

Maigret's only reply was a grimace, leaving her in no doubt as to his feelings.

'I'm not surprised. I had a feeling that he wasn't particularly happy in his home life. His real life was here. I've always said that when the blow fell he was the hardest hit of all. Especially when you think that he was at the age when it's difficult to change the habits of a lifetime.'

'How old was he?'

'Forty-five or forty-six, I'd say.'

'Do you know what he did after he left here?'

'He never spoke of it. He must have been through some hard times. For a long time after he left, I never saw him. Then one day, when I was out shopping and in a tearing hurry as usual, I caught sight of him sitting on a bench. It was a shock. You just wouldn't expect to see a man like him idle in the middle of the day. I was on the point of going up to him, when it struck me that it could only cause him embarrassment, so I turned off into a side street.'

'How long was this after the business closed down?'

It was even colder here, under the glass roof, than in the courtyard.

'Would you like to come into the lodge, and warm up?' she suggested. 'It's hard to say how long after. It wasn't in the spring. There were no leaves on the trees. It was probably just about the end of the winter.'

'When was the next time you saw him?'

'Oh! long afterwards, in mid-summer. The thing that struck me most was that he was wearing goose-dung shoes. Why are you looking at me like that?'

'No reason. Please go on.'

"It was so out of character. He invariably wore black shoes when he worked here. He came into the lodge, and put a small parcel down on the table. It was wrapped in white paper and tied with gold ribbon. It was a box of chocolates. He sat down in this chair here. I made him a cup of coffee, and slipped out to get half-bottle of Calvados from the shop on the corner, leaving him to keep an eye on things in the lodge.'

'What did he have to say for himself?'

'Nothing special. But you could see that it made him happy, just to be breathing the air of this place again.'

'Didn't he refer to the change in his life?'

'I asked him how things were going, and he said he had nothing to complain of. At any rate, he obviously wasn't working office hours, seeing that he was able to call on me between ten and eleven in the morning. Another time, he came in the afternoon, and he was wearing a light tie. I teased him about it, and remarked that it made him look years younger. He was never one to take offence. Then I asked about his daughter. I've never met her, but he always carried photographs of her, right from the time she was a few months old. He was a proud father all right, and was always ready to show the photographs to anyone.'

No recent photographs of Monique had been found on him, only the one taken when she was a baby.

'Is that all you can tell me?'

'How should I know anything more? I'm shut up in this place from morning to night. Since Kaplan's closed down, and the hairdresser vacated the first floor premises, things haven't been any too lively here.'

'Did you and he talk about that?'

'Yes. We chatted about all sorts of things, such as the number of tenants who had moved out, one after another, the lawsuits, the architects who came in from time to time studying the plans for their wretched cinema, while the walls slowly crumbled in ruins about us.'

She did not sound bitter. All the same, he was sure that she would hang on long after everyone else had left.

'How did it happen?' she asked in her turn. 'Did he suffer much?'

Neither Madame Thouret nor Monique had thought to put this question to him.

'The doctor says not. Apparently he died instantly.'

'Where did it happen?'

'Not very far from here, in an alleyway off the Boulevard Saint-Martin.'

'Near the jeweller's, do you mean?'

'Yes. Someone must have been following him in the dusk. At any rate, he was found with a knife in his back.

Maigret had telephoned the Forensic Laboratory the previous night from his home, and again this morning. The knife was a very ordinary mass-produced article, to be found on the shelves of almost any ironmonger's. It was new, and there were no fingerprints on it.

'Poor Monsieur Louis! He did so enjoy life!'

'You mean he was always cheerful?'

'It's hard to explain. He certainly wasn't an unhappy man. He always had a smile and a kind word for everyone. He was very considerate, and modest with it.'

'Was he interested in women?'

'Never! And yet there were plenty of opportunities here. Apart from Monsieur Max and the old book-keeper, he was the only man around, and women who take jobs as packers aren't exactly strait-laced as a rule.'

'Did he drink?'

'Just a glass of wine, like everyone else. Occasionally, he would have a liqueur with his coffee.'

'Where did he go for lunch?'

'He hardly ever went out. He nearly always brought sand-wiches wrapped in oilcloth. I can see him now. He ate standing up, with his packet of sandwiches open on the table. Afterwards, he would go out into the courtyard and smoke his pipe, before returning to the stockroom. Very occasionally he would go out, announcing to me that he was having lunch with his daughter. This was towards the end of his time here. His daughter was quite grown-up by then, and had an office job in the Rue de Rivoli.

' "Why not bring her back here, Monsieur Louis? I would so love to meet her."

' "I will one day. . . ." he promised.

'But he never did. I've often wondered why.'

'Have you lost touch with Mademoiselle Léone?'

'No, indeed. In fact, I have her address. She lives with her mother. She doesn't work in an office any more. She's opened a little shop in the Rue de Clignancourt in Mont-martre. She may be able to tell you more than I can. He used to go and see her too. On one occasion, when we were talking about her, he told me that she was selling layettes and other things for babies. It seems odd, somehow.'

'What's odd about it?'

'That she, of all people, should be selling things for babies.'

People were beginning to come into the lodge to collect their mail. They looked at Maigret uneasily, assuming, no doubt, that he, like others before him, had come to evict them.

'Thanks for your help. I'll be back before very long, I daresay.'

'Have you any idea who might have done it?'

'None,' he frankly admitted.

'Was his wallet stolen?'

'No, nor his watch.'

'Well, then, he must have been mistaken for someone else.'

The Rue de Clignancourt was right on the other side of town. Maigret went into a little bar, and made straight for the telephone box.

'Who's speaking?'

'Janvier here, Chief.'

'Any news?'

'In accordance with your instructions, the men are already out on the job.'

These were the five inspectors, each assigned to a different district, who had been detailed to comb all the hardware shops in Paris. As for Santoni, Maigret had instructed him to find out everything he could about Monique Thouret. By now, he must be in the Rue de Rivoli, sniffing round the offices of Geber et Bachelier, Solicitors.

If Madame Thouret had been on the telephone, Maigret would have rung her in Juvisy, to ask whether, during the past three years, her husband had continued to leave home every morning with his lunch wrapped in a square of black oilcloth.

'I'd be glad if you'd send a car for me.'

'Where are you?'

'In the Rue de Bondy. Tell the driver I'll be waiting opposite *La Renaissance.*'

He was on the point of instructing Janvier, who for once was not snowed under with work, to assist with the inquiries among the shopkeepers in the Boulevard Saint-Martin. Inspector Neveu was already on the job, but for work of that sort extra help was always appreciated.

But he thought better of it, mainly because he had an urge to return to the district himself.

'Any other instructions?'

'I want photographs sent to all the newspapers. They've played down the story so far, and I'd be grateful if they'd keep it that way.'

'I get it. I'll send you a car right away.'

Partly because the concierge happened to have mentioned Calvados, and partly on account of the extreme cold, Maigret went into a bar and ordered a glass. Then, with his hands in his pockets, he crossed the boulevard to have another look at the cul-de-sac where Monsieur Louis had been found stabbed.

So reticent had the newspapers been on the subject of the murder that not a single one of the passers-by stopped to peer at the paving stones, in the hope of finding traces of blood.

He stood for quite a time gazing into one of the two display windows of the jeweller's shop. Inside, he could see five or six assistants of both sexes. The jewellery was, for the most part, second-rate stuff. Many of the pieces on view were described as *bargain offers*. Both windows were crammed with goods: wedding rings, paste diamonds, and possibly one or two genuine ones, alarm clocks, watches, and hideous mantle clocks.

A little old man, who had been watching Maigret from inside the shop, must have decided that he was a potential customer, since he came to the door with a smile on his face, intending to invite him in. But the Chief Superintendent thought it was time he took himself off, and a few minutes later he was getting into the Headquarters car.

'Rue de Clignancourt,' he said to the driver.

It was a good deal quieter than the Boulevard Saint-Martin, but this too was a district of small tradespeople, and Mademoiselle Léone's shop—from the sign above it, he gathered it was called *Le Bébé Rose*—was so completely eclipsed by a horsemeat butcher's on one side and a cabmen's eating place on the other that one would have to be in the know to find it.

Going into the shop, he could see in the back room an old woman in an armchair, with a cat on her lap. Another, younger woman came forward to meet him. He looked at her with slight sense of shock. She did not conform to his preconceived notion of what a shorthand typist who had worked for the firm of Kaplan should look like. What was it about her? he wondered. He could not say. Presumably she was wearing felt slippers, as her footsteps made no sound. For this reason, she reminded him a little of a nun, and her deportment also was that of a nun, for she advanced seemingly without moving her body.

She wore a faint smile, which was not confined to her mouth, but played about all her features. She had a very gentle expression and a self-effacing manner.

How strange that she should be called Léone, the more so as she had a broad pug-nose, such as one might see on an aged lion slumbering in a cage.

'What can I do for you, Monsieur?'

She was dressed in black. Her face and hands were colourless, ethereal. Comforting gusts of warmth blew into the shop from the big stove in the back room, and everywhere, on the shelves and on the counter, there were fragile knitted garments, bootees threaded through with pink or blue ribbons, bonnets, christening robes.

'I am Chief Superintendent Maigret of the *Police Judiciaire*.'

'Oh?'

'I have to inform you that Louis Thouret, a former colleague of yours, I believe, was murdered yesterday.'

No one else had taken the news to heart as she did. And yet, she didn't cry, or fumble for a handkerchief, or screw up her face. The shock of it froze her where she stood and, for a moment, he could have sworn, arrested the beating of her heart. And he saw her lips, which were pale anyway, turn as white as the baby clothes all around her.

'Please forgive me. I ought not to have put it so bluntly.'

She shook her head, wishing him to understand that she did not hold it against him. The old lady in the back room stirred.

'If I am to find his murderer, I need to learn everything there is to be known about him.'

She nodded, but still did not speak.

'I believe you knew him well?'

173

For an instant, her face lit up.

'How did it happen?' she finally asked, with a lump in her throat.

The must have been ugly even as a little girl, and, no doubt, she had always been conscious of the fact. Glancing towards the other room, she murmured:

'I'm sure you'd be more comfortable sitting down.'

'I don't think your mother . . .'

'We can talk freely in front of mother. She's stone deaf. But she does like company.'

He could not possibly have admitted to her that he felt suffocated in this airless room, where the two women spent the greater part of their cramped existence.

Léne was ageless. In all probability she was over fifty, perhaps a lot older than that. Her mother looked all of eighty, as she darted a glance at the Chief Superintendent with her bright little bird-like eyes. It was not from her that Léone had inherited her broad pug-nose, but from her father, if the enlarged photograph on the wall was anything to go by.

'I've just come from seeing the concierge in the Rue de Bondy.'

'It must have been a great shock to her.'

'Yes. She was very fond of him.'

'Everyone was.'

She coloured a little as she spoke.

'He was such a good man!' she hastened to add.

'You saw quite a lot of him, isn't that so?'

'He came to see me several times. You couldn't say I saw him often. He was a very busy man, and he lived a long way out of town.'

'Do you happen to know how he spent his time latterly?'

'I never asked him. He seemed to be doing well. I presumed he was self-employed, as he didn't have to keep office hours.'

'Did he never talk to you about the people he met?'

'We mostly reminisced about the Rue de Bondy, and Kaplan's, and Monsieur Max, and stocktaking. What an upheaval that used to be every year, with more than a thousand different lines in stock.

She hesitated.

'I presume you've seen his wife?'

'Yesterday evening, yes.'

'How did she take it?'

'She couldn't understand how her husband came to be wearing light brown shoes when he was killed. She claims that the murderer must have put them on him.'

She, like the concierge, had noticed the shoes.

'No. He often wore them.'

'Even when he was working in the Rue de Bondy?'

'No, only after he left. Some time after.'

'How long after?'

'About a year.'

'Did it surprise you that he should be wearing light brown shoes?'

'Yes. It was different from his usual style of dress.'

'What did you think about it?'

'That he had changed.'

'He wasn't quite the same man. His sense of fun had changed. Sometimes he laughed as if he would never stop.'

'Did he never laugh in the old days?'

'Not in that way. Something new had come into his life.'

'A woman?'

It was cruel, but he had to ask.

'Perhaps.'

'Did he never confide in you?'

'No.'

'Did he ever make love to you?'

Vehemently, she protested: 'Never! I swear it! I'm sure no such thought ever entered his head.'

The cat had jumped off the old lady's lap and on to Maigret's.

'Let it stay,' he said, as Léone was about to shoo it off.

He had not the courage to light his pipe.

'I daresay it was a bitter blow to you all when Monsieur Kaplan announced that he was about to close down the business?'

'We were all hard hit, yes.'

'And especially Louis Thouret?'

'Monsieur Louis was particularly attached to the firm. It had become a habit with him. Just think of it, he'd been working there from the age of fourteen, when he joined as a messenger boy.'

'Where was he from?'

'From Belleville. From what he told me, his mother was a widow. She brought him along one day to see old Monsieur Kaplan. He was still in short trousers. He had had practically no schooling.'

'Is his mother dead?'

'She has been for many years.'

Why was it that Maigret had the feeling that she was hiding something? She had spoken freely, and had looked him straight in the eye, and yet there was something evasive about her, as though she were gliding furtively away from him on silent, felt-shod feet.

'I believe he had some difficulty in finding another job?'

'Who told you that?'

'I gathered it from some of the things the concierge told me.'

It's never easy for someone over forty to find work, particularly if one has no specialist qualifications. I myself . . .'

'Did you look for a job?'

'Only for a few weeks.'

'And Monsieur Louis?'

'He persisted longer.'

'Is that just a supposition, or do you actually know he did?'

'I know he did.'

'Did he ever come and see you during that period?'

'Yes.'

'Did you help him financially?'

He was by now convinced that Léone was the sort of person to have saved every penny she could.

'Why do you want to know?'

'Because, until I have a clear picture of the kind of man he was during the last few years of his life, I have no hope of laying my hands on his murderer.'

'It's true,' she admitted, after a pause for thought. 'I'll tell you the whole story, but I'd be grateful if you would keep it to yourself. Above all, his wife mustn't find out. It would be a bitter blow to her pride.'

'Do you know her then?'

'No, he told me. His brothers-in-law both occupy positions of responsibility, and both had houses built for them.'

'So did he.'

'He had no choice. His wife had set her heart on it. She was the one who insisted on moving to Juvisy, like her two sisters.'

Her voice had somehow changed, and one could sense the underlying rancour, that must have been festering for a long time.

'Was he afraid of his wife?'

'He hated to hurt anyone. When we all got the sack, a few weeks before the Christmas holidays, he was determined to see that it didn't cast a blight on the family festivities.'

'You mean he didn't say anything to them, but just let them go on believing that he was still working in the Rue de Bondy?'

'He thought at first it would only be a matter of days before he got another job. Later, he thought it might take weeks. The only thing that worried him was the house.'

'I don't understand.'

'He was paying off the mortgage, and I gathered that it would have been a very serious matter if he had fallen behind with his monthly payments.'

'Who lent him the money?'

'Monsieur Saimbron and I between us.'

'Who is Monsieur Saimbron?'

'He was the book-keeper. He's retired now. He lives alone in rooms on the Quai de la Mégisserie.'

'Has he got money?'

'He's very poor.'

'And yet you both lent money to Monsieur Louis?'

'Yes. If we had not done so, the house would have been sold over their heads, and they would have been out in the street.'

'Why didn't he go to Monsieur Kaplan?'

'He knew he would get no help from him. That's the way he is. When he told us that the firm was closing down, he handed each of us an envelope containing three months' salary. Monsieur Louis dared not keep his share at home, because his wife would have been sure to find it.'

'Used she to go through his wallet?'

'I don't know. Probably she did. At any rate, I kept the money for him, and every month I would hand over the equivalent of his salary. Then, when there was no more left . . .'

'I understand.'

'He paid me back.'

'After how long?'

'Eight or nine months. Almost a year.'

'When did you next see him, after you'd lent him the money?'

'I lent him the money in February, and didn't see him again until August.'

'Didn't that worry you?'

'No. I knew he'd be back eventually. And, besides, even if he had not paid me back . . .'

'Did he tell you whether he'd found another job?'

'He said he was in work.'

'Was that when he took to wearing brown shoes?'

'Yes. After that, he came to see me several times. He always had some little present for me, and sweets for Mother.'

Maybe that was why the old woman was looking so crestfallen. No doubt most of her visitors arrived armed with sweets for her, and here was Maigret empty-handed. He made a mental note to bring a box of sweets if ever he had occasion to visit the shop again.

'Did he ever mention any names to you?'

'What sort of names?'

'I don't know. Employers, friends, workmates, perhaps.'

'No.'

'Did he ever refer to any particular district of Paris?'

'Only the Rue de Bondy. He went back there several times. It made him feel bitter to see that they hadn't even started on the demolition work.

' "We could have stayed on another year at least," he used to say, with a sigh.'

The door-bell tinkled. Léone poked her head forward, as no doubt she did many times in the course of a day, to see who was in the shop.

Maigret stood up. 'I mustn't keep you any longer.'

'Come back whenever you like. You'll always be welcome.'

A pregnant woman was standing beside the counter. He picked up his hat and made for the door.

'I'm much obliged to you.'

He got into the car, watched by the two women, who were gazing at him over the pink and white woollies piled on the counter.

'Where to now, Chief?'

It was just eleven o'clock.

'Stop at the first bistro you come to.'

'There's one next door to the shop.'

Somehow, he felt shy of going in there, under Léone's watchful eye.

'We'll find one round the corner.'

He wanted to ring Monsieur Kaplan, and to consult the street guide, to find Monsieur Saimbron's exact address on the Quai de la Mégisserie.

While he was there, having started the day with a Calvados, he thought he might as well have another, and drank it standing at the bar counter.

## 3. The Boiled Egg

MAIGRET lunched alone at his usual table in the *Brasserie Dauphine*. This was significant, especially as nothing urgent had cropped up to prevent him from going home to lunch. As usual, there were several inspectors from the Quai having an aperitif at the bar, and they turned to look at him, as he made his way to his own special table near a window, from which he could watch the Seine flow by.

Without a word, the inspectors exchanged glances, although none worked directly under him. When Maigret walked with a heavy tread, his eyes somewhat glazed and his expression, as some mistakenly supposed, ill-humoured, everyone in the *Police Judiciare* knew what it all signified. And even though it might make them smile, they nevertheless viewed the signs with some respect, because they always pointed to the same conclusion: sooner or later someone, man or woman, would be persuaded to confess to their crime.

'What's the *Veau Marengo* like?'

'Excellent, Monsieur Maigret.'

Without realizing it, he was subjecting the waiter to a look that could not have been sterner if he had been a suspect under interrogation.

'Beer, sir?'

'No. A half-bottle of claret.'

He was just being perverse. If the waiter had suggested wine, he would have ordered beer.

So far today, he had not set foot in his office. He had just come from calling on Saimbron on the Quai de la Mégisserie, and the experience had left him feeling a little queasy.

As a first step, he had telephoned Monsieur Max Kaplan at his home address, only to be told that he was staying at his villa in Antibes, and that it was not known when he would be returning to Paris.

The entrance to the building on the Quai de la Mégisserie was sandwiched between two pet shops selling birds, many of which, in their cages, were strung out along the pavement.

'Monsieur Saimbron?' he had inquired of the concierge.

'Top floor. You can't miss it.'

He searched in vain for a lift. There was none, so he had to climb six flights of stairs. The building was old, with dark and dingy walls. Right at the top, the landing was comparatively bright, due to a skylight let into the ceiling. There was a door on the left, beside which hung a thick red and black cord, resembling the cord of a dressing-gown. He pulled it. This produced an absurd little tinkle inside the flat. Then he heard light footsteps, the door was opened, and he saw a ghostly face, narrow, pale and bony, covered with white bristles of several days' growth, and a pair of watering eyes.

'Monsieur Saimbron?'

'I am Monsieur Saimbron. Do please come in.'

This little speech, brief as it was, brought on a fit of hoarse coughing.

'I'm sorry. It's my bronchitis.'

Inside, there was a pervasive smell, stale and nauseating. Maigret could hear the hissing of a gas ring. There was a pan of water on the boil.

'I am Chief Superintendent Maigret of the *Police Judiciaire*.'

'Yes. I've been expecting a visit from you or one of your inspectors.'

On a table, which was covered with a flower-embroidered cloth such as are now only to be found on flea market junk stalls, lay a morning paper, open at the page on which Louis Thouret's death was reported in a few brief lines.

'Were you about to have lunch?'

Next to the newspaper stood a plate, a glass of water to which a drop of wine had been added, and a hunk of bread.

'There's no hurry.'

'Do please carry on, just as if I wasn't here.'

'My egg will be hard by this time, anyway.'

All the same, the old man decided to go and fetch it. The hissing of the gas ceased.

'Do please sit down, Chief Superintendent. I advise you to take off your coat. I am obliged to keep the place excessively warm, on account of my rusty bronchial tubes.'

He must have been almost as old as Mademoiselle Léone's mother, but he had no one to take care of him. In all probability, no one ever came to see him in his lodgings, the only merit of which was a view of the Seine and of the *Palais de Justice* and the flower market beyond.

'How long ago did you last see Monsieur Louis?'

Their conversation had lasted half an hour, partly because of the old man's frequent bouts of coughing, and partly because he was so incredibly slow over eating his egg.

And what, in the end, had Maigret learned from him? Nothing that Léone and the concierge in the Rue de Bondy had not already told him.

The liquidation of the firm of Kaplan had been a tragedy for Saimbron as well. He had not even attempted to find another job. He had saved a little money. For years and years, he had believed that it was enough to keep him in his old age. But owing to successive devaluations of the franc he now literally had barely enough to stave off total starvation. That boiled egg was probably his only solid food for that day.

'I'm one of the lucky ones. I have at least been able to call this place home for the last forty years!'

He was a widower. He had no children, and no surviving relatives.

When Louis Thouret had been to see him and asked him for a loan, he had lent him the money without hesitation.

'He told me it was a matter of life and death, and I could tell that he was speaking the truth.'

Mademoiselle Léone had also been only too glad to lend him money.

'He paid me back a few months later.'

But had he never wondered, during those months, whether he would ever see Monsieur Louis again? If he had not done so, how would Monsieur Saimbron have managed to pay for his daily boiled egg?

'Did he come and see you often?'

'Two or three times. The first time was when he came to return the money. He brought me a present, a meerschaum pipe.'

He went to fetch it from the drawer of a whatnot. No doubt he had to be sparing with his tobacco as well.

'How long is it since you saw him last?'

'About three weeks. He was sitting on a bench in the Boulevard Bonne-Nouvelle.'

Was it that the old book-keeper was so much attached to the district where he had worked for so long that he returned to it from time to time by way of pilgrimage?

'Did you speak to him?'

'I sat down beside him. He offered to buy me a drink in a café nearby, but I declined. The sun was shining. We chatted, and watched the world go by.'

'Was he wearing light brown shoes?'

'I didn't pay any attention to his shoes. I can't tell you, I'm afraid.'

'Did he say anything about his job?'

Monsieur Saimbron shook his head. Like Mademoiselle Léone, he was reluctant to discuss it. Maigret could understand why. He was growing quite attached to Monsieur Louis, though he had never seen him, except as a corpse that had met death with a wide-eyed stare of astonishment.

'How did your meeting end?'

'Someone was hovering around the bench. I had the impression that he was trying to attract my friend's attention.'

'A man?'

'Yes. A middle-aged man.'

'What was he like?'

'The sort of person one often sees sitting on a bench in that particular district. In the end, he came and sat beside us, but he didn't speak. I got up and left. When I looked back, the two of them were deep in conversation.'

'Did they seem friendly?'

'They certainly weren't having an argument.'

And that was that. Maigret had gone down the stairs, intending to return home for lunch, but in the end had decided to eat at his usual table in the *Brasserie Dauphine*.

It was a grey day. There were no glittering flecks on the Seine. He drank another small glass of Calvados with his coffee, and returned to his office, where a mass of paper work awaited him. A little later, Coméliau, the Examining Magistrate on the case, rang through to him.

'What do you think of this business of Thouret? The Public Prosecutor took it upon himself this morning to tell me that you were working on the case. It was the usual sort of thing, a mugging or a case of thieves falling out, I presume?'

Maigret merely grunted, preferring not to commit himself one way or the other.

'The family want to know when they can have the body. I didn't want to say anything definite until I had consulted you. Have you finished with it yet?'

'Has Doctor Paul completed his examination?'

'He's just rung me to let me know the result. I shall have his written report by tonight. The knife punctured the left ventricle, and death was virtually instantaneous.'

'Any signs of a struggle?'

'None.'

'I see no reason why the family shouldn't collect the body as soon as they like. There's just one thing, though. I'd be glad if you'd arrange for the clothes to be sent on to the Forensic Laboratory.'

'I'll see to that. Keep me in the picture, won't you?'

Judge Coméliau was unusually affable. This was, no doubt, because the press had barely mentioned the matter, and because he himself had come to the conclusion that it was just an ordinary case of mugging. He was not interested. No one was interested.

Maigret poked the fire in the stove, filled his pipe and, for the next hour or so, immersed himself in his paper work, scribbling notes in the margins of some documents, and signing others. Then he made a few unimportant telephone calls.

'May I come in, Chief?'

It was Santoni, dressed up to the nines as usual. And, as usual, reeking of hair oil, a habit which frequently caused his colleagues to protest:

'You smell like a tart!'

Santoni was looking very pleased with himself.

'I think I'm on to something.'

Maigret, evincing no emotion, looked at him with wide, troubled eyes.

'First of all, it may interest you to know that Geber et Bachelier, the firm where the Thouret girl works, are debt collectors. Nothing very big. What they actually do is to take over hopeless defaulters for a small consideration, and then squeeze the money out of them. It isn't so much a matter of office work as of house-to-house harassment. Mademoiselle Thouret is only in her office in the Rue de Rivoli in the mornings. Every afternoon, she's out and about visiting the defaulters in their homes.'

'I get it.'

'They're little people, mostly, because they are the ones most likely to be intimidated, and to pay up in the end. I didn't see either of the partners. I waited outside until the staff came out at lunch-time. I took good care to avoid being seen by the young lady, and spoke to one of the other employees, a woman past her first youth, who, as it turned out, had no very warm feelings towards her colleague.'

'And what did you find out?'

'That our little Monique has a boyfriend.'

'Do you know his name?'

'All in good time, Chief. They've known each other for about four months, and they meet every day for a set lunch at a restaurant in the Boulevard Sébastopol. He's very young, only nineteen, and has a job as a salesman in a big bookshop in the Boulevard Saint-Michel.'

Maigret was fiddling with the row of pipes strung out on his desk, then, although the one he was smoking was still alight, he started to fill another.

'The kid's name is Albert Jorisse. I thought I might as well take a look at him, so I went along to the restaurant. You never saw such a crowd! In the end, I managed to spot Monique sitting at a table, but she was on her own. I sat at a table on the opposite side of the room, and had a very nasty meal. The young lady seemed very much on edge, and never stopped glancing towards the door.'

'Did he arrive eventually?'

'No. She made her food last as long as she could. In a dump of that sort, the meals are served with the utmost speed, and dawdling is frowned on. In the end, she had no choice but to get up and go, but she hung about outside, pacing up and down for nearly a quarter of an hour.'

'What happened next?'

'She was so concerned about the young man, that she didn't notice me. Next she made for the Boulevard Saint-Michel. I followed her. You know that big corner bookshop, where they have trays of books outside on the pavement?'

'Yes, I know the one you mean.'

'Well, she went in there, and spoke to one of the salesmen, who referred her to the cashier. I could see that she was being very persistent, but to no avail. In the end, looking very crestfallen, she left.'

'Didn't you follow her?'

'I thought I'd do better to concentrate on the young man, so I, in my turn, went into the bookshop, and asked the manager whether he knew anyone of the name of Albert Jorisse. He said yes, he worked in the shop, but only in the mornings. When I expressed surprise, he explained that it was common practice with them, as most of their employees were students, who were unable to work full-time.'

'Is Jorisse a student?'

'Give me a chance! I wanted to know how long he'd been working there. The manager had to consult his records. He's been with the firm for just over a year. At the beginning, he worked full-time. Then, after he'd been there for about three months, he said he was going to work for a law degree, and henceforth could only come in in the mornings.'

'Do you know his address?'

'He lives with his parents in the Avenue de Châtillon, almost opposite the church of Montrouge. But that's not all. Albert Jorisse didn't turn up at the shop today. It's not the first time, it happens two or three times a year, but, up to now, he's always telephoned to let them know. Today, he didn't.'

'Was he there yesterday?'

'Yes. I thought you'd be interested, so I took a taxi to the Avenue de Châtillon. His parents are thoroughly respectable people. They have a flat on the third floor. It's spotlessly clean. His mother was busy ironing.'

'Did you tell her you were a police officer?'

'No. I said her son was a friend of mine, and I needed to see him urgently.'

'Did she suggest you went to the bookshop?'

'Exactly. She doesn't know a thing. He left home this morning at a quarter past eight, as usual. She's never heard a word about this law degree project. Her husband works for a wholesaler in fabrics in the Rue de la Victoire. They couldn't afford to pay for a higher education for their son.'

'What did you do next?'

'I pretended I thought I was on the wrong tack, and that her son probably wasn't the Jorisse I was looking for. I asked her whether she had a photograph of her son. She took me to see the one on the dresser in the dining-room. She's a good soul, and she doesn't suspect a thing. All she ever thinks about is re-heating her iron, and making sure she doesn't scorch the linen. I stayed on for a while, talking sweet nothings. . . .'

Maigret made no comment, but listened with a marked lack of enthusiasm. It was plain to see that Santoni had not been working under him for long. Everything he said—and even his manner of saying it—was out of tune with the way Maigret's mind, and indeed the minds of his closest associates, worked.

'On the way out, taking care not to let her see what I was doing. . . .'

Maigret held out his hand.

'Give it here.'

As if he didn't know that Santoni had pinched the photograph! It showed a thin youth with a nervous expression and very long hair, the sort whom women often find attractive, and who know it.

'Is that all?'

'We'll have to wait and see whether he goes home tonight, won't we?'

Maigret sighed. 'Yes, we'll have to wait and see.'

'Anything the matter?'

'Of course not.'

What was the use? Santoni would learn in time, as others had learned before him. It was always the same when one took on an inspector from some other branch of the Service.

'The reason I didn't follow the girl was that I know where to find her. Every evening at about half-past five, or a quarter to six at the latest, she calls in at the office to hand over the money she has collected, and write her report. Do you want me to go there?'

Maigret hesitated on the brink of telling him to drop the whole thing. But he thought better of it. It would have been unfair. After all, the inspector had done his best.

'Just check that she does go back to the office, as usual, and then make sure she goes off to catch her train.'

'Maybe her boyfriend will be waiting for her there?'

'Maybe. What time does he usually get home in the evening?'

'They have dinner at seven. He's always in by then, even if he has to go out again later.'

'They're not on the telephone, I suppose?'

'No.'

'What about the concierge?'

'I don't think she is either. It's not the sort of place where you'd expect to find telephones. But I'll check.'

He consulted the street directory.

'You'd better go back there some time after seven, and see what you can find out from the concierge. Leave the photograph with me.'

Santoni had taken the photograph, there was no going back on it, Maigret thought. So he might as well keep it. It could come in useful.

'Will you be staying here in your office?'

'I don't know where I shall be, but keep in touch with our people here.'

'What shall I do between now and then? I've got nearly two hours to kill before setting out for the Rue de Rivoli.'

'Go down and have a word with the Licensed Premises chaps. They may have a registration form in the name of Louis Thouret.'

'You mean you think he took a room somewhere in town?'

'Where do you suppose he left his brown shoes and colourful tie when he went home?'

'That's a thought.'

It was now fully two hours since Monsieur Louis's photograph had appeared in the afternoon editions of the newspapers. It was only a small photograph, tucked away in a corner, and the caption read:

*Louis Thouret, murdered yesterday afternoon in a cul-de-sac off the Boulevard Saint-Martin. The police are on the track of the killer.*

It wasn't true, but that was what the papers invariably said. It was odd, come to think of it, that the Chief Superintendent had not yet received a single telephone call. If the truth were told, it was chiefly on this account that he had decided to return to the office and, while he was about it, clear his in-tray.

Almost always, in a case of this sort, there were people who believed, rightly or wrongly, that they recognized the victim. Or they claimed to have seen an unsavoury-looking character lurking near the scene of the crime. More often than not such claims were unfounded. All the same, every now and again, one or more of these people would lead him to the truth.

For the past three years, Monsieur Louis, as he was known to his former colleagues and to the concierge in the Rue de Bondy, had left Juvisy at the same time every morning. He continued to take his lunch with him, wrapped in a square of oilcloth, as he had always done.

But how had he spent his time, after he had got off the train at the Gare de Lyon? That was still a mystery.

Except, that is, for the first few months, when, in all probability, he had spent every moment desperately looking for another job. Like so many others, he must have joined the queues outside the offices of one of the newspapers, waiting to pounce on the Situations Vacant columns. Maybe he had even tried his hand at selling vacuum cleaners from door to door?

Apparently he had not succeeded, since he had been driven to borrow money from Mademoiselle Léone and the old book-keeper.

After that, for several months, he had disappeared from view. By this time, he had not only somehow had to lay his hands on a sum of money equivalent to his salary at Kaplan's, but also to pay back the two loans.

During all that time, he had returned home every evening, just as if nothing had happened, and looking every inch the family breadwinner.

His wife had suspected nothing. Nor had his daughter, nor his sisters-in-law, nor his two brothers-in-law, who both worked on the railways.

And then, one day, he had turned up at the Rue de Clignancourt to pay his debt to Mademoiselle Léone, armed with a present for her, and sweets for her aged mother.

Not to mention the fact that he had taken to wearing light brown shoes!

Had those brown shoes of his anything to do with the keen interest that Maigret was beginning to take in the fellow? He would certainly never admit it, even to himself.

He too had longed at one time to own a pair of goose-dung shoes. They had been all the rage then, like those very short fawn raincoats, known at that time as bum-freezers.

Once, early on in his married life, he had made up his mind to buy a pair of light brown shoes, and had felt himself blushing as he went into the shop. Come to think of it, the shop was in the Boulevard Saint-Martin, just opposite the *Théâtre de l'Ambigu*. He had not dared to put them on at first. Then, when he had finally plucked up the courage to open the parcel in the presence of his wife, she had looked at him, and then laughed in rather an odd way.

'You surely don't intend to wear those things?'

He never had worn them. It was she who had taken them back to the shop, on the pretext that they pinched his feet.

Louis Thouret had also bought a pair of light brown shoes, and that, in Maigret's view, was symbolic.

It was above all, Maigret was convinced, a symbol of liberation. Whenever he wore those shoes, he must have thought of himself as a free man, which meant that, until the moment when he changed back into his black shoes, his wife, sisters-in-law and brothers-in-law had no hold on him.

The shoes meant something else as well. On the day when Maigret had bought his pair, he had just been informed by the Superintendent of the Saint-Georges District, whose subordinate he was at the time, that he was to have a rise in salary of ten francs a month. And, in those days, ten francs really were ten francs.

Monsieur Louis, too, must have been feeling weighed down with riches. He had presented a meerschaum pipe to the old book-keeper, and repaid the two people who had been prepared to trust him. As a result, he had been able to go back from time to time and see them both, especially Mademoiselle Léone. And at the same time, he had felt free to call on the concierge in the Rue de Bondy. Why had he never told any of them how he spent his time?

Quite by chance, the concierge had seen him one morning round about eleven sitting on a bench in Boulevard Saint-Martin.

She had not spoken to him, but had gone back by a round-about route, so that he should not see her. Maigret could understand that. It was the bench that had ruffled her. For a man like Monsieur Louis, who had worked ten hours a day for most of his life, to be caught idling on a park bench! Not on a Sunday! Not after working hours! At eleven in the morning, when there was always a bustle of activity in every shop and every office.

Monsieur Saimbron had also recently spotted his former colleague sitting on a bench. In his case, in the Boulevard Bonne-Nouvelle, within easy walking distance of the Boulevard Saint-Martin and the Rue de Bondy.

This had been in the afternoon, and Monsieur Saimbron, showing less delicacy than the concierge, had spoken to him.

Or perhaps Louis Thouret had seen him first.

Had the former storekeeper come there by appointment? Who was the man who had hovered near the bench, apparently waiting for an invitation to sit down?

Monsieur Saimbron had not described him. Probably, he had not paid much attention to him. All the same, his comment had been illuminating:

*'He was the sort of man one often sees sitting on a bench in that area.'*

In other words, one of those individuals without any visible means of support, who spend hours sitting on benches on the boulevards, absently watching the world go by. The occupants of the benches in the Saint-Martin district were different from those to be seen in many of the squares and public gardens of the city, such as the Parc Montsouris, which are mostly patronized by local residents with private means.

People of that sort are not to be found sitting in the Boulevard Saint-Martin, or if they are, it is on the terrace of a café.

There were the light brown shoes on the one hand, and the bench on the other. As far as the Chief Superintendent was concerned, they did not seem to fit together.

Finally, there was the overriding fact that, at about half-past four on a wet and gloomy afternoon, Monsieur Louis, for no apparent reason, had turned into a cul-de-sac, followed soundlessly by someone who had knifed him between the shoulder blades, barely ten yards from the milling throng of people on the Boulevard.

His photograph had appeared in all the papers, and no one had telephoned. Maigret was still making notes on documents and signing official forms. Outside, the dusk was deepening, and would soon turn to darkness. He had to switch on the light, and when he saw that the hands of the mantel clock stood at three, he got up, and took his heavy winter overcoat down from its hook.

Before leaving, he put his head round the door of the Inspectors' Duty Room.

'I'll be back in an hour or two.'

There was no point in using a car. At the end of the Quai, he jumped on to the platform of a bus, from which he alighted a few minutes later at the junction of the Boulevard Sébastopol and the Grands Boulevards.

At this same hour on the previous day, Louis Thouret had still been alive. He too had roamed around the district, with plenty of time to spare, before having to change back into his black shoes, and make his way to the Gare de Lyon, to catch his train to Juvisy.

The pavements were jammed with people. On every corner they were bunched together like grapes, waiting to cross the road, and when the traffic lights changed, they all surged forward.

That must be the bench, he thought, noticing one on the pavement opposite, in the Boulevard Bonne-Nouvelle.

It was unoccupied, but even at that distance he could see a piece of crumpled, greasy paper which, he could have sworn, had recently contained ham or slices of pork sausage.

Prostitutes were to be seen loitering on the corner of the Rue Saint-Martin. There were more of them in one of the little bars, and, at a round, tripod table, four men could be seen playing cards.

A familiar figure was standing at the bar counter. It was Inspector Neveu. Maigret stopped to wait for him, and one of the women thought that he was interested in her. Absently, he shook his head.

If Neveu was there, it meant that he had already questioned them. This was home ground to him, and he knew them all.

'Everything all right?' Maigret asked him, when he came out of the bistro.

'So you're here too?'

'Just looking around.'

'I've been wandering about here since eight this morning. If I've questioned one person I must have questioned five hundred.'

'Have you found out where he used to go for lunch?'

'How did you guess?'

'I felt sure he must have eaten his midday meal somewhere in this district, and his sort would be likely always to go back to the same place.'

'Over there,' said Neveu, pointing to what looked like a quiet little restaurant. 'He even had his own napkin and ring.'

'What did they tell you?'

'He always sat at the same table, at the back near the bar. I got that from the waitress who always served him. She's tall and dark, with a face like a horse and hairs on her chin. Do you know what she called him?'

How could the Chief Superintendent be expected to know!

'Her little man. She told me so herself:

' "Well, little man, what do you fancy today?"

'She says he was always cheerful. Rain or shine, he never failed to mention the weather. He never attempted to get fresh with her.

'All the waitresses in the restaurant get two hours off between clearing away the lunch and laying the tables for dinner.

'Apparently, several times, on her way out at about three o'clock she saw Monsieur Louis sitting on a bench. Each time, he waved to her.

'One day she said, to tease him:

' "You take things easy, little man, I must say!"

'He replied that he worked at night.'

'Did she believe him?'

'Yes. She seemed quite besotted on him.'

'Has she seen the papers?'

'No. The first she'd heard of his death was from me. She didn't want to believe it.

'It's not an expensive restaurant, but it isn't one of those fixed-price places either. Every lunch-time Monsieur Louis would treat himself to a half-bottle of good wine.'

'Did you find anyone else who had seen him around?'

'About ten people so far. One of the girls whose beat is over there on the corner saw him almost every day. She accosted him the first time, but he said no, very kindly. No getting on his high horse for him, and after that she got into the way of calling out every time she saw him:

' "Well, is it to be today, then?" '

'It was just a little game they played. Whenever she hooked a client, he would give her a broad wink.'

'Did he never go with any of them?'

'No.'

'Did none of them ever see him with a woman?'

'Not them. One of the salesmen in the jeweller's did, though.'

'The one next to the place where he was killed?'

'Yes. I showed the photograph to all the staff, but he was the only one who recognized him.

' "That's the man who came in and bought a ring last week!" he exclaimed.'

'Did Monsieur Louis have a young woman with him?'

'She wasn't particularly young. The salesman hardly noticed her. He thought they were husband and wife. What he did notice, though, was that she was wearing a silver fox fur draped round her shoulders, and a chain with a pendant in the shape of a four-leaf clover.

' "We sell pendants just like it!" '

'Was the ring valuable?'

'A paste diamond in a gold-plated setting.'

'Did they say anything of interest in his presence?'

'They talked like any other married couple. He can't remember their exact words. Nothing that mattered, anyway.'

'Had he ever seen her before?'

'He wasn't sure. She was dressed in black, and wearing

gloves. She nearly left them behind on the counter, having taken them off to try on the ring. It was Monsieur Louis who came back for them. She waited outside. She was taller than he was. When he went out, he took her arm, and they went off in the direction of the Place de la République.'

'Nothing else?'

'These things take time. I began my inquiries higher up the Boulevard, near where it joins the Rue Montmartre, but I drew a blank there. Oh! I nearly forgot: you know those waffle stalls in the Rue de la Lune?'

They toasted the waffles in open-fronted booths, almost completely exposed to the elements, as at a fair, and the sweetish smell of the cooking dough hit one as soon as one turned into the street.

'They remember him. He often bought waffles there, always three at a time. He didn't eat them there and then, but took them away with him.'

The waffles were enormous. They were advertised as the largest in Paris. It was unlikely that little Monsieur Louis, having eaten a substantial lunch, could have managed to put away three of them all by himself.

Nor was he the sort of man who would sit munching on a bench. Had he shared them with the woman for whom he had bought the ring? In that case, she must have lived somewhere close at hand.

On the other hand, the waffles could have been intended for the man seen by Monsieur Saimbron.

'Am I to carry on?'

'Of course.'

Maigret felt a pang. He wished he could do the job himself, as he used to when he was only an inspector.

'Where are you going, Chief?'

'I'm going over there, to have another look.'

He didn't suppose it would do any good. It was just that, as the cul-de-sac where Monsieur Louis had been killed was barely a hundred yards away, he had an itch to return to the spot. It was practically the same time of day. Today there was no fog, but all the same it was pitch dark in the little passage, and being dazzled by the harsh lights in the jeweller's window didn't help.

The waffles had reminded Maigret of fairs he had been to in the past, and, because of this, he had had the idea that Thouret might have gone into the cul-de-sac to relieve himself. But this notion was soon dispelled by the sight of a urinal just across the street.

'If only I could find that woman!' sighed Neveu, whose feet must have been aching after all the walking he had had to do.

Maigret, for his part, was more anxious to find the man who, in response to a silent signal, had come and sat beside Monsieur Louis and the old book-keeper while they were still in conversation. Which was why his searching glance rested on every bench they passed. On one of them sat an old man, a vagrant, with a half-empty litre bottle of red wine next to him. But he was not the one. If he had been a tramp, Monsieur Saimbron would have said so.

A little farther along, a fat woman from the provinces was sitting waiting for her husband to come out of the urinal, no doubt glad of the chance to rest her swollen feet.

'If I were you, I'd concentrate less on the shops and more on the people on the benches.'

At the start of his career, he had spent long enough pounding the beat to know that every bench has its regulars, who are always to be found there at certain times of the day.

They were ignored by the passers-by, who seldom so much as glanced at them. But the occupants of the various benches were known to one another. Had it not, after all, been due to Madame Maigret's getting into conversation with the mother of a little boy, while sitting on a bench in the square gardens of the Place d'Anvers, awaiting her dental appointment, that a murderer had been tracked down?

'You mean you want them rounded up?'

'Anything but! I just want you to sit down beside them and get into conversation.'

'Very well, Chief,' said Neveu with a sigh, not overjoyed at the prospect. Even walking the streets seemed preferable.

He never dreamed that the Chief Superintendent would have leapt at the chance of taking his place.

## 4. A Funeral in the Rain

THE NEXT DAY, Wednesday, Maigret had to attend the Assizes to give evidence, and wasted most of the afternoon kicking his heels in the dingy room reserved for witnesses. No one had thought to turn up the central heating, and everyone was shivering. When, at last, someone did turn it up, the room became stiflingly hot within ten minutes, and there was a pervasive smell of unwashed bodies and clothes that had never been properly aired.

The name of the man on trial was René Lecœur. Seven months earlier, he had battered his aunt to death with a bottle.

He was only twenty-two and broad-shouldered as a coal heaver, with the face of a naughty schoolboy.

Why on earth couldn't they use stronger lighting in the *Palais de Justice,* considering how the dark grey paint, the dust and the shadows soaked up all the natural light?

Maigret left the witnesses' waiting-room feeling depressed. A young lawyer, who was just beginning to get himself talked about, chiefly on account of his aggressive manner, was fiercely hectoring the witnesses, as they followed one another into the box.

The line he took with Maigret was that the accused would never have confessed but for the rough treatment to which he had been subjected at the Quai des Orfèvres. Which was an out-and-out lie. And not only was it a lie, but the lawyer perfectly well knew that it was.

'Will the witness kindly tell the court how long my client was subjected to interrogation on the first occasion?'

The Chief Superintendent had been expecting this.

'Seventeen hours.'

'And during all that time, he had nothing to eat?'

'Lecœur was offered sandwiches, but he refused.'

The lawyer turned an eloquent glance upon the jury, as if to say: *You see, gentlemen! Seventeen hours without a morsel of food!*

And what of Maigret himself? Throughout the whole of that time he had eaten nothing but a couple of sandwiches. And he hadn't killed anyone!

197

'Does the witness deny that, on the 7th of March, at three o'clock in the morning, he struck the accused without provocation, in spite of the fact that the poor young man was handcuffed?'

'I do deny it.'

'Is the witness denying that he ever struck the accused?'

'I did slap his face at one point, but lightly, as I might have slapped my own daughter.'

The lawyer was going the wrong way about it. But all he cared about was to impress those present in court and get himself written up in the papers.

This time, contrary to accepted practice, he addressed himself directly to Maigret, adopting a tone of voice that was at once honeyed and biting.

'Have you a daughter, Chief Superintendent?'

'No.'

'Have you ever had children . . . ? Speak up, please . . . I can't hear you.'

The Chief Superintendent was obliged to repeat audibly that he had had a little girl who had died at birth.

And that was the end of it. He left the witness box, went to have a drink in the *Palais de Justice* bar, and then returned to his office. Lucas, who had been working solidly on another case for the past fortnight, was now free to turn his attention to the Thouret murder.

'Any news of young Jorisse?'

'Nothing so far.'

Monique Thouret's boy friend had not returned home the previous night, nor had he put in an appearance at the bookshop in the morning, and he had not turned up for lunch at the fixed-price restaurant in the Boulevard Sébastopol, where he had been in the habit of meeting the girl.

It was Lucas who was in charge of the search. He was in close touch with all the railway stations, police stations and frontier posts.

As for Janvier, he and four of his colleagues were still combing the hardware shops, hoping to track down the man who had sold the knife to the murderer.

'Any word from Neveu?'

Maigret had been expected back in his office earlier.

'He rang through half an hour ago. He said he'd try again at six.'

Maigret was feeling a little weary. He was haunted by the memory of René Lecœur sitting in the dock. And also by the voice of the lawyer, the judges still as statues, the crowds of people in the dimly lit courtroom, with its dark oak panelling. It was no longer any concern of his. Once a suspect left Police Headquarters to be handed over to the Examining Magistrate, the Chief Superintendent's responsibility was ended. He was not always happy at the way things were done from then on. He could never be quite sure of what would happen next. And if it had been left to him. . . .

'Nothing from Lapointe?'

By now, each one of his men had been assigned to a specific task. Young Lapointe's was to go from one lodging house to another, outward in ever widening circles from the Boulevard Saint-Martin. Monsieur Louis must have taken a room somewhere, if only so as to be able to change his shoes. He had rented the room either in his own name or in the name of someone else, such as the woman with the fox fur, towards whom he behaved as if she were his wife, and for whom he had bought a ring. As for Santoni, he was still on Monique's tail, in the hope that Albert Jorisse would try and get in touch with her, either in person or by way of a message.

The family had claimed Thouret's body the previous day. An undertaker's van had collected it. The funeral was to take place next day.

There were more documents to be signed; the paperwork never seemed to end. A number of telephone calls were put through to him, none of them of any interest. It was odd that not a single person had telephoned, written or called in person on the subject of Monsieur Louis. It was almost as if he had vanished, leaving no trace behind.

'Hello! Maigret speaking.'

It was Inspector Neveu, calling from a bistro. Maigret could hear music in the background, coming from a radio, no doubt.

'There's still nothing very positive to go on, Chief. I've found three more people, one of them an old woman, who spend a great deal of their time sitting on benches in the boulevards. They all remember him, and they all say the same thing: he was very likeable, always polite, and never slow to enter into conversation. According to the old woman, when he left her he always made towards the Place de la République, but she would soon lose sight of him in the crowd.

'Was he never with anyone else when she saw him?'

'No. But one of the others, a tramp, said to me:

' "He was always waiting for someone. As soon as the man turned up, they would go off together."

'But he couldn't give me a description of the other man. All he could say was:

' "There was nothing special about him. One sees thousands like him every day." '

'Keep up the good work!' said Maigret, with a sigh.

He telephoned his wife to say that he would be late home, then went down into the forecourt, got into the car, and told the driver to take him to Madame Thouret's address in Juvisy.

There was a strong wind blowing. Dense clouds made the sky appear low overhead. They swirled about, as they do on the coast when a storm is brewing. The driver had difficulty in finding the Rue des Peupliers. When they finally got there, not only were the kitchen lights on, but also those in the bedroom on the floor above.

The bell wasn't working. It had been disconnected as a sign of mourning. But someone had heard him arrive. The door was opened by a woman whom he had not seen before. She bore a family resemblance to Madame Thouret, but was four or five years older.

'Chief Superintendent Maigret . . .' he said.

She looked towards the kitchen, and called out:

'Emilie!'

'I heard. Bring him in.'

He was shown into the kitchen, the dining-room having been transformed into a memorial chapel. The narrow entrance was filled with the scent of flowers and candles. A cold supper was laid out, and several people were seated at the table.

'I'm sorry to have to disturb you. . . .'

'Allow me to introduce my brother-in-law, Monsieur Magnin, who is a railway inspector.'

'Pleased to meet you.'

Magnin was both humourless and stupid. He had a ginger moustache, and an Adam's apple that bobbed up and down.

'You've already met my sister Jeanne. This is my elder sister Céline.'

There was barely room for all of them in the cramped little kitchen. Monique alone had not risen to greet him. She was subjecting the Chief Superintendent to an unwavering stare. She must have been thinking that he had come for her, to question her on the subject of Albert Jorisse, and she was frozen with terror.

'My brother-in-law Landin, Céline's husband, will be coming home on the Blue Train tonight. He'll just be in time for the funeral. Won't you sit down?'

He shook his head.

'Would you like to see him?'

She wanted him to know that they had done things in style. He followed her into the adjoining room, where Louis Thouret was laid out in his coffin. The lid had not yet been screwed down. Very softly, she whispered:

'He looks as if he was asleep.'

He went through all the proper motions, dipping a sprig of rosemary into a bowl of holy water, crossing himself, moving his lips as if in prayer, and crossing himself again.

'He never thought about dying,' she said, and added: 'He did so love life!'

They tiptoed out, and she shut the door behind her. The others were waiting for Maigret to leave, before returning to their meal.

'Will you be attending the funeral, Chief Superintendent?'

'I'll be there. As a matter of fact, that was what I came to see you about.'

Monique still did not stir, but she was obviously relieved to hear this. Maigret did not seem to have noticed her, so she kept very still, almost as if, in that way, she could ward off what fate had in store for her.

'I take it you and your sisters know most of the people who will be attending the funeral? I don't, of course.'

'I understand!' said Magnin, the brother-in-law, implying that great minds think alike.

And he turned to the others, as if to say: 'This is going to be good!'

"All I'm asking is that, if you should spot anyone there whose presence strikes you as odd, you should simply point them out to me.'

'You mean you think the murderer might be there?'

'Not necessarily the murderer. I can't afford to ignore any possibility, however remote. You must remember that much of your husband's life during the past three years is still shrouded in mystery.'

'Are you insinuating that he was mixed up with another woman?'

It was not only her face that had assumed a hard expression, but those of her two sisters as well.

'I'm not insinuating anything. I'm just feeling my way. If you notice anything out of the way tomorrow, just give me a sign. I shall understand.'

'Do you mean we should be on the lookout for any stranger?'

He nodded, and then apologized again for disturbing them. It was Magnin who saw him to the door.

'Have you anything to go on yet?' he asked, man to man, in the tone of voice one adopts with the doctor just after he has seen the patient.

'No.'

'Not even the tiniest glimmer of an idea?'

'None at all. Goodnight.'

His purpose in visiting the Rue des Peupliers had not been to alleviate the feeling of oppression which had weighed upon him ever since he had sat waiting to be called as a witness in the Lecœur trial. In the car, on the way back to Paris, he was occupied with random and seemingly irrelevant thoughts. He was remembering that when, at the age of twenty, he had first arrived in the capital, what had most disturbed him about it was the unremitting ferment of the great city, in which hundreds of thousands of people were all milling about, apparently on some private quest of their own.

In some places, one might almost call them strategic points, such as Les Halles, the Place Clichy, the Bastille and the Boulevard Saint-Martin, where Monsieur Louis had met his death, the ferment was even more intense than elsewhere.

In the old days he had been particularly struck, even one might say romantically stirred, by the sight of those who, discouraged and defeated, had given up the struggle, being swept along willy-nilly by the great, surging tide of humanity.

Since then, he had come to know many such people, and it was no longer them whom he most admired, but rather those just one step above them on the ladder, who were clean and decent and not in the least picturesque, and who fought day in and day out to keep their heads above water, or to nurture the illusion, or perhaps the faith, that they were alive and that life was worth living.

For twenty-five long years, Monsieur Louis had caught the same train every morning, sharing a compartment with the same people, his oilcloth packet of sandwiches tucked under his arm, and, in the evening, he had returned to what Maigret could not help thinking of as the House of the Three Sisters, since, although Céline and Jeanne had homes of their own several streets away, all three were ever-present, shutting off the wider horizon like a stone wall.

'Back to Headquarters, Chief?'

'No. Drive me home.'

That evening, as he so often did, he took Madame Maigret to a cinema in the Boulevard Bonne-Nouvelle. On the way there and back, with his arm through his wife's, he walked past the cul-de-sac off the Boulevard Saint-Martin.

'Is there something upsetting you?'

'No.'

'You haven't said a word all evening.'

'I wasn't aware of it.'

The rain began to fall at about three or four in the morning, and, in his sleep, he could hear the water gurgling in the gutters. By breakfast time it was coming down in buckets, accompanied by squally winds, and the people in the streets were clutching on to their umbrellas for fear they should be blown inside out.

'Proper All Saints' Day weather,' remarked Madame Maigret.

But in his recollection, All Saints' Day had always been overcast, windy and cold, but not wet. Why this should be, he had no idea.

'Have you a lot to do?'

'I don't know yet.'

'You'd better wear your galoshes.'

He did as he was told. By the time he found a taxi, his shoulders were already wet through, and, when he got in, the rain dripped off his hat-brim on to the floor.

'Quai des Orfèvres.'

The funeral was at ten. He looked in at the Chief Commissioner's office, but did not stay for the daily briefing. He was waiting for Neveu, who would be driving him to the cemetery. He was taking him on the off-chance that he might recognize someone. After all, the Inspector knew an enormous number of people in the Saint-Martin district, and Maigret had high hopes of this particular line of inquiry.

'Still no news of Jorisse?' he asked Lucas.

Although he couldn't explain why, Maigret was convinced that the young man was still somewhere in Paris.

'Better make a list of all his friends, all the people he went about with, during the last few years.'

'I've made a start on it already.'

'Good. Keep at it!'

Neveu appeared in the doorway. He too was sopping wet. Maigret and he went off together.

'What a day for a funeral!' grumbled the Inspector. 'I hope they've laid on cars.'

'I very much doubt it.'

It was ten minutes to ten when they arrived at the house of mourning. Black curtains embroidered in silver had been hung over the door. People, sheltering under their umbrellas, were standing about on the unmade pavement, where the rain was soaking into the yellowish clay soil and running in rivulets.

Some of the bystanders went into the house to pay their respects to the dead, and came out looking solemn and pompous, conscious of having done their duty. There must have been about fifty people clustered round the house, and more sheltering in the neighbouring doorways. There were also the neighbours, watching from their windows, determined to remain indoors until the last possible moment.

'Aren't you going in, Chief?'

'I was here yesterday.'

'Not very cheerful in there, is it?'

Neveu, needless to say, was not referring to the funeral atmosphere of the occasion, but to the house itself. And yet there were thousands and thousands of people whose dream it was to own just such a house.

'Whatever possessed them to come and live here?'

'She wanted to be near her sisters and brothers-in-law.'

They noticed several men in railwaymen's uniform. The house was not far from the marshalling yard. Most of the houses on the estate were occupied by people connected in one way or another with the railways.

The hearse arrived, followed at a brisk pace by a priest under an umbrella. He, in turn, was followed by a choir boy carrying his cross.

The wind whistled unimpeded down the street, flattening wet clothes against shivering bodies. The rain beat down on the coffin. Madame Thouret and her sisters, who were waiting in the entrance lobby, conferred together in whispers. Maybe they should have seen to it that there were more umbrellas?

All three were dressed in deep mourning, as were the two brothers-in-law. Behind them came the girls, Monique and her three cousins.

Which made seven women in all. As far as Maigret could see, the girls, like their mothers, closely resembled one another. It was a family of women, in which the men seemed uneasily aware that they were in a minority.

The horses whinnied. The family closed ranks behind the hearse, followed by such neighbours and friends as considered themselves entitled to precede the others in the procession.

The remainder straggled behind in a ragged line, some sheltering as best they could from the squally showers by hugging the inside of the pavement.

'Do you see anyone you recognize?'

There was no one of the sort they were looking for. None of the women, for example, could have been the woman with the ring. True, one of them was wearing a fox fur, but the Chief Superintendent had himself seen her come out of one of the houses in the street, locking the door behind her. As for the men, it was impossible to imagine any one of them sitting on a bench in the Boulevard Saint-Martin.

Nevertheless, Maigret and Neveu stayed right to the end. Fortunately, there was no Mass, just a prayer so short that it was not thought worth while to shut the church doors, with the result that the tiled floor was soon wet all over.

Twice, the Chief Superintendent found himself looking straight into Monique's eyes, and each time he could sense the fear clutching at the girl's heart.

'Are we going on to the cemetery?'

'It's not far. We might as well.'

They found themselves up to their ankles in mud, because the grave was in a new part of the cemetery, where the paths were nothing more than slimy tracks. Every time Madame Thouret caught Maigret's eye, she looked about her ostentatiously, to show that she had not forgotten his request. When he went forward, like all the others, to offer his condolences to the family as they stood at the graveside, she murmured:

'I don't see anyone who shouldn't be here.'

Her nose was red because of the cold, and the rain had washed off her face powder. The four cousins also had shiny noses and cheeks.

Maigret and Neveu hung around for a little while outside the gate, then they went into the dingy little bar opposite, and Maigret ordered two glasses of hot toddy. They were not the only ones. A few minutes later, half the people who had attended the funeral poured into the little bar, stamping their feet on the tiled floor to get their circulation going.

There was a great deal of chatter, but Maigret was struck by one remark only:

'Will she get a pension?'

Her sisters certainly would, because their husbands

worked on the railways. In short, Monsieur Louis had always been the poor relation. Not only had he been a lowly storekeeper, he had also had no pension rights.

'How will they manage?'

'The daughter has a job. They'll take in a lodger, I daresay.'

'Coming Neveu?'

The rain dogged them all the way to Paris, where it was lashing the pavements. There were thick moustaches of muddy water on the windscreens of all the cars.

'Where do you want to be dropped, Neveu?'

'There's no point in going home to change. I'll still have to wear the same wet coat. Drop me at the Quai. I'll take a taxi on from there.'

The corridors of Police Headquarters were covered in wet footprints, like the tiled floor of the church. Here, too, it was damp and cold. A man wearing handcuffs was sitting on a bench outside the office of the Chief Superintendent of the Gaming Squad.

'Anything new, Lucas?'

'Lapointe telephoned from the *Brasserie de la République*. He's found the room.'

'The room rented by Louis?'

'So he says, although apparently the landlady is being anything but co-operative.'

'Does he want me to ring him back?'

'Either that, or that you should meet him there.'

Maigret preferred the second alternative. There was nothing he disliked more than sitting in his office in wet clothes.

'Any other news?'

'Only a false alarm about the young man. They thought they'd picked him up in the waiting-room of the Gare Montparnasse. It wasn't him, just some other fellow who fitted the description.'

Maigret returned to the little black car, and within a few minutes was going through the door of the *brasserie* in the Place de la République, where he found Lapointe sitting beside the stove, having a cup of coffee. Maigret ordered another hot toddy for himself. He felt as if a good deal of the icy rain that had been falling had poured into his nostrils. He felt sure he was going to get a cold. Maybe he was just going along with the old superstition that one always catches cold at a funeral.

'Where is this place?'

'Only a few yards from here. I came upon it quite by chance, because it isn't registered as a lodging house with furnished rooms to let.'

'Are you sure it's the right place?'

'You can ask the landlady yourself. I was going along the Rue d'Angoulême, cutting across from one boulevard to another, when I saw a *Room to Let* sign in a window. It was a small house. There was no concierge. I rang the bell and asked to see the room. It was the landlady herself who opened the door to me. She's an elderly woman. She must have been a red-head in her youth, and possibly a beauty. But her hair is thin and faded now, and her body looked flabby under the sky-blue dressing-gown she was wearing.

' "Is it for yourself?" she asked, with the door still on the chain. "Are you on your own?"

'I heard a door on the floor above, and then I caught a glimpse of a very pretty girl leaning over the banister. She was in a dressing-gown too.'

'A brothel?'

'I wouldn't go as far as that, but it wouldn't surprise me to learn that the landlady had worked in a brothel at some time, perhaps as an assistant to the Madame.

' "Are you thinking of renting it by the month? Whereabouts do you work?"

'I persuaded her in the end to show me the room, which was on the second floor. It overlooks the courtyard, and the furniture isn't too bad. A bit overstuffed for my taste, with lots of cheap velvet and silk about it, and a doll on the divan bed. There were still lingering traces of a woman's scent.

' "Who gave you my address?"

'I nearly let out that I had read the sign in the window. All the time we were talking, I could see a flabby breast seemingly about to escape from her dressing-gown at any minute, and it bothered me.

' "You were recommended to me by a friend," I said at last.

'On the off-chance, I added: "He said he lived here."

' "What's his name?"

' "Monsieur Louis."

'It was then that I realized that she knew him. Her face changed. Even her voice sounded different.

' "Never heard of him!" she said curtly. "Are you in the habit of coming in late?"

'She couldn't wait to get rid of me.

' "I thought my friend might be here now," I said, playing the innocent. "He doesn't work in the day time, and he usually gets up late."

' "Do you want the room, or don't you?"

' "I do want it, but . . ."

' "The rent is payable in advance."

'I took out my wallet, and then, as if coming on it by accident, I produced the photograph of Monsieur Louis.

' "Would you believe it! Here's a photograph of the friend I mentioned."

'She barely glanced at it.

' "I somehow don't think you and I would get on together," she declared, making for the door.

' "But . . ."

' "I hope you don't mind seeing yourself out. If I don't hurry, my dinner will be spoilt."

'I'm certain she knew him. As I went out, I saw a curtain twitch. I fancy she was more than a little jumpy.'

'Let's go!' said Maigret.

Although it was no distance, they got into the car, which drew up opposite the house. Once again, the curtain twitched. The woman who came to the door was still not dressed, and no colour could have been more unbecoming to her than the blue of her dressing-gown.

'Who's there?'

'The *Police Judiciaire*.'

'What do you want? I knew that young imp of Satan was going to make trouble for me!' she grumbled, giving Lapointe a dirty look.

'We could talk better inside.'

'Well, I'm not stopping you. I have nothing to hide.'

'Why did you deny that Monsieur Louis was your lodger?'

'Because that young man had no business to be snooping around here.'

She opened a door leading to a little sitting-room. It was overheated, and there were garish cushions scattered about everywhere, embroidered with cats, hearts, and musical notes. As the drawn curtains were so thick as to exclude almost all the daylight, she switched on a standard lamp with a huge orange shade.

'What exactly do you want of me?'

Maigret, in his turn, showed her a photograph of Monsieur Louis, whose funeral he had attended that morning.

'He did rent a room here, didn't he?'

'Yes. I suppose you were bound to find out sooner or later.'

'How long was he with you?'

'About two years. Maybe longer.'

'Do you have many?'

'Lodgers, you mean? This house is too big for a woman living alone. And it's not easy nowadays finding somewhere to live.'

'How many?'

'Three, at the moment.'

'And one room vacant?'

'Yes. The one I showed this young fellow here. I should have been more careful.'

'What can you tell me about Monsieur Louis?'

'Only that he was a quiet sort of man. He never gave any trouble. And as he worked at night . . .'

'Do you know where he worked?'

'As it was no concern of mine, I never bothered to ask him. He used to leave at night and return in the morning. He didn't seem to need much sleep. I often told him he didn't get enough, but apparently it's the same with all night workers.'

'Did he have many visitors?'

'What exactly are you getting at?'

'You read the papers. . . .'

There was a morning paper open on a table.

'I see what you mean. But first I have to be sure that you're not going to make trouble for me. I know the police and their methods.'

Maigret was certain that, if they were to look through the Vice Squad records, they would find a file on this woman.

'I do take in lodgers, but I don't shout it from the house-tops, and I don't tell tales about them to the police. It's not a crime. All the same, if I'm going to have any trouble. . . .'

'That depends on you.'

'Have I your word for that? To start with, what is your rank?'

'I am Chief Superintendent Maigret.'

'Right then! Now I know where I stand! It must be more serious than I thought. It's your colleagues in the Vice Squad who . . .'

She came out with an expression so coarse that Lapointe felt himself blushing.

'I admit I know he's been murdered. But that's all I do know.'

'What did he say his name was?'

'Monsieur Louis. Just that.'

'There was a woman who used to visit him, a dark woman, past her first youth.'

'A fine-looking woman, not a day over forty. She was a real lady.'

'Did she come often?'

'Three or four times a week.'

'Do you know her name?'

'I knew her only as Madame Antoinette.'

'You seem to make a habit of calling people only by their first names.'

'I don't pry into other people's business, if that's what you mean.'

'Used she to stay with him long?'

'As long as was necessary.'

'The whole afternoon?'

'On two occasions, yes. Usually she didn't stay more than an hour or two.'

'Did she ever come in the morning?'

'No. Well, perhaps she may have done once or twice, but not often.'

'Have you got her address?'

'I never asked her.'

'Are all your other lodgers women?'

'Yes. Monsieur Louis was the only man who . . .'

'Did he never have relations with any of them?'

'Do you mean did he ever make love to them? If that's what you're getting at, no, he didn't. He just didn't seem keen, that's all. If he'd wanted to . . .'

'Was he friendly with them?'

'He used to talk to them. They'd often knock on his door, to borrow a match or a cigarette, or to look at his newspaper.'

'Is that all?'

'They chatted to him. And occasionally he'd play a two-handed game of *belote* with Lucille.'

'Is Lucille up there now?'

'She's been out on the tiles for the past two days. It often happens. I daresay she's found some man to shack up with. You've promised not to make trouble for me, remember? And the same applies to my lodgers.'

He did not remind her that he had made no promises of any kind.

'Did he never have any other visitors?'

'There was one who called two or three times quite recently, asking for him.'

'A young girl?'

'Yes. She never went up to his room. She just asked me to tell him she was here.'

'Did she give her name?'

'Monique. She always waited out in the hall. She wouldn't even come into the sitting-room.'

'Did he come down?'

'The first time they talked in whispers for a few minutes, and then she left. The other times, they went out together.'

'Didn't he tell you who she was?'

'He just asked me if I thought she was pretty.'

'What did you say to that?'

'That she was quite sweet, as girls of her age go nowadays, but that she'd be a real stunner in a few years' time.'

'Who else came to see him?'

'Won't you sit down?'

'No thanks. I'm soaking wet, and I wouldn't want to ruin your cushions.'

'I like to keep everything just so, as far as possible. Wait a minute. There was someone else, a young man, but he didn't give his name. When I went up to tell Monsieur Louis that he was here, he seemed a little upset. He asked me to show him up. The young man only stayed about ten minutes.'

'How long ago was that?'

'It was in the middle of August. I remember because of the heat and the flies.'

'Did you ever see him again?'

'On one occasion they came into the house together. I got the impression that they'd met by chance in the street. They went upstairs, but the young man left almost at once.'

'Is that all?'

'Isn't that enough for you? Now, I suppose you'll be wanting to see his room as well?'

'Yes.'

'It's on the second floor, the room opposite the one I showed to your underling here. It looks out on to the street, and we call it the green room.'

'I'd be obliged if you would come with us.'

She sighed, and went on sighing all the way up the two flights of stairs.

'Don't forget, you promised. . . .'

He shrugged.

'And what's more, if you try any dirty tricks with me, I'll tell the court that everything you say is a pack of lies.'

'Have you got the key?'

On the floor below, inside a half-open door, he had seen a young woman. She had stared at them, standing there stark naked with a bath towel in her hand.

'I have a pass-key.'

And turning back, she called over the stairs:

'Don't worry, Yvette, it's not the Vice Squad!'

# 5. The Policeman's Widow

ALL THE FURNITURE in the room must have been bought sometime at a local auction. It was made of 'solid' walnut in a style fashionable fifty or sixty years ago, and included an enormous mirror-fronted wardrobe.

The first thing that struck Maigret as he went in was a canary in a cage, on a table covered with a printed cotton cloth. As soon as he appeared, the bird began hopping about excitedly.

It reminded Maigret of Monsieur Saimbron's place on the Quai de la Mégisserie, and he was convinced that the old book-keeper's bird had been a present from Louis Thouret.

'Did the bird belong to him?'

'He brought it here about a year ago. He was cheated over it, because it doesn't sing. He was told it was a male bird, but in fact it's a female.'

'Who does the housework?'

'I let furnished rooms. I provide linen, but no service. I used to in the old days, but I had a lot of trouble with maids. As my lodgers are nearly all women . . .'

'Did Monsieur Louis clean his own room?'

'He made his bed, cleaned the wash basin, and dusted around. Once a week, as a special favour to him, I used to go up and do a little extra cleaning and polishing.'

She remained standing in the doorway, and the Chief Superintendent found this a little disconcerting. In his eyes this was no ordinary room. It was the place that Monsieur Louis had chosen as a retreat. In other words, his furnishings and possessions were not, as is usual, just the ordinary necessities of life, but an expression of his own personal, intimate tastes.

In the glass-fronted wardrobe there was not a single three-piece suit, but there were three pairs of light-brown shoes, lovingly polished to a high gloss, each pair with its own shoe-trees. Furthermore, on the bedside table lay a pearl-grey hat, almost new, which he must have bought one day in a fit of wild extravagance, as a protest against the atmosphere of the house in Juvisy.

'Did he ever go to the races?'

'I don't think so. He never mentioned racing.'

'Did he talk to you much?'

'Sometimes, in passing, he would come into the sitting-room for a chat.'

'Was he generally cheerful?'

'He seemed to enjoy life.'

Also by way of flouting his wife's notions of good taste, he had bought himself a flowered dressing-gown and a pair of scarlet kid slippers.

The room was tidy, with everything in its proper place, and not a speck of dust anywhere. In a cupboard, Maigret found an open bottle of port and two wine glasses on stems. And, hanging from a hook, a raincoat.

He had not thought of that. If a rainy day should be followed by a fine evening, Monsieur Louis couldn't risk arriving home with wet clothes.

Clearly, he had spent hours reading. On the chest of drawers stood a whole row of books in cheap editions, popular novels, cloak and dagger romances, and one or two detective stories. Maigret suspected that he had not cared for these, since he had not added to his store.

His armchair was placed near the window. Next to it was a small table, on which stood a photograph of a woman in a mahogany frame. She was about forty, with very dark hair, and was dressed in black. She fitted the description given by the jeweller's assistant. She seemed tall, about the same height as Madame Thouret, big-boned as she was, and almost equally lacking in suppleness. She was what the people of the neighbourhood would no doubt call a fine figure of a woman.

'Is she the one who came to see him fairly regularly?'

'Yes.'

In the drawer he found some other photographs, poly-fotos mostly, including a somewhat blurred one of Monsieur Louis himself, wearing the pearl-grey hat.

Apart from two pairs of socks and several ties, there were no personal possessions to be seen, no shirts or pants, no papers of any sort, no old letters; in fact, none of the usual clutter which tends to fill up most people's drawers.

Maigret, recalling the many occasions in his childhood when he had something he wanted to hide from his family, picked up a chair and carried it across to the glass-fronted wardrobe. He climbed on to it to take a look at the top of the wardrobe. As in most houses, it was covered in a thick layer of dust, but plainly to be seen in the middle was a large, clean rectangle, where something like a big envelope or a book, or perhaps a box, had recently lain.

He made no comment. The woman was watching him intently, and, just as Lapointe had said, one of her breasts, always the same one, limp and soggy as dough, seemed to be on the point of slipping out of her dressing-gown.

'Did he have a key to this room?'

The only key found on him had been the key of his house in Juvisy.

'Yes, he did, but he always left it with me when he went out.'

'Is that common practice?'

'No. He said he had a habit of losing things, so he'd rather I kept it for him, and gave it to him when he got in. And as he never came in in the evening, or late at night . . .'

Maigret took the photograph out of its frame. Before leaving, he gave the canary some fresh drinking water, and wandered about the room for a few more minutes.

'I'll be back soon, I daresay,' he said.

She led him downstairs.

'I suppose I can't tempt you to a little something to drink?'

'Are you on the telephone? I'd be obliged if you'd let me have your number. I may need to call on you for assistance again.'

'It's Bastille 2251.'

'What's your name?'

'Mariette. Mariette Gibon.'

'Thanks.'

'Is that all?'

'For the moment.'

He and Lapointe almost had to swim to the car through the rain, which was still pelting down.

'Drive us to the corner,' ordered Maigret.

216

And to Lapointe:

'You'll have to go back there. I'm afraid I forgot my pipe in the room upstairs.'

Maigret had never forgotten his pipe anywhere. And besides, he never carried less than two in his pockets.

'Did you do it on purpose?'

'Yes. Keep the glamorous Mariette talking for a few minutes, and then come back and join me here.'

He pointed to a little bar, which also sold coal and logs. He himself made a dash for the telephone, and dialled the number of Police Headquarters.

'Put me through to Lucas, please. . . . Is that you, Lucas? I want you to make arrangements immediately to have this telephone number tapped: Bastille 2251.'

Then, as he had nothing to do while waiting for Lapointe but to sip his liqueur at the bar counter, he took a closer look at the photograph. It surprised him that Louis should have picked on a mistress who, outwardly at least, so closely resembled his wife. He wondered if there was any similarity of temperament. It was not impossible.

'Your pipe, Chief.'

'Was she, by any chance, on the telephone when you arrived?'

'I don't know. She had two women with her.'

'Including the naked girl?'

'Yes, but she had slipped on a dressing-gown.'

'You can go off to lunch now. I'll see you at the Quai this afternoon. I'll keep the car.'

He told the driver to take him to Léone's little shop in the Rue de Clignancourt. On the way. he stopped at a confectioner's to buy a box of chocolates. He hid it under his coat, before crossing the pavement to get into the car. He felt that the last place he should be visiting with his clothes sopping wet was a shop like this one, overflowing with so many light and fragile garments. But he had no choice. Awkwardly he held out the box of chocolates, saying:

'For your mother.'

'How kind of you to think of her.'

Probably on account of the humidity, the place was even hotter than last time.

'Wouldn't you like to give them to her yourself?'

He preferred to remain in the shop, which had at least some slight contact with the world outside.

'I just wanted you to take a look at this photograph.' She glanced at it, and said, without hesitation:

'Why, it's Madame Machère!'

This was most satisfactory. It wasn't a sensational discovery, such as the newspapers revel in. It was nothing really, but it did prove that he had not been mistaken in his assessment of Monsieur Louis's character. He was not the sort of man to pick up a woman on the street or in a bar. The Chief Superintendent could not see him making advances to a strange woman.

'How did you get to know her?'

'She worked at Kaplan's. Not for very long, though. Only about six or seven months. Why did you want me to see her photograph?'

'She was a very close friend of Monsieur Louis.'

'Oh!'

He would have spared her the pain if he could, but there was no way of avoiding it.

'Didn't you suspect anything when they were both working in the Rue de Bondy?'

'There was nothing to suspect, I'm sure of it. She worked with ten to fifteen other women in the packing room, depending on the time of year. She was married to a policeman. I remember her well.'

'Why did she leave the job?'

'I believe she needed to have an operation.'

'Thank you. Please forgive me for troubling you again.'

'It's no trouble. Have you been to see Monsieur Saimbron?'

'Yes.'

'One other question. Was Monsieur Louis living with that woman?'

'He had rented a room near the Place de la République. She used to visit him there. I'm convinced that she was just a friend, and that there was nothing else between them.'

'You may be right.'

'If the business records haven't been destroyed, I could

218

find out her address for you, but I have no idea what's become of them.'

'If, as you say, she's the wife of a policeman, I shouldn't have any difficulty in tracing her. You did say the name was Machère, didn't you?'

'Yes, and if my memory serves me right, her first name was Antoinette.'

'Au revoir, Mademoiselle Léone.'

'Au revoir, Chief Superintendent.'

He beat a hasty retreat. The old woman in the back room was showing signs of agitation, and he just couldn't face having to go in there to see her.

'The *Préfecture*.'

'At the Quai?'

'No. The one at City Police Headquarters.'

It was midday. The people pouring out of shops and offices teetered on the edge of the pavements, waiting for a chance to dash across the road to their favourite restaurants. There were groups of people sheltering in every doorway. They all looked glum but resigned. On the news-stands, the papers were all sodden.

'Wait here for me.'

He found his way to the office of the Head of Personnel, and asked for information about a man of the name of Machère. A few minutes later, he learned that there had been a police constable called Machère, but that he had been killed in a scuffle in the line of duty two years before. At that time, he had been living in the Avenue Daumesnil. His widow was in receipt of a pension. The couple had had no children.

Maigret made a note of the address. To gain time, he telephoned Lucas, which saved him having to cross the road from one side of the Boulevard du Palais to the other.

'Has she made any telephone calls?'

'Not so far.'

'Hasn't she received any calls either?'

'Not for her. Someone rang asking to speak to one of the girls, name of Olga. Something to do with a fitting. We checked that the call really was from a dressmaker, one of those in the Place Saint-Georges.'

He would eat later. For the time being, he made do with an aperitif, which he gulped down in a bar, before returning to the little black car.

'Avenue Daumesnil.'

It was some distance away, not far from the Metro. It was a very ordinary building, somewhat seedy by now, and no doubt mainly occupied by small tradespeople.

'Could you please direct me to Madame Machère's flat?'

'Fourth floor, left-hand side.'

There was a lift, but it ascended in jerks, being inclined to stop several times between each floor. The brass bell beside the door was brightly polished, and the doormat clean. He pressed the bell. He could hear footsteps coming towards him.

'One minute!' a woman called through the door.

No doubt she was changing from a housecoat into a dress. She wasn't the sort of woman to show herself in a dressing-gown, even to the man who came to read the gas meter.

She looked at Maigret without speaking, but he could tell that she was upset.

'Please come in, Chief Superintendent.'

She looked just like her photographs. The jeweller's assistant had accurately described her as being tall and heavily built, with a serene expression and a good deal of self-assurance. She had recognized Maigret. And, needless to say, she knew why he had come.

'This way. . . . I was in the middle of doing my house-work. . . .'

In spite of that, her hair was neatly brushed, and she was wearing a dark dress with every button fastened. The floor boards gleamed. Next to the door were two felt pads, which she no doubt slipped under her feet whenever she came in with wet shoes.

'I'm afraid I'm leaving dirty marks all over the place.'

'It doesn't matter.'

The interior, though older and better kept, was very similar to that of the house in Juvisy. There were the same sort of ornaments on top of the furniture, and on the dresser stood a framed photograph of a police constable, with a medal attached to it.

He had no wish to embarrass her, or to take her by surprise. Anyway, there was no question of surprise. He said simply: 'I've come to talk to you about Louis.'

'I've been expecting you.'

Although she looked sad, there were no tears in her eyes. She was preserving a decent composure.

'Please sit down.'

'I'm afraid I'll make your chair cover all wet. You and Louis Thouret were very good friends, were you not?'

'He was fond of me.'

'No more than that?'

'It could have been that he loved me. He'd never been happy at home.'

'Did your relationship begin when you were both working in the Rue de Bondy?'

'Aren't you forgetting that my husband was still alive at that time?'

'Was Louis particularly attentive to you?'

'He never treated me any differently from any of the other women in the packing department.'

'So it wasn't until later, after the firm of Kaplan had gone out of business, that you really got to know one another?'

'It was eight or nine months after my husband's death.'

'Did you meet again just by chance?'

'You know as well as I do that a widow's pension isn't enough to live on. I had to find work. Even when my husband was alive, I took a job every now and then. That's how I came to be working at Kaplan's. But I never worked full-time. Anyway, one of my neighbours introduced me to the personnel officer of the *Châtelet*, and I was taken on to show people to their seats.'

'Is that where . . . ?'

'Yes. It was a matinee. The play was *Round the World in Eighty Days*, I remember. I was showing Monsieur Louis to his seat, when I suddenly realized who he was. He recognized me, too. And that was all there was to it. But he came back to the theatre often, always for the matinee, and he got into the way of looking out for me. This went on for quite some time, because, apart from Sundays, there were only two matinees a week. Then one day, after the show, he invited me to have an aperitif with him, and I accepted. We ate a hurried snack together, because I had to get back in time for the evening performance.'

'Had he, at that time, already taken the room in the Rue d'Angoulême?'

'I imagine so.'

'Did he tell you that he had no job?'

'He didn't say that, just that he was free in the afternoon.'

'Did you ever find out what he did for a living?'

'No. I didn't feel it was my place to ask.'

'Did he talk much about his wife and daughter?'

'A great deal.'

'What did he say?'

'It's not the sort of thing one cares to repeat, you know. When a man is unhappy in his home life, and confides in one. . . .'

'Was he unhappy at home?'

'They treated him like dirt, on account of his brothers-in-law.'

'I don't quite understand.'

Maigret understood perfectly well, and had done for some time, but he wanted to encourage her to talk.

'They both had very good jobs, with free travel for themselves and their families thrown in. . . .'

'And a pension at the end of it.'

'Yes. They despised Louis for his lack of ambition, and his willingness to spend the rest of his life as a miserable storekeeper.'

'When he took you out, where did you go?'

'Almost always to the same little café in the Rue Saint-Antoine. We used to stay there for hours, just chatting.'

'Do you like waffles?'

She blushed.

'How did you guess?'

'He used to buy them for you in the Rue de la Lune.'

'That was much later, when . . .'

'When you began visiting him in the Rue d'Angoulême?'

'Yes. He wanted me to see the place where he spent so much of his time. He called it his den. He was very proud of it.'

'Did he ever tell you what made him decide to take a room in town?'

'Just so as he could have somewhere he could call his own, if only for a few hours a day.'

'Did you become lovers, eventually?'

'I often went to his room.'

'Did he ever buy you jewellery?'

'Just a pair of drop ear-rings about six months ago, and, more recently, a ring.'

She was wearing it.

'He was too kind, too sensitive. He needed cheering up. Whatever you may think, I was, first and foremost, his friend, the only friend he had.'

'Did he ever come and see you here?'

'Never! It wouldn't have done, on account of the concierge and the neighbours. It would have been the talk of the district in no time.'

'Did you see him on Monday?'

'I was with him for about an hour.'

'What time of day was that?'

'Early afternoon. I was out shopping.'

'Did you know where to find him?'

'We had arranged to meet.'

'On the telephone?'

'No. I never telephoned him. We fixed it up when I was with him the time before.'

'Where used you to meet?'

'Nearly always at our usual little café. Sometimes on the corner, at the junction of the Rue Saint-Martin and the Grands Boulevards.'

'Was he on time?'

'He was never late. On Monday, it was cold and foggy. I have a sensitive throat. We went to a news cinema.'

'In the Boulevard Bonne-Nouvelle?'

'How did you know?'

'What time did you part?'

'Round about four. Half an hour or so before he died, according to the newspapers.'

'Did you know he was going to meet someone?'

'He said nothing about it to me.'

'Did he never mention any people he went about with?'

She shook her head. Looking towards the glass-fronted dresser in the dining-room, she said, 'Would you care for a drink? I only have a little Vermouth. I gave up drinking myself a long time ago.'

To please her, he accepted. There was a thick sediment at the bottom of the bottle, which, no doubt, had been there since the late police constable's time.

'When I read about it in the paper, I almost went to see you. I'd heard a lot about you from my husband. I recognized you at once just now, because I've often seen photographs of you in the papers.'

'Did Louis ever consider getting a divorce and marrying you?'

'He was too scared of his wife.'

'And his daughter?'

'He was very fond of his daughter. There's nothing he wouldn't have done for her. All the same, I had the feeling that he was a little disappointed in her.'

'Why?'

'It was no more than an impression. He often seemed sad.'

She wasn't all that cheerful herself, with her monotonous, uninflected voice. He wondered if she was the one who had polished the furniture for him in the course of her visits to the Rue d'Angoulême.

He couldn't imagine her undressing in Louis's presence, and stretching out on the bed. He couldn't even imagine her naked or wearing just a bra and briefs. To his way of thinking, they must have been most at home together sitting at a table in a dark corner of their little café, as she called it, talking in undertones, and glancing from time to time at the clock over the bar.

'Did he spend money freely?'

'It depends what you mean by freely. He didn't stint himself. One had the feeling that he was comfortably off. If I had let him, he would have loaded me with presents, mostly the sort of useless fripperies one sees in gift shops.'

'Did you ever come across him sitting on a bench?'

'On a bench?' she repeated, as though the question somehow troubled her.

She hesitated.

'Once, when I was shopping in the morning. He was in conversation with a man, a thin man. I felt that there was something odd about him.'

'In what way?'

'He reminded me, I don't quite know why, of a clown or a comic without the make-up. I didn't really see his face, but I noticed that his shoes were worn, and the bottoms of his trousers frayed.'

'Did you ask Louis about him?'

'Yes. He said one came across all sorts of people sitting on benches, and he enjoyed talking to them.'

'And that's all you know? By the way, I'm surprised you didn't go to the funeral.'

'I didn't dare show my face. In a day or two, I shall go and put some flowers on his grave. I presume there will be someone to show me where it is? Will the newspapers have to be told about me?'

'Certainly not.'

'That's a great relief. They're very strait-laced at the *Châtelet*, and they wouldn't hesitate to sack me.'

It wasn't all that far to the Boulevard Richard-Lenoir, so after he had left the widow, he got the driver to run him home, and said:

'You'd better go off and get some lunch. Come back here for me in about an hour.'

During lunch, his wife watched him more closely than was her wont. In the end, she plucked up the courage to ask:

'What's the matter?'

'What should be the matter?'

'I don't know. You don't seem like yourself, but like someone quite different.'

'Who for instance?'

'It might be anyone. But it's certainly not Maigret.'

He laughed. He had been thinking so much about Louis that he had begun to behave in the way that he imagined Louis would have behaved, even to the extent of aping what he supposed to have been his facial expressions and mannerisms.

'I hope you're going to change your suit?'

'What's the use? I'll be soaking wet again in no time.'

'Why? Are you going to another funeral?'

He decided to give in, and changed into the clothes she had laid out for him. It was a pleasant sensation, he had to admit, to be wearing dry things again for however short a time.

At the Quai des Orfèvres he did not go straight to his office, but looked in on the Vice Squad first.

'Do you know anyone by the name of Mariette or Marie Gibon? I'd be very grateful if you'd have a look through your records.'

'Is she young?'

'Fiftyish.'

Without further delay, the Inspector got out several boxes filled with dusty, yellowing registration forms. He did not have to look far. The Gibon girl, born in Saint-Malo, had been a licensed prostitute for eleven years. She had been referred three times to Saint-Lazare, in the days before it was closed down. She had been arrested twice for stealing from clients.

'Was she convicted?'

'She was released for lack of evidence.'

'Anything else?'

'Just a second. I'll have a look through this other box.'

Her name appeared again on more recent registration forms, but all were at least ten years old.

'Before the war, she was assistant manageress at a massage parlour in the Rue des Martyrs. At that time she was living with a man called Philippe Natali, otherwise known as Philippi, who was sentenced to ten years for murder. I remember the case. It was a gang killing. Two or three men killed a bloke from a rival gang, in a tobacconist's in the Rue de la Fontaine. It was never established who actually fired the shot, so they nabbed them all.'

'Is he still in prison?'

'He died in Fontevrault.'

That didn't help matters.

'And what became of her?'

'Don't know. She may be dead too. . . .'

'She isn't.'

'She must have had quite a packet salted away. She's probably set up an establishment of her own in her home town.'

'She lets furnished rooms in the Rue d'Angoulême. She's not registered with the Licensed Premises people. Most of her tenants are girls, but I don't think they ply their trade on the premises.'

'That makes sense.'

'I'd like a watch kept on the house, and as much information as possible about the inmates.'

'That shouldn't be difficult.'

'I'd prefer to have someone from the Vice Squad on the job. My men couldn't be sure of identifying the people involved.'

'I'll see to it.'

At last Maigret was able to sit down, or rather collapse into the armchair in his office. No sooner was he comfortably settled than Lucas put his head round the door.

'Any news?'

'Nothing on the telephone front. There have been no outgoing calls. But there was one rather odd incident this morning. A woman by the name of Madame Thévenard, who lives with her nephew in the Rue Gay-Lussac, went out to attend a funeral.'

'Really?'

'Not the same funeral. This took place in a local cemetery. The flat was empty while she was out. When she got home, having done her household shopping on the way back, she went into her larder to put her provisions away, and discovered that a sausage which had been there two hours previously had disappeared.'

'Is she quite sure. . . ?'

'Absolutely sure. And besides, when she had a good look round the flat . . .'

'Wasn't she frightened?'

'She had an old service revolver in her hand. Her husband had kept it from the First World War. Apparently, she's an odd sort of woman, very tiny and plump, and she never stops laughing. She says she found a handkerchief that doesn't belong to him under her nephew's bed, and a few crumbs.'

'What does the nephew do?'

'He's a student, and his Christian name is Hubert. As the Thévenards aren't all that well off, he works in the daytime as an assistant in the bookshop in the Boulevard Saint-Michel. Do you see what I'm driving at?'

'Yes. Did the aunt notify the police?'

'Yes. She telephoned the local station from the lodge. The Inspector who took the call got in touch with me straight away. I sent Leroy off to the bookshop, to see what he could get out of Hubert. The lad was shaking all over, and then he burst into tears.'

'Is he a friend of Albert Jorisse?'

'Yes, and Jorisse pleaded with him, until he agreed to hide him in his room for a few days.'

'What did Jorisse say was the matter?'

'He said he'd quarrelled with his parents, and that his father had such a fearful temper, he was quite capable of doing him a serious mischief.'

'And so Hubert agreed to let him spend two days and nights hidden under his bed?'

'No. He was only there twenty-four hours. He spent the first night wandering about the streets, or so he told his friend. I've notified all police stations. The kid must be out and about somewhere in the town.'

'Has he any money?'

'Hubert Thévenard couldn't say.'

'Have you alerted all the railway stations?'

'I think we've provided for everything, Chief. I'd be surprised if he wasn't brought in sometime between now and tomorrow morning.'

He wondered what the family was doing in Juvisy. No doubt the widow's sisters, along with their husbands and daughters, had rallied round. They had probably all dined there, in the house of mourning. A substantial meal, without a doubt, as was only fitting after a funeral. They must have discussed Madame Thouret's future, and Monique's as well.

Maigret could just see them, the two men lounging in the best armchairs, with drinks and good cigars.

'Do have a drop of something, Emilie. It will do you good.'

Had they talked of the dead man? Probably someone had remarked that, in spite of the shocking weather, the funeral had been well attended.

Maigret was almost tempted to go and see for himself. He was particularly anxious to have a serious talk with Monique. But not at her home. At the same time, he was reluctant to summon her officially.

Almost without thinking, he asked the operator to put him through to her place of work.

'Are you Geber et Bachelier?'

'Georges Bachelier speaking.'

'I wonder if you are expecting Mademoiselle Thouret to be back at work tomorrow morning?'

'Certainly. She had today off to attend to family matters, but I can't see any reason why she shouldn't . . . Who is that speaking?'

Maigret hung up.

'Isn't Santoni back yet?'

'He hasn't been in since early this morning.'

'Leave him a note, will you, telling him that I want a watch kept, from first thing tomorrow morning, on the entrance to Geber et Bachelier. As soon as Mademoiselle Thouret arrives, I want her brought here. Tell him to treat her gently.'

'You want her brought here?'

'Yes, to my office.'

'Anything else?'

'No, nothing. I shall be working in here for a time. I don't want to be disturbed.'

He had had enough of one day of Louis Thouret, his family and his mistress. If it hadn't been for his sense of duty, he would have walked straight out and gone to a cinema.

He stayed until seven, ploughing through a mass of paperwork as if the fate of the world depended on it. Not only did he polish off everything in his pending tray, he also dealt with several files that had been kicking around for weeks or even months, and which were of no importance whatsoever.

When finally he left, his vision blurred from having spent so long poring over print and typescript, he was aware of a change. At first, he couldn't think what it was. Then he held out his hand, and realized that it was no longer raining. He felt an odd sense of deprivation.

## 6. The Beggars

'WHAT'S SHE DOING?'

'Nothing. She's sitting bolt upright, with her head held high, staring into space.'

She had chosen to sit not in one of the armchairs in the waiting-room but on a hard upright chair.

Maigret had intentionally left her to stew, as he put it. When Santoni had looked in at about twenty-past nine to tell him that Monique was in the waiting-room, Maigret had growled, 'Leave her in the cage for a while.'

This was his name for the glass-walled waiting-room, with its velvet armchairs, where so many before Monique Thouret had sat for hours, until their nerve gave way.

'How does she look?'

'She's wearing mourning.'

'That's not what I meant.'

'I almost had the feeling that she'd been expecting to find me there. I waited a few yards from the door of the offices in the Rue de Rivoli. As soon as she arrived, I came forward to meet her, saying:

' "Excuse me Mademoiselle. . . ."'

'She screwed up her eyes and peered at me. I think she must be short-sighted. Then she said:

' "Oh! It's you."'

' "The Chief Superintendent would like a word with you."'

'She didn't protest. I hailed a taxi. She never opened her mouth all the way here.'

Not only was it not raining, but the sun was actually shining. The light seemed even more diffused than usual, because of the humidity in the air.

Maigret, on his way to the daily briefing, had seen her in the distance, sitting in a corner of the waiting-room. Half an hour later, when he passed by on his way back to his office, she was still there, exactly as before. Some time after that, he had sent Lucas to see what she was doing.

'Is she reading?'

'No. She's not doing anything.'

From where she sat, her view of Police Headquarters was similar to the view of a restaurant as seen from the kitchen area. She could see the long corridor with its many doors, and the inspectors coming and going, with files under their arms, visiting one another in their different rooms, and then returning to their own offices. Occasionally, they would stop in their tracks to discuss some current problem with a colleague, and from time to time one would arrive escorting a handcuffed prisoner or a weeping woman.

Other people, who had arrived long after she had, had already been interviewed by those whom they had come to see, yet she still showed no signs of impatience.

The telephone in the Rue d'Angoulême remained silent. Did Mariette Gibon suspect that it was being tapped?

Maybe the ruse of pretending he had forgotten his pipe had put the wind up her?

Neveu, who had by now been relieved by a local colleague, reported that he had observed nothing unusual while keeping watch on the house.

As for Albert Jorisse, it was now practically certain that he had still been in Paris at six o'clock the previous night. Police Constable Dambois, who, like everyone else, had been issued with a description of him, had spotted him round about that time at the junction of the Place Clichy and the Boulevard des Batignolles. The young man had been coming out of a bar. Had the constable perhaps been too eager in his attempt to apprehend him? At any rate, Jorisse had made a run for it, and was soon lost in the crowd, which was particularly dense at that time of the evening. The constable had blown his whistle to summon help.

But, inevitably, it had been to no avail. They had combed the area, in vain. They had questioned the proprietor of the café, who had told them that the young man had not used the telephone, but that he had wolfed down five hard-boiled eggs with buttered rolls, and drunk three cups of coffee.

'He looked famished to me.'

Judge Coméliau had been on to Maigret.

'Any fresh news?'

'I'm hoping to be in a position to arrest the murderer within the next couple of days.'

'Was it a mugging, as we thought?'

He had said yes.

There was still the business of the knife to be settled. A letter had arrived by the morning post from the firm who manufactured them. As a first step in his inquiries, Janvier had personally gone to see one of the high-ups in the firm, only to be told that there was no way of finding out which hardware shop had been supplied with that particular knife. With considerable pride, he had quoted to Janvier the astronomic figure representing the number of such knives made in their factories.

Now someone with the words *Joint Managing Director* typed beneath his signature had written to the Chief Commissioner to inform him that, according to the serial number on the handle, the murder weapon had formed part of a consignment of knives delivered about four months ago to a wholesaler in Marseilles.

So five inspectors had wasted three days combing the hardware shops of Paris. Janvier was hopping mad.

'What should I do next, Chief?'

'Pass the word to Marseilles. Next, get hold of Moers or someone else from the Forensic Lab, go with him to the Rue d'Angoulême, and get him to fingerprint Louis Thouret's room. Tell him not to forget to give the top of the glass-fronted wardrobe a thorough going-over.'

During all this time, Monique was still waiting. Every now and then, Maigret sent someone to have another look at her.

'What's she doing?'

'Nothing.'

He had seen people much tougher than she was reduced to nervous wrecks after an hour of waiting in the glass-walled cage.

By a quarter to eleven, he could stand no more of it.

'Send her in,' he said, with a sigh.

He stood up as she came in, and apologized for keeping her waiting.

'As I am anxious that we should have a long talk, I thought it best to get my paperwork out of the way first.'

'I quite understand.'

'Do please sit down.'

She did so, smoothing down her hair on either side of her face, and rested her handbag flat on her lap. He sat down opposite her, raised a pipe to his lips and, before striking a match, said, 'Do you mind?'

'My father smoked. So do both my uncles.'

She was less strung up, less uneasy than when she had first been to see him in this same office. The weather had been so mild that day that the Chief Superintendent had left his window open, and the street noises, though muted, had floated up to them.

'Needless to say, it's your father I want to talk about.'

She nodded.

'And about you, too, and one or two other people.'

She gave him no help, nor did she look away from him. She just waited, as if she knew what he was going to say.

'Are you very attached to your mother, Mademoiselle Monique?'

It had been his intention to adopt a bantering, affable approach, leading her on by degrees until, in the end, she would be left with no choice but to tell him the truth. But he was disconcerted by her blunt reply.

With complete composure, as if it were the most natural thing in the world, she said:

'No.'

'You mean you and she don't see eye to eye?'

'I hate her.'

'May I ask why?'

She gave a little shrug.

'You've been to the house. You've seen her.'

'Could you elaborate on that?'

'My mother thinks only of herself, and her own social position, and providing for her old age. She never stops fretting at having married less advantageously than her sisters, though she tries hard to pretend that she is every bit as well off as they are.'

He had difficulty in suppressing a smile, though she had spoken with great intensity of feeling.

'Were you fond of your father?'

She was silent for a moment. He repeated the question.

'I'm trying to think. I'm not sure. I hate having to admit it, now that he's dead.'

'You mean you didn't think much of him?'

'He was pretty spineless.'

'What do you mean by that?'

'He would never take a stand over things.'

'What sort of things?'

'Everything.'

Then, with a sudden burst of feeling:

'You can't imagine the sort of life we led. If you can call it living. I got fed up with it long ago. Now I have only one thought in my head, to get away.'

'To get married, you mean?'

'Not necessarily. I just want to get out.'

'In the near future?'

'Perhaps not, but one day.'

'Did you ever talk it over with your parents?'

'What good would it have done?'

'Did you intend to leave without saying a word?'

'Why not? What difference would it have made to them?'

He was watching her with growing interest, so much so that from time to time he let his pipe go out. He had to relight it several times.

'When did you discover that your father was no longer working in the Rue de Bondy?' he asked bluntly.

He had thought that she would at least start in surprise, but she didn't. She must have anticipated his line of questioning, and had her answers ready. It was the only possible explanation for her attitude.

'Nearly three years ago. I can't remember the exact date. It was sometime in January, I think. January or February. It was freezing cold.'

The firm of Kaplan had closed down at the end of October. In January and February, Monsieur Louis had still been looking for another job. It was at that period that, having exhausted his reserves, he had reluctantly borrowed money from Mademoiselle Léone and the old bookkeeper.

'Did your father tell you himself?'

'No. It was simpler than that. One afternoon, when I was out on my rounds . . .'

'Were you working in the Rue de Rivoli at that time?'

'I began working for the firm when I was eighteen. It so happened that one of the people I had to see was a ladies' hairdresser with premises in the building where my father worked. I looked out into the courtyard. It was past four o'clock. It was pitch dark. There were no lights on in the building opposite. I couldn't understand it, so I inquired of the concierge, who informed me that Kaplan's had gone out of business.'

'Did you say nothing to your mother when you got home?'

'No.'

'Nor to your father?'

'He wouldn't have told me the truth.'

'Was he a habitual liar?'

'It's hard to explain. He hated domestic strife, so, in order to avoid it, he would say and do anything to keep my mother happy.'

'Was he afraid of her?'

'He just wanted to keep the peace.'

She spoke with some contempt.

'Did you follow him?'

'Yes. Not the next day, because the opportunity didn't arise. It was two or three days later. I caught an earlier train than usual, saying that there was an urgent job waiting for me in the office, and I hung about near the station.'

'What did he do that day?'

'He went into several offices. I got the impression that he was looking for a job. At lunch time he went into a little bar and ate a couple of croissants, and then he rushed into a newspaper office to read the Situations Vacant columns. I realized what it all meant.'

'How did you feel about it?'

'What do you mean?'

'Didn't it surprise you that he had not mentioned it to either your mother or yourself?'

'No. He wouldn't have dared. It would only have led to a scene. My uncles and aunts would have taken advantage of the occasion to overwhelm him with advice, and reproach him for his lack of initiative. I've had that word "initiative" dinned into me ever since I was born.'

'And yet, at the end of each month, your father brought home his salary as usual, didn't he?'

'That really did puzzle me. As the months went by, I became more and more certain that, before very long, he would have no choice but to return home empty-handed. But instead of that, he announced one day that he had "demanded" a rise and got it.'

'When was this?'

'A good while after. In the summer. Sometime in August.'

'I presume you thought your father had managed to get another job?'

'Yes. I wanted to find out more, so I followed him again. But he still had no work. He wandered around, and every now and then he sat down on a bench. I thought, perhaps, it was his day off, so I waited a couple of weeks and then, deliberately picking a different day, I followed him yet again. On that occasion, he spotted me. He had just sat down on a bench on one of the Grands Boulevards. He turned very pale, hesitated, and then got up and came towards me.'

'Did he know you had been following him?'

'I don't think so. He must have thought it was just a chance meeting. We went and had an Espresso on the terrace of a café. It was very hot. He told me a lot of things then.'

'What did he say?'

'That Kaplan's had been bought up, and that he had suddenly found himself out of a job. He said he had decided not to tell my mother, in order to spare her anxiety, as he had been quite sure that he would have no difficulty in finding another job.'

'Was he wearing light brown shoes?'

'Not that day. He went on to say that it had not been as easy as he had expected, but that everything was all right now. He was selling insurance, which gave him plenty of free time.'

'Why had he still said nothing at home?'

'Still on account of my mother. She despised door-to-door salesmen. It made no difference whether they were selling insurance or vacuum cleaners. She referred to them as good-for-nothings and beggars. If she had found out that her husband had joined their ranks, she would have felt so humiliated that she would have made life unendurable for him. Especially in relation to her sisters.'

'Your mother sets good store by her sisters' good opinion, doesn't she?'

'Keeping up with them is the sole object of her existence.'

'Did you believe your father, when he told you he was selling insurance?'

'At the time I did.'

'And later?'

'I began to wonder.'

'Why?'

'First of all, because he was making too much money.'

'As much as all that?'

'I don't know what you mean by "as much as all that"! After a few months, he announced that he had been promoted to assistant manager, at an increased salary, still at Kaplan's, of course. I remember they had words about that. Mother wanted him to change the entry under "Occupation" on his identity card. She had always felt humiliated by the title of storekeeper. He said it wasn't worth the trouble, it was such a trivial matter.'

'I daresay you and your father exchanged knowing glances at that point?'

'When he was sure my mother wasn't looking, he winked at me. From time to time, in the morning, he would slip a banknote into my bag.'

'In order to buy your silence?'

'No, it gave him pleasure to be able to give me money.'

'You mentioned that you and he sometimes met for lunch.'

'That's right. He used to arrange to meet me, in whispers, in the entrance lobby at home. In the restaurant he'd always make me have the most expensive dishes, and would offer to take me to a cinema afterwards.'

'Did you ever see him wearing light brown shoes?'

'Once. It was then that I asked him where he went to change his shoes, and he told me that, for business reasons, he had had to rent a room in town.'

'Did he give you the address?'

'Not at first. All this took place over a long period of time.'

'Had you a boy friend then?'

'No.'

'When did you first make the acquaintance of Albert Jorisse?'

She neither blushed nor stammered. This was another question she had been expecting.

'Four or five months ago.'

'Are you in love with him?'

'We're planning to go away together.'

'To get married?'

'Not until he's of age. He's only nineteen. He can't marry without his parents' consent.'

'Would they refuse to give their consent?'

'I'm quite sure they would.'

'Why?'

'Because he has his way to make in the world. That's all his parents ever think of. Just like my mother.'

'Where are you planning to go?'

'South America. I've already applied for a passport.'

'Have you any money?'

'A little. I'm allowed to keep part of what I earn.'

'When did you first ask your father to let you have the money?'

She stared at him for a moment, then said, with a sigh:
'So you know that too!'

Then, without hesitation:

'I thought you might. That's why I'm telling you the truth. I'm sure you wouldn't be such a louse as to repeat all this to my mother. Unless, of course, you and she are two of a kind!'

'I have no intention of discussing your affairs with your mother.'

'Even if you did, it wouldn't make the slightest difference!'

'You mean you'd go anyway?'

'In my own good time, yes.'

'How did you find out the address of your father's lodgings?'

This time, she seemed on the point of telling a lie.

'I got it from Albert.'

'How did he find out? Did he follow him?'

'Yes. We were both curious as to how he earned his money. We decided that the best way to find out was for Albert to follow him.'

'What business was it of yours?'

'Albert was sure that whatever my father was up to, it was something illegal.'

'And supposing it was, what was to be gained by pursuing your investigations?'

'Whatever it was, it must have been very lucrative.'

'Did you intend to ask for a share of the money?'

'We expected that he would at least pay our fares.'

'Blackmail, in other words.'

'It's only natural for a father . . .'

'The long and the short of it is that your friend Albert set about spying on your father.'

'He followed him for three days.'

'What did he find out?'

'What have you found out?'

'I asked you a question.'

'First, that my father had taken a room in the Rue d'Angoulême. Next, that he was not connected in any way with insurance, but that he spent most of his time loafing about on the Grands Boulevards, and sitting on benches. And finally . . .'

'Finally?'

'That he had a mistress.'

'What effect did this discovery have on you?'

'I wouldn't have minded so much if she had been young and attractive. In fact she was very like Mother.'

'Have you seen her?'

'Albert pointed out the place where they were in the habit of meeting.'

'In the Rue Saint-Antoine?'

'Yes. It was a little café. I strolled past, as if I were there just by chance, and looked in. I didn't have time to get a good look at her, but I could see the sort of woman she was. It can't have been much more fun for him being with her than with my mother.'

'And then you went to see him in the Rue d'Angoulême?'

'Yes.'

'Did your father give you money?'

'Yes.'

'Did you use threats?'

'No. I told him I'd lost the envelope containing the money I had collected for my firm that afternoon, and that, unless I made it up to them, I'd be out on my ear. I also said that they would prosecute me for theft.'

'How did he react to that?'

'He looked embarrassed. Then I noticed a photograph of a woman on the bedside table. I snatched it up, and exclaimed:

' "Who's that?" '

'What was his answer?'

'That she was just a childhood friend, whom he happened to have run into again recently.'

'Aren't you ashamed of yourself?'

'I was only acting in self-defence.'

'Against whom?'

'Against the whole world. I am determined not to end up like my mother, slowly stifling to death in some caricature of a house.'

'Did Albert go and see your father as well?'

'I've no idea.'

'My dear child, that's a plain lie.'

She looked at him thoughtfully. then said:

'Yes.'

'Why did you choose to lie about that, in particular?'

'Because, ever since I found out that my father had been murdered, I have realized that Albert was in for trouble.'

'You know that he's disappeared?'

'He telephoned me.'

'When?'

'Before he disappeared, as you put it. Two days ago.'

'Did he tell you where he was going?'

'No. He was terribly distressed. He was convinced that he was going to be charged with murder.'

'What put that idea into his head?'

'Because he had been to the Rue d'Angoulême.'

'When did you find out that we were on his track?'

'After your inspector had questioned that old sourpuss, Mademoiselle Blanche. She hates me. Afterwards, she boasted that she'd said enough to make sure, as she put it, that my goose was well and truly cooked. I tried to calm Albert down. I told him that he was behaving like an idiot, because nothing was more likely to arouse the suspicions of the police than that he should go into hiding.'

'But you couldn't make him see reason?'

'No. He was in such a state that he was scarcely coherent on the telephone.'

'What makes you so sure he didn't kill your father?'

'What possible motive could he have had?'

Very calmly, to show that she had thought it all out, like the rational being she was, she added:

'We could have asked my father for as much money as we wanted.'

'What if he had refused?'

'He couldn't have done that. Albert had only to threaten to tell my mother all he knew. I know what you're thinking. You think I'm a bitch, you almost said as much, but if you had wasted the best years of your life, as they say, in a hole like Juvisy. . . .'

'Did you see your father on the day of his death?'

'No.'

'What about Albert?'

'I'm almost sure he didn't. We hadn't planned anything

for that particular day. We had lunch together, as usual, and he never mentioned my father.'

'Do you know where your father kept his money? As I understand it, your mother was in the habit of going through his pockets and his wallet every evening, when he got home.'

'She always did.'

'Why?'

'Because on one occasion, ten years ago or more, she found a handkerchief with lipstick on it. My mother doesn't use lipstick, you see.'

'You must have been very young at the time.'

'I was ten or twelve years old. All the same, I'll never forget it. They'd forgotten I was there. My father's story was that one of the women in the packing room had fainted on account of the heat, and that he'd poured alcohol on to his handkerchief and held it under her nose until she came round.'

'He was probably telling the truth.'

'My mother didn't believe him.'

'To return to my question, your father couldn't come home with more money in his pocket than could be accounted for by his so-called salary.'

'He kept it in his room.'

'On top of the glass-fronted wardrobe?'

'How did you know?'

'How did you?'

'Once, when I went to see him to ask for some money, he climbed up on a chair and took a buff envelope from the top of the wardrobe. It was stuffed with thousand-franc notes.'

'A lot?'

'A thick bundle.'

'Did Albert know about it too?'

'That's no reason for killing him. I'm certain he didn't do it. And besides, he would never have used a knife.'

'How can you be so sure?'

'I've seen him near to passing out when he's pricked his finger with a penknife. The sight of blood makes him ill.'

'Do you go to bed with him?'

Once again she shrugged, then said:

'What a question!'

'Where?'

'Anywhere. There are enough hotels in Paris which exist solely for that purpose. You're surely not suggesting that the police don't know about them?'

'Be that as it may, let us return to a more interesting topic. You and Albert were blackmailing your father, intending, as soon as you had squeezed enough money out of him, to elope to South America?'

For all the feeling she showed, she might not have heard him.

'Furthermore, I gather, for all your spying on him, you were not able to find out how your father got his money.'

'We didn't try all that hard.'

'I see. All that mattered was that he had the money, not how he made it.'

From time to time, Maigret had the feeling that she was looking at him with a kind of pitying indulgence. She must have been thinking that he, Chief Superintendent of the Crime Squad, was proving to be almost as naïve as her mother and her aunts and uncles.

'Now you know everything,' she said, making as if to get up. 'You'll have noticed, I hope, that I haven't pretended to be anything but what I am. As to what you may think of me. I couldn't care less.'

All the same, she was uneasy about something.

'Can I have your assurance that you won't say anything to my mother?'

'Why should you care? You'll be out of it soon anyway.'

'For one thing, it will take time to make all the arrangements, and for another, I'd prefer to avoid a scene.'

'I understand.'

'Albert is still a minor, and his parents might . . .'

'I should very much like to have a talk with Albert.'

'If it was up to me, he'd be here now. He's a fool. I can just see him, huddling out of sight somewhere, shaking from head to foot.'

'You don't seem to have a very high opinion of him.'

'I haven't a high opinion of anyone.'

'Except yourself.'

'I don't think much of myself either. I'm only looking after my own interests.'

What was the use of arguing with her?

'Have you told my employers that I was being brought here?'

'I telephoned them, and said we needed you here in connection with certain legal formalities.'

'What time are they expecting me back?'

'I didn't say any particular time.'

'Can I go?'

'I'm not stopping you.'

'Will I still be followed around by one of your inspectors?'

He felt like laughing, but managed to keep a straight face.

'Possibly.'

'He'll be wasting his time.'

'Thank you for your assistance.'

Maigret did, in fact, have her followed, though he was convinced that nothing would come of it. It was Janvier, who happened to be free at the moment, who took over the assignment.

As for the Chief Superintendent, he sat for ten minutes or more with his elbows on his desk and his pipe clenched between his teeth, gazing absently at the window. In the end, he had to shake himself back to consciousness, like someone waking from a deep sleep. He got up, grumbling to himself under his breath, 'Silly little fool!'

Feeling somewhat at a loose end, he went into the Inspectors' Duty Room.

'Still no news of the boy?'

Albert must be itching to get in touch with Monique. But how could he manage it without risk of arrest. There was one question that Maigret had neglected to ask. And yet it was a matter of some importance. Which of the two of them was actually in possession of the money that they had amassed, in order to finance their journey to South America? If it was Albert, he was probably still carrying it about in his pocket. If it was not, presumably he had barely enough to buy food.

For a few minutes more he paced restlessly between the two rooms, then he telephoned the offices of Geber et Bachelier.

'May I speak to Mademoiselle Monique Thouret, please?'

'One moment, I think she's just coming in.'

'Hello!' It was Monique's voice.

'I hope you're not too disappointed. It's not Albert, only the Chief Superintendent. There's just one thing I forgot to ask you. Which of you has the money?'

She was quick to grasp his meaning.

'I have.'

'Where is it?'

'Here. I keep it locked in one of the drawers of my desk.'

'Has he any money of his own?'

'Very little, I should think.'

'Thanks. That's all I wanted to know.'

Lucas was making signs to him, indicating that he was wanted on another line. It was Lapointe.

'Are you speaking from the Rue d'Angoulême?' asked Maigret, in surprise.

'Not from the house. From the bistro on the corner.'

'What's been happening?'

' I don't know if it was done on purpose, but I thought you ought to be told. They've turned out the room and cleaned it thoroughly. The furniture and the floor are gleaming with wax polish, and there isn't a speck of dust anywhere.'

'What about the top of the wardrobe?'

'That's been dusted too. I could feel, from the way that woman looked at me, that she had put one across me. I asked her when the cleaning had been done. She said that her charwoman was there yesterday afternoon—she only goes in twice a week—so she thought she'd take advantage of her being there to give it a thorough turn-out.

'You said nothing about leaving it as it was, she said, and as she'd have to let it again. . . .'

Maigret had made a blunder. He ought to have foreseen this. 'Where is Moers?'

'He's still up there, in the hope that one or two finger-prints at least may have been overlooked. He hasn't found anything yet. If it really was done by the charwoman, she's made a thorough job of it. Do you want me to go back to the Quai?'

'Not just yet. Find out the name and address of the charwoman, and go and see her. Ask her to tell you exactly what happened, what her instructions were, whether anyone else was in the room with her. . . .'

'I get it.'

'Moers may as well give up. Just one more thing. Did you notice anyone from the Vice Squad watching the house?'

'Yes, Dumoncel. I've just had a word with him.'

'Tell him to ring Headquarters and ask for reinforcements. If any one of the women leaves the house, I want her followed.'

'They're not ready to go out yet. One of them seems to have a mania for trailing up and down the stairs stark naked, another is having a bath. As for the third one, apparently no one has seen her for several days.'

Maigret decided to go and see the Chief Commissioner, not for any particular reason, but just because, as sometimes happened, he felt like an informal chat about the case and other matters. He liked the atmosphere of the Chief's office. He always stood near the window, to enjoy the view of the Pont Saint-Michel and the Quais.

'Tired, are you?'

'I feel as if I've been engaged in an endless game of patience. I'm itching to be everywhere at once, so I end up just pacing up and down in my office. This morning I had one of the most . . .'

He paused, groping for the right word to describe his interview with Monique, but it eluded him. He felt whacked, or perhaps drained would be a better word, as if he were suffering from a severe hangover.

'And yet she was only a girl, scarcely more than a kid.'

'The Thouret girl, do you mean?'

The telephone rang. The Chief Commissioner answered it. 'Yes, he's here.' And turning to Maigret:

'It's for you. Neveu has arrived, bringing someone with him. He can't wait to show you his prize.'

As he went past the waiting-room, he could see Inspector

Neveu, on his feet, apparently in a state of great excitement, and, sitting beside him on one of the upright chairs, a pale, sickly-looking man of indeterminate age, whose face seemed somehow familiar. It was more than that, he felt as if he had known the man all his life, but still, he couldn't put a name to him.

'Do you want a word with me in private first?' he said to Neveu.

'There wouldn't be any point. And, besides, I wouldn't risk letting this joker out of my sight for a single second.'

Then Maigret realized that the man was handcuffed.

He went into his office, followed by the prisoner. Neveu, bringing up the rear, locked the door behind him and removed the handcuffs from the man's wrists.

'Don't you recognize him, Chief?'

Maigret still could not put a name to him. All the same, one thing was suddenly clear. The man had the look of a clown stripped of his make-up, cheeks that seemed to be made of rubber, a wide mouth twisted in an expression of bitterness mingled with drollery.

Who was it who had spoken recently of a man with a face like a clown? Mademoiselle Léone? The old bookkeeper, Monsieur Saimbron? At any rate, whoever it was, that person had seen Monsieur Louis sitting on a bench in the Boulevard Saint-Martin or the Boulevard Bonne-Nouvelle in the company of another man.

'Take a seat.'

The man answered, as if he felt completely at home:

'Thanks, Chief.'

## 7. The Rainwear Shop

'JEF SCHRAMECK, otherwise known as Fred the Clown, also the Acrobat, born at Riquewhir in the Upper Rhine, sixty-three years of age.'

Flushed with triumph, Inspector Neveu introduced his captive with all the flourish of a ringmaster.

'Do you remember him now, Chief?'

Neveu was referring to something that had occurred fifteen years ago or more. Now Maigret came to think of it, it had happened not so very far from the Boulevard Saint-Martin, somewhere between the Rue de Richelieu and the Rue Drouet.

'Sixty-three?' repeated Maigret, looking at the man, who, taking this as a compliment, responded with a broad smile.

Possibly because he was so thin, he didn't look his age. In fact, he was ageless. It was his expression, most of all, that made it impossible to think of him as a man getting on in years. Terrified though he must be, he still looked as if he couldn't take anyone seriously, not even himself. No doubt it was simply a mannerism acquired over the years, like the capacity to pull extraordinary faces. He just had to make people laugh.

The amazing thing was that, at the time of that business on the Boulevards which had turned him into a celebrity for a few weeks, he was already past the age of forty-five.

Maigret pressed the buzzer, and lifted the receiver of the internal telephone.

'Would you please send me down the file on Schrameck, Jef Schrameck, born at Riquewhir, in the Upper Rhine.'

He could not remember how it had started. It had been an evening in early spring, for it was already pitch dark by eight o'clock. The Grands Boulevards had been crowded, and there was not a single vacant chair on any of the café terraces.

Had someone noticed a dim light flickering in one of the windows of an office block? At any rate, the police were alerted, and came running to the spot. As usual, a crowd had gathered, though most of the people had had no idea of what was going on.

No one had dreamed that the spectacle would last nearly two hours, and provide much drama interspersed with comic interludes, or that, towards the end, the crowd would be such that it would become necessary to erect barriers.

Trapped in the office building, the intruder had opened a window and, with the help of a strip of guttering, had crawled sideways along the entire length of the façade. He had just found a foothold on the sill of a window on the floor above, when a policeman appeared. The man had persisted with his hazardous climb, to the accompaniment of terrified shrieks from the women in the crowd below.

It had been one of the most exciting chases in police history, with the pursuers inside the building hurrying from one floor to the next, flinging windows open as they went, and the quarry nimbly eluding them, as if performing a circus turn entirely for his own amusement.

He had been the first to reach the roof, a steeply sloping roof, which the police had been reluctant to risk climbing. The man, apparently impervious to vertigo, had taken a flying leap on to the next roof, and so on from one building to the next, until he had reached the corner of the Rue Drouet, where he had vanished through a skylight.

They had lost sight of him, but had found him again a quarter of an hour later, on another roof farther on. The people in the street had pointed upwards, shouting: 'There he is!'

No one had known either what he had been doing in the first place or whether he was armed. Someone had started a rumour that he had killed several people.

The climax of the show, as far as the spectators were concerned, had been the arrival of the Fire Brigade with their ladders. Some time had gone by before powerful floodlights were set up and trained on the rooftops.

When, at last, he had been arrested in the Rue de la Grande-Batelière, he was not even out of breath. He was very cocky, and had poured amiable scorn on the police. Then, at the very moment when he was being bundled into a car, he had wriggled out of the grasp of his captors like an eel, and managed, heaven knows how, to worm his way to freedom through the crowd.

The name of the man was Schrameck. For several days, the Acrobat had hogged the headlines in all the newspapers, until he was recaptured, quite by chance, at a race meeting.

He had made his debut as a circus performer at a very early age, appearing mainly in Germany and Alsace-Lorraine. Later, he had come to Paris and, except for brief spells in prison for theft, had always found employment at various fairgrounds.

'I never dreamed,' Inspector Neveu was saying, 'that he was spending his declining years in my manor.'

The man remarked in all seriousness:

'I turned over a new leaf years ago.'

'I'd got a description of a tall, thin, elderly man who had been seen in conversation with Monsieur Louis on benches on the Boulevards.'

Hadn't someone said to Maigret: 'The sort of man one often sees sitting on a bench?'

Fred the Clown was the kind of individual whom one would not be in the least surprised to find lounging about for hours, watching the passers-by or feeding the pigeons. His colouring blended with the grey paving stones, and he had the look of a man who had nothing to do and nowhere to go.

'Before I hand him over to you, I think I ought to tell you how I happened to catch up with him. I was in a bar in the Rue Blondel, very near the Porte Saint-Martin. The bar also serves as a betting shop. It's called *Chez Fernand*. Fernand is a former jockey. I know him well. I showed him a photograph of Monsier Louis, and I could tell from the way he looked at it that he recognized him.'

' "Is he a customer of yours?" I asked him.

' "He isn't, himself. But he's been in here two or three times in company with one of my best customers."

' "Who's that?"

' "Fred the Clown."

' "The Acrobat? I thought he had either died long ago or was in prison!"

' "He's very much alive, and he comes in here every afternoon for a glass of something, and to place his bets. But, come to think of it, I haven't seen him for some days now."

' "How long exactly?"

'Fernand considered the matter, and then went and had a word with his wife in the kitchen.

' "Monday was the last time he came in."

' "Was Monsieur Louis with him?"

'He couldn't remember, but he was quite sure he hadn't set eyes on the Acrobat since last Monday. Do you see what I'm getting at?

'The next step was to find him. I now knew where to look. I had found out the name of the woman he's been living with for the past few years. She used to sell vegetables off a barrow. Her name is Françoise Bidou.

'I had then only to get her address. She lives on the Quai de Valmy, overlooking the canal.

'I found my man, skulking in her bedroom. He hadn't set foot outside since Monday. The first thing I did was to clap him in handcuffs. I didn't want him slipping through my fingers.'

'I'm not as agile as I used to be,' quipped Schrameck.

There was a knock on the door. A thick, buff-coloured file was deposited on Maigret's desk. It contained Schrameck's life history, or, more precisely, the history of his brushes with the Law.

Unhurriedly, puffing at his pipe, Maigret skimmed through it.

As far as he was concerned, this was the best time of day for conducting interviews. Between twelve and two, most of the offices were deserted, there were fewer interruptions, and hardly any telephone calls. He had the same feeling he had often experienced late at night of having the whole place to himself.

'You must be hungry,' he said to Neveu.

As Neveu seemed at a loss as to how he should reply, Maigret persisted.

'You'd better go out and have a snack now. I may want you to relieve me here later.'

'Whatever you say, Chief.'

Neveu, much against his will, went out. The prisoner watched him go with a mocking expression on his face. Maigret lit a fresh pipe, laid his broad hand on the file, looked Fred the Clown straight in the eye, and murmured:

'Alone, at last!'

He felt more at his ease with this man than he had with Monique. All the same, before getting down to business, he took the precaution of locking his door, and even went so far as to bolt the door communicating with the Inspectors' Duty Room. Then, catching him glancing at the window, Jef protested, with a comic grimace.

'Have no fear. I'm past keeping my balance on narrow ledges.'

'I suppose you know why you're here?'

Ever the clown, he protested plaintively:

'It's always the same people who get arrested! It reminds me of the good old days. Nothing of this sort has happened to me for years.'

'Your friend Louis has been murdered. It's no good putting on that bewildered expression. You know very well who I mean. You are also well aware that there's every likelihood of your being charged with the crime.'

'That would be just one more miscarriage of justice.'

Maigret picked up the telephone.

'Get me *Chez Fernand*. It's a bar in the Rue Blondel.'

When he had Fernand on the line, he said:

'Chief Superintendent Maigret speaking. It's about one of your regulars, Jef Schrameck. . . . The Acrobat, that's right . . . I want to know whether he gambled heavily. . . . What? . . . Yes, I see. . . . And latterly? . . . Saturday? . . . I'm much obliged to you. . . . No. That's all for the present.'

He seemed satisfied. Jef, on the other hand, was looking a little uneasy.

'Do you wish me to repeat what I have just been told?'

'People will say anything!'

'All your life, you've been losing money on horses.'

'If the Government had put a stop to it, I should have been spared the expense.'

'You've been backing on the *Pari-Mutuel* with Fernand for some years now.'

'He's a registered agent of the *Pari-Mutuel*.'

'Be that as it may, you must have got the money to bet with from somewhere. Now until about two and a half years ago, you bet only in very small sums. On occasion, you hadn't even the wherewithal to pay for your drinks, and Fernand would let you have them on credit.'

'He shouldn't have done! It only encouraged me to keep at it.'

'Then, all of a sudden, you began staking larger sums of money, sometimes very large sums. And a few days later, you were cleaned out all over again.'

'What does that prove?'

'Last Saturday, you staked an enormous sum.'

'What of it? The owners are often prepared to risk as much as a million francs on a horse!'

'Where did you get the money?'

'My lady friend is earning.'

'What does she do?'

'Housework. Occasionally she gives a hand in one of the bistros on the Quai.'

'Do you take me for a fool?'

'Such a thought never crossed my mind, Superintendent.'

'Now look here, we've wasted enough time already.'

'I assure you, I have no pressing engagements. . . .'

'Never mind that. I'm going to tell you just where you stand. You were seen by several witnesses in Monsieur Louis's company.'

'A finer man you couldn't wish to meet.'

'That's neither here nor there. I don't mean recently. This was about two and a half years ago. At that time Monsieur Louis had been out of work for months. He was at the end of his tether.'

'I know the feeling all too well!' sighed Jef. 'However long the tether, we all come to the end of it sometime!'

'As to what you were living on in those days, I have no idea, but I'm prepared to believe that you were being kept by your friend Françoise. You hung about on benches, occasionally venturing a few francs on a horse, and getting your drinks on credit in various bars. As for Monsieur Louis, he was driven to borrowing money from at least two old friends.'

'Which only goes to show that the world is full of people on their uppers.'

Maigret ignored this remark. Jef had been so long accustomed to the laughter of an audience that he had developed a craving for it, which was why he could never stop clowning. Doggedly, the Chief Superintendent pursued his own line of thought.

'The fact remains that, all of a sudden, you were both very flush. The evidence, with exact dates, will emerge in the course of the inquiry.'

'I can never remember dates.'

'After that, there were times when you gambled heavily, and others when you couldn't even pay for your drinks. Nobody could fail to draw the conclusion that you and Monsieur Louis had found a means of laying your hands on very large sums of money. Whatever the means, it was not legal. But we'll come to that later.'

'What a pity! I'm dying to hear how we managed it.'

'You'll soon be laughing on the other side of your face. I repeat that on Saturday you were loaded with money, but you lost it all in the space of a few hours. On Monday afternoon, your associate, Monsieur Louis, was murdered in a cul-de-sac off the Boulevard Saint-Martin.'

'It was a tragic loss for me.'

'Have you ever been up for trial at the Assizes?'

'No. Only in the lower courts. Several times.'

'Well, I may as well tell you that juries as a whole don't much care for clowning, especially from a man with your record. Nothing is more calculated to persuade them that you are the only person who would know where to find Monsieur Louis at all times of day, and the only one with a motive for murder.'

'In that case, they must be a lot of idiots.'

'That's all I have to say to you. It is now half-past twelve. We are both here in my office. At one o'clock Judge Coméliau will be back in his chambers.

'As soon as he arrives, I'll hand you over to him, and he will deal with you as he thinks fit.'

'Isn't he a little dark man, with a toothbrush moustache?'

'Yes.'

'He and I have met before. He's a right so-and-so. Come to think of it, he can't be all that young any more. What if I say I don't want to see him?'

'It rests entirely with you, as you very well know.'

Jef the Clown heaved a long sigh.

'You don't by any chance happen to have a spare cigarette?'

Maigret took a packet from his drawer, and held it out to him.

'Have you a match?'

He smoked for a while in silence.

'I don't suppose you keep any liquor in here?'

'Are you going to come clean?'

'I'm not sure yet. I'm still considering whether there's anything I can usefully say.'

This might turn out to be a very long session. Maigret knew his sort. On impulse, he went across to the door leading to the Inspectors' room, and called out:

'Lucas! Do me a favour. Go to the Quai de Valmy, and find a woman called Françoise Bidou. I want her brought here.'

At this the Clown wriggled in his chair, and held up his hand like a schoolboy in the classroom.

'You wouldn't do that to me, Chief Superintendent!'

'Will you talk?'

'It would help a lot if I could have a little something to drink.'

'Hold on, Lucas. Don't go until I tell you.'

And to Jef:

'Are you afraid of her?'

'You promised to give me a drink.'

Maigret shut the door, went to the cupboard, and got out the bottle of liqueur brandy that he always kept there. He poured a small tot into a tumbler.

'Aren't you going to join me?'

'Well, what have you to say?'

'Ask me whatever questions you like. I'd be obliged if you would take note that I am making no attempt to impede the course of justice, as the lawyers put it.'

'Where did you first meet Monsieur Louis?'

'On a bench in the Boulevard Bonne-Nouvelle.'

'How did you strike up an acquaintance with him?'

'The way one does, sitting next to someone on a bench. I remarked on the weather, and he agreed that it was cold for early spring, but said that it was milder than it had been the week before.'

'Would this have been about two and a half years ago?'

'Something like that. I didn't make a note of the date in my diary. We met every day on the same bench after that. He seemed glad to have someone to talk to.'

'Did he mention that he was out of work?'

'By degrees, he told me the whole story of his life. He said he'd been twenty-five years with the same firm, and that the boss had then decided, without a word of warning to anyone, to close down the business. He said he hadn't dared tell his wife—just between ourselves, she sounds like a right cow—and she believed that he was still working at the same job. I fancy it was the first chance he'd had of getting it all off his chest, and it was a great relief to him.'

'Did he know who you were?'

'All I told him was that I used to be a circus performer.'

'And then?'

'What exactly do you want to know?'

'Everything.'

'I'd be obliged if you'd first take another look at my file and tot up the number of convictions. What I want to know is whether this new charge is likely to get me transported. I shouldn't care for that.'

Maigret did as he asked.

'Unless the charge is murder, you're still two short of the requisite number of convictions.'

'That's what I thought. I wasn't sure your total would tally with mine.'

'What was the racket? Stealing?'

'It wasn't as simple as that.'

'Whose idea was it?'

'His, of course. I haven't the wits to dream up a scheme like that. Don't you think I've earned another little tot?'

'When I've heard all you have to tell me.'

'That's going to take a long time. Well, you leave me with no choice but to cut it as short as possible.'

The Chief Superintendent yielded, and poured him another mouthful of brandy.

'As a matter of fact, it was the bench that first gave him the idea.'

'How do you mean?'

'As he spent most of his time sitting on a bench, usually the same bench, he began to take notice of his surroundings. Do you, by any chance, know the shop in the boulevard where they sell raincoats?'

'I know the one you mean.'

'The bench where Louis usually sat was just opposite. So, almost without realizing it, he became very familiar with the comings and goings in the shop and the habits of the employees. And that's what put the idea into his head. When you have the whole day before you, and nothing to do, you get to thinking. You plan projects, even projects that haven't a hope of being realized. One day, he began telling me about one of these projects of his, just to pass the time. That particular shop is always very crowded. It sells nothing but raincoats, of every shape and size, raincoats for men, women and children. The children's raincoats are tucked away in a corner. And there are more on the first floor. On the left of the building, as with so many in that district, there is a little cul-de-sac leading on to a courtyard.

'Would you like me to draw you a plan?' he suggested.

'Not now. Go on.'

'Louis said to me:

' "I'm surprised no one has ever robbed the till. It would be the easiest thing in the world!" '

'You couldn't wait to hear more, I daresay.'

'Naturally, I was interested. He explained to me that at about twelve, or a quarter past at the latest, everyone was turned out of the shop, and the employees all went off to lunch. And that included the boss, a little old man with a wisp of a beard, who always lunched at the *Chope du Nègre*, not far from where we were sitting.

' "Suppose one of the customers were to stay behind and get locked in?"

'Don't say it couldn't be done. My first reaction, too, was that it was impossible. But Louis had been studying the lay-out of the shop for weeks. The staff never bothered to look in all the dark corners and behind the racks of raincoats, to satisfy themselves that there was no one left in the shop. It never occurred to them that anyone might stay behind on purpose, see?

'Everything turned on that. The boss was always the last to leave, locking the door carefully behind him.'

'And you were the one to stay behind, I suppose? And

after that, all you had to do was force the lock and slip away with the takings?'

'You're quite mistaken. And that's what made it such a lark. Even if I'd got caught, they wouldn't have found a shred of evidence. Admittedly, I did empty the till. After that I went into the lavatories. Next to the urinals, there is a tiny skylight too small even for a child of three to squeeze through, but quite big enough for throwing out a parcel containing bank-notes. It overlooks the courtyard. As if by sheer chance, Louis was passing by underneath, and he picked up the parcel. As for me, all I had to do was wait until the staff returned, and there were enough customers in the shop for me to slip out unnoticed, by the way I came in. Which is what I did.'

'How did you share out the money?'

'Fifty-fifty, like brothers. The hardest thing was to persuade Louis to make up his mind. The whole plan was just an imaginative exercise to him. He took a pride in it, the way a painter does in his work. When I first suggested that we should put it into practice, he was shocked. What finally tipped the scales was the thought of having to tell his wife that he was broke to the wide. You will have noticed that the plan had one further advantage. It's true that, having admitted the offence, I shall be convicted of theft, but as there's no question of breaking and entering, that will mean, if I'm not mistaken, two years lopped off my sentence.'

'I'll have a look at the Criminal Code later.'

'Well, I've told you all there is to tell. Louis and I did very nicely out of it, and I have no regrets. The proceeds of that little venture kept us going for over three months. Well, to be perfectly frank, my share didn't last quite that long, on account of all those broken-down hacks, but Louis used to slip me a bank-note from time to time.

'When we realized we were coming to the end of our resources, we moved to a different bench.'

'With the intention of planning another job?'

'Well, why not? The scheme was an excellent one, and there was no point in trying anything new. Now that you know the trick, you only have to look at the files to spot all the jobs I brought off by getting myself locked into a shop. The next time, it was a shop that sold electrical goods, in the same boulevard, but a bit higher up. There was no cul-de-sac, but the back of the shop overlooked the courtyard of the building opposite, which was just as good. In that district, the lavatories nearly always have a small window or vent overlooking a courtyard or passageway.

'I was only caught once, by a salesgirl opening a cupboard in which I was hiding. I pretended to be drunk and incapable. She called the manager, and the two of them hustled me out, threatening to call the police if I didn't clear off.

'Now will you be so good as to explain what possible motive I could have had for killing Louis? We were buddies. I even introduced him to Françoise, to reassure her, because she was beginning to wonder what I was up to. He brought her a box of chocolates, and she thought him most distinguished.'

'Did you pull off a job last week?'

'It was all in the papers. A dress shop in the Boulevard Montmartre.'

'I take it that, when Louis was killed, he was in the cul-de-sac to check that there was a suitable window at the back of the jeweller's overlooking the courtyard?'

'Very likely. He was always the one to case the joint, because of his respectable appearance. People tend to be more suspicious of a man like me. Even when I'm dressed up to the nines, they look sideways at me.'

'Who killed him?'

'Why ask me?'

'Who would have had a motive for killing him?'

'I don't know. His wife, maybe.'

'Why should his wife have wanted to kill him?'

'I told you she was a right cow. Supposing she found out that he'd been cocking a snook at her for over two years, and that he had a lady friend. . . .'

'Do you know her?'

'He never introduced me to her, but he often talked about her, and I saw her once or twice from a distance. He was very fond of her. He was a man who needed affection. Well, come to think of it, don't we all? I've got my Françoise. I daresay you've got someone of your own too. They got on very well. They used to go to the cinema, or else they'd go into a café and chat.'

'Did she know what was going on?'

'I'm sure she didn't.'

'Who did know?'

'I did for a start.'

'That's obvious.'

'His daughter, possibly. He worried a lot about his daughter. He said that the older she got, the more like her mother she was. She was always badgering him for money.'

'Did you ever go and see him in the Rue d'Angoulême?'

'Never.'

'But you know the house?'

'He pointed it out to me.'

'Why did you never go in?'

'Because I didn't want to spoil things for him. His landlady thought him a very respectable man. If she'd seen me. . . .'

'What if I were to tell you that we've found your fingerprints in his room?'

'I would reply that fingerprints are a load of tripe.'

He talked as if he hadn't a care in the world. He believed he was on a winning streak. Every now and then, he would take a quick look at the bottle.

'Who else knew?'

'See here, Chief Superintendent, I am what I am, but I've never grassed in all my life.'

'You mean you'd rather take the rap yourself?'

'That would be a miscarriage of justice.'

'Who else knew?'

'The young madam's boy friend. Now there's a one for you. I wouldn't stake a fortune on his innocence. I don't know whether he was acting on orders from his lady love, but he took to following Louis in the afternoon for days at a time. He went to see him twice, to extort money from him. Louis was scared stiff the kid would blow the gaff to his wife, or write her an anonymous letter.'

'Do you know him?'

'No. I know he's very young, and that he works in a bookshop in the mornings. Latterly, Louis was haunted by a sense of impending catastrophe. He said things couldn't go on as they were, and that his wife was bound to learn the truth in the end.'

'Did he ever mention his brothers-in-law?'

'Often. They were always being held up to him as an example. They were made use of to show him up as a failure, a good-for-nothing, a namby-pamby, a nobody. He was told that, if he was content with his miserable lot, he ought never to have married. It was a shock to me, I can tell you.'

'What was?'

'Reading in the papers that he was dead. Especially as I wasn't very far away when it happened. Fernand will confirm that I was in his bar having a drink at the time.'

'Did Louis carry much money on him?'

'I don't know about that, but I do know that, two days earlier, we pulled off quite a lucrative job.'

'Was he in the habit of carrying the money about with him?'

'Either that, or he'd leave it in his room. The joke was that, every evening, he had to go back to his room to change his shoes and tie before catching his train. On one occasion, he forgot his tie. He told me all this himself. It was only when he got to the Gare de Lyon that he realized. He couldn't go and buy just any other tie. It had to be the same as the one he'd been wearing when he left home in the morning. He had to go all the way back to the Rue d'Angoulême, and when he got home he made up a story about having been kept late at work, to attend to some rush job or other.'

'Why have you been hiding in Françoise's room since Tuesday?'

'What would you have done in my place? When I read the paper on Tuesday morning I realized that someone must have seen Louis and me together at some time, and that they'd be sure to tell the police. They always pick on people of my sort anyway.'

'Did you never consider leaving Paris?'

'No, I just lay low, in the hope that they wouldn't get on to me. This morning, when I heard your inspector calling out to me, I knew I was done for.'

'Does Françoise know what you've been up to?'

'No.'

'How does she suppose you managed to get hold of all that money?'

'To begin with, she hasn't seen much of it, only what I had left after my racing losses. And then she believes I'm still picking pockets in the Metro.'

'Is that what you used to do?'

'Surely you don't expect me to answer that? By the way, don't you ever get thirsty?'

Maigret poured him another tot.

'Are you quite sure there's nothing you haven't told me?'

'As sure as I'm sitting here!'

Maigret opened the door to the Inspectors' Duty Room, and called out to Lucas.

'Take him down to the cells.'

Then, looking towards Jef Schrameck, who stood up with a sigh, he added, 'He'd better be handcuffed, just to be on the safe side.'

As he was going out, the Acrobat turned back with an odd little smile on his mobile face, and Maigret said, 'Tell them not to be too hard on him.'

'Thank you, Chief Superintendent. Oh! and there's one other thing. Please don't tell Françoise that I gambled away all that money. She's quite capable of punishing me by not sending me any little extras in prison.'

Maigret put on his coat, took his hat down from the hook, and decided to go to the *Brasserie Dauphine* for a bite to eat. He was going down the main staircase, which was, as usual, grey with dust, when he heard sounds of a scuffle coming from the ground floor. He looked over the banister.

A young man, with his hair all over the place, was struggling in the grip of a giant of a constable with a bleeding scratch on his cheek. He was growling:

'Cool it, kiddo, if you don't want a smack in the chops!'

The Chief Superintendent was sorely tempted to laugh.

It was Albert Jorisse on his unwilling way to see him. He was still struggling and shouting.

'Let go of me! I told you, I won't run away. . . .'

At this point, the two of them came face to face with Maigret on the stairs.

'I arrested him a couple of minutes ago on the Pont Saint-Michel. I knew him at once. When I apprehended him, he tried to get away.'

'That's not true! He's lying!'

The young man was red in the face and panting, and his eyes were feverishly bright. The policeman had hold of his coat collar, which he had pulled up high, as if he were manipulating a puppet.

'Tell him to let go of me.'

He kicked out with his foot, but missed.

'I told you I wanted to see Chief Superintendent Maigret. I came here, didn't I? I came here of my own free will.'

His clothes were crumpled, his trousers still streaked with mud after last night's downpour. He had huge black circles under his eyes.

'I am Chief Superintendent Maigret.'

'Well, then, order him to let go of me.'

'It's all right, son, you can let go now.'

'Whatever you say, sir, but . . .'

The constable was convinced that the young man was as slippery as an eel.

'He's a beastly bully,' panted Albert Jorisse. 'He treated me as if . . . as if . . .'

He was stammering with rage.

Smiling in spite of himself, the Chief Superintendent pointed to the constable's bleeding cheek.

'It looks to me rather as if he was the one who . . .'

Jorisse, who had not noticed the gash until now, looked at him with flashing eyes, and shouted:

'Serve him right!'

## 8. Monique's Secret

'SIT DOWN, you young ruffian.'

'I'm not a young ruffian,' protested Jorisse.

He had still not quite got his breath back, and was wheezing a little, but he had calmed down a lot.

'I wouldn't have expected it of you, Chief Superintendent Maigret, using insulting language like that before even giving me time to explain.'

Maigret, somewhat taken aback, looked at him, frowning.

'Have you had any lunch?'

'I'm not hungry.'

He spoke like a sulky kid.

'Hello!' Maigret said into the phone. 'Get me the *Brasserie Dauphine* . . . Hello! Is that you, Joseph? . . . Maigret here . . . I'd be obliged if you'd bring over some sandwiches. Six . . . Ham for me . . . Just a minute . . .'

And to Jorisse: 'Ham or cheese?'

'I don't really mind. Ham.'

'Beer or red wine?'

'Water, if you don't mind. I'm thirsty.'

'Joseph? Six ham sandwiches, cut nice and thick, and four halves of beer. . . . Hang on a second. . . .You may as well bring us two cups of black coffee while you're about it. . . . And be as quick as you can, won't you?'

He replaced the receiver, and then immediately lifted it again and dialled an internal number, never taking his eyes off the young man, whose appearance interested him. Jorisse was thin and frail-looking, jumpy to the point of neurosis, suggesting that his staple diet was black coffee rather than nourishing steaks. Otherwise he wasn't bad-looking, with his long brown hair, which he had to shake out of his eyes by tossing his head every now and again.

Perhaps because he was still very worked up, his nostrils twitched from time to time. He was still looking reproachfully at the Chief Superintendent, with his head on one side.

'Hello! You can call off the search for Jorisse. Pass the message on to all police and railway stations.'

The youth opened his mouth, but Maigret didn't give him time to speak.

'Later!'

The sky was once more overcast. There was more rain in the offing. No doubt it would come down in buckets, as it had done on the day of the funeral. Maigret went over to the window and shut it, then, still without a word, he returned to his desk and rearranged his pipes, as a typist, before getting down to work, rearranges her machine, her shorthand pad and her carbons.

There was a knock on the door.

'Come in,' he said, testily.

It was Inspector Neveu. . . . He just put his head round the door, assuming that the Chief was right in the middle of an interrogation.

'Excuse me. I just wanted to ask what . . .'

'You can go off now. And thanks!'

When he had gone, the Chief Superintendent began pacing up and down, to fill in time until the waiter arrived from the *Brasserie Dauphine*. He also made another call, this time to his wife:

'I shan't be in for lunch.'

'I was beginning to wonder. Do you know what time it is?'

'No. Does it matter?'

She burst out laughing. He couldn't imagine why.

'I came here to tell you . . .'

'It'll keep.'

It was his third interrogation that day. He was thirsty. Then he noticed, all of a sudden, that the young man was staring at the bottle of brandy and the used tumbler that had been left standing on his desk.

Maigret blushed like a child, and only just stopped himself from blurting out that it wasn't he who had been drinking brandy out of a tall glass, but Jef Schrameck, who had left the office just before Albert arrived.

Had the boy's reproachful words struck home? Was Chief Superintendent Maigret regretting that he had forfeited his good opinion?

'Come in, Joseph. Put the tray down on the desk. Everything's there, I take it?'

And when at last they were alone with the tray of food:
'Let's eat.'

Jorisse ate heartily, in spite of having said that he wasn't
hungry. Right through the meal, he kept darting inquiring
glances at the Chief Superintendent, but by the time he
had finished his first glass of beer, he seemed to have regained a little self-confidence.

'Feeling better?'

'Yes, thanks. All the same, you did call me a ruffian.'

'We'll discuss that later.'

'It really is true that I was on my way to see you.'

'What for?'

'Because I was sick of running away.'

'Why did you run away?'

'So as not to get myself arrested.'

'Why should anyone have wanted to arrest you?'

'You know very well why.'

'No, I don't.'

'Because I am Monique's friend.'

'Why were you so sure we'd find out?'

'You were bound to.'

'And you think that because you and Monique were
friends, we would have arrested you?'

'You wanted to make me talk.'

'I did, to be sure!'

'You've made up your mind that I'm going to lie to you,
and you won't be happy until you've tripped me up.'

'I'm afraid you've been reading too many detective
stories.'

'No. But I read the papers. I know how you people go
about things.'

'In that case, what exactly are you doing here?'

'I've come to tell you that I didn't kill Monsieur Louis
Thouret.'

Maigret, puffing at his pipe, slowly sipped his second
glass of beer. He was seated at his desk. The green-shaded
light was switched on, and the first few drops of rain were
spreading on the window panes.

'Do you understand the implications of what you have
just said?'

'I don't know what you mean.'

'You assumed that you were under threat of arrest. Which means that there were good reasons why we should arrest you.'

'You've been to the Rue d'Angoulême, haven't you?'

'How do you know that?'

'You found out by the merest chance that he had a room in town. It was because of the light brown shoes, wasn't it?'

The Chief Superintendent looked at him with an amused little smile. 'So what?'

'The woman there must surely have told you that I'd been to see him.'

'Is that a reason for arresting you?'

'You've interrogated Monique.'

'Do you really believe she would give you away?'

'It wouldn't surprise me to learn that you'd managed to make her talk.'

'In that case what was the point of hiding under a friend's bed?'

'So you know that too?'

'Please answer my question.'

'I wasn't thinking. I got into a panic. I was afraid I might be browbeaten into saying things that weren't true.'

'Did you get that from the newspapers as well?'

After all, had not René Lecœur's lawyer referred in open court to the brutality of the police, and had not the words been quoted in every newspaper in the land? In fact, there had been a letter from Lecœur in the morning post. In despair, being under sentence of death, he had written to beg the Chief Superintendent to visit him in prison.

Maigret was tempted to show the letter to the youngster. He would do so later, if it should prove necessary.

'Why didn't you remain in hiding in the Rue Gay-Lussac?'

'Because I couldn't stand spending the whole day hiding under a bed. It was ghastly. I ached all over. I kept thinking all the time that I was going to sneeze. It's a small flat, and the doors are left open. I could hear my friend's aunt moving about the whole time. If I'd so much as moved, she would have been bound to hear me.'

'Is that the only reason?'

'I was hungry.'

'What did you do?'

'I wandered about the streets. At night, I managed to get a couple of hours' sleep by lying on a sack of vegetables in Les Halles. Twice I got myself as far as the Pont Saint-Michel. I saw Monique come out of this building. I walked to the Rue d'Angoulême, and there was a man there who looked as if he was watching the house. I assumed he must be from the police.'

'What reason would you have had for killing Monsieur Louis?'

'Don't you know that I borrowed money from him?'

'Borrowed?'

'All right, I asked him for money, if you like.'

'Asked?'

'What are you suggesting?'

'There are different ways of asking. Among others, there is a way which makes it almost impossible for the person concerned to refuse. In plain terms, blackmail.'

He was silent, gazing fixedly at the floor.

'What have you to say to that?'

'In actual fact, I would never have told Madame Thouret.'

'All the same, you threatened to do so?'

'That wasn't necessary.'

'Because a hint that you might talk was enough?'

'I don't know. You're confusing me.'

He added, in a weary voice:

'I'm dropping with sleep.'

'Drink your coffee.'

He obeyed meekly, never taking his eyes off Maigret.

'How often did you go and see him?'

'Only twice.'

'Did Monique know?'

'What did she say about it?'

'Never you mind what she said. I want to get at the truth.'

'She did know.'

'What did you say to him?'

268

'To whom?'

'To Louis Thouret, of course.'

'That we were in need of money.'

'Who's "we"?'

'Monique and I.'

'What did you say you wanted it for?'

'To go to South America.'

'So you told him you intended to run away together?'

'Yes.'

'How did he react?'

'In the end, he agreed he had no choice in the matter.'

There was something wrong, somewhere. It was beginning to dawn on him that the youngster thought Maigret knew more than he actually did. He would have to proceed with caution.

'Did you ask his permission to marry her?'

'Yes. But he knew very well it was out of the question. Firstly, I am under age, and would have to get my parents' consent. Secondly, even if they were to agree, Madame Thouret would never have put up with a son-in-law who still had his way to make in the world. Monsieur Thouret himself was the first to discourage me from introducing myself to his wife.'

'Did you tell him that you and Monique had been making love in heaven knows how many different hotel rooms?'

'I didn't go into details.'

For the second time he blushed.

'I simply told him that she was pregnant.'

Maigret didn't start or show any other sign of surprise. All the same, it was a shock. He blamed his own lack of insight. Because it was, he had to admit, the one possibility that had never occurred to him.

'How far gone is she?'

'Just over two months.'

'You've seen a doctor, I presume?'

'She wouldn't let me go in with her.'

'But she has seen someone?'

'Yes.'

'Did you wait for her outside?'

'No.'

269

Maigret changed his position slightly, and began mechanically to fill another pipe.

'What had you in mind to do, when you got to South America?'

'Anything at all. I'm not afraid of work. I could have become a cowhand.'

He said this with great seriousness, even a touch of pride, and Maigret had a mental image of the many six-foot roughnecks that he had encountered on ranches in Texas and Arizona.

'A cowhand,' he echoed.

'Or I could have prospected for gold.'

'Of course!'

'I would have managed somehow.'

'And you and Monique would have got married?'

'Yes. I imagine it would be easier there than here.'

'Do you love Monique?'

'She's my wife, or as good as, isn't she? Just because we haven't been through the formalities. . . .'

'How did Monsieur Louis react to this news?'

'He couldn't believe his daughter could have done such a thing. He cried.'

'In your presence?'

'Yes. I swore to him that my intentions . . .'

'Were honourable. But of course. What happened then?'

'He promised he'd help us. He couldn't give us all the money at once, but he gave me some.'

'Where is this money?'

'Monique has it. She keeps it hidden in the desk in her office.'

'What about the rest of the money?'

'He promised he'd let me have it on Tuesday. He was expecting a large remittance.'

'Who from?'

'I don't know.'

'Didn't he tell you how he earned his money?'

'He couldn't, obviously.'

'Why not?'

'Because he hadn't a job. I was never able to find out how he got the money. There were two of them involved.'

'Did you ever see the other one?'

'Once, in the boulevard.'

'A tall, thin man, with the face of a clown?'

'Yes.'

'He was with me here until just a few minutes before you arrived. The brandy was for him.'

'In that case, you know it all.'

'What I want to know is whether you do.'

'I don't know anything. My guess is that they were blackmailing someone.'

'And you didn't see any reason why you shouldn't have a share of the loot?'

'We needed money, on account of the baby.'

Maigret lifted the receiver of the internal telephone.

'Lucas? I want you in here for a moment.'

As soon as Lucas arrived, Maigret introduced the young man: 'This is Albert Jorisse. He and Monique are expecting a baby.'

He spoke with great solemnity, and Lucas, who did not know what to think, nodded.

'The young lady may still be in her office, as she wasn't able to be there this morning. I want you to go and fetch her, and then take her to a doctor. Let her decide which one. If she has no preference, it might as well be the one at the *Préfecture*. I want to know how many months pregnant she is.'

'What if she refuses to be examined?'

'Tell her that, if she does refuse, I shall have no choice but to arrest her, as well as her boy friend, who is here in my office. Take a car, and telephone and let me know what she says.'

When they were alone again, Jorisse asked:

'What was all that about?'

'It's my job to check up on everything.'

'Don't you believe me?'

'I believe *you*, yes.'

'But you don't believe her, is that it?'

The ringing of the telephone saved Maigret the embarrassment of replying. The call had nothing to do with the matter in hand. It was with reference to a lunatic who had been to see him some days earlier, and who had later been arrested in the street for riotous behaviour. Instead of answering the query in a few words, as he could have done, Maigret spun out the conversation for as long as possible.

When he had replaced the receiver, he asked, pretending that he had forgotten where they had got to:

'What do you intend to do now?'

'Do you accept my assurance that I didn't kill him?'

'I've always known that. You see, it's not as easy as is generally supposed to stab someone in the back. It's even more difficult to prevent the victim from crying out.'

'You mean I would be incapable of carrying it out?'

'Sure.'

He seemed almost offended. After all, he had had dreams of becoming a cowhand or a gold prospector in South America.

'Do you intend to go and see Madame Thouret?'

'I suppose I'll have to.'

Maigret was sorely tempted to burst out laughing at the thought of the lad going to the house in Juvisy, with his tail between his legs, in an attempt to butter up Monique's mother.

'Do you believe that, as things are, she'll be prepared to regard you as an acceptable son-in-law?'

'I don't know.'

'You don't deny, do you, that you didn't play altogether straight?'

'What do you mean?'

'It isn't only that you asked Monsieur Louis to give you the money to take Monique to South America, but that, knowing Monique spends every afternoon going from house to house collecting debts, you decided you might as well take advantage of the fact.

'She could always hurry through her round with an hour or two to spare, which she got into the habit of spending shut up with you in some hotel room or other.'

'We did meet like that sometimes.'

'In order to do so, you were forced to give up your afternoon stint in the bookshop. And hotel rooms cost money.'

'We did spend a little of . . .'

'You knew where Monsieur Louis kept his money, didn't you?'

He was watching the young man closely. He answered without a moment's hesitation:

'On top of his glass-fronted wardrobe.'

'When he gave you the money, did he get it from there?'

'Yes. But Monique had already told me about it.'

'I take it you never went near the house in the Rue d'Angoulême on Monday?'

'No, I didn't. Ask the landlady, if you like. I had an appointment to go and see him on Tuesday at five.'

'When were you intending to leave for South America?'

'There's a ship sailing in three weeks' time. That would have given us time to get our visas. I have already applied for a passport.'

'I thought that, in the case of a minor, parental consent was obligatory.'

'I forged my father's signature.'

There was a pause. Then, for the first time, Jorisse asked for permission to smoke.

Maigret nodded. The absurd thing was that, having had his coffee, he really was longing now for a glass of liqueur brandy, but he had not the courage to take out the bottle, which was now back in the cupboard.

'You called me a ruffian.'

'Don't you think you deserved it?'

'I had no choice but to do what I did.'

'How would you like it, if your son were to behave as you did?'

'I intend to bring up my son differently. He won't have to . . .'

Once again they were interrupted by the telephone.

'Is that you, Chief?'

Maigret frowned. It was Neveu. He had not sent him out on any assignment.

'I've got the money!'

'You must be joking!'

He glanced at Jorisse, and said to the Inspector, 'Just a second. I'll go on to the other line.'

He went into the adjoining room, and told the first inspector he saw to go and keep an eye on the young man.

'That's better. Now you can talk freely. Where are you?'

'In a bistro on the Quai de Valmy.'

'What are you doing there?'

'You're not angry with me?'

'Carry on.'

'I meant it for the best. It's ten years now since Jef moved in with Françoise. From all I hear, he's fonder of her than he likes to make out. I suddenly had a yen to take a look round her place.'

'What for?'

'I thought it odd that he should have left her without money. I was lucky enough to find her at home. There are only two rooms, plus a kind of cupboard they use as a kitchen. In the bedroom there is an iron bedstead with brass knobs. The walls are whitewashed, country style, but it's all very clean.'

Feeling a little cross, Maigret waited for Neveu to finish his story. He didn't care for over-zealousness, especially in the case of someone like Neveu, who belonged to a different branch of the service.

'Did you tell her Jef had been arrested?'

'Shouldn't I have done?'

'Go on.'

'To begin with, judging by her reactions, I was convinced she didn't know what he'd been up to. Her first thought was that I had caught him picking pockets in the Metro or on a bus. Presumably, that's his usual racket.'

It was one of the many talents cultivated by Schrameck when he was still working in fairgrounds. One of his convictions had been for purse-stealing.

'Ignoring her protests, I set about searching the place. It wasn't until right at the end that it occurred to me to unscrew the brass bed-knobs. They're hollow inside, and two of them were stuffed full of tightly rolled notes. They add up to a fortune! Françoise couldn't believe her eyes.

' "To think that he let me go out charing, when he had all that money hidden away! He'll never get to heaven! Just let him come back here, and he'll see what . . ."

'She's still in the most fearful rage, calling him every name under the sun. She didn't even calm down when I suggested that he had put the money aside to provide for her, in case anything happened to him.

'"What amazes me," she snarled, "is how he managed to avoid gambling it all away."

'Do you see what I'm getting at now, Chief? They must have had a big share-out last Saturday. I've got more than two hundred thousand francs here. Jef wouldn't have dared to gamble all that lot away, especially at Fernand's place. He only lost a fraction of the money. If they split it down the middle, Monsieur Louis must have had a packet salted away as well.'

'I'm very grateful to you.'

'What shall I do with the money?'

'Have you got it with you?'

'I should say I have! I couldn't very well leave it there. . . .'

'Go and have a word with your Chief Superintendent, and ask him to get things sorted out according to the rule book.'

'Must I?'

'Heavens above! I don't want the defence lawyers accusing us of having planted the notes!'

'Have I put my foot in it?'

'You have, rather.'

'I'm sorry. I only wanted . . .'

Maigret hung up. He turned to Torrence, who was working at his desk. 'Are you very busy?'

'It's nothing that can't wait.'

'I want you to go and see Chief Superintendent Antoine. Ask him to arrange for one of his men to get out a list of all the thefts committed in shops in the Grands Boulevards during the last two and a half years or so, especially those that took place while they were shut for lunch.'

Such cases were not the concern of his Department, but of Antoine's, whose office was at the end of the passage.

He went back to Albert Jorisse, who had just lit another cigarette, and released the inspector who had been keeping an eye on him.

'I had no intention of running away, you know.'

'I daresay. But you might have been tempted to take a peep at the files on my desk. Go on, you may as well admit it.'

'Perhaps.'

'That makes all the difference.'

'What does?'

'Never mind. I know what I'm talking about.'

'What do you intend to do with me?'

'For the time being, you're staying here with me.'

Maigret glanced at his watch, and calculated that Lucas and Monique must have arrived at the doctor's by now. No doubt they were in the waiting-room, reading the magazines.

'You despise me, don't you?'

He shrugged.

'I've never had a chance.'

'A chance to do what?'

'To escape.'

'To escape from what?'

Maigret sounded almost aggressive.

'You don't understand, I can see that. If you'd heard nothing but money, money, money ever since you were a child, and if you'd seen your mother shaking with anxiety at the end of every month. . . .'

'I had no mother.'

The boy was silenced. For nearly ten minutes, not a word was spoken. For a while, Maigret stood by the window with his back to the room, watching the rain trickling down the window panes. Then he began pacing up and down, and finally, almost defiantly, he made up his mind to open the cupboard. He had washed the glass in the enamel drinking fountain some time before. He rinsed it again, and poured a tot of brandy into it.

'Would you care for a drop of this?'

'No, thanks.'

Albert Jorisse was finding it hard to keep awake. His cheeks were flushed, and Maigret was sure his eyes were smarting. From time to time, he swayed in his chair.

'In time, I daresay, you'll prove yourself to be a man.'

He could hear footsteps in the passage, those of a man and a woman, and he knew that it was Monique, accompanied by Lucas. He had a decision to make. That was what he had been brooding over for the last quarter of an hour. Should he have the girl brought into his office, or should he interview her next door?

With a little shrug, he went across and opened the door. Both of them had glistening drops of rain on their shoulders. Monique was no longer her old confident self, and when she caught sight of Albert, she stopped dead in her tracks, clutched her bag more tightly, and glared furiously at the Chief Superintendent.

'Did you take her to see a doctor?'

'At first, she flatly refused to go. I . . .'

'What did he find?'

Jorisse stood up, and seemed on the point of grovelling at her feet to beg her forgiveness.

'Nothing.'

'You mean she's not pregnant?'

'She never has been.'

Jorisse, scarcely able to believe his ears, didn't know which way to turn. He made a sudden move as if to spring at Maigret, whom he seemed to regard as the cruellest man on earth.

Maigret, after shutting the door, indicated a chair to the young woman.

'Have you anything to say?'

'I did believe . . .'

'No.'

'What do you know about it? You're not a woman.'

Then, turning to the young man:

'I swear to you, Albert, that I truly believed I was going to have a child.'

Maigret, unmoved, but not wishing to be unfair, said:

'For how long?'

'For several days.'

'And then?'

'When I discovered it was a false alarm, I didn't want him to be disappointed.'

'Disappointed?'

277

Maigret exchanged glances with Lucas. The two of them went out together into the adjoining office. They shut the door, leaving the young lovers to themselves.

'As soon as I spoke of taking her to a doctor, I could see that there was something amiss. She protested violently. It wasn't until I threatened to arrest her and Albert. . . .'

Maigret was not listening. Lucas was not telling him anything he didn't already know. Torrence was back at his desk.

'Did you do as I asked?'

'They're still working on the list. It's going to be a long one. For the last two years or more, Chief Superintendent Antoine and his Squad have been plugging away at it. Apparently . . .'

Maigret went over to the communicating door, and put his ear to it.

'What are they up to?' asked Lucas.

'Nothing.'

'Are they talking?'

'They're not saying a word.'

He decided to look in on the Chief Commissioner, and put him in the picture. They talked for a while about this and that. Maigret spent the next hour or so dropping in on various colleagues for a chat.

When he returned to his office, Albert and Monique looked as if they had not stirred during his absence. They were still sitting upright on their chairs, ten feet or so apart. The girl's face was unrevealing, her jaw, so like her mother's and aunts', resolutely set.

Whenever her eyes chanced to meet the young man's, it was hard to tell whether there was more of contempt or loathing in her glance.

As for Jorisse, he was utterly crushed. His eyes were red, either with exhaustion or with weeping.

'You are both free to go.' Maigret said, without preamble, as he went towards his chair.

It was Monique who asked, 'Will there be anything in the papers?'

'There's no reason why there should be.'

'Will my mother have to be told?'

'I don't think that will be necessary.'

'And my employers?'

He shook his head, and she got swiftly to her feet and made for the door, without so much as sparing a glance for Jorisse. With her hand on the doorknob, she turned to the Chief Superintendent, and said:

'You knew all along, didn't you?'

'Yes,' he replied. Then, with a sigh, he said to Albert:

'You're free to go as well.'

And seeing that the youngster did not stir:

'You'd better hurry, if you want to catch up with her. . . .'

She was already on the stairs.

'Should I, do you think?'

'What did she say to you?'

'She called me an idiot.'

'Is that all?'

'She added that on no account would she ever permit me to speak to her again.'

'And then?'

'Nothing. I don't know.'

'As I've already said, you're free to go.'

'What am I to say to my parents?'

'Whatever you like. They'll be only too delighted to have you back.'

'Do you really think so?'

In the end, he almost had to push him out. He still seemed to have something on his mind.

'Off you go, you young idiot!'

'I'm not a ruffian then?'

'No, only an idiot! She was quite right.'

He turned his head away, sniffed and murmured:

'Thanks.'

Presently, alone in his office at last, Maigret was able to pour himself another drop of liqueur brandy.

# 9. Judge Coméliau Grows Restive

'IS THAT YOU, MAIGRET?'

'Yes, Judge.'

He telephoned every day, and if one of Maigret's colleagues happened to be in the room at the time, Maigret would give him a wink. His voice sounded unusually bland when he was talking to the Examining Magistrate.

'How are things on the Thouret front?'

'Progressing! Progressing!'

'Don't you think it's been dragging on a bit too long?'

'You know how it is with a crime of this sort, it takes time to clear things up.'

'Are you sure it's a case of thieves falling out?'

'You've said so yourself, right from the start. Your words were:

' "It's as plain as a pikestaff." '

'Do you believe this Schrameck fellow's story?'

'I'm convinced he was telling the truth.'

'In that case, who did kill Louis Thouret?'

'Someone who wanted his money.'

'At any rate, do the best you can to speed things up.'

'You have my word on that, Judge.'

He did nothing about it, however, but instead turned his attention to two other cases, which kept him busy for most of the day. Three men, Janvier and young Lapointe among them, were taking it in turn to keep an eye on the house in the Rue d'Angoulême, twenty-four hours a day. The telephone was still being tapped.

He was no longer interested either in Madame Thouret or in her daughter. Jorisse, too, who was now once more working full-time at the bookshop in the Boulevard Saint-Michel, had been eliminated from the case. It was as if he had never known them.

As to the thefts, he had turned the file over to his colleague, Antoine, who was having Jef the Clown, alias the Acrobat, brought up for further questioning nearly every day.

Maigret occasionally ran into Jef in the corridor.

'Everything O.K.?'

'Everything's fine, Chief Superintendent.'

The weather was cold, but dry. The proprietress of the house in the Rue d'Angoulême had not succeeded in finding other tenants, so that two of her rooms were still vacant. As for the three girls who were still living there, knowing that the house was being watched, they no longer dared ply their usual trade. They scarcely ever went out, except to have a meal in a nearby restaurant, or to buy something from the delicatessen, or when one of them went to a cinema.

'What do they do with themselves all day?' Maigret asked Janvier, when things had been going on in this way for some days.

'They sleep, or play cards or patience. One of them, the one they call Arlette, puts her tongue out at me every time she sees me from the window. Yesterday, she tried something different. She hitched up her dressing-gown and showed me her behind.'

The Mobile Squad in Marseilles had taken over the inquiries concerning the knife. They were searching not only in the town itself, but in the surrounding villages as well. They were also taking an interest in any shady local characters who had recently moved to Paris.

All these routine inquiries were being conducted unhurriedly and without fuss. And yet Maigret had not forgotten Monsieur Louis. Once, when he had to go to the Rue de Clignancourt on some other business, he had even gone so far as to look in on Mademoiselle Léone, not forgetting to buy a cream cake for the old lady on his way.

'Have you still not solved the mystery?'

'Sooner or later, the truth will come to light.'

He said nothing to the former shorthand typist of Monsieur Louis's activities.

'Do you know why he was killed?'

'For his money.'

'Surely he can't have had all that much!'

'He had a very large income.'

'Poor man! What a shame to have to die, just when all his troubles were over!'

He did not venture on the long climb up to Monsieur Saimbron's lodgings, but ran across him by chance one day in the Flower Market. They exchanged greetings.

Then one morning, at long last, he received a telephone call from Marseilles. It lasted a long time. Afterwards, he went up to the Registry, and was there for nearly an hour, looking through hundreds of registration forms. Then he went downstairs to Records, where he spent nearly as long again.

It was round about eleven when he went out into the courtyard, and got into one of the little Headquarters cars.

'The Rue d'Angoulême.'

It was young Lapointe who was on guard outside the house.

'Everybody at home?'

'Only one of them is out. She's doing her shopping locally.'

'Which one?'

'Olga. She's the dark one.'

He rang the bell. The curtains twitched. Mariette Gibon, the landlady, flip-flopped to the door in her bedroom slippers.

'Well, well! If it isn't the Big White Chief himself! Your men must be getting fed up with wearing down the paving stones outside my door.'

'Is Arlette at home?'

'Shall I call her down?'

'No, thanks. I'd rather go up to her room.'

She stayed out in the entrance lobby, looking very uneasy, and he went upstairs and knocked at the door on the first floor.

'Come in!'

As usual, she was in her dressing-gown, lying on the unmade bed, reading a romantic novel.

'Oh! So it's you.'

'In person,' he said, putting his hat on the chest of drawers, and sitting down on a chair by the bed.

She seemed both surprised and amused.

'Don't tell me you're still on about that same old business?'

'The case will not be closed until the murderer is found.'

'You don't mean you still haven't found him? I thought you were such a cunning old fox. I hope it doesn't embarrass you, me being in my dressing-gown like this?'

'Not in the least.'

'I daresay you must be used to it by now.'

Without stirring from the bed, she moved so that her dressing-gown flew open. As Maigret did not seem to have noticed, she said, provocatively:

'What do you say to this?'

'What?'

'Seeing all this.'

As he still remained impassive, she made a vulgar gesture, and said impatiently, 'How about it?'

'Thanks.'

'Yes, thanks, do you mean?'

'No, thanks.'

'Well, really, old man. . . . You are the . . .'

'Do you get a kick out of being coarse?'

'You're surely not going to lecture me, on top of everything else?'

All the same, she gathered together the folds of her dressing-gown, and sat up on the edge of the bed.

'What exactly is it you want of me?'

'Do your parents know that you are no longer working in the Avenue Matignon?'

'What are you on about now?'

'You worked for a year at *Chez Hélène et Hélène* in the Avenue Matignon.'

'What of it?'

'I was just wondering if your father knew you'd changed your occupation.'

'What business is it of yours?'

'Your father is a good man.'

'He's an old fool, and that's a fact.'

'If he should ever find out what you've been up to . . .'

'Are you thinking of telling him?'

'I might.'

This time, she was unable to conceal her agitation.

'You haven't been to Clermont-Ferrand to see my parents?'

'Not yet. . . .'

She got up, made a dash for the door, and flung it open to reveal Mariette Gibon, who had no doubt been standing there for some time, with her ear glued to the door panel.

'My God! You've got a nerve!'

'May I come in?'

'No. Shove off. And if I ever catch you spying again . . .'

Maigret had not moved from his chair.

'Well?' he said.

'Well, what? I can't think what you want from me.'

'You know perfectly well.'

'No, I don't. You'll need to spell it out.'

'You've been living in this house for the past six months.'

'So what?'

'You hardly ever go out in the daytime, so you must be aware of most of what goes on.'

'Well?'

'There's one person who used to be a regular visitor, but who hasn't set foot in the house since Monsieur Louis's death.'

Her pupils seemed to contract. Once again she went to the door, but there was no one behind it.

'Well, anyway, he didn't come here to see me.'

'Who then?'

'You must know the answer to that. I think I'd better get dressed.'

'Why?'

'Because, after this little talk of ours, I'd be safer out of this house.'

She let her dressing-gown slip to the floor, but this time with no thought of being provocative. Then she snatched up a bra and a pair of briefs, and opened the wardrobe.

'I might have known that this was how it would end.'

She was talking to herself.

'You're a clever bastard, I'll say that for you.'

'Arresting criminals is my job.'

'Have you arrested him?'

She had taken a black dress from the wardrobe, and was now wearing it. She proceeded to daub her mouth with lipstick.

'Not yet.'

'But you do know who he is?'

'You are going to tell me.'

'You seem very sure of yourself.'

He took his wallet from his pocket, and extracted a photograph of a man. He was about thirty, and there was a scar on his left temple. She glanced at the photograph, but said nothing.

'Is that him?'

'You seem to think so.'

'Am I wrong?'

'Where can I go to be safe while he's still at large?'

'I'll arrange for one of my inspectors to look after you.'

'Which one?'

'Which would you prefer?'

'The dark one with lots of hair.'

'That's Inspector Lapointe.'

Returning to the subject of the photograph, Maigret asked:

'What do you know about Marco?'

'That he was the landlady's lover. Must we talk here?'

'Where is he now?'

Without replying, she began bundling all her clothes and personal possessions into a large suitcase. She couldn't wait to be out of the house, it seemed.

'We can finish this conversation somewhere else.'

And, as he bent down to pick up her suitcase, she added:

'Well, well! So you can be chivalrous, when you want to!'

The door of the downstairs sitting-room was open. Mariette Gibon was standing in the doorway, looking drawn and anxious.

'Where are you going?'

'Wherever the Chief Superintendent is taking me.'

'Is she under arrest?'

She dared not question them further. She watched them go out, then she went to the window and raised the curtain a little. Maigret pushed the suitcase into the back of the car, and said to Lapointe:

'I'll send someone along here to relieve you. As soon

as he arrives, come and join us at the *Brasserie de la République*.'

'Right you are, Chief.' He gave instructions to the driver, but did not get into the car.

'Let's go.'

'To the *Brasserie de la République*?'

'For the time being, yes.'

It was only a few hundred yards away. They sat down at a table at the back of the room.

'I have to make a phone call. Take my word for it, it will be better for you if you don't try and give me the slip.'

'I understand.'

He telephoned the Quai, to give instructions to Torrence. When he got back to the table, he ordered two aperitifs.

'Where is Marco?'

'I don't know. After you came to the house that first time, the landlady told me to telephone him and tell him not to attempt to get in touch with her until he heard from her again.'

'When did you give him the message?'

'Half an hour after you left. I rang from a restaurant in the Boulevard Voltaire.'

'Did you actually speak to him?'

'No. I left a message with one of the waiters in a bar in the Rue de Douai.'

'Do you know his name?'

'Félix.'

'And the name of the bar?'

'*Le Poker d'As*.'

'Hasn't she had any news of him since?'

'No. She's going through hell. She's not blind to the fact that she's twenty years older than he is, and she's for ever imagining him chasing girls.'

'Is he the one who's got the money?'

'I don't know. But he was in the house that day.'

'What day?'

'The Monday that Monsieur Louis was murdered.'

'What time did he get to the Rue d'Angoulême?'

'About five. He and the landlady went and shut themselves up in her room.'

'Did she, at any time, go into Monsieur Louis's room?'

'She may have done. I didn't notice. He left after about an hour. I heard the door slam behind him.'

'Didn't she attempt to get in touch with him again through one of you girls?'

'She was afraid we might be followed.'

'Did she know that the telephone was being tapped?'

'She wasn't taken in by that business of your pipe. She's quick on the uptake. I don't like her much, but she's really rather pathetic. She's absolutely crazy about him. It's making her ill.'

Young Lapointe found them sitting contentedly over their drinks.

'What will you have?'

The girl was looking Lapointe over from head to foot, and smiling. Lapointe was studiously avoiding her eyes.

'The same as you.'

'I want you to take her to some quiet little hotel, and book a couple of adjoining rooms with a communicating door. You're not to let her out of your sight until I give you the word. As soon as you're settled in, ring me and let me know where you are. You shouldn't have to go very far. They might have rooms at the *Hôtel Moderne* just opposite. I'd rather she didn't talk to anyone. You'd better arrange to have her meals sent up to her room.'

When she and Lapointe went off together, it looked to Maigret as if she were taking him into custody, rather than the other way round.

The search continued for another two days. Someone —no one ever found out who—must have tipped off Félix, the barman in the Rue de Douai. At any rate, he had gone into hiding with a friend, and was not traced until the following night.

It took the greater part of the night to get him to admit that he knew Marco, and to persuade him to reveal his whereabouts.

Marco had left Paris, and taken a room in a country inn on the banks of the Seine, mainly patronized by anglers. At this time of year, he had the place to himself.

Before the police could disarm him, he fired two shots.

Mercifully, no one was hurt. He had the banknotes stolen from Monsieur Louis in a money belt that had probably been made for him by Mariette Gibon.

'Is that you, Maigret?'

'Yes, Judge.'

'How are things progressing in the Thouret case?'

'It's all over. I'll be handing the murderer and his accomplice over to you very shortly.'

'Who are they? Shady characters, as we thought?'

'They couldn't be shadier. The woman runs a bawdy house, and the man is a thug from Marseilles. Monsieur Louis was fool enough to hide the money on top of the wardrobe and . . .'

'What's that you said . . . ?'

'He couldn't possibly be allowed to find out that the money had gone. Marco saw to that. We've found the shop where he bought the knife. My report will be on your desk by tonight. . . .'

This was always the most boring part. Maigret spent all afternoon writing, with the tip of his tongue protruding, like a schoolboy.

It wasn't until after dinner that night that he suddenly remembered Arlette and young Lapointe.

'Damn! There's something I forgot to do!' he exclaimed.

'Is it important!' asked Madame Maigret.

'Not all that important, come to think of it. It's so late, I might as well leave it till the morning. Let's go to bed.'

*19 September, 1952*